FALSE FLAG

A Behind the Curtain Novel

David Axson

ISBN-13: 979-8-9928140-0-2

Library of Congress Control Number: 2025904322

Printed in the United States of America
Published by Sonax Group

Cover design by: Nick Castle

Also by David Axson

Fiction
>Berlin Bitte (coming late-2025)
>Détente Dawn (coming 2026)

Non-fiction
>Best Practices in Planning and Management Reporting (Wiley 2003)
>Best Practice in Planning and Performance Management – From Data to Decisions (Wiley 2007)
>Best Practice in Planning and Performance Management (Wiley 2010)
>The Management Mythbuster (Wiley 2010)
>Half The World Away (Countinghouse Press 2010)

"From Stettin in the Baltic to Trieste in the Adriatic, an iron curtain has descended across the Continent."

Winston Churchill, 5th March 1946

Prologue

The Soviet T-62 tank passed within inches of Nic Slater. He was lying prone in long grass beside a little-used farm track about a hundred metres from the border between Finland and the Soviet Union.

Looking to his right, he saw two members of the SAS team lift their weapons, ready to engage any infantry following in the tank's wake. Their faces were a study in concentration, no hint of fear. Nic wished he felt so calm. Despite the early morning chill, he was sweating, and his heart felt like it was beating inside his head. The machine pistol in his right hand was secured in a near-death grip. He was a spy not a soldier. He had not expected to be on the front lines. Yet in amongst the fear was an intense feeling of exhilaration. At this moment, he mattered. Nic Slater, a working-class kid from Sheffield, was important.

The tank neared the gate where the SAS team had laid explosives designed immobilise it. Nic could already see the second and third tanks in the column rumbling down the track. It was mismatch. A sixteen-man SAS squad and a petrified MI6 agent against four Soviet tanks and who knew how much infantry.

Time seemed to move in slow motion as the lead tank hit the tripwire and the first batch of explosives detonated. For a split second, it seemed as if the whole tank levitated off the ground before crashing back to earth.

1

Three Years Earlier

Nic Slater had not planned on becoming a spy. Growing up in a small village just outside Sheffield, the steel-making capital of Britain, a future working in a mill or down a coal mine had seemed more likely. However, his parents were determined that Nic and his older sister, Margaret, would escape the grind of working-class life.

His father, George, was a shift supervisor and union shop steward at the local steel mill. His mother, Kath, was a nurse. They had met just before the outbreak of World War II and married after a whirlwind courtship, prompted by the imminent arrival of Nic's sister, Margaret, or Mags as the family called her. This created quite a scandal in the local community at the time.

Dominic followed three years later. He was named after Saint Dominic, the founder of the Dominican order. His mother had found great comfort in her Catholic faith after the trauma she experienced as a child.

Kath was Russian by birth; her given name was Katarina. Her father was a founding member of the Bolshevik movement in 1912 and an associate of Lenin and Trotsky. He had been killed during the early days of the Russian Revolution while leading a team tasked with blowing up a key railway supply line just outside Moscow.

Just over a year later, Katarina was an orphan; her mother a victim of the brutal civil war that followed the revolution. Aged eight, she was evacuated to England. After spending six months in a children's home just outside London, she was adopted by a family living in the same village as her future husband.

While proud of her Russian heritage, she had no love for the Soviet Union. In her opinion, the revolution failed to achieve the goals her parents had so passionately believed in and died for. One ruling elite, the Tsars, had been replaced by another, communist party apparatchiks. She hoped that one day, the totalitarian regime would collapse and be replaced by a truly democratic socialist system.

Once in Britain, Kath worked hard to eradicate any trace of her accent and rarely spoke of her childhood. The only concession to her heritage was to insist that both her children learn to speak Russian fluently.

George had served in the British Army during the war and was awarded the Distinguished Conduct Medal, the second highest military honour for non-officers. Nic was not sure what his father had done to deserve the medal; like so many veterans, he never talked about his wartime service. Nic suspected it was related to his time in North Africa, where George had been one of the founding members of the Special Air Service (SAS). George was both a patriot and a proud socialist, as many working-class men who had served were. He was a long-time member of the Labour Party but never a communist. Partly influenced by his wife, he was no fan of the Soviet Union. He had been an ardent supporter of Clement Atlee, who, as Britain's first post-war Prime Minister, had overseen the creation of the National Health Service, the independence of India, and the nationalisation of many industries.

Some of his more radical friends wanted to see a worker-led revolution in Britain, but George believed democracy was the way to achieve lasting socialism in Britain. To his mind, any right-minded individual would see that socialism was preferable to unchecked capitalism. He was disappointed that many of his fellow countrymen did not seem to agree.

Growing up in the immediate aftermath of the war had not been glamorous for Nic and his sister. Food rationing was pervasive, local industry was declining, and the promised post-war economic boom had taken its time materialising. Notwithstanding the challenges, the Slater home was a loving, safe environment. Both parents had doted on their children.

The Slater's were not wealthy, but George and Kath ensured their children never wanted for anything. Despite having little formal education themselves, they emphasised its importance to their children. They were proud when both children passed the dreaded eleven-plus exam, earning places at the local grammar school.

In 1950's Britain, the eleven-plus largely determined a child's academic future. Pass and grammar school beckoned. The curriculum included foreign languages, English literature, biology, physics, and chemistry. Fail, as over eighty percent of children did, and you were consigned to less academically focused schools, leading to an apprenticeship at best. Despite benefiting from the system, Nic thought it unfair that a single exam at such a young age dictated a child's future educational and career choices.

Nic had been a decent student, a bit lazy, but blessed with a good memory upon which he relied heavily. However, he lived in the shadow of his sister, the star pupil in her year. Nic was not sufficiently motivated to match her work ethic. Mags earned top marks in every exam and won a scholarship to Oxford—the first girl from their school to do so. She had graduated with a first in Greats—an archaic curriculum focused on all things Latin and Greek—before becoming one of the first female barristers in London.

Nic's path had been less starry. He was a good all-round athlete, playing rugby in the winter and cricket in the summer. He passed his exams with middling grades and secured a place at Leeds University to study Economics. Leeds was one of the rapidly expanding provincial universities, a notch or two below the elites of Oxford and Cambridge. He arrived having little idea what he wanted to do with his life. His father suggested he become an accountant. His mother saw him as a bank manager, becoming a pillar of local society. Neither prospect excited him much.

Rather than make the tough choices, Nic enjoyed the social side of university far more than the academics. He studied just enough while playing rugby, unsuccessfully chasing girls, and drinking a lot of beer. He had no real direction until a strange encounter in his final year.

2

October 1962 – Oxford

The Leeds University rugby team was drinking in the Turf Tavern, one of Oxford's oldest pubs, dating back to the 14th century. They were celebrating a victory over Lincoln College. Nic was working on his third pint; they were slipping down very smoothly.

As was usual for rugby, both teams enjoyed a post-game pint together. The barriers of class between the largely public-school-educated Oxford players and the grammar school lads from Leeds dissipated in direct proportion to the amount of alcohol consumed.

For Nic, the beer's numbing effect was beginning to ease his aches and pains. He was enjoying himself. There was the usual barbed but good-natured banter and communal singing of bawdy tunes whose lyrics would make a nun blush.

Nic was leaning on the roughhewn oak bar, his head brushing against the low-beamed ceiling, when he felt a hearty slap on his back. He turned to see the hulking figure of one of the Lincoln players.

'You were a little fortunate today,' said the wild-haired, ruddy-faced man blessed with an accent that screamed posh twat.

'How can 37-12 be lucky?' Nic responded tartly.

'You caught us on an off day. We all got a bit tipsy last night. Bit of a session at the college smoker.'

Seeing Nic's bemused expression, he elaborated. 'A smoker is a college dinner, lots of booze and inedible food! Great fun, but one does tend to overindulge.'

Nic nodded, 'We don't have those up north. We make do with a few pints of Tetley's and Yorkshire pudding with onion gravy.'

'Good northern grub, that,' said Seb in a terrible attempt at a Yorkshire accent.

'Want another pint?' Nic said, gesturing to Seb's empty glass.

'That's very generous of you. A pint of Abbot, please.'

'Two pints of Abbot, please,' Nic said to the barmaid. She took their empty glasses and using a hand pump, filled them with a rich, chestnut-brown liquid.

'Name's Sebastian Harmes, but everyone calls me Seb,' the man said, reaching out to shake Nic's hand.

'Dominic Slater, but everyone calls me Nic,' he replied. For some reason, when confronted with a member of the upper class, he always used his full first name. Perhaps it was some forlorn attempt to bridge the class divide.

The radio behind the bar was tuned to the BBC. John Webster was reading the football results. Nic gestured for quiet, 'Hang on a second.' Today had been the big derby match between his team, Sheffield United, and their arch-rivals, Sheffield Wednesday.

'Don't tell me you follow football? Dreadful game. Rugby is the only sport for a gentleman.'

'You won't find many gentlemen in Sheffield,' Nic replied, eliciting a throaty laugh from Seb.

Webster's distinctive voice said, Sheffield United, two, Sheffield Wednesday, two.

'At least we didn't lose,' he said to no one in particular.

Mavis handed them their pints. Looking at Nic, she said, 'I

wouldn't waste your time with this posh knob.'

Seb feigned indignation, 'Now Maeve, you know you love me, really.'

Nic was conscious of his new friend unashamedly ogling Mavis's ample cleavage. 'Get away with you,' she replied, 'I'm far too good for you.'

Nic laughed and took a sip from the fresh pint. He always enjoyed that first taste; the blend of beer and foam from the head provided a refreshing taste of what was to come. He placed a few coins on the bar, 'Have one yourself, Mavis.'

'Thank you, kind sir,' she replied, winking.

'Let's take a load off,' Seb suggested. 'My legs need to recover from the run-around you gave us.'

They found a table and sat down. Seb took a large pull on his pint, draining almost half its contents before setting his glass down on a sodden beer mat next to an overflowing ashtray. English pubs were such classy places.

Nic recognised Seb as the annoying opponent who had spent most of the match seeking to do grievous harm to his reproductive organs.

'By the way, you're a dirty bastard,' added Nic.

Seb laughed uproariously. 'I had to be. I am too fat and too slow to keep up with you!'

Seb was right. Although almost six feet tall, he was well upholstered, probably tipping the scales at eighteen stone in his jockstrap.

'What do you do when you are not engaged in casual GBH on the rugby pitch?' Nic asked.

'I read Russian literature.'

Nic replied in fluent Russian. Seb held up his hands in mock surrender.

'We only read the English translations of the bloody books!

'What use is a degree in Russian literature?' Nic questioned.

'None at all. I am only studying it because there were no places on any other course for someone of my middling abilities. I will be lucky to graduate with a Richard.'

'A Richard?' Nic queried

'Richard III, a third.'

'What are you going to do when you graduate?'

'Off to the Foreign Office. I have been working there during the long vac.' Again, Nic looked puzzled. 'That is the summer holidays to you. I start full time after I go down in January, that is graduate, in provincial terms.'

Nic just shook his head. The toffs even had their own bloody language. His exposure to the upper classes was limited to the occasional costume drama on television and an English teacher who spoke as if he had a thumb stuck up his bum. He had attended a minor public school, which he seemed to think entitled him to talk down to the plebs in his classroom.

Nic's father had nothing but disdain for the entitled and privileged class who still ran Britain. He frequently ranted that they have "never done an honest day's work in their lives."

Despite his innate prejudices, Nic found himself warming to Seb. He was erudite, funny, and companionable.

'Why the Foreign Office?' Nic asked when Seb returned with two more pints.

'Father wanted me to become a barrister, but I am too bloody lazy. Even for a privileged oik like me, a third is not good enough to take the bar, so he pulled a few strings with his chums at the FO.'

Nic was not surprised.

'What about you?' he asked Nic.

'Not sure. Dad is pushing me towards accountancy; Mum thinks I should become a bank manager. It all sounds a bit dull, but at least I won't be down the pit like most of my mates.'

'Sounds bloody awful, dear chap. Ever thought about working for the government?'

Nic laughed, 'Not bloody likely! The civil service makes accountancy look sexy.'

Seb stared intently at Nic, 'It's not all boring,' he said cryptically. 'Parts of the Foreign Service can be quite exciting.'

'What are you doing? Recruiting spies?' Nic said sarcastically.

Seb smiled and whispered, 'Well, yes, actually, I am. But keep your voice down.'

Nic blanched, taking a sip from his pint, 'You want to recruit me?' he said incredulously.

Seb nodded, 'One of my jobs over the summer has been to seek out potential recruits for the Secret Intelligence Service. Earlier this week, my future boss came up to Oxford and told me about this chap on the Leeds rugby team who is a fluent Russian speaker.'

Nic was astonished. He did not know whether to be impressed or angry.

'What are you talking about?

 Seb looked a little sheepish. 'Sorry if I blindsided you. Let me try and explain. You've heard of the Cold War?' Seb asked.

'I'm from Sheffield, not Outer Mongolia!' Nic replied testily.

'Yes, yes. I am not handling this very well, am I? Let me start again. Since the end of the war, the Soviets have been itching to extend the Iron Curtain further west. That is why NATO was established. Everyone knows it was a mistake to let Stalin take control of Eastern Europe after the war. Now, we are locked in an ideological, political, and military battle between East and West. There is a real threat Soviet tanks will burst through the Iron Curtain and roll across Western Europe. We could all be speaking Russian!

'NATO is ill-equipped to respond, and individual governments, including ours, seem more interested in appeasing the Soviets, just like we did with the Nazis in the thirties, and we know how that ended. Look what has happened since the end of the war. Stalin annexed most of Eastern Europe. They stole the knowledge to build their atom bomb, blockaded Berlin, backed the north in the Korean War, murdered millions of their citizens, rolled tanks into Hungary, and built the Berlin Wall. All the while, we stood by and let them get on with it; only when they put nukes in Cuba did JFK finally stand up to them.'

Nic took a couple of deep breaths. He suddenly felt very sober. He paid enough attention to world events to understand the trajectory of the Cold War. He knew from his mother's stories how brutal the Soviet regime could be. She had lost all her extended family to Stalin's purges. Seb's passion resonated with him. He listened as Seb explained that the Foreign Office needed to recruit a new generation of agents to work for MI5 and MI6. He was intrigued. It could be a way to make a difference, and it sounded a lot more interesting than being an accountant or a banker.

Seb looked at his empty glass, turned and shouted, 'Two more, please, Maeve.'

That had been the start.

3

Nic sat in the lobby of the Foreign Office, one block away from Downing Street. Everything about the building intimidated him. Designed by George Gilbert Scott, the classically designed building was built on a scale intended to demonstrate the might of the British Empire. Frankly, it all looked a bit shabby. Two world wars had drained government resources, and routine maintenance had been neglected.

He wondered if accepting Seb's invitation to a follow-up meeting had been a mistake. The Foreign Office did not seem the sort of place where he would fit in.

In preparation for the meeting, he had done a little research. He discovered that Seb's full name was Sebastian James Merryweather Hyde Harmes. He was a bone-fide aristocrat with a title, Viscount Weston. As the eldest son of Baron Ebdale, he would inherit the baronetcy upon his father's death. Seb and his father had extensive entries in Debrett's Peerage, a sort of Who's Who for the upper classes.

The family owned a large estate in Oxfordshire, which included a village complete with a church and two pubs, a townhouse in Mayfair, a mews house in Marylebone, an estate in Scotland offering fly fishing on the river Spey, and a villa on the isle of Capri.

Seb was not just posh; he was from the uppermost echelon of the upper class, one step removed from royalty. Class-wise, he was about as far removed from Nic as it was possible to be.

When Seb reached out a few weeks after their first meeting in Oxford and suggested a follow-up meeting in London, Nic accepted, more out of curiosity than anything else. Now, as he sat looking up at the Grand Staircase, the defining feature of the FO building, he felt rather stupid.

'Mr. Slater?' said an attractive young woman standing before him. She was dressed demurely in a twinset and pearls more suited to someone twice her age. 'Hello, I am Miss Webster.'

'Call me Nic, Mr. Slater is my father,' Nic replied.

'Right you are, Nic. I am Suzy,' she said, smiling. Follow me, and I will show you to Viscount Weston's office.'

Nic smiled upon hearing Seb's title. Why was a working-class lad from Sheffield meeting with a member of the aristocracy to discuss spying for Her Majesty's Government? Aside from his fluency in Russian, he had nothing to offer.

Minutes later, he was laughing as Seb regaled him with a bawdy tale about the exploits of his younger brother and a housemaster's daughter at Eton. He may be upper class, but some of his language came straight from the gutter.

Seb's storytelling was interrupted by a knock on the door. Without waiting for a response, the door opened, and a tall, balding man in an immaculately tailored three-piece suit entered. He nodded at Seb and turned to Nic. 'You must be Slater. I am Sir Nicholas Crombie. Pleased to meet you,' he said, reaching out a hand.

Nic wondered if a Viscount outranked a Sir—he suspected they did, but Crombie was clearly in charge here. Nic shook the proffered hand. Crombie sat down, smoothing the perfect creases in his chalk pinstripe trousers before looking at Nic over the top of his half-moon glasses. 'Has Harmes told you what we are about here at Six?'

'A little, Sir. Although, to be honest, I am a bit bemused as to why I am here.'

'Don't worry about that,' Crombie said dismissively, 'All will become clear.'

The door opened, and Suzy reappeared carrying a tea tray and a small plate of biscuits. It took her a few minutes to complete the ritual of pouring milk, straining tea, and adding sugar. Nic offered to help, drawing surprised looks from Seb and Crombie. Serving tea was beneath them. Suzy smiled and thanked Nic.

'My pleasure,' Nic replied.

Seb laughed, 'You move fast. Miss Webster has worked for me for three months, and I never knew her first name.'

'Well, in your position, it is probably not a good idea to get too friendly with the help.' Nic said, smirking,

Crombie looked disapproving at such familiarity but said nothing. With the tea poured, Suzy left the room, and Crombie started talking. 'Historically, we have recruited agents from Oxford and Cambridge. Chaps from good families who know how to shoot, pass the port—that sort of thing.'

Nic did not know but said nothing.

'Unfortunately, during the thirties, a strong communist sentiment took root at both seats of learning. The Soviets found a fertile recruiting ground. English intellectuals were seduced by the idealism of Marxism and believed the Soviet Union offered the best hope for a new, more egalitarian society. The KGB successfully recruited quite a few young men who went on to occupy highly influential positions in government and the security services.

After the war, when the Soviet Union morphed from our ally to our enemy, these traitors started to do real damage. In 1951, Donald Maclean and Guy Burgess, who had met at Cambridge in the early thirties, defected. Both held senior posts in the Foreign Office and had supplied information to the Soviets since leaving Cambridge. Then, last month, Kim Philby defected, and all hell broke loose.

'Philby was the most senior of them all. I worked closely with him during the war and never suspected a thing. He was investigated after Maclean and Burgess defected, as we all were, but was given the all-clear. Now it transpires he was the one who warned them.

'We are conducting a root and branch review of our recruiting policies. One immediate effect is that we are looking beyond Oxbridge for talent. Clearly, upper-class intellectuals are not as sound as we previously thought.'

As he said this, Crombie looked pointedly at Seb, who just smiled. 'We are looking for intelligent, loyal, and mature young men to join the service. Your fluency in Russian makes you a perfect candidate for our intelligence officer training program. What do you think?'

Seb had warned him that Crombie would be direct.

'I'm not sure what an intelligence officer does,' Nic replied. 'My knowledge of espionage is limited to reading Graeme Greene and Ian Fleming; however, it does sound a bit more interesting than banking or accountancy.'

Crombie snorted, 'But not as well paid, I dare say.'

'The idea of serving my country is appealing. My mother feels she owes her life to Britain, and my dad fought in the war,' Nic said.

'And very brave he was too,' said Crombie.

They had done their homework. The meeting lasted another two hours. Crombie explained that the work could be dangerous. Nic would be eligible for a government pension; if anything untoward happened, his family would receive a generous life insurance payout. Nic did not know if that was supposed to assuage his fears.

He asked lots of questions. There was one answer that he particularly enjoyed hearing. He asked Crombie why the intelligence services had not hired more people from his background in the past. Crombie frowned, saying, 'Historically, the Foreign Office functioned as a rather cosy club, reuniting men from the same backgrounds, schools, and colleges, like Sebastian and me. There was a mistaken belief that those from the so-called lower classes were somehow less intelligent and less patriotic. Frankly, the outstanding performance of men like your father in the war started to change perceptions. Then the defections highlighted a critical failing at the FO.'

Nic was not surprised at the institutional arrogance but appreciated the honesty of the answer.

The more Crombie talked, the more intrigued he became. It sounded exciting but, more importantly, meaningful. He left the meeting having agreed in principle to sign on. Before leaving the building,

Nic was ushered into a small room where his photograph and fingerprints were taken. He also signed the Official Secrets Act and warned of the dire consequences if he revealed anything about that day's meeting to anyone, including his immediate family.

As he approached the exit, he saw Seb waiting for him.

'I think you have earned a drink,' he said.

'I certainly need one,' Nic replied.

They walked over to the Two Chairmen pub on Dartmouth Street, which Seb described as the local FO bar. Once they had their drinks, Seb raised his glass and said, 'Welcome to the Circus!'

Nic smiled. He had just finished reading John Le Carre's new novel The Spy Who Came in from the Cold, in which the Circus was the nickname of a fictional intelligence organisation that bore a striking similarity to MI6.

'What am I going to be? A performing monkey?'

4

'Welcome to the SIS, or the Secret Intelligence Service, for the mentally challenged amongst you,' barked the senior training officer standing at the front of the class. He had all the charm of an Army Sergeant Major. 'My job over the next few months is to break you into little pieces and put you back together so you can function as an agent in the field,'

One week earlier, Nic had walked across the stage of the Great Hall at Leeds University to receive his degree. His delighted parents had looked on with pride, and his sister had goaded him about graduating from a third-rate institution.

'I hear they give degrees away here with three Corn Flake box tops,' she teased.

'At least my degree deals with the real world. All you did was study dead languages and dead cultures.'

'Stop bickering,' said George. 'Margaret, your brother has done ever so well,' Kath said as she hugged her son. George patted him on the back and said, 'Well done, son,' which was about as demonstrative as he ever got.

The family's reaction to the news that he had accepted a job as an economics analyst at the Foreign Office was a mix of pride and surprise. His mother did not seem too disappointed; it was a respectable position, albeit not as prestigious as being a bank manager. His father offered no opinion, but as a die-hard socialist, he could hardly object to his son working for the state. Mags teased him by saying, 'So, you are going to be a spy!' He hoped his cover was not already blown.

The No. 1 Military Training Establishment at Fort Monckton sat four miles outside Portsmouth on the south coast of England, overlooking the Solent estuary. Much of the fort remained intact, including the drawbridge. Nic pondered the symbolism. Was he pulling up the drawbridge on his former life?

There were thirty recruits in the class—all men. Since the war, the only women in the SIS were secretaries and tea ladies, despite the outstanding performance of female operatives in occupied France. Crombie's assertion that the recruitment profile was changing seemed a stretch: there were only four non-Oxbridge members in the class. Nic, a cockney, Barry Finnis, who had graduated from Kings College London, and two army NCOs who had joined up at eighteen.

A gruelling six-month training program was ahead. Seb had warned him that fewer than half of all recruits successfully completed the course. Those who did would be assigned to either MI5, domestic intelligence, or MI6, overseas intelligence.

The training officer explained that they would spend the first two months at the fort, then move to Scotland for two months of field training and finish up with two months in London.

After the briefing was over, the recruits were ushered into a chilly gymnasium and ordered to strip down to their underpants. They had their vital signs checked, probes inserted into various orifices, reactions, eyesight, and hearing tested. An irregular heartbeat immediately reduced the class to twenty-nine.

After the medical, gym clothes were issued in preparation for a fitness test. Push-ups, pull-ups, rope climbing, vaulting, shuttle runs in the gym, a quarter-mile swim in the pool, and a five-mile run round the castle grounds were completed under the watchful eye and abusive voices of a group of Army NCOs. One unfortunate recruit landed awkwardly from a vault and had to be stretchered out of the gym with a broken ankle. Two down, and they were only three hours into the program.

The next two months followed a similar pattern: up at 06:00, an hour in the gym before breakfast, and three hours of classroom training on topics such as global politics, the characteristics of different national spy agencies, and the local customs of every Eastern European country.

After lunch, there was usually a four-hour exercise. Nic learned to build bridges, bug telephones, make bombs, and jump from a moving train. He swam in The Solent, dived down to the wreck of a Spanish galleon, and parachuted into the New Forest. Each evening, the exhausted recruits prepared their dinner and enjoyed two hours of free time before lights out at 22:00. Verbal, written, and physical tests were never announced and could occur at any time of day or night.

By the end of the second month, four more had left, so twenty-four trainee agents boarded the Flying Scotsman for the journey to Scotland. While first-class passengers sipped cocktails and dined on smoked salmon and roast beef, Nic and his classmates sat in an empty mail carriage devoid of any seats, windows, or heating at the back of the train. Apart from a ten-minute stop at Crewe to stretch their legs, they sat huddled together on the floor, cursing their plight.

Upon arrival in Fort William, they travelled by lorry to a remote camp in the Highlands. It was a bleak and desolate place situated at the end of Loch Arkaig. Sheep appeared to be the only other living things in the area.

The train ride's deprivations were nothing compared to what

they experienced over the next two months. The camp had been a commando and SAS training facility during the War. Nic wondered if his father had been there.

Not much seemed to have changed in the intervening years. An assortment of prefabricated single-story huts stood in a valley surrounded on three sides by mountains, through which ran a small burn that emptied into the loch.

Nic found the training exhausting but exhilarating. Fifty-mile treks through the Highlands, numerous nights spent out in the open with no tent, foraging for food, rock climbing, weapons training, self-defence, and mastering various types of watercraft were just some of the skills he learned. Again, sleep was frequently disturbed for a night hike, swim, or sabotage exercise.

One unfortunate recruit died of exposure during an overnight exercise after becoming detached from the rest of his team and fell into a snow-covered crevasse in the dark. His lifeless body was not found until the following day. Nic was shocked, not just by the death but also by the dismissive attitude of the instructors. When one trainee became emotional, an NCO told him to, 'Get his shit together. You should have been at Arnhem; then you would know the meaning of senseless death.'

In addition to the fatality, six other recruits flamed out while in Scotland. That left seventeen of the original thirty, and they were only two-thirds of the way through their training.

While others complained about the rigour of the exercises, Nic thrived. He became fitter and stronger. He realised that the intensity of the training was in his best interests. The better trained he was, the better prepared he would be to face challenges in the field.

He also liked how he looked. His body had transformed from that of a reasonably fit twenty-three-year-old with the beginnings of a beer belly to a lean, strong athlete with well-defined abdominals, muscled calves, and bulging biceps. He gained a stone in weight, all of it muscle. He had muscles in all the right places and not a scrap of excess fat. Even the pain diminished over time.

5

September 1963 – London

Nic stepped off the southbound Metropolitan Line train, walked quickly across the platform at Finchley Road, and boarded a southbound Bakerloo Line train just as the doors closed. It was the seventh tube train he had taken in the last hour.

Now based in London, the remaining recruits were in week two of the final three months of training. Today's exercise was to identify and lose a four-man surveillance team. Starting at Victoria, Nic had taken the Circle Line to Charing Cross, Bakerloo Line to Oxford Circus, Central Line to Tottenham Court Road, Northern Line to Euston, walked to Euston Square, boarded a Metropolitan Line train to Wembley Park, and reversed direction back to Finchley Road. He was certain he had lost all his tails.

The instructors had taught the apprentice agents how to spot a tail. Sudden bouts of window shopping, reading a newspaper but never turning the pages, or standing in random doorways were all useful indicators.

The program was just as intensive as Scotland's, but in a different way. The focus was more on the brain than the body. Courses covering evasion skills, dead drops, brush contacts, codes and ciphers, and disguises were punctuated with long practical exercises on the streets and in the parks of the capital.

The instructors were an eclectic group. The code and cipher instructor was a delightful middle-aged lady who reminded Nic of his aunt. She arrived each day dressed in a twinset and pearls, her hair tightly permed, and carrying a capacious Mary Poppins-style handbag. Rumour had it that she had helped win the war by decoding Enigma messages at Bletchley Park. In addition to encoding messages, she taught them all manner of communication methods, from chalk marks on lampposts to semaphore, using curtains and laundry hanging on a clothesline.

The two instructors teaching disguise both worked at Shepperton Film Studios. The make-up artist had worked with Joseph Cotton, Orson Welles, and Trevor Howard on The Third Man. The clothing designer had recently dressed Gregory Peck and David Niven for The Guns of Navarone. After working with them, Nic could age himself by thirty years, fake a limp, and pass himself off as a Russian Orthodox priest.

Two of the more interesting sessions addressed the essential tradecrafts of smoking and seduction. Nic was not a smoker. His father's early morning cough had deterred him from doing much more than trying a sneaky Players No. 6 behind the bike sheds at school. Not smoking made him the exception amongst his peers. The boys smoked to look cool; the girls smoked to look sexy. At least, that was the message conveyed by Hollywood. It seemed to have worked work for Lauren Bacall and Humphrey Bogart.

The instructor explained that smoking could cover a multitude of covert actions. Human nature draws attention to movement. Observers focus on the actions of the smoker, from removing a cigarette from the packet to lighting, inhaling, and exhaling, to stubbing out the spent butt. Each movement could mask a sleight of hand involving a discrete handoff, retrieval, or signal. Stopping to light a cigarette was also a fine way to interrupt a pursuit and reduce the risk of observation.

When Nic mentioned the recent furore linking smoking to cancer, his instructor reminded him that he was training to be a spy. A job that could easily result in him ending up dead in a dark alley or entombed in a cell in the basement of the Lubyanka, so getting a bad cough should be the least of his concerns.

The seduction, or "shagging", course, as it was universally known, was very popular with the group of testosterone-filled young men. There were three instructors, two women and one man.

Molly Staines was an elegant lady in her early fifties. Although she looked nothing like a temptress, she did have a very seductive smile and a wicked sense of humour. It was rumoured that she had been a successful spy operating in Paris during the war. Numerous senior Nazi officers had succumbed to her charms and shared their secrets across the pillow.

Much to the delight of the trainees, she frequently brought young actresses into the classroom to role-play. She directed role-playing scenes demonstrating different seduction techniques. Flattery, teasing, humour, nonchalance, anger, and disinterest all played a role. She also taught the group how to analyse someone's personality. Were they outgoing, shy, serious, frivolous, or intellectual? Did the way they dressed accentuate or hide their true persona?

Nic gained a newfound appreciation for feminine wiles, knowledge he wished he had a few years earlier. Despite frequent boasting to the contrary, he was not experienced in relationships with the opposite sex, having had only one girlfriend. It was a chaste relationship that lasted for two years while at university. It ended just before graduation when she decided that a prospective civil servant was not ideal husband material and dumped him. His mother, who had adored the girl, continued to remind him that she was now engaged to a doctor.

The second instructor, Jean McDonald, was a psychologist in her mid-thirties. She had a lovely, soft Edinburgh accent and a slender figure. All the recruits fancied her. Her specialty was interpreting non-verbal cues such as gestures and mannerisms. She taught the boys how to read feminine signals and respond appropriately. She regularly used her skills to flirt outrageously. She would lead someone on, and then just when they thought they were making progress, she would humiliate them in front of their peers. Everyone loved her sessions. Nic had no idea that so much could be discerned from an eye movement, a flick of the hair, or the crossing and uncrossing of the legs.

The best sessions were when Jean took them out in groups of four or five on field trips around London. They went to pubs and restaurants, had picnics in the park, and sat in the lobbies of grand London hotels to observe interactions between people. Jean pointed out different situations and the characteristics she used to identify them. A couple meeting for the first time, a man approaching a woman for a clandestine rendezvous, a cheating husband or wife meeting their lover, a prostitute soliciting for business, a homosexual approaching a prospective partner.

Jean decoded the signals people used to communicate, such as a concierge's nod to a bellman indicating the arrival of a valued guest or a two-person surveillance team using hand gestures to communicate. More interesting were the unconscious signals people exhibited, such as a man mentally undressing a woman, the frowns of a couple who had just had a row, or the distant expression of a woman bored stiff by her companion.

After one such outing, Nic said to Jean, 'Who needs words when you can tell everything about a person by their gestures and mannerisms?'

'Precisely my point, dear boy. For example, you have very little experience with women, do not like smoking, and are uncomfortable around the upper classes. Correct?'

Nic blushed. Was it that obvious?

'Don't be embarrassed. It is my job. I will teach you how to suppress those signals.'

The third instructor, Paolo Giovani, ran an Italian restaurant in South London and was fluent in Italian, German, and English. He had moved to London in 1930 to escape the rise of fascism in his homeland. He was recruited by MI5 at the outbreak of World War II for his language skills and had become a key member of the "Double Cross" team at MI5, which successfully turned numerous captured German and Italian spies to work as double agents and feed disinformation back to their employers

While in London, Seb insisted Nic stay with him at his house in Wimpole Mews, near Marylebone Station. The building was originally the family stables where Seb's ancestors had saddled up their horses for rides through Regents Park. In the early 20th century, the stables were converted into a very desirable townhouse with a garage on the ground floor and three floors of living accommodations above. It was a vast improvement on the spartan digs in Scotland.

Despite the gulf in their heritage, social background, and political views, they were becoming good friends. Seb's coarse sense of humour kept Nic from stressing too much about the potential dangers of his new job.

Since their first meeting on the rugby field, Seb had enjoyed the good life rather too much. He had given up any form of strenuous activity, save for passing the port, developing the corpulent frame of a dedicated connoisseur of the long lunch, usually at one of the many clubs he belonged to. His sartorial style could best be described as "scruffy country gentleman," blending woollen waistcoats with generously tailored tweed suits, always accessorised with a bow tie and pocket square, which was frequently used to clean his glasses, wipe his nose, or mop up minor spills before being stuffed back into place.

On evenings when Seb was not dining out, they enjoyed long conversations over bottles of very good wine. Nic sensed that Seb was a bit of a disappointment to his father, Baron Ebdale. He had only been admitted to Oxford because four generations of the Harmes male line had attended Lincoln College and made significant donations to their alma mater.

His lowly third-class degree was no reflection of his intellect; he was very smart and had a quick mind. Nic was constantly amazed at his ability to have seemingly intelligent conversations about anything with anyone. His lacklustre academic record was more the result of lack of application than lack of ability.

While at Eton, he ran a lucrative business blackmailing the teachers with information gained from his wide circle of spies in the lower years of the school. No affair, assignation, or clumsy fumble went unreported to Seb.

At Oxford, in addition to his performances on the rugby pitch, he was a leading light of the Oxford Union debating society and Oxford Revue comedy group. In his spare time, he ran an illegal betting operation that counted two future MPs, three barristers, a Church of England vicar, and a fellow Viscount among its clientele. The fruits of this scheme were reflected in the gorgeous 1951 Bentley Mark VI drop-head that he piloted around London.

Ironically, it was Seb's money-making skills that led to his recruitment by the Security Services. One of the best customers of his betting syndicate was the son of the permanent secretary at the Foreign Office. He had followed in his father's footsteps and joined the Foreign Office. One evening, Seb ran into him at their mutual club in London and bemoaned the drudgery of his position as an articled clerk at a law firm. His friend immediately recruited him despite Seb falling short of the academic requirements. Nic suspected his passage might also have been smoothed by his father's membership of the House of Lords and friendship with numerous cabinet ministers.

Like most members of his class, Seb seemed to know everyone who was anyone. He had partied with Princess Margaret, been in Berlin with actress Vanessa Redgrave when The Wall first appeared and was friends with the Beyond the Fringe cast of Jonathan Miller, Peter Cook, Dudley Moore, and Alan Bennett.

In comparison, Nic's only encounter with anyone remotely famous was seeing England goalkeeper Ron Springett walking down the street in Sheffield.

One evening, over an excellent claret, Seb told Nic the story of his walk-on part in the Profumo Affair. Sometime in late 1962, Seb had been sitting in the mews house reading when he heard gunshots in the street outside. Rushing to investigate, he found a man brandishing a gun and hurling insults at the home of one of his neighbours. The subject of the man's ire was

Stephen Ward, an osteopath who moved in London's most fashionable social circles. The gunman was Johnny Edgecombe, a former lover of a young showgirl, Christine Keeler, who frequently stayed at Ward's house.

Not long after, with Ward's help, Keeler had accomplished the remarkable feat of having simultaneous affairs with the then Minister of War, John Profumo, and a Soviet naval attaché, Yevgeny Ivanov, who happened to work for the KGB.

When news of the affairs became public, the proverbial excrement hit the fan. Profumo resigned in disgrace, Ward committed suicide, and the nineteen-year-old Keeler was branded a scarlet woman.

Seb was interviewed by the police, but his witness statement strangely disappeared, and all mention of him relating to the case disappeared soon after he joined the Foreign Office. MI5 had considered using Keeler as bait to try and get Ivanov to defect. Still, once the affair became public, they erased all trace of intelligence service involvement, including Seb's role as an innocent bystander.

Seb admitted that he had been rather jealous of the parade of beautiful young women who flitted in and out of Ward's house. He had particularly noticed a vivacious blonde by the name of Mandy Rice-Davis. 'I met her at one of Ward's parties. A feisty young thing!'

Seb had an endless supply of sordid and salacious tales. It opened Nic's eyes. The upper class was not much different from anyone else—except their tales involved Taittinger rather than Tetley's!

On another evening, much to Nic's surprise, Seb said he believed Nic was far better equipped for the real world, given his grittier life experience. Nic responded, 'You mean because I am a working-class oik?' Seb demurred.

Nic's time in London was exhausting. It was not just the long training days; Seb insisted on introducing him to a side of London he had only read about in the newspapers: debutante balls, garden parties, dinner parties, and long lunches at gentlemen's clubs.

It was expensive; he had to rent a top hat and tails to attend the Boat Race, Royal Ascot, and the Henley Rowing Regatta, and it required a lot of preparation. Seb showed him how to tie a bow tie and trained him on dinner table etiquette.

Nic wondered what his father would say about all the hobnobbing he was doing. Comments about bloody toffs and upper-class twits came to mind. While he found each new experience intimidating, he also found them enjoyable. Not least because, much to Seb's annoyance, he was hugely popular with the female members of Seb's social circle. The combination of his provincial accent, modest upbringing, handsome features, and chiselled abs seemed to have a remarkable effect on the young debs of high society who fancied a bit of rough. He had ample opportunities to put Jean McDonald's techniques to the test—some of them even worked,

6

September 1963 – Oxfordshire

Nic coaxed Sadie, his sister's aging Morris Minor, through the gates of Sangster Hall, the Harmes family estate. He didn't own a car but had prevailed upon his big sister to borrow hers for the weekend. Despite the inevitable sibling bickering, Mags spoiled her little brother. In return, he would do anything for his big sis.

Seb had been pestering Nic to visit for some time, and he had finally run out of excuses. He enjoyed knocking around with Seb in London but was petrified about meeting his family. How do you address a Baron? Should he bow? What should he wear? Would his table manners pass muster?

Seb warned him that hunting, shooting, and fishing would all be on the agenda. Apart from a few rainy Saturdays fishing in the polluted canal back home, Nic had no experience of such country pursuits and was convinced he would make a fool of himself.

Sadie bumped down a long driveway flanked on both sides by tall elm trees. According to Seb, his great-grandfather had planted them after visiting Blenheim Palace and seeing the elms lining both sides of the mile-long Great Avenue.

Eventually, the drive opened onto a wide gravel area in front of a house that was part castle, part palace. Seb had told him to park in the courtyard to the side of the house. He pulled up beside Seb's Bentley, a Rolls, and a Daimler. He patted the steering wheel and said, 'We are in elite company, Sadie. Do not let me down.'

The side door opened, and a man dressed in a dark three-piece suit appeared, 'Good afternoon, Sir. I am Hayes, Baron Ebdale's butler. May I take your case?'

Nic was embarrassed to hand over his battered cardboard suitcase; Hayes was probably more used to handling Louis Vuitton.

Nic followed Hayes down a long corridor through a magnificent entrance hall and into what the butler called the drawing room. His parents' two-up, two-down terrace could comfortably fit inside several times over. He counted twelve windows, each at least twelve feet tall. A hodgepodge of mismatched chairs, sofas, and tables lay scattered around the room. The windows overlooked a formal garden, beyond which were rolling fields punctuated by small stands of trees for as far as the eye could see.

Hanging on the walls were a series of enormous oil paintings. Nic assumed they were portraits of Seb's ancestors. Upper-class fashion could be traced through the ages, from when men powdered their faces and wore stockings to the present day, when the roles were reversed. Nic gazed at what he thought maybe a 17th-century Baron Ebdale when one of the many doors flew open, and Seb burst in.

'Welcome to our humble abode, old chap. I see you are studying the family tree.'

He pointed to a picture of a very elegant lady in Edwardian garb, her expression not unlike Queen Victoria's in mourning. That is Granny, and next to her is Mumsy.

'Where are you?' Nic asked.

'I don't qualify yet. You only get a painting when you become Baron or Baroness. I must wait for Papa to fall off the twig before I join this rogue's gallery. Time for a welcome drink, don't you think?' It was not a question. Seb walked over to a sideboard laden with various shaped decanters and poured two generous whiskies. He handed one to Nic and said, 'Take a seat. The family will be assembling shortly.'

Various family members wandered in, and Nic was introduced to the Baron, his wife, the Baroness, Seb's twin sister, Viola, and his younger brother, Fabian. They all spoke with the same slightly nasal intonation. Nic felt like a museum exhibit as each one cast an appraising eye over the strange working-class specimen who had clearly escaped from the servants' quarters.

After drinks, dinner was served in a dining room that was only slightly smaller than the drawing room. Apart from some confusion over what to do with what turned out to be a fish knife, Nic felt he acquitted himself quite well.

Dinner conversation revolved around topics upon which Nic either had no opinion: death duties, declining quality of the food in the House of Lords, the rising cost of domestic help, or where he prudently kept his opinions to himself such as the unchecked rise of trade union power, lack of common decency amongst today's youth, communist infiltration of the Labour Party. The only sign the family had evolved in the last couple of hundred years was that the ladies did not retire after dinner to allow the men to smoke cigars and drink brandy.

He sat next to Viola during dinner. She took an instant liking to Nic and flirted with him throughout dinner. During dessert, she made it clear he was welcome to visit her bedroom later. He tried to politely demur. She looked disappointed, 'Well then, you can ride me in the morning.'

Nic thought he had missed the word "with" and said, 'I am

not much of a horseman.'

'Who said anything about horses?'

Nic felt himself blushing. She laughed. 'I am just teasing; I will be at the stables at seven.'

Training to be a spy was much easier than dining with the aristocracy. By the time he got back to his room, he was exhausted.

The rest of the weekend was no more relaxing. The next morning, Nic presented himself, as ordered, to the stables, where Viola was waiting. He noted that her jodhpurs and riding boots fit her very well. After a near tumble while trying to mount his horse, a huge thing called Brutus, he was pleased to avoid falling off as they trotted across the muddy fields of the estate. At one point, Vi galloped off into the distance. Mercifully, Brutus did not follow. When they returned to the stables, he felt he was getting the hang of it. Thankfully, Viola did not try to seduce him further, and they were back in time to join the others for an early lunch. Another half dozen guests had arrived; most seemed to be members of the huntin', shootin', and fishin' set with names like Gerald and Veronica.

After lunch everyone piled into a couple of Land Rovers to go shooting. Nic was thankful the targets were clay pigeons not grouse. His training proved invaluable as he impressed everyone with his marksmanship, eliciting many comments about how good the shooting must be 'up north.'

As the weekend progressed, he struggled to master the bewildering set of protocols that governed every aspect of country life. He thanked Hayes so many times for small services that he was finally told, 'Sir, there is no need to thank me every time I do something. It is my job.'

Nic found Baron Ebdale charming in that smug way of the English upper class. He asked questions and listened attentively to the answers, but Nic could tell he had little appreciation of what it meant to be working class. All the other guests were regular members of the Harmes' social circle. Nic, Seb, and his siblings were the only ones under fifty.

While walking back from the shoot, Nic asked Seb about the family's choice of names. Sebastian, Viola, and Fabian were uncommon in the West Riding of Yorkshire. Seb sighed and informed Nic that if he knew his Shakespeare, he would know that Sebastian and Viola were the twins in Twelfth Night and Fabian was the clown. Baron Ebdale had met the future Baroness during a college theatre production of Twelfth Night at Oxford.

When Nic asked Seb if Viola was always quite so forward, he laughed. 'Tried to seduce you, did she? She is insatiable. All my chums are desperate to get into her knickers. By all accounts, she has been bonking her way around London all summer!'

He managed to mostly avoid Viola for the rest of the weekend, although she did manage to slide her tongue into his mouth when giving him a goodbye kiss on Sunday afternoon.

He was mentally exhausted by the time he was reunited with Sadie for the drive back to London. He had only embarrassed himself a few times. He returned the car to Mags and took the train back into London. When he emptied his pockets, back in his flat, he found a piece of paper in his pocket with Viola's London phone number written on it and the words, 'Call me soon, lover boy.'

7

October 1963 – London

As the training intensified, Nic had less time for social pursuits. Night-time exercises became common. Twenty-four-hour days were not unusual, and sleep deprivation became the norm.

Everyone was ordered to move into a bleak dormitory in deepest, darkest Bermondsey, south of the River Thames, in the heart of Docklands. The instructors explained that Bermondsey was a useful surrogate for the working-class neighbourhoods of Eastern Europe, where they would soon spend a lot of time. It was a desolate landscape. Undeveloped bomb sites, decaying housing, putrid smells, and thick early-morning smog created an oppressive environment. All this in a country that had supposedly won the war.

Despite the squalor and deprivation, Nic felt more at home than in Mayfair. The locals exhibited the same spirit he had grown up with in Sheffield. Housewives scrubbed their front steps with pride. Children played cricket and football on any vacant piece of ground. Men supped their pints at the local while debating the prospects of the local football team. Substitute Sheffield United for Millwall, and he could have been at home.

One of the briefings described how the Communist Party had tried to foment unrest in areas like Bermondsey. However, after some initial success before and during the war, support for the Communist Party cratered after the drawing of the Iron Curtain and the brutal crushing of the Hungarian uprising. The area was rough but not revolutionary. The locals were socialists but also monarchists and nationalists, much like Nic and his dad.

The accommodations were far from salubrious. The twelve remaining agents shared a single dormitory on the first floor of an abandoned workhouse. A temperamental coal-burning stove that belched acrid smoke offered the only heating. The windows had no curtains, and some lacked glass. Each agent had a wire-framed bed with a thin mattress, one sheet, and one blanket. Possessions were stowed in a footlocker at the end of their bed. There was one bathroom with a single shower, no hot water, and two toilet stalls, each with a limited supply of very rough toilet paper. Meals were served in a draughty canteen on the ground floor and appeared to consist of multiple variations of beef stew without the beef.

Nic thought that if this accurately represented conditions behind the Iron Curtain, then the West did not have much to fear.

During his little free time, Nic walked the streets of the East End with one of his classmates, Barry Finnis. Barry was the only other civilian, working-class kid in the class. He was the son of an East End market trader blessed with a brain that had earned him a scholarship to Kings College, London. He had a gift for languages and spoke some Russian, albeit with a strong Cockney accent. He appointed himself as Nic's tour guide.

Despite the decline of the British Empire, the Port of London remained a bustling hub of global trade, a twenty-four-hour-a-day operation that handled almost sixty million tonnes of goods a year. The area adjacent to the docks was a hive of activity. Factories processed the imported materials, making everything from cigars to briefcases. Warehouses stored goods waiting for transport, and dozens of pubs served an always thirsty workforce.

As they navigated the cobbled streets, he and Barry tried out various disguises and developed their dead drops and brush contacts. Barry also co-opted Nic into some minor criminal activity. They breached buildings, conducted searches, and surreptitiously followed and photographed people, usually attractive young ladies.

As their training neared its end, the primary topic of conversation amongst the trainees turned to their first assignment. Everyone wanted a plum posting to either Berlin, Moscow, or Istanbul. Nic expected a Moscow posting as hc was the class's only truly fluent Russian speaker. Barry also hoped to go to Moscow and insisted he and Nic only speak Russian to each other to improve his fluency.

8

November 1963 – Langley, Virginia, USA

For the final week of training, the remaining ten trainees were shipped to the CIA headquarters in Langley, Virginia, just outside Washington, D.C.

After the bleak conditions in Scotland and Bermondsey, the group was excited to experience America. Unfortunately, the trip over was not on a plush airliner. They boarded a huge US Air Force Lockheed C-121 Constellation at Greenham Common Air Base for the nine-hour flight to Andrews Air Force Base in Maryland. The seats were metal benches along the side of the fuselage, the middle of the plane was filled with assorted crates, and there were no flight attendants. After landing, they were taken to CIA Headquarters in a yellow school bus.

Much to the group's disappointment, the first few days of the course consisted of twelve hours of classes conducted in windowless basement rooms. As Barry noted, 'They could have done this in bloody Slough and saved a ton of money.'

Nic was not too disappointed. Fifteen CIA trainees were also attending the course, and Nic took every opportunity to quiz them on all things American, from baseball to burgers.

The instructors were all seasoned CIA operatives. On the second day, one of them, a six-foot, four-inch-tall black Marine Major named Moses Ranger, delivered a compelling lecture on the origins of the Cold War from a US perspective. He traced the roots of the current conflict back to Churchill and Eisenhower's failure to confront Stalin while the Soviet Union was still an ally during the last days of World War II. They allowed the Russians to enter Berlin first and gifted them most of Eastern Europe. The West had created its own new enemy. Nic corralled Ranger after the lecture and bombarded him with questions. Eventually, Ranger said, 'Bro, I need a beer. Let's grab some steak and suds?'

'I am not sure I'm allowed out,' Nic said.

'You are if you're with me.'

Twenty minutes later, Nic was sitting in the passenger seat of Ranger's cherry red 1963 Corvette Stingray as they shot through the front gates of CIA Headquarters. Heading west into the Virginia countryside, the V8 engine roared as Ranger accelerated to 60mph in less than six seconds while still in second gear. It contrasted sharply with Sadie's more sedate 0-60 time of just over 30 seconds!

Being on the right-hand side of the road felt strange, with yellow instead of white lines down the middle. They passed a gas station, and Nic saw a uniformed attendant wiping the windscreen of a car while pumping gas. It looked like a scene from a movie.

Ranger pulled up at what looked like a corrugated iron shack by the side of the road. A faded wooden sign announced they had arrived at 'Hals Steak Shack.' An assortment of pick-up trucks and sports cars were parked outside.

'This is our local,' Ranger said, 'Don't worry, the beer is cold, and the steaks are rare.'

The place was packed. About half the clientele were in uniform. As they walked to the bar, Ranger acknowledged greetings from many of them.

'You seem pretty popular around here,' Nic commented.

'I tend to stand out,' Ranger said, smiling.

Two cold beer bottles with tops removed were already sitting on the bar.

'Thanks, Hal,' Ranger said. 'We will take two ribeyes, medium rare.'

'Sure thing. Take a seat, and I will bring the food over,' replied a grey-haired man with a thick beard and a large tattoo of a dagger on his forearm.

The décor could best be described as minimalist. The walls were black-painted plywood adorned with numerous patches representing different military units and pictures of scantily clad girls. The floor was covered in discarded peanut shells.

'A bit different to your local, isn't it?' Ranger asked.

'Just a tad,' Nic replied. He took a swig of beer. As Ranger had promised, it was cold but also tasteless. The food proved more satisfying. The steaks were huge and accompanied by an enormous baked potato slathered with butter, cheese, bacon, and some white stuff Nic could not identify.

'What is this?' he asked.

Ranger laughed, 'Sour cream. It's good.'

He was right. The steak was tender and juicy, unlike the overdone cuts so prevalent in England. Ranger talked about how the CIA and MI6 worked together as they ate. He candidly explained that there was a lack of trust on both sides. The British were upset that they were now very much the junior partner, and the Americans were incensed at the damage done by the recent defections.

'It's a strange time,' Ranger explained. 'We are supposed to be allies, but sometimes it feels like we spend more time fighting each other than the Soviets.' Nic appreciated his honesty.

After dinner, Ranger dropped Nic back at Langley. He felt

like he just had his first authentic American experience.

'Where have you been?' shouted Barry as he walked into the dormitory wing.

'Just doing my homework,' Nic replied.

'No, bloody way! You've been on the piss; how did you swing that?'

'Didn't you know? I am the teacher's pet.'

Barry scoffed, shaking his head, 'I thought you were just some northern plonker, but you're not as dumb as you look.'

Nic was not sure if that was a compliment or not. The next few evenings followed the same pattern. Over more beer and beef, Nic and Ranger discussed everything from the influence of the blues on rock' n roll to the possibility of the Soviets launching a nuclear first strike. Nic felt he was getting private tuition—learning more from these extracurricular sessions than from the formal classes.

He wondered why Ranger had chosen him for special treatment. When he asked, the reply was succinct and honest: 'You are a little different than the usual Brit, not quite so pompous, and now you owe me. I need a man on the inside at MI6.'

Nic wasn't sure how to take that. Was he now a double agent serving at Ranger's beck and call? He was beginning to suss out how the spy game worked. Everything was about leverage. A good spy needed collateral to make deals, be it favours owed or 'kompromat' as the Russians called it. Was that what Ranger planned for him?

On the final day of the course, the combined British and American group boarded a bus for a tour of Washington, D.C., followed by dinner at a restaurant on the Potomac. Nic was impressed by the Capitol Building, White House, Lincoln Memorial, and other grand buildings surrounding the National Mall. It was so different from London, which had evolved over centuries rather than been planned from the start.

The tour ended with a visit to Arlington National Cemetery. Founded immediately after the Civil War, 1964 marked the Cemetery's centennial. It was a moving and sombre experience. The rows of graves along the hillside and the Tomb of the Unknown Soldier brought home the sacrifices that successive generations had made in the name of peace and freedom.

As they walked through the cemetery, Ranger guided Nic away from the main group to section twenty-four. He pointed to the markings on the marble gravestones. Each had the letters U.S.C.T. engraved on them.

'What does that stand for?' Nic asked.

'United States Coloured Troops,' Ranger replied.

Nic looked at him, 'Coloured troops were kept separate?'

'Yes. In both life and death. They are buried in different sections to white soldiers.'

Nic knew a little about America's racist history, but this was his first direct exposure. He wondered how Ranger felt about serving in the military, which treated him as a second-class citizen until just a few years ago.

The evening turned into a riotous affair. Much to the delight of the all-male class, a group of young women had been bussed in from Langley and the Pentagon to join them for dinner. Fuelled by alcohol, the dancing became frenetic and the petting heavy. Nic suspected that one or two clandestine couplings took place along the banks of the Potomac.

The next morning, a very subdued group emerged for the

short ride to Andrews and the flight back to the UK. One recruit failed to show up, having apparently decided to go to a young lady's apartment after dinner, leaving only nine to return to London.

9

December 1963 – Moscow

Irina Sashkaya walked through the Kremlin Palace of Congresses, a massive concrete and glass structure built to Khrushchev's orders in the late 1950s. She was trying to find one of the eight hundred rooms within, having been summoned to a meeting with Foreign Minister Andrei Gromyko and KGB Chief Vladimir Semichastny. What could be so important? Irina was only three years removed from the KGB academy; Politburo members rarely engaged with such junior staff.

After twice asking for directions, she found the room. The Politburo had just finished a meeting as Khrushchev and his three most senior deputies, Kosygin, Podgorny, and Brezhnev, left the room. They did not attempt to disguise their appraisal of her; eyes moved from head to foot and back again. She was subjected to such treatment multiple times a day. It was one of the many cracks in the façade of the perfect socialist state offering equality to all. Women were not equal; they were merely there to serve men.

She stood aside to let the three men pass before moving cautiously towards the door. She saw her friend and fellow agent, Yuri Kovlev, standing inside the room. As she entered, he turned, smiled, and said, 'You as well? Do you know why we are here?' She shook her head, but a gruff voice summoned them both to sit at the table before she could say anything.

Gromyko had been Minister of Foreign Affairs since 1957. He was one of the few Soviet leaders who had been a close confidante of both Stalin and Khrushchev. Semichastny had headed the KGB since 1961. At only forty, he was young to be in such a senior position. Irina had only met him once before. He had a reputation as ideologically rigid, decrying Nobel prize winner Boris Pasternak, author of Doctor Zhivago, as "a pig that shits in its own sty." He also was known for his disdain for women serving in the KGB.

Gromyko smiled, 'Thank you both for coming so promptly,' he said unnecessarily. The summons had been an order, not a request.

'You are probably wondering about the purpose of this meeting, so let me get straight to the point.'

He slid a piece of paper across the table. The typed heading read Pobezhdat, the Russian word for Vanquish.

Below were a series of dates and places:

"61-Berlin/London, 62-Cuba, 63-Dallas, 64-Vietnam, 65-Finland/Iran, 66-The Moon."

'Do either of you understand the significance of this list?' he asked.

Yuri slowly shook his head. Irina nodded. 'I think so, Comrade,' she said hesitantly.

'Go on,' Gromyko urged.

'Berlin refers to the construction of the Berlin Wall, and London could be the entrapment of British Minister of War John Profumo. Cuba is our siting of nuclear missiles on the island, and President Kennedy was assassinated in Dallas.'

'Do you know what connects them?'

'I am not sure, other than they were all embarrassing for the West,' Irina said.

'True, but there is more to it than that. All these events were orchestrated directly by the Soviet Union as part of a long-term strategy to destabilize the West.'

Yuri gasped. Gromyko smiled, 'Clever, don't you think?'

'Yes, comrade,' said Irina, 'Why have the Americans or the British not discovered the link?"

'Because they are stupid,' Semichastny interjected.

'That may be so,' Gromyko conceded, 'but we have also executed a successful deception. After Hungary in 1956, the Politburo became concerned about the growing gap in nuclear capability between us and the United States. The Americans had over 3,600 nuclear weapons compared to our 400. We needed to reduce the threat of the Americans thinking they could launch a successful nuclear attack. Khrushchev started to talk about "peaceful co-existence," whereby socialist states could live in peace alongside capitalist ones. We attempted to reduce the rising tension and back away from the policy of trying to bring about a Marxist-Leninist world revolution. We backed it up with concrete action. We participated in peace conferences, Khrushchev visited the United States in 1959, and we signed the nuclear test ban treaty. However, peaceful co-existence was a cover for a series of clandestine operations we collectively called Vanquish.'

'We have completely fooled the American imperialists,' added Semichastny.

Irina and Yuri exchanged shocked looks. Never mind the Americans having no idea; neither did most of the KGB. It was an audacious strategy that had worked flawlessly. However, if the Americans ever learned that the Soviet Union instigated Kennedy's assassination, nuclear war could easily be on the agenda.

Semichastny took over, 'This year, Vanquish is focused on Indochina. We are equipping the North Vietnamese and Viet

Cong to drag the Americans further into an unwinnable conflict. Next year, we will see how serious NATO is about defending Europe by invading Finland and Iran. In 1966, we will win the space race by landing a man on the moon.'

'In parallel, we are prosecuting longer-term missions to sow civil unrest across the globe,' added Gromyko. 'Since 1962, we have been working to incite racial unrest across the United States to ignite a civil war. Comrade Khrushchev has just approved a mission to assassinate a leading civil rights leader in the next few weeks.'

Irina assumed he was referring to Martin Luther King.

'In Europe, we already fund the French and Italian communist parties, are preparing the ground for a military coup in Greece, and are running a propaganda campaign in West Germany, pushing for re-unification under a socialist regime. As for Britain, the new Labour government is full of Soviet sympathisers, many of whom are on our payroll. Brezhnev, First Secretary of the Communist Party, has recently said that Britain was ripe for revolution before the decade's end.

'Why are you telling us all this, comrade?' Yuri asked.

'As the pace and scope of Vanquish increases, we need to ensure that no leaks occur. Until recently, we had highly placed sources in the CIA, FBI, MI5, and MI6 who could help disguise what we were doing. Now, almost all our sources have either defected or been exposed. That is where the two of you come in.' Yuri glanced at Irina. He saw apprehension in her eyes.

For the next hour, Semichastny explained that the continued success of Vanquish required an effective program of disinformation, deception, and diversion. Defections had decimated the CIA and MI6 networks behind the Iron Curtain, but both agencies were actively working to rebuild. Finally, he got to their mission, 'You will infiltrate these new networks, posing as recruitable double agents and serve as conduits for a flow of disinformation that will mask the truth about Vanquish.'

After a few more minutes of briefing, they were dismissed and told to await further instructions. As they left the room, Irina turned to Yuri and said, 'I need a drink.'

Once outside, Irina said, 'Can you believe what we just heard?'

'It's a lot to take in, but all those events did happen, so I suppose we could have been behind them.'

'If so, it's our most successful operation since the end of the Great Patriotic War.'

Yuri nodded, 'By the sound of it, it's only going to get bigger. Do you really think we can put a man on the moon in under three years?

'Maybe, but I am unsure we could bring them back alive! What concerns me more are the other operations. Surely, the Americans will connect the dots.'

'I think it is our job to ensure that does not happen,' Yuri replied. He pushed open the door to a small bar tucked away in a back street near the Lenkom Theatre. They were far enough away from the Kremlin and Lubyanka to avoid other KGB officers. The place was packed. The clientele an eclectic mix of mix of students, actors, and musicians. Loud western pop music blared through a thick cloud of cigarette smoke. Elvis Presley was singing about his Blue Suede Shoes. A small group of boys and girls were dancing energetically, an activity still frowned upon by the authorities.

There was no chance anyone could eavesdrop on them here.

Irina found two stools, and Yuri got their drinks. He returned with two beers and a bottle of vodka.

'I figured we might need more than one,' he said.

10

December 1963 – London

With his training complete, Nic moved into his newly rented flat in Edith Grove, the less posh part of Chelsea. The Foreign Office provided a small accommodation allowance, so while the flat was a considerable step down from the luxury he had enjoyed at Seb's, it gave him his own base in London.

He spent the next few weeks waiting for news of his first posting. Seb was confident it would be Moscow, but nothing would be confirmed until C had made his decision.

Nic used the time to explore another part of London. Edith Grove was a short walk from the Chelsea and Fulham football grounds. He took the opportunity to see his beloved Sheffield United play at both. Just to the south of his flat, the King's Road was fast becoming a magnet for the young as new boutiques, cafes, and clubs opened.

One night, he got talking to three aspiring young musicians in one of the clubs. It transpired that they lived in a rather squalid bedsit in the house next door to Nic's flat. It also served as their rehearsal space, explaining the loud music most evenings.

A few days later, he saw them play in a room above a pub in Hammersmith. The place was packed, and the atmosphere was unlike anything he had experienced. It was loud, sweaty, and very sexual. After the gig, the boys invited him back to the bedsit. It was a mess, save for many beautiful girls arrayed across various rugs and blankets. Part of him envied their seemingly bohemian lifestyle, apparently unconcerned with anything other than having a good time.

Finally, he received his summons to meet with Dick White, the Head of MI6. White's code name was C, not M, as Ian Fleming was using in the James Bond books, which had recently become very popular after the release of the first two Bond films. The C designation had originated with the first head of the service, Captain Sir Mansfield Smith-Cumming, who had signed his letters with a capital C in green ink.

On the day of the meeting, Nic was running late. He had underestimated the impact of the January sale crowds on his journey time. Kings Road and Victoria Street thronged with shoppers, and traffic was at a standstill. He abandoned the bus and carved a mazy path through the crowds, arriving at 54 Broadway, MI6's headquarters above St. James's Park tube station just in time.

There was no sign that the building housed Her Majesty's Secret Service, but a brass plate suggested the tenant was the Minimax Fire Extinguisher Company. Nic showed his identity card to the guard, signed in, and rushed up the stairs. Out of breath, he caught up with Seb outside C's office.

'You are cutting it fine,' Seb chastised.

'Bloody Christmas shoppers,' Nic cursed.

Seb sighed but had no time to respond; a secretary motioned them into C's office. This meeting would determine Nic's immediate future. Only eight of the original twenty-nine recruits had made it through to the end of the training program. One unfortunate chap had literally fallen at the final hurdle. After a drunken night out to celebrate the end of training, he tripped over a curb and broke his leg.

Nic had completed the course with flying colours, placing second in the class behind a cocky Scotsman with a PhD in

Physics, a Scottish rugby cap, and an unbounded capacity to consume alcohol with minimal effect.

Dick White sat behind his desk. He was in his mid-fifties, with greying hair that reminded Nic of his old headmaster. Unusually, he was, like Nic, from a working-class background. His father had been an ironmonger. White had broken free of his working-class roots by taking a first-class degree from Oxford and being recruited into MI5 in 1936. He had the unique distinction of having headed both MI5 and MI6.

He looked up as Nic and Seb entered. 'Sit down, gentlemen.' He wasted no time getting to the point. 'Congratulations, Slater. Now the real work starts. Remember, those mistakes you made in training may be fatal in the future.'

It was a chastening thought. White continued, 'I am sure it will be no surprise that you are going to Moscow. You will serve as an economic affairs attaché focused on Anglo-Soviet trade. You will report to Sir Roderick Barker, our economic consul, and Six station chief. SirRod is a legend in the service. He was one of our best agents during the war. In the immediate aftermath, he was among the first to realise that the Russians were no longer our ally but our enemy. There is nothing he does not know about the Soviet mindset. Listen carefully to what he says; it will probably save your life.'

Nic tried to keep a straight face even though he was elated. He could see Seb grinning out of the corner of his eye.

'This is an important assignment. Philby and the others have decimated our agent ranks. The Americans don't trust us, and the Soviets laugh at us. We need to rebuild our credibility on all fronts. The old way of public schoolboys playing at spying is dead.'

Nic thought he saw C give a sly glance in Seb's direction.

'Your mission is to identify and recruit Soviet agents to work for us. We need people who have access to high-grade intelligence. The Soviets will be alert for any signs we are trying to rebuild our network, so beware of potential traps. They will do anything to gain leverage: blackmail, coercion, deception, sex.'

He looked at Seb and said, 'Harmes will be your handler. You leave for Moscow on 17th January and will report to Sir Roderick first thing the next day. Spend some time with your family and ensure your affairs are in order. Be back here the week before for a briefing. Good luck.'

C stood up and reached across his desk to shake Nic's hand. 'Thank you, Sir. I will not let you down,' Nic said.

'You better not,' he replied sternly.

As they walked down the corridor, Seb said, 'So?'

'It all just got very real!'

'What do you think of him?'

'I like him. He is clear and direct. None of the usual bureaucratic claptrap.'

Seb clapped Nic on the shoulders and said, 'It's time to celebrate!'

They walked around the corner to the Caxton Bar at the St. Ermin's Hotel, unofficially known in Six as the "works canteen."

Seb ordered a bottle of chilled Pol Roger, Churchill's favourite champagne. Seb chattered, but Nic had a hard time concentrating. In less than a month, he would be a spy operating behind the Iron Curtain. Perhaps accountancy would not have been such a bad career choice.

11

10th January 1964 – London

The Master Cutler pulled into Kings Cross just a few minutes behind schedule. The Pullman coaches had provided a comfortable ride from Sheffield; however, the diesel locomotive possessed none of the charm of the steam engines that had excited Nic as a child. He fondly remembered his father taking him to the railway bridge near their home to watch the trains. They had to time it just right to duck down as the engine passed below to avoid being engulfed in smoke.

The last week had passed in a blur. After the drunken evening of celebration with Seb, Nic had passed out on the sofa at the Mews house. Early the next morning, he returned to Edith Grove, packed some clothes, took the tube to Kings Cross, and boarded the train for Sheffield.

His father met him at the station, and they took the bus to the family home. Mags, her husband Norman, and their two children had driven up for the weekend to see him off. Nic liked Norman, who, despite being an actuary, had a sense of humour.

Nic's mother tried to build him up with enormous meals while fussing about the dangers he would face in the Soviet Union. She had visions of him disappearing into the gulags, never to be heard from again. Nic was glad she did not know the true nature of his assignment.

On Saturday evening, the family went to the pub. His father spent most of the evening boasting to his mates that his son would teach the Russkies a lesson. Just before closing time, after quite a few brandies, he put his arm around Nic's shoulders and said in a slightly slurred voice, 'I love you, son.'

Nic was surprised; he had never heard his father express such a sentiment. Mags was the one he doted on. She was the apple of his eye, smart, beautiful, and successful while also being the mother to his two grandchildren. Nic knew his father loved him, but their bond was different.

Looking at his family, he wondered when, or was it if, they would all be together again. As they weaved their way home, Mags teased him about being a spy. Did she know something? She was well connected, counting a couple of peers and a junior government minister amongst her clients, but he doubted there had been a leak. He deflected her jests by asking how someone as intellectually inferior and undisciplined as him could ever be a spy. She acknowledged he had a good point.

By Sunday afternoon, he was relieved to be heading back to London. He loved his family, but it became suffocating after a few days in their company. Both he and Mags felt increasingly detached from their working-class roots. Few of their friends had gone to university; most still lived in Sheffield, worked in the steel mills, factories, or local shops, went to the pub every night, and stood on the terraces at Hillsborough or Bramall Lane every Saturday. Nowadays, Nic was more likely to be found at the theatre or in a trattoria drinking Chianti.

12

17ᵗʰ January 1964 – Moscow

The Boeing 707 touched down at Sheremetyevo Airport, a former military airfield outside Moscow converted for commercial use in the late 1950s. Numerous military aircraft still sat on the tarmac.

It was early evening. The five-hour flight from London had been uneventful, and he had even managed a couple of hours of sleep despite the adrenaline coursing through his body.

As the plane taxied to the gate, he felt a mix of excitement and trepidation. That morning, Seb had given him a final briefing. He wondered what sort of reception he would get. Theoretically, his diplomatic passport entitled him to expedited immigration, but Seb had warned him to expect a thorough interrogation. The Soviets liked to intimidate new diplomatic staff upon arrival.

The stewardess announced that passengers could unfasten their seatbelts and prepare to disembark. Nic retrieved his briefcase from the overhead compartment. His other luggage had been sent ahead and should be waiting for him at the Embassy residence house.

The plane was only half full. Looking around at the other travellers, most appeared to be foreigners like himself. It was hard for ordinary Russians to obtain permission to travel abroad; the authorities feared they might not return. The Berlin Wall was designed to keep people in, not out.

There were only two female passengers; one looked like the wife or mistress of an elegantly dressed businessman, and the other appeared to be traveling alone. That was unusual. She was

tall, slim, and looked Latino, except she had light blonde hair–
an unusual combination. Maybe it was dyed, Nic thought.

He took care while exiting the plane down rusty, ice-coated
steps. An icy wind whipped across the tarmac. Three passengers
were ushered to a waiting limousine, no doubt bypassing
customs and immigration. Everyone else boarded a battered old
bus belching fumes into the cold night air. The windows were
covered in ice, barring any view of the world outside. When
everyone was on board, the bus crawled towards the terminal
building. It lacked any heating, and most of the passengers were
shivering.

When the bus stopped, an armed soldier opened the doors
and ushered the passengers through glass double doors and up a
staircase to the main concourse. The terminal was dimly lit and
not much warmer than the bus—a queue formed at a solitary
staffed immigration desk. Nic saw a sign reading Дипломат,
the Russian for Diplomat, pointing to the right. He followed the
arrow, earning angry looks from some of the passengers he
bypassed.

Behind him, he heard the click of heels and turned to see the
single woman from the plane following him. He nodded and
said, 'Are you a diplomat as well?' in Russian.

She smiled and replied in unaccented English, 'No, I was just
following you!'

Nic realised the stupidity of his question and laughed. She
introduced herself, 'Hello, I am Rosa Klein. I work at the
Brazilian Embassy as a cultural attaché.'

'Nic Slater, economics attaché at the British Embassy. Well,
I will be, starting tomorrow.'

'Ah, a rookie,' she said, 'Welcome to the second most spy-infested city in the world.'

Nic looked at her quizzically, 'Second most?'

'Berlin tops the list. Everyone is a spy there.'

Their conversation was interrupted by a stern-faced official who frowned at Nic and said, 'Documents.'

Nic handed over his passport and diplomatic introduction letter. The officer took the letter and flipped open the passport. He studied the photograph, holding it up to compare it to the real thing. He consulted a list, checked off a name, and handed the documents back. For a moment, Nic thought he had successfully entered the Soviet Union.

However, the official turned and signalled to another officer standing to the side and said, 'First-time entry.'

Nic heard Rosa's voice behind him, 'Now you get the "welcome to paradise" speech. Don't worry; they will probably let you keep your trousers on.'

The officer summoned Nic to follow him to a small office in the corner of the immigration hall. Behind him, Nic heard the first officer greet Rosa. His tone changed completely when confronted by a beautiful woman. Nic turned to look, but Rosa just rolled her eyes. The officer stamped her passport and ushered her through.

She waved to Nic and said, 'See you later, Agent Slater.'

Why did everyone assume he was a spy? The officer directed him to take a seat. The room was devoid of decoration except for a black-and-white picture of Khrushchev hanging on one wall. A single bare lightbulb hung from the ceiling that illuminated the middle of the room but dissipated into shadow at the corners. The only furniture was a wooden desk and two chairs. The officer took the other chair, looked at Nic, and said in Russian, 'There is a mandatory set of rules that all diplomats operating in the Soviet Union must follow. These are in addition to, and where appropriate, supersede those contained in the Vienna Convention on Diplomatic Relations.'

Nic knew any such rules directly contravened the convention but kept quiet.

The officer spoke rapidly for the next ten minutes, only pausing for Nic to nod to confirm his understanding. Nic was informed that possessing a diplomatic passport was a courtesy that could be revoked for any reason. Diplomats were subject to all laws currently in force in the Soviet Union and punished for any violation. Again, this directly contradicted the convention, which stated that diplomats would not be arrested or detained.

When the lecture ended, the officer returned his passport and ushered him from the room. He breathed a sigh of relief as he walked through a set of doors leading to the baggage claim area. Rosa was standing by the carousel, waiting for her bags.

'You must have passed,' she said.

Nic rolled his eyes, 'What a waste of time.'

Rosa smiled, 'Welcome to the Soviet Socialist utopia.'

He nodded wryly before saying, 'I have a driver meeting me. Do you want to share a ride into the city?'

'I would love to, but we are not allowed to travel with foreign diplomats in case they try to seduce us,' said a smirking Rosa.

Nic felt himself blush. Rosa laughed. 'Here, take my card. Let's meet for a drink once you have settled in.'

She handed him a small rectangular business card. Her name, Rosa Velasquez Klein, was printed in an elegant font, followed by a Moscow address and phone number. There was no job title or indication that she worked at the Embassy.

Nic nodded, 'Thanks. Maybe you can explain the nuances of Moscow life to me?'

'I certainly can, Agent Slater,' she said, winking.

Was she teasing? It was the third time she had called him agent. She leaned forward and kissed him on both cheeks. His English reserve caused him to flinch.

She laughed, 'I don't bite, well, not often.'

Nic remembered something Molly had said during his training, "In the espionage game, beautiful women always have an ulterior motive when they flirt." He wondered about Rosa's motive.

Her suitcase appeared on the carousel. Nic stepped forward and lifted it onto her baggage trolley. 'Thank you, kind sir,' she said, 'and don't forget to call.'

She turned on her heels and strode gracefully towards the exit. Nic watched, wondering whether he would call. Once in the arrival hall, he saw a man holding a small sign with his name on it.

Nic nodded, and the man said, 'Welcome to Moscow, Mr Slater. My name is Anna.'

Seeing the confused look on Nic's face, he explained, 'Anna is a girl's name in your country, yes? But it wasn't always so. There was an English king in the 7th century called Anna. My father was a Professor of English History at Kyiv State University and decided to name me after the king. He had a strange sense of humour.'

As they walked to the car park, Nic asked, 'Do you work for the embassy?'

Anna nodded, 'I have worked for the British for seven years. They treat me very well.'

'Don't they worry you are spying on them?'

'Of course. Occasionally, the police pull me in for a grilling, but I am neither communist nor Russian. I am Ukrainian. We have our own language, culture, and customs. There is no love lost between us and the Russians. My country has, at various times, been ruled by the Poles, Austrians, Turks, and now the Russians. We hate them all. But one day, we will be an independent nation.'

Nic nodded. He knew the USSR was an amalgam of many different ethnic and national groups, which Moscow ruled through a combination of fear and force.

Anna opened the back door of what had once probably been a white car. It was covered in a layer of dirt punctuated by small rust holes. Once behind the wheel, Anna edged out into the traffic. 'We should be at the residence in about an hour,' he said.

It was slow progress until they got onto the new Moscow ring road, the MKaD. Anna accelerated, the car began to rattle, and the suspect suspension transferred every bump to Nic's bottom. Anna seemed unconcerned, 'Don't worry. She will hold together for a little longer.' he said reassuringly. Nic was reminded of Sadie bumping along the gravel drive of Sangster Hall.

When they exited the ring road, the city skyline came into view. Ornate churches vied for attention with utilitarian, grey tower blocks. As they neared the centre, the slabs of Soviet-era concrete gave way to more elaborate, pre-revolutionary architecture. In the distance, Nic saw the distinctive domes atop the four-hundred-year-old St. Basil's cathedral. He remembered reading that it had been commissioned by Ivan the Terrible to celebrate his military victories. The cathedral was really nine different churches, each with its own dome.

Anna stopped outside an imposing art deco building, a style that had been all the rage in Russia before the revolution.

'Here we are, Sir.'

'Call me Nic.'

Anna opened the rear door and said, 'Okay, Nic. Welcome to Kandinsky House.'

Nic attempted to slip a ten rouble note into Anna's hand as he stepped out. 'Oh no, Sir. Your government pays me very well. They pay me in pounds worth five times the official exchange rate on the black market.'

'I will remember that next time,' said Nic, 'Maybe a bottle of scotch?'

Anna smiled broadly, 'That would be most welcome! I will pick you up at 10:00 to take you to the Embassy.'

'Can I walk?' Nic enquired.

'You can,' Anna replied, 'But we don't want you getting lost on your first day, do we?'

"Good point, I'll see you at ten.'

He climbed the steps and rang the doorbell. He saw the blurred image of a woman approaching the frosted glass door panels. The door opened, and an elegant, grey-haired lady came into focus. She wore a dark green two-piece suit, a white blouse, thick black stockings, and sensible black court shoes. A pair of reading glasses hung from a chain around her neck. She looked to be about the same age as his Mum.

'You must be Dominic. Welcome, I am Mary Canover, the manager here at Kandinsky House.'

'Call me Nic; my mother is the only person who calls me Dominic.'

'Okay, Nic, it is.' She reminded Nic of one of his kind primary school teachers, although he suspected Mary could be quite strict if necessary.

The entrance hall was very grand, the vaulted ceiling spanning two stories. The floor looked like a giant chessboard, with alternating black and white tiles. An abstract brass sculpture stood against one wall. Two high-backed, black leather armchairs sat on either side of a small table along the other wall. There was no other furniture. The walls were painted one of those designer shades of white, giving the whole area a clean but sterile look. Mary led Nic to a small office off to the side of the hallway.

'Take a seat, my dear boy. How was the journey?'

'Very good, Mrs. Canover,' Nic replied.

'If I am to call you Nic, you will call me Mary. I need to go over a few house rules with you. It won't take long, and then we can get you settled in your rooms. You will need some rest before meeting SirRod in the morning.'

'Sorry?'

'Sir Roderick Barker, everyone calls him SirRod, just not to his face.'

Mary explained that the building had nineteen apartments, all housing Embassy staff and their families. She gave him the keys to the front door and his apartment.

'You can come and go as you please, but no visitors are allowed without the prior approval of the Embassy security officer. Cameras cover all the building entrances, and the security team is on duty 24/7. Their office is in the basement.

Meals are served in the dining room. Just let us know in advance if you will be eating out.'

Nic signed a form acknowledging that he understood all the rules. 'Right, I will give you a quick tour.'

On the ground floor was the dining room and a spacious lounge cum library. There were only two people in the lounge. An elegantly dressed lady reading Vogue and smoking a cigarette lodged in a gold holder, and an Asian man sipping tea while reading a report. Mary introduced the lady as Victoria Cummings, the wife of a deputy undersecretary. She barely acknowledged him, merely peering at him over her reading glasses.

Mary whispered, 'She is a stuck-up cow. She thinks she's above the rest of us. Why, I don't know. She was just a slapper from Southend before she met her husband.'

Nic struggled not to laugh. The Indian gentleman rose and introduced himself as Leo Puri, an Indian government official from the United Nations on secondment.

Mary led the way up the stairs to the first floor. There was a lift, but she said she needed the exercise. Taking Nic's room key, she opened the door to his apartment. Stepping through the door, Nic was impressed by the grandeur of his new accommodations—more Harmes mews house than Bermondsey warehouse.

The front door opened onto a large sitting room furnished in art deco style—straight lines everywhere with Mission-style chairs, tables, and bookcases. Three tall brass lamps, all very angular, were dotted around the room. The floor continued the black and white motif from the hallway. Several large rugs had been artfully placed around the room. Each had a geometric design in various shades of grey. The walls were painted the same shade of white as the entrance hall. The effect was stunning. The light brown wood of the furniture jumped out from the predominantly black and white background.

'Impressive, isn't it? You are one lucky boy,' Mary said. 'This is the best suite in the building. It was designed and furnished by a former deputy ambassador in the early-1950s. He was a connoisseur of the art deco style.'

'It's bigger than my parent's house,' Nic exclaimed.

Mary showed him the rest of the apartment. There was a large master bedroom with an enormous four-poster bed. Nic's suitcases sat on the floor next to the wardrobe. The shabby cardboard rather spoiled the ambiance of the room. The bathroom featured a huge white, enamel bath in the middle of the room. Brass pipes and taps contrasted with the black tiled walls. There was a small but functional kitchen with a fridge and two electric cooking rings. The final room was equipped as an office. Mary handed him the keys and stepped out into the corridor, 'I will leave you alone to make yourself at home. Don't hesitate to contact me if you need anything. Just dial nine on the phone. Nic thanked her and closed the door. He leaned against the wall, marvelling at his new accommodations. The incongruity of having such decadent rooms in the heart of communist Russia was not lost on him.

He started unpacking his clothes. It was apparent his bags had been opened and searched. He laid them all out on the bed. Apart from the purchases he had made for his weekend at the Harmes' estate, his wardrobe was limited.

He had intended to buy some new clothes before leaving London. The problem had been cash flow. During his training, his salary had been a meagre £150 per month before tax. He had hoped to save most of it, but too many trips to the pub in Scotland and nights out with Seb in London put paid to that. Now, as the equivalent of a clerical officer in the civil service, his pay had risen to £200 per month. However, all his first month's salary had gone towards paying off his debts.

After unpacking, he realised how tired he was. Within seconds of his head hitting the pillow, he was asleep.

13

18th January 1964 – Moscow

The alarm shattered Nic's slumber. He opened his eyes and stared at the ceiling. It took a few seconds for him to remember he was in Moscow and that he would be working as a spy from today.

He thought back to his training—was he really equipped for his new role? Despite the gruelling nature of the training, mentally and physically, he knew that nothing could prepare you for a job where the price of failure was most likely death.

His training had covered all the different techniques the Soviets were known to use to compromise agents. Everything was fair game: blackmail, bribery, drugs, booze, and sex. Seb had told him they would probably use all of them simultaneously. It sounded surreal but was about to get very real.

He gazed at the glass chandelier hanging from the ceiling and wondered which crystals hid a microphone or maybe even a camera. He had been told to assume that every room he entered was bugged, even those at the Embassy. The security staff conducted monthly sweeps, but the technology was advancing rapidly. Cameras were the size of a matchbox, and microphones looked like tie pins. In Moscow, bugs and cameras would follow close behind whenever a workman entered a building.

After an excellent "Full English" breakfast, he returned to his room, cleaned his teeth, and ensured his tie was correctly knotted. Walking down the stairs, he felt beads of nervous sweat forming on his neck. Mary was in the hallway and wished him good luck. Anna was waiting in the car outside. Nic climbed into the front seat. He had felt awkward sitting in the back on the way from the airport.

'You don't mind, do you?' he asked.

'You can ride on the roof as far as I am concerned,' Anna replied.

Nic laughed, 'Might be a bit chilly up there.'

'You would be fine; it is only a ten-minute drive to the Embassy!'

They sat in silence for the short journey. Nic was apprehensive but excited. He stared out the window as Anna expertly navigated the narrow streets until they turned onto Smolenskaya Naberezhnaya, a wide boulevard running along the north bank of the Moskva River.

Moscow's architecture was alternately spectacular and drab. Elegant Moscow Baroque from the 17th century was juxtaposed with ugly slabs of Stalinist concrete and glass. Nic thought it could be seen as a metaphor for the transformation after the Revolution. He was no fan of dictatorial monarchies, but it seemed that the Russian people had swapped one sort of tyranny for another.

Anna turned into the courtyard in front of the Embassy. As Nic got out of the car, he said, 'Remember, do not trust anyone, not even me.'

Nic nodded. He wondered why Anna was a mere Embassy driver; he was shrewd and intelligent.

The Same Day – KGB Headquarters, Moscow

'What about Dominic Slater?' Irina Sashkaya asked, looking at the next photograph in the briefing book.

'He is an interesting one,' Yuri replied. 'Not your typical British diplomat. He is from a solid socialist, working-class family. He grew up in the industrial north of England and was one of the few from his cohort to succeed academically and go on to university. We think that is where MI6 recruited him.'

'Interesting,' Irina said, smiling. 'He looks quite handsome.'

'He does,' Yuri replied.

'I'll fight you for him,' Irina challenged.

Yuri laughed, 'I wouldn't stand a chance.'

Irina and Yuri met on their first day at a special KGB school when they were twelve years old. They formed a close sibling-like bond. They surreptitiously helped each other through training and graduated as the top two in their class. Since then, they had not worked together until summoned by Gromyko.

'Back to business,' Yuri said. 'He could be a good target. His mother is Russian by birth. Her parents were active in the Revolution, but both died when she was young. An English charity moved her to England, where she was adopted. She met Slater's father while still in her teens and became pregnant, forcing them to marry. She taught both her children—Slater has an older sister, Margaret—to speak fluent Russian. The recommendation is to appeal to his proletarian roots, emphasising the damage the British ruling elites have inflicted on the working class. We should downplay the more authoritarian aspects of the Soviet system.'

Irina smiled wryly. Both she and Yuri were aware of the vast gulf between Marxism-Leninism's theory and its practical manifestation in the Soviet Union.

'Surely the British are not stupid enough to send someone here who we flip so easily?'

Yuri nodded, 'You would think so, but remember, these are the same people who allowed Blake, Burgess, Philby, and

Maclean to rise to senior positions while working for us. Slater appears to be part of an attempt by MI6 to reduce their reliance on the bourgeois elite for agents. We think they have relaxed their standards in the haste to rebuild their network.'

'When does he arrive in Moscow?'

'He arrived yesterday. He is staying at Kandinsky House, the British Embassy residence house. He will be one of the UK delegates to the Anglo-Soviet Economic Council.'

'Then we must now be members of our delegation?' Irina asked.

Yuri nodded, 'We need a plan of attack to reel him in. Unfortunately, he seems to heterosexual, so you will have to be the bait in the trap.'

'Don't look so disappointed,' Irina said, 'maybe he has a friend?'

'Ha ha,' Yuri replied. I suggest we take it slowly. Why don't I attend the first two meetings, make casual contact with him, and observe how he behaves? I will report back to you, and then you can make your entrance and work your magic.

Irina nodded, 'Make sure observing is all you do.'

'Very funny.'

The Same Day – The British Embassy, Moscow

The Embassy sat on the banks of the Moskva River directly across from the Kremlin. The views were spectacular, but Nic was too nervous to take them in.

It seemed like only yesterday that his biggest concern had been completing his latest course assignment in time to make last orders at the pub. Now, he was sitting in the Embassy library awaiting an audience with Sir Roderick Barker, Six's Moscow

Station chief's newest warrior in the Cold War. It was all a bit much for a lad from Sheffield.

The Embassy was even more imposing than Kandinsky House. He felt out of his depth, much like he had at Seb's country estate. The library was a two-story affair. Glass-fronted bookcases lined the first floor. An enormous Persian rug covered most of the polished wooden floor, upon which sat a plush leather sofa and various armchairs. A wrought iron spiral staircase led to the balcony surrounding the room, which held more bookshelves. The door opened as he gazed at the rows of books, and an elegantly dressed middle-aged woman entered.

'You must be Dominic.' It was not a question. 'I am Vera, SirRod's secretary. He will see you now. Follow me.'

Nic had heard all about the formidable Vera Gray. Rumour had it that she was the real force behind British intelligence operations in the Soviet Union. During the war, she had been a codebreaker at Beaumanor Hall in Leicestershire, a sister operation to the more famous Bletchley Park. There, she had met Sir Roderick, who had the good sense to hire her as his assistant. It was said that Khrushchev could not take a shit without Vera Gray knowing about it.

Nic followed as she purposefully strode along an oak-panelled corridor, the heels of her court shoes tapping a steady beat. She turned and motioned for Nic to knock on the door at the end of the corridor. A deeply resonant but muffled voice barked, 'Enter.' Nic pushed down on the wrought iron handle. Despite the weight of the door, it swung open easily, and Nic walked in.

Sir Roderick Barker, the scion of a blue-chip merchant banking family, had chosen not to follow his siblings into the family firm. In 1926, after graduating from Cambridge, he joined the Foreign Office.

There was constant speculation he would soon return to England and retire, but he seemed reluctant to leave the service. Nic was both intimidated and excited at the prospect of working for him.

'Ah, Slater, my dear boy, welcome to Moscow,' said Barker from behind a large oak desk. He had a full head of dark brown hair with just a hint of grey. His most striking feature was his piercing blue eyes. They made him look much younger than his sixty-three years.

His office continued the English country house theme from the rest of the Embassy. Two walls were lined with bookcases packed tight with dusty, leather-bound volumes; richly patterned burgundy and gold-flocked wallpaper filled the gaps. An oversized fireplace was flanked by two large, arched windows looking out over the Embassy courtyard. The early morning sun slanting through the glass cast shadows onto the polished wooden floor. Logs crackled in the fireplace, giving off just enough heat to take the chill out of the January air.

Sir Roderick stood up, revealing that he was almost as tall as Nic. He walked around his desk and shook Nic's hand, motioning for him to sit in one of the brown leather Chesterfields in front of the fireplace.

'Time for a drink, don't you think?' The question was rhetorical, as without waiting for a response, Barker lifted a crystal decanter from a side table and poured two generous measures of what looked like a very fine malt whisky into two cut glass tumblers. Nic glanced at his watch; it was only 10:00.

Sir Roderick lowered himself into the other chair. He wore a crumpled tweed blazer, a brown and green checked shirt, and a green tie with an embroidered coat of arms, no doubt denoting a former school, regiment, or club. His trousers were baggy brown corduroy, slightly worn at the knees. His highly polished, brown brogue shoes were the only item of clothing that appeared well-maintained. He looked like an older version of Seb. Maybe this was the unofficial uniform of the upper classes.

'How are you settling in? Digs ok?' SirRod asked.

'Very grand, Sir. I was expecting something a little more utilitarian,' Nic replied.

'Ah, yes. Everyone thinks the Soviets are Communists, but they are just as bourgeois as the rest of us. All the Politburo members live in grand Tsarist era apartments replete with antique furniture and priceless works of art, and they have luxury lakeside Dachas to escape to when the going gets a bit tough.'

'A true workers paradise,' Nic commented.

SirRod laughed. 'Very true. Anyway, we like to provide decent accommodation for our chaps. Kandinsky House was home to Mathilde Kschessinska; she was a ballet dancer but, more importantly, a mistress of Tsar Nicolas. She must have been an energetic lass as she was also bonking two other dukes from the Romanov family.'

Nic smiled. The upper class could be so elegantly crude and indiscreet. SirRod must be confident his office was not bugged, or maybe he didn't care. Seb was the same way. He was always sharing some little tidbit told to him in confidence. He wondered if this trait contributed to the numerous leaks plaguing security services.

'We signed a long lease on the place in 1929. Did you know we were the first nation to establish diplomatic relations with the Soviets after the Revolution?'

'No, Sir.'

'They desperately want it back, but we will not surrender it any time soon.'

Sir Roderick picked up his glass and took a generous swig. Nic took a small sip. As a connoisseur might say, it was an excellent malt, rich and smoky with a peaty bottom.

'How much do you know about your assignment here?'

'A little, Sir. C and Harmes explained that we are trying to rebuild our intelligence network behind the Iron Curtain as the Cold War heats up.' He cringed at his unintended pun, but SirRod's expression remained impassive.

'That is partially correct. Philby and the others destroyed our network. Many good men and women lost their lives because of those bastards. I still don't know how they got away with it for so long. Philby was head of our Soviet counter-intelligence division and passed details of every operation to Moscow.'

Just like C, SirRod felt betrayed by his former colleagues. They were his contemporaries, although there had never been any suggestion that SirRod was suspect. Nic understood the anger, although he suspected it was magnified by the shattering of an illusion that spying was a game played by gentlemen.

SirRod picked up a pipe from the table, filling it with tobacco from a pouch he took from his jacket pocket. He tamped it down with his thumb before setting it on fire. Nic enjoyed watching pipe smokers prepare their fixes. It was one ritual that cut across class boundaries. His father did the same thing while sitting in his favourite chair in front of the fire at home. Of course, SirRod used a polished gold lighter rather than a Bryant and May. Plumes of blueish smoke rose into the air, and SirRod sighed, his anger dissipating.

'The Soviets are also trying to rebuild their network. There is a new generation of KGB agents trained to operate either as sleeper agents in the West or develop new sources within our intelligence services. Unlike the previous generation, who learned their trade under Stalin, they are less cowed by his legacy and more attuned to Western culture. That is a weakness we can exploit. They know about the widening gulf in living standards and see we have so much more to offer than empty shelves and gulags. Despite all the propaganda, things are not going well in Khrushchev's socialist utopia. The economy is kept afloat by a theoretically illegal but unofficially sanctioned black market. There are shortages of everything from food to foreign currency, and despite their apparent successes in space, they are falling further behind in technology. It turns out our former Nazi scientists are better than theirs.'

Nic knew about the race after the war between the US and Soviet Union to capture the best Nazi scientists. The space program was the most obvious manifestation, but the advances in advanced weaponry and other systems were much more significant in relation to the Cold War.

'There is one bright spot from the defection of Philby and the others. It deprived the Soviets of their own very highly placed moles. Both sides are trying to infiltrate the other. It's a high-stakes game. We want the KGB to think that our new agents, like you, from working class, dare I say, socialist backgrounds, are susceptible to being turned. We suspect they have a rather simplistic view of the world. As a product of the proletariat, naturally, you will be susceptible to propaganda about the utopian Soviet system and the moral bankruptcy of capitalism. We expect they will try to recruit you. If they do, you will play along, then we can channel disinformation through you.'

Nic thought it a naïve rationale. During his recruitment, he had been surprised at the emphasis on his background. Now he understood—in the simplistic mind of the British ruling class, recruits from the proletariat would be attractive targets for the KGB. After all, the working class were all closet communists.

It reflected the growing gulf between the generation whose worldview was shaped by World War II and his generation, whose attitudes toward Nic were shaped by changes in social norms, politics, and culture rather than economic depression, war, and rationing.

Nic agreed with some of socialism's tenets, such as equality of opportunity and universal access to basic needs such as housing, healthcare, and education. However, he could see that the Soviet system, which relied on dictatorial control and was rooted in a class war between rich and poor, was fundamentally flawed.

'Sir, am I right in thinking you want me to pretend to be a double agent?' he said.

'Exactly. You will be a triple agent: working for us while working for them, but still working for us.'

Barker chuckled and sucked hard on his pipe, partially disappearing behind a cloud of smoke. Nic took another small sip of whisky; he would have preferred a cup of tea.

'Your cover story will be that you are an economic advisor to the ambassador. Your role is to foster mutual understanding between our two countries with a view to expanding trade links.

Large-scale trade is politically impossible in the current environment. However, the Mandarins in London want to be somewhat collaborative. You will be a delegate to a newly formed joint Anglo-Soviet economic collaboration working party looking for common ground. Everyone knows it is a charade. Both sides will use it as a forum to recruit people from the other side while going through the motions of cooperation. Our deputy station chief, Jeremy Webbe, will brief you further. Vera will show you to his office.'

SirRod stood up, Nic followed suit, and they shook hands, 'Good luck, Dominic.'

Nic turned to leave and saw Vera waiting at the door. She led him down the corridor, knocked on a door, opened it without waiting for a reply, and said, 'Jeremy, Dominic is here for your briefing.'

'What?' spluttered a voice from within. 'Oh hell, is it that time already? Show him in.'

Vera rolled her eyes and whispered, 'Good luck,' she said, stepping aside to let Nic pass.

The office was nowhere near as grand as SirRod's. About one-fifth the size, it had one small window and was furnished with what Seb would describe as civil service tat. There were no plush rugs, polished wooden floors, or walls lined with antique bookcases.

A prematurely bald man, Nic estimated to be in his mid-thirties, peered at him through half-moon glasses from behind a metal desk. The desk and much of the floor were covered with papers and files.

'Sit down, Slater,' the man said sharply. Nic moved a pile of files from the single chair in front of the desk. 'I hear you are part of the new breed of plebian agents who are going to save the intelligence services?'

Nic did not bother to respond. Seb had warned him that Webbe was a bully and a snob.

'I will take this slowly. Hopefully, you can keep up,' Webbe said condescendingly. 'We live in a complex world.'

For the next three hours, he lectured Nic on Anglo-Soviet relations, the current situation in Moscow, and all manner of other topics. He just kept talking, barely pausing for breath, and not tolerating any interruptions.

The gist of his briefing was that tensions between East and West had eased somewhat after Stalin's death. Khrushchev had focused on consolidating his power internally and shoring up Soviet control over Eastern Europe through the formation of the Warsaw Pact in 1955. The Cold War had become less East versus West and more a direct ideological and economic conflict between the Soviet Union and the United States. Outwardly, the Soviets had backed away from trying to foment a global socialist revolution. However, there had still been a series of provocations, such as the brutal suppression of the Hungarian uprising, the construction of the Berlin Wall, and the Cuban missile crisis. During the latter, Kennedy had forced Khrushchev into a humiliating climbdown, but for a few tense days, the world had been on the edge of nuclear war. In the immediate aftermath, both sides signed a nuclear test ban treaty in 1963.

As for Britain, the defection of Philby and others damaged Britain's standing in the Americans' eyes. Webbe derisively suggested the Americans had a traitor problem of their own— they just had not found them yet.

The Russians were convinced Britain was a weak link in the NATO alliance that could be further exploited. Webbe insisted that was false, and they were in for a rude awakening.

Webbe ended his lecture by saying, 'Personally, I think letting your sort into the service is a mistake. Your type simply does not have the intelligence or aptitude for espionage. I give you six weeks before you screw up.'

Nic ignored the jibe but wondered if Webbe was expressing a commonly held view. Did everyone else expect him to fail?

His next meeting was with Vera, and it cheered him up considerably. She started by telling him to ignore everything Webbe had told him. 'He is an idiot. He is only still in the service because this father plays golf with C. He was sent here so that SirRod could keep an eye on him.'

Nic expected a briefing on administrative procedures like filing expense claims; however, Vera walked him through a fascinating session on Soviet communication, code, and counter-espionage protocols. She even provided tea and biscuits. He devoured the custard creams—his favourite.

The gossip was true; Vera was no mere secretary. He wondered if she was the deputy station chief—she was much more competent than Webbe.

As the meeting wrapped, she said, 'You will do well here. Just remember, in Moscow, there is no such thing as an insignificant gesture or meaningless piece of information— everything has value.'

Nic was flattered. He valued her opinion far more than that of Webbe.

Back at this apartment, he reflected on the day. It had been a rollercoaster. His meetings with SirRod and Vera had counterbalanced the one with Webbe. The more he thought about Webbe's worldview, the more simplistic it seemed. It was not a case of capitalism, good, socialism, evil. While both systems had their merits, the practical manifestations were riddled with iniquities. The Cold War was more nuanced than good versus evil.

Despite relative prosperity, many people in Britain still lived in poverty. More broadly, the huge wealth and privilege gap between the upper class and working class was widening all over the Western world. On the other hand, the totalitarian nature of the Eastern bloc was anathema to him. The lack of freedom and constant state intrusion into the lives of the people were abhorrent.

The biggest travesty was the billions of dollars, pounds, and roubles being wasted by both sides in an arms race with no good outcome. Every day, the world was edging closer to a nuclear Armageddon.

He would keep his thoughts to himself. Openly expressing them would be career-limiting, maybe even life-limiting.

14

Darkness came early during the Moscow winter, and the air turned icy as the sun set. Nic walked through the darkened streets on his way back from the first Anglo-Soviet Economic Cooperation Symposium (ASECS) meeting. It had been dull and unproductive. The idea of meaningful trade between the UK and USSR was, as SirRod had said, a sham.

The meeting was held in the Narkomfin Building, an avant-garde housing development for employees of the Soviet Ministry of Finance. Nic suspected the Soviets were trying to show off. Built in 1930, it was supposed to showcase a collectivist model for housing based on sound socialist principles. Nic thought it looked more like a dilapidated and soulless office block.

The discussions had been amusing in their pointlessness. The Soviet delegation bombarded the British with propaganda about the Soviet economic miracle while highlighting the moral and financial bankruptcy of the West. Apparently, there had been zero price inflation in the Soviet Union since 1945, while the average income of a Soviet citizen had quadrupled. One of Nic's colleagues commented wryly that there was no inflation because there was nothing to buy in the shops, and as for income growth, four times nothing was still nothing--remarks that had not gone down well with the Russian delegation.

The British did not try to refute any Soviet "facts" but did emphasise areas where the West was clearly in the lead, such as data processing, transportation, medical research, financial services, and, most significantly, living standards.

The Soviet response was to argue that all these claims were meaningless propaganda. The Soviet Union led in the areas that mattered—free education and healthcare for all and an economic system based upon the needs of all the people, not one corrupted by the capitalist profit motive. Like all such arguments devoid of facts, there could be no winner.

More interesting than the meeting was the reception afterward. Each side took turns hosting, with the Soviets going first. It started off as a rather stilted affair, but as the vodka flowed, more stimulating conversations began to break out. The Soviets teased the Brits about losing their empire, while the Brits challenged the Soviets to justify the Berlin Wall. It was mostly light-hearted but with an edge.

Nic controlled his alcohol consumption, wary that the slightest verbal indiscretion would probably be captured on tape. He surreptitiously peered into the vases of flowers dotted around the room, looking for microphones.

By the time he left, he had talked to most members of the Soviet delegation. Only two interactions were of note. The first occurred when a nondescript man suggested they meet later while discretely cupping Nic's left buttock in his hand.

The second encounter showed more promise. A tall man with dark blond hair and hooded eyes introduced himself as Yuri Kovlev. He said he was from Siberia and was an economics professor at Moscow State University. They talked about the differences between Britain and the Soviet Union. Yuri was the first person Nic had encountered who seemed to have any real knowledge of what was happening beyond the Iron Curtain. The more they talked, the more he wondered if Yuri was KGB. His questions were too penetrating to be those of a humble university professor. Was this the first stage of a recruitment dance?

15

18th March 1964

Over the next few weeks, Nic's life settled into a dull routine. After a short initiation on the work undertaken by the different Embassy departments, given his fluency in Russian, he was assigned to monitor Soviet communications. He set to work translating intercepted messages between various arms of the Soviet government. It was a job where long periods of tedium were occasionally interrupted by a few seconds of excitement when some vaguely interesting material crossed his desk. He met with SirRod every two weeks but rarely had anything of substance to report. He became impatient and had to keep reminding himself that espionage was a long game.

Outside work, he spent time exploring the city. He was surprised to find that few areas were out of bounds. He could even walk through most of the Kremlin. In some ways, Moscow reminded him of London. The Moskva River wound its way through the city much as the Thames did in London. Red Square approximated to Trafalgar Square—everything radiated out from there. His favourite feature was that Moscow, like London, had numerous parks and open spaces.

The growing tedium of his daily routine was briefly interrupted by the March A-SECS meeting, which the British hosted at the Embassy. Nic found it amusing to see the Embassy security staff following the Soviet delegates around to ensure they did not leave any bugs behind.

The discussion focused on potential areas of economic cooperation. The best idea the group came up with was for Britain to export Raleigh bicycles to Russia in exchange for animal furs, as there was a chronic shortage of bicycles in the Soviet Union. Nic suspected this would do little to solve Britain's looming balance of payments problem.

In typical British style, the reception after the meeting was a formal affair, complete with cucumber sandwiches and tea served by white-gloved waiters while a string quartet played in the background. Nic thought the Embassy did a fine job living up to every preconceived notion of English elitism and decadence.

The absence of any alcohol subdued the whole affair. The ambassador had vowed not to waste one bottle from the Embassy's extensive wine cellar on bloody communists. Yuri commented that if he had known it was a "dry do," he would have smuggled a bottle of vodka into his briefcase. Rather than taking offense, he just laughed. Nic was finding out that he was not your typical Russian. He was outgoing, politically incorrect, and funny.

Meaningful social interaction was stunted by the presence of the ambassador, Geoffrey Harrison, and the Soviet Foreign Minister, Andrei Gromyko. These two senior diplomats exchanged pleasantries with each other for all of thirty seconds before spending the rest of the time comically introducing themselves to members of their own delegation, whom they clearly had never met before.

SirRod attended in his official role as Britain's official trade representative. Even he saw the incongruity in his title. As he freely admitted, there was no trade to speak of between Britain, and the Soviets knew full well that he was MI6 station chief. He also knew next to nothing about economics. Despite being a member of the Barker banking family, he had studied music at Cambridge and could barely balance his cheque book.

Nic left after an hour, wondering if he was cut out for this line of work. It had sounded so glamorous. He would be in the vanguard of rebuilding Britain's intelligence network behind the Iron Curtain. So far, he had attended two pointless meetings and translated hundreds of dull messages sent between various branches of the Soviet government. He suspected that the excuses given for a shortfall in grain production in the chernozem, or the black earth region between Kazakhstan and Ukraine, would be unlikely to trigger a breakthrough in the Cold War.

When he complained to Seb, he got a blistering response telling him to stop whinging and get on with his job. Suitably chastened, he resolved to change his attitude.

16

One week later

The phone rang, jolting Nic from another daydream. He picked up the receiver, and the switchboard operator said brusquely, 'Miss Klein for Mr Slater.'

A click signified that the operator had hung up and that recording of the call had begun.

'How is my favourite British spy?' Rosa asked. Nic winced at the thought of those words being recorded.

'Rosa, good to hear from you. Are you missing meat and Malbec yet?' Nic replied.

'More than you can imagine,' she replied, 'Speaking of Malbec, are you ready to have that drink?

'That would be great,' he replied. He needed to get away from the Embassy and his apartment.

'Be in the bar of the National Hotel at seven,' she ordered.

'I'll be there,' he replied, excited at the prospect of some intelligent and attractive company. There was another click as Rosa hung up.

The sound of her voice had lifted his spirits, but should he have agreed to meet her so readily? He picked up the phone and dialled Vera's extension.

'Ma'am, Nic Slater here,' he said when she picked up.

'Don't ever call me Ma'am again; I am not the Queen,' she snapped.

'Sorry,' he stammered. There were gales of laughter from the other end of the line, 'Just teasing. How are you settling in?'

'Very well, thank you.'

'Good. How can I help?'

'I have a question.'

'Go ahead.'

'I have been invited for drinks this evening by the cultural attaché at the Brazilian Embassy. Is there any reason why I should not accept her invitation?'

'I assume she is attractive?'

'Does that make a difference?' Nic stammered.

'No,' she replied. 'I am just being nosy. She is probably Brazilian intelligence, so be careful. Brazil is a basket case right now. There was a coup a few months ago. Our analysts think it could usher in a military dictatorship, so things are a little unstable. Make sure you write up a contact report after your meeting. If you take her to bed, don't report that, but you must tell me all the details.' Nic could feel himself blushing. 'I will let Sir Roderick know and get back to you if there is a problem.'

There was no return call from Vera, so he was clear to meet Rosa. The National Hotel was not far from the Embassy. For the first time since arriving in Moscow, he felt excited. This would be his first social interaction outside of drinks with colleagues and the dire A-SECS receptions.

The National was a slightly faded, grand old hotel but remained a popular destination for the rich and famous. H.G. Wells, Paul Robeson, and Prokofiev had all been guests. The hotel was rumoured to be the most bugged building in Moscow. Nic wondered why Rosa had chosen to meet there.

He spotted her as soon as he entered the bar. She sat on a barstool in a striking red dress that fell just below her knees. Lean calves led to red, four-inch stilettos. Her blonde hair cascaded over her shoulders. She represented the only splash of colour in a room where everyone else was clad in various shades of grey.

As he approached, she stood, and they did the kiss-on-both-cheeks thing again. He had not mastered the technique yet and found himself kissing her ear. Intimate gestures were not the done thing in England; they might crease the stiff upper lip.

Rosa nodded to the barman, and he started mixing a drink. It was not the first time she had been to this bar.

'How are you finding Moscow?' she asked.

'The city is fascinating, but the people are less so,' Nic replied.

Rosa nodded, 'Russians are very reserved. They are not as outgoing as Westerners and certainly not as expressive as we South Americans. You might be a little guarded if the penalty for saying the wrong thing was a life sentence to a labour camp in the frozen north.'

'Fair point. I wonder why the people put up with it.'

'Don't underestimate the Soviets. They have developed a system that exerts frighteningly control over what people think. They have mastered the art of propaganda and disinformation. Most Russians feel they are well looked after. The basics of education, healthcare, and housing are provided. There are periodic food shortages, and consumer goods that you and I take for granted are scarce, but the state works hard to prevent the people from finding out about the gap in living standards compared to the West. It has worked well for forty-five years. It will take something dramatic to change things. We should talk about something else; these walls have ears.'

'Not just the walls, from what I hear.' Nic replied.

Rosa nodded.

'How did you end up in Moscow?' he asked.

Rosa began to tell her story. Her father had fled Germany in the mid-1930s to avoid the persecution of the Jews. His parents, brother, and sister had all stayed behind and perished in the camps. After a short period in Buenos Aires, he moved to Brazil, where he met Rosa's mother, the daughter of a Brazilian factory owner. Her father had taken over his father-in-law's business, which had boomed during the war years, making the Kleins one of the wealthiest families in the country. Rosa had been born just after the war started. Her mixed parentage explained her blonde-haired, Latino look.

After the war, her father became influential in the hunt for Nazis who had escaped to South America. He was a member of the team led by Simon Wiesenthal that had tracked down Adolf Eichmann, one of the architects of the Holocaust, in Buenos Aires and smuggled him to Israel to face trial.

At school, Rosa discovered she had a knack for languages, becoming fluent in Portuguese, German, Spanish, and English as a teenager. She added Russian while at university. After graduation, she joined the civil service and had been posted to Moscow two years earlier.

'I am sure you are as much a cultural attaché as I am an economics one,' Nic challenged.

She smiled enigmatically.

'How has the coup impacted you?' Nic asked.

'None of us knows if we still have a job. We are just carrying on as if nothing happened. Eventually, someone will get around to telling us what's what.'

Nic shared as much of his own story as he thought prudent. She smiled when he described himself as an outsider amongst the clubby public-school boys who still ran Britain.

'You don't know what it means to be an outsider unless you are Jewish,' she said.

They were now on their third martini, and Nic felt very relaxed.

'Do you have a girl back home?' she asked.

'No, no one back home,' he replied. Rosa smiled. Was she trying to seduce him? Did he mind?

'Come on, let's go for a walk,' she suggested while placing a few kopeks on the bar.

Nic helped her down from the stool, and they walked into the lobby. A bellboy stepped forward and opened the door. Rosa gave him a dazzling smile and slipped him a few coins, causing him to blush.

Once outside, they walked across Manezhnaya Square towards Alexander Gardens, which ran along the western side of the Kremlin. They stopped at the recently constructed Tomb of the Unknown Soldier. Fashioned in red granite with an eternal flame at its centre, the tomb contained the remains of soldiers killed during the Battle of Moscow in 1941. The Germans had come close to capturing the city before being stopped just forty kilometres short.

'What a senseless waste,' she said, tears forming in her eyes. Nic slipped his arm around her waist. She turned towards him, and for a moment, he thought she was going to kiss him, but the moment passed, and they just hugged.

He walked her back to her apartment. She asked if he wanted to come up for a nightcap. The look on her face made it a tempting offer. He wanted to say yes, but seducing beautiful Brazilians was not in his remit. He resisted temptation and politely declined.

A brief look of disappointment flashed across her face, but she quickly regained her composure. Leaning forward, she gave Nic a passionate kiss on the lips and whispered huskily in his ear, 'You don't know what you are missing.'

He looked at her and said regretfully, 'Unfortunately, I think I do.'

She smiled, 'We should do this again. Remember, if you ever need help, you have my number.'

'Thank you. I will.'

He watched as she walked gracefully up the steps. She turned and gave him a little wave before disappearing inside. He sighed and started walking down the street. Moments later, he spotted a man stepping out of a nearby doorway and following him.

17

May was another tedious month. There was no A-SECS meeting as the Soviet delegation, like most of the country, seemed to have taken most of the month off to celebrate International Labour Day and Victory Day, which commemorated the defeat of the Nazis.

The only excitement in the foreign intelligence community had been the discovery of forty hidden microphones in the walls and floors of the American Embassy. They had gone undetected for months despite frequent sweeps. They had only been discovered when a wall had been demolished during internal building works. Even the toilets were found to be bugged. This set off a mild wave of paranoia at the British Embassy. SirRod dismissed the fuss by saying, 'What did the Americans expect? Assume everywhere is bugged and act accordingly,' was his simple advice.

Nic could not resist sending a teasing telex to Ranger, mocking the flaws in American security. He was surprised to receive a reply from the US Embassy in London that read, "Very funny. I should warn you I am now the senior London-based CIA liaison officer with MI5 and MI6. I might have to warn C that one of his agents is making disparaging comments about the UK's most important ally."

Nic smiled. Ranger was sure to make an impact in London.

The June A-SECS meeting was being held at Moscow State University. Nic had few expectations. SirRod suggested he engage more with Yuri to better understand whether he was a possible recruitment target.

The topic was Indochina, which was becoming the nexus of the Cold War as Soviet and Chinese-backed North Vietnamese troops engaged with US-backed South Vietnamese. It was not yet a full-scale war, but it looked to be heading in that direction.

Having nothing better to do, Nic did some research in preparation for the meeting. He headed to the Embassy's research department, where he found Simon and Charlotte, the resident research analysts. As he entered their lair in the basement, he heard them bickering like an old married couple, adding some weight to the rumours that their relationship was not purely professional.

Charlotte looked up as Nic entered and said, 'Well, well, what have we done to deserve a visit from our very own James Bond?'

'He's more like double-oh-three-and-a-half than double-oh-seven,' said Simon.

Nic laughed, 'As I am licensed to kill, you may want to rethink that comment.'

Stacks of books, magazines, and newspapers littered the small room. Nic took a seat at the large table in the centre of the room, which was surrounded on all four sides by shelving containing books, files, old newspapers, maps, and photograph albums.

'Tell me all about Indochina,' he said.

Both their faces lit up, and like a well-rehearsed double act, they were off. Vietnam, Cambodia, and Laos had been part of French Indochina since the 19th century. During World War II, the Japanese had invaded, overthrowing the colonial government. However, with Japan's defeat, the French, with British help, had reclaimed control. Not long after, the Viet Minh, who had fought against the Japanese occupation during the war, turned on France. In 1954, the French withdrew, and Vietnam was split into two. North Vietnam was ruled by Ho Chi Minh's communists and the South by Bao Dai, the thirteenth and last emperor of the Nguyen dynasty.

While Ho consolidated power in the North, the South was plagued by political instability. In 1955, Dai was overthrown and replaced by his pro-American prime minister. Ho exploited the situation, and the Americans became increasingly paranoid that the communists would roll through South Vietnam and conquer the whole region.

Since the late fifties, a new communist force, the Viet Cong, with backing from Ho, had been fighting a guerrilla warfare to overthrow the South Vietnamese government. The Americans began supplying military advisors to help the South fight the Viet Cong, and now they were starting to deploy combat troops. In Charlotte's opinion, the Americans would get bogged down trying to fight an enemy that shunned conventional warfare. The Viet Cong hid in the jungle amidst the civilian population, blunting the effectiveness of American firepower. Simon suggested that while the Americans were a far superior military force, they were underestimating the will of the Viet Cong and North Vietnamese, 'They are prepared to accept staggering losses over the long haul, for them it is a war being fought in their homeland against an imperialist foe. How long will America be willing to send its young men to fight a war thousands of miles away from home?'

To Nic, it sounded similar to the losses the Russians were prepared to accept to stop Hitler from reaching Moscow. He left thinking it could be an entertaining discussion at the A-SECS meeting. It was topical, divisive, and pitted the bad guys of communism against the good guys of capitalism.

He arranged for Anna to drive him to the university in the city's Lenin Hills district. As usual, he sat in the passenger seat. Anna accelerated smoothly out of the Embassy courtyard. He appeared to be the only driver in Moscow who did not crunch the gears. Russian cars had very suspect gear boxes, they required a unique blend of brute force and gentle coaxing to function effectively.

It was hot inside the car. The only ventilation provided by the numerous gaps between different parts of the poorly made vehicle. Winding down the windows provided some relief.

The warmer weather had brought people onto the streets. Nic noticed that even in Moscow, hemlines were starting to rise. He wondered whether the Politburo would legislate on skirt length to prevent the nation's moral decay. Mags had told him that some schools in England now measured the length of girls' skirts to ensure they remained suitably demure.

'How are you liking Moscow?' Anna asked.

'I love it,' he replied. 'It is easy to walk around, some of the architecture is stunning, and the parks are beautiful. It's just a shame the shops are empty, and the people look so miserable.'

Anna nodded, 'You can blame the bloody communists for that!' Nic wasn't sure if he was joking or not.

Anna dropped Nic by the park in front of the university. It was an imposing sight. At just under 750 feet, the main building was the tallest structure in Europe. It had been built by gulag labour during Stalin's rule. Nic wondered whether the inside matched the grandeur of the outside.

He walked up the steps to the porticoed entrance. Pools of sweat formed on his neck and back. He pushed open one of the heavy wooden outer doors, crossed the porch, and went through a revolving door that opened out onto the marble-floored and columned entrance hall. That answered his question: the inside was just as grand as the outside.

After signing in at the reception desk, he was escorted to a large conference room on the third floor. There were significantly more attendees than at previous meetings— perhaps thirty. Nic nodded hello to those he recognised before his attention was drawn to a new face and the only woman in the room.

She was stunning. Of above-average height, she wore a well-tailored suit that looked like it had escaped from Paris. Her long legs were accentuated by the heels she was wearing. Her dark brown hair was cut in a fashionable style Nic had seen in London: a centre parting with hair falling straight down to just above the shoulder, then curled outwards on both sides. He thought it was a style made popular by Jackie Kennedy. A simple gold chain around her neck was the only jewellery she wore. Her make-up was light, not that she needed much.

She was talking to Yuri, who nodded to Nic over her shoulder. She turned to see who Yuri was acknowledging. The hint of a smile emanated from her lips, but it did not reach her arched eyebrows, piercing blue eyes, and perfect cheekbones. It was a beguiling look, to say the least.

Nic made sure to take the seat opposite her at the long table. She did not look at him as she continued talking animatedly to Yuri. For some reason, he felt jealous.

Once all the delegates were seated, the chairman opened the session and asked each new delegate to introduce themselves. When it came to her turn, she looked directly at Nic and said, 'My name is Irina Sashkaya. I work with Yuri here at the university.'

Nic hoped he was not blushing. He tried to remember Molly's advice—keep a straight face and maintain eye contact. Looking away was a sign of weakness. Easier said than done, he thought.

The first presentation was delivered by one of the Russian delegates, who explained the Soviet perspective on Indochina. The gist of his message was that the region was yet another product of failed European colonialism, in this case, French colonialism. He argued that recent American involvement in the region was an attempt to reimpose colonial rule over an already oppressed region. Nic did not completely disagree. The American motive might have been to stop the spread of communism, but was that so different from earlier colonial adventures aimed at civilising the natives?

The speaker stated that the Soviet Union and China were committed to supporting the establishment of independent nation-states in the region. He argued that the UK should support this goal rather than backing American imperialism. One member of the UK delegation interrupted to object. 'You are talking rubbish,' he said angrily. The Soviet Union and China are only focused on extending communist rule across the whole region.'

This triggered a loud denial from the speaker and other members of the Soviet delegation. Soon, arguments broke out all around the table. Nic looked at Irina and saw her gently shaking her head and smiling at him. He thought he saw her mouth the word "children".

It took the chairman some time to restore order. He called for a short break before reconvening for what he suggested should be a more civilised discussion.

Nic wanted to introduce himself to Sashkaya, but she quickly left the room and only returned as the discussion session began. It did not disappoint. Moving from an ideological debate on the pros and cons of communism and capitalism to an argument that the Soviet Union's creation of the Warsaw Pact was just another form of imperialism.

Sashkaya made only one comment, noting that all nations should have the right to self-determination. This stunned the room into silence. A Soviet delegate was arguing that any form of control by one nation over another was wrong. She explicitly condemned Soviet control in Eastern Europe. She was either very brave or foolish. Nic noted the wry smile on her face and suspected she had deliberately wanted to shock the room.

As he listened to her speak, he thought about SirRod's warning that most of the Soviet delegation would be KGB. Was she one of them? He couldn't be sure. She was clearly intelligent and articulate, consistent with her work at the university. However, the Soviets were well known for using attractive female agents to try to compromise their enemies.

Nic made a few contributions of his own based on his briefing from Charlotte and Simon. He incurred the wrath of the Soviet delegation by declaring that communism would do little to move Vietnam from a largely subsistence, agrarian economy, given how spectacularly collective farming had failed in Russia.

After the meeting ended, the chairman invited everyone downstairs for the reception in one of the student social clubs. Having consumed too much Russian tea during the meeting, Nic needed to stop at the toilet. By the time he reached the reception room, Irina was surrounded by men from both delegations. He cursed his bladder.

He wandered over to the bar, where he was handed a glass of Nastoiki. A vodka resembling cherry-flavoured paint stripper. Yuri joined him and nodded in the direction of the mob surrounding Sashkaya. 'What is the expression you use in English? Wasps at the honey pot?'

Nic laughed, 'It's bees at the honey pot.'

Yuri nodded, though Nic suspected he knew the correct expression perfectly well.

'She said she works with you?' Nic said.

'Yes, but not as much as I would like,' he said, grinning. 'If you are planning to make a move, I urge caution. I have known Irina for years—she eats men alive.'

'Introduce me,' Nic said.

Yuri laughed, 'Weren't you listening to me?'

'I just want to talk to her,' Nic replied.

'That's what they all say. Very well, if you insist, follow me.'

When she saw Yuri approaching, she detached herself from the mob. 'Irina, let me introduce Nic Slater, the new economics attaché at the British Embassy.'

'Mr Slater, my pleasure,' she said as her smile finally expanded to her whole face.

Nic found himself bowing slightly, 'Likewise,' he said. 'I thought your comments were very insightful.'

She laughed, 'So Mr Slater, what do you think America's' real goals are in Vietnam?'

'Call me Nic, please. The same as they were in Korea: stop the spread of communism.'

'Why are they so worried about something happening so far away from their shores?'

'Since the war, America sees itself as the leader of the free world. They realised they had made a big mistake letting Stalin draw an Iron Curtain across Europe. Then, there were communist takeovers in China, North Korea, and Cuba. They are terrified of any further spread of communism. It doesn't matter where it is.'

'But surely partitioning Vietnam, like Korea, is not a long-term solution?'

'The Americans would agree,' Nic replied, 'the real question is under what political and economic system should reunification take place.'

'If things escalate, it won't matter. We will all be vapourised in a nuclear war.'

Again, Nic was surprised by her candour. The Soviets were not known for straying from the party line. He was about to probe further when Barry Finnis stumbled over. Barry had got his posting to Moscow and had rapidly developed a taste for strong vodka.

He leered at Irina and said drunkenly, 'Hello, darling. Fancy getting out of here and having a shag?'

Nic noticed that rather than anger, there was a hint of a smile on Irina's face. Before she could reply, Nic said, 'Behave Bazza. You're pissed.'

Barry glared at Nic before dissolving into laughter and saying, 'You're right, mate, but I had to try.'

Turning to Irina, he said, 'Sorry, darling. I was bang out of order.'

Irina frowned at him and, in a perfect impression of a prim English schoolteacher, said, 'Young man, you need to remember your manners. This is not Saturday night down the Dog and Duck.'

Barry's jaw dropped. It was the first time Nic had ever seen him rendered speechless.

'Sorry about my friend,' Nic said as Barry wove his way towards the door.

'Not a problem. Just tell him we have a camp in Siberia for misbehaving foreign spies.'

Nic wasn't sure whether she was joking.

'Anyone fancy joining me for dinner?' she asked.

Yuri quickly apologised and mumbled something about another appointment. She turned to Nic and said, 'Well?'

He wasn't sure how to react. Instinct told him it was a set-up, but it could also be an opportunity, 'I would love to,' he said.

'Good. I will meet you outside in five minutes.'

Nic made for the toilets. He needed to steady his breathing. As he splashed water on his face, he stared in the mirror. 'Don't screw this up, Slater,' he said out loud.

Irina was waiting at the bottom of the steps.

'Follow me,' she ordered.

Despite wearing heels, she walked briskly down the hill to Novoslobodskaya station. Like many of Moscow's subway stations, it was ornately decorated, in this case with a series of stained-glass windows.

'This is beautiful,' Nic said.

'You sound surprised,' she snapped, 'not everything in the Soviet Union is ugly.'

Nic was taken aback. If her sudden mood changes were designed to unsettle him, it worked.

'Where are we going?' he asked tentatively.

'Not far; it is only three stops. I promise you it will be worth your while,' Irina said, winking. There it was again, another mood change.

He tried to rationalise what was happening. A beautiful woman had asked him out to dinner. Usually, he would have been surprised and delighted. Instead, he was surprised and apprehensive. She was probably KGB, and this was all an act. She spoke perfect English with no trace of an accent and had already demonstrated a talent for mimicry and misdirection. Was this part of her entrapment strategy? He rather hoped so.

It was precisely the type of scenario he had been told to expect. The KGB researched new Embassy staff arriving in the Soviet Union and was adept at identifying those who were ripe for turning. Was he a target? Maybe he and Irina had the same objective—to recruit a foreign agent. He needed to be careful.

The train approached the platform, pushing a mass of humid air ahead of it. Irina's hair flew everywhere as she tried vainly to smooth it down. Nic was transfixed; her every movement was elegant. He chided himself. He must not let his emotions and attraction to her get in the way of his job. When the doors opened, they boarded the train and sat beside each other.

'What did you think of the meeting?' she asked.

Was this a casual question or the first phase of an interrogation? He needed to stop overthinking and go with the flow.

'It was the first interesting discussion we have had. The previous two sessions were pretty dull.'

'Why do you say that?' Irina asked.

'First, you were not there,' he said boldly. His training had emphasised that the easiest way to respond to any situation was to mirror the other party's behaviour.

She playfully thumped his leg, 'Be serious,' she said.

'There was no real discussion. It descended into a simplistic battle between two philosophies: Capitalism, good, communism, bad, or vice versa. Today was different. It was more nuanced and constructive.'

Irina leaned over and whispered in his ear, 'What you really mean is that at the first two meetings, everyone was trying to work out who the spies were?'

'That's the game. He said, smiling.

'Well, are you a spy?' she asked

'Are you?'

'No. I teach economics at the university.'

The train pulled into Kiyevskaya station. 'This is us,' she said, rising from her seat. Nic could not help but notice that the eyes of every man in the carriage watched as she moved towards the doors.

The restaurant was on a quiet side street just outside the station. Only one table was occupied where an elderly couple were finishing dessert. The woman looked up as they entered and smiled at Irina, who walked over to the table and embraced them both. Nic took a seat at a table by the window.

'Friends of yours?' he asked.

She nodded, 'I have been coming here for years; it's cheap, and the food is good. They always seem to be here. The man fought in the war but then got caught up in Stalin's purges. He was lucky to survive. She was a ballerina with the Bolshoi and managed to use her connections to save him. Most of his contemporaries got a bullet in the head. He merely had to endure eight years of hard labour in Siberia.'

Nic nodded. Her voice was angry. She was no apologist for the Soviet regime.

A waiter appeared, and upon seeing Irina, he exclaimed, 'Where have you been, moya dorogaya (my love)?'

Irina stood and they did the triple cheek kissing thing.

'Anatoly, it has not been that long.'

'Who is your friend?'

'This is Nic, he is a British spy.'

Nic was beginning to understand her game, 'Well, that's my cover blown,' he replied.

They all laughed. One of his instructors had told him that the more often you say you are a spy, the less likely they are to believe you. It was the furtive and secretive ones who were found out.

'We will both have my usual order,' Irina said.

'Your wish is my command, Princess.'

Anatoly disappeared into the back of the restaurant, returning shortly with their tea. It was hot and black, served in glasses encased in elegant silver holders.

After taking a sip, Irina started telling her story. She was born in a small town south of Moscow during the Great Patriotic War, as the Soviet Union called World War II. Her mother, Luda, was only seventeen at the time. Her father, Valery, had been a commissar in the NKVD, the forerunner of the KGB. Irina was the product of a brief wartime liaison just before he shipped out to Stalingrad as a political officer with the 95th Rifle Division. Less than a year after Irina was born and without ever seeing his daughter, he became one of the million Russian casualties incurred during the bloody battle for Stalin's namesake city. Luda was left as one of tens of thousands of widows left to bring up the children of fallen soldiers. She was luckier than most, as she and baby Irina were able to move in with her parents.

Her next revelation surprised Nic. Luda's parents were Scottish. Before World War I, her father had worked in the shipyards on the Clyde in Glasgow. During the war, he had been a founding member of the Clyde Workers' Committee, an organisation set up to incite a communist revolution in Britain.

After the war, there was little appetite for revolution in Britain, so Luda's parents left Scotland to start a new life in the socialist paradise being built in the Soviet Union.

They settled in Petrograd, where her father found work in the shipyards. Luda was born in 1924, just before the city was renamed Leningrad. Her father rose rapidly through the ranks of the workers' committees at the shipyards. In 1928, he transferred to Moscow as a co-ordinator of foreign workers in the USSR. The family spoke only English at home, so Luda was bilingual from an early age. After the General Strike in Britain in 1926, her parents were convinced that a communist revolution was inevitable, and they would move back to Scotland.

No such revolution was forthcoming, and by the start of World War II, Luda was working in the kitchen of the Moscow Komsomol, where she met Valery, the handsome young NKVD officer who was Irina's father.

After his death, Luda's language skills landed her a job as an interpreter with the NKVD, the position partly a reward for doing her patriotic duty in bearing a fallen NKVD officer's child.

Irina was primarily raised by her grandmother while Luda worked. After the war, Luda, who was still only twenty-two, married a professor of politics at Moscow State University who was more than a decade older than her. He accepted Irina as his daughter, and she considered him her father.

As she spoke, Nic looked for signs that she was following a carefully crafted script, but everything she said was plausible and probably verifiable.

Anatoly reappeared carrying two large bowls of borscht, a beetroot soup laden with vegetables. He set the steaming bowls down along with a plate of black bread.

'This is the second-best borscht in Moscow,' Irina explained. Anatoly looked offended, 'The best is obviously my mother's,' she quickly added, 'no Russian would dare say otherwise.'

Suitably placated, Anatoly left them to their meal.

'Enough about me,' she said. 'Tell me about Dominic Slater?'

Nic suspected she already knew quite a bit about him.

He had spent hours rehearsing his answer to this question, trying to get just the right blend of fact and fiction to be convincing.

'I grew up in a small village outside Sheffield in northern England. I have an older sister, Margaret, who we call Mags.

'Why is that?' Irina asked.

'I could not pronounce her full name when I was little, so I just called her Mags.'

Irina smiled and nodded.

'My mother and father met during the war. Dad is a few years older than Mum, but he insists she made the first move by flirting with him at a church dance. It was a typical wartime courtship. It was only recently I worked out they had to get married because Mum became pregnant with my sister. Dad fought in the British Army in North Africa and Italy during the war.'

'Where did you learn to speak Russian?'

'My Mum was a refugee from the Soviet Union. She was born near Leningrad. She insisted Mags and I both learnt Russian.'

Irina acted surprised. Nic thought she was a good actress. He went on to tell the story of how his mother had been orphaned and ended up in England.

They took their time eating, dunking pieces of bread into the borscht, and sipping tea. It was delicious and very filling.

Nic described his time at school and university and even mentioned his recruitment to the Foreign Office. However, he told her he had been hired as an economist, not a spy.

'What's London like?' she asked, 'I hear it is very exciting.'

'It is,' he replied, 'but quite different to the rest of the country—much more cosmopolitan and livelier. The rest of Britain still seems slightly hungover from the war. A new attitude is appearing in my generation. We were born during the war but don't remember it. Women are more liberated and independent; men do not have to do two years of national service. We have different attitudes, wear different clothes, and listen to different music.

'Like The Beats?'

He laughed, 'You mean the Beatles and, yes, they are a big part of the so-called youth revolution. How do you know about them?'

'I attended a lecture about the sources of moral decay in the West. The Beats, sorry Beatles, were cited as an example. The lecturer played one of their songs, "She Loves You". He compared it to Shostakovich's first symphony to illustrate Western cultural decay.'

'Not exactly a fair comparison. Do you believe all that stuff about moral decay?'

A slight frown crossed her face, 'Of course, all anyone seems to care about is the length of boys' hair and girls' skirts.'

Nic knew he was being teased. It was time to fight back a little. 'Okay, we may be morally bankrupt, but at least we can feed our people and don't need to build walls to stop them leaving.'

'The Berlin Wall was built to stop the infiltration of fascist agitators.'

'You seriously believe that?' Nic said.

'Our leaders would not lie to us, would they?' she said with a look of mock incredulity. The conversation continued similarly—more light-hearted banter than serious argument. Each taking cheap shots at the other. As Irina sipped the last of her tea, she looked at her watch and said, 'It is past my bedtime. This has been fun.'

'It has, but why did you ask me out to dinner?'

'I think you know the answer to that question,' she said, smiling.

Nic tried to help Irina with her coat as they stood up to leave. She turned and snapped at him, 'I am capable of putting my own coat on, thank you,' she said sternly. 'I am not some delicate English rose who needs the assistance of a man all the time.'

Nic was taken aback and stammered an apology. Irina looked at him sternly before dissolving into laughter.

'I am only teasing,' she said.

'Good,' he replied, 'anyway, I would never have thought of you as a rose, more like a thistle.'

That earned him a withering stare. Anatoly reappeared. He was probably ready to close for the night but showed no sign of irritation. He thanked them for their custom, kissed Irina and shook Nic's hand. 'Come back soon,' he said.

Outside, the street was dimly lit; only about half of the lamps were on. 'My apartment is not far from here,' Irina said, 'I will walk. You can take the Metro.'

'Are you sure you don't want me to walk you home?'

'Weren't you listening to a word I said?'

He was about to apologise when she leaned forward and kissed him on both cheeks, whispering, 'Men are so gullible.'

Before he could respond, she was striding off down the road.

As he walked back to Kandinsky House from the station, he tried to analyse the evening. His meeting with Irina and the dinner that followed had been no accident. Yuri was somehow involved. Perhaps they were both KGB, and he was now bait in a Soviet trap. SirRod and Seb would be pleased, but who was trying to recruit whom?

Back at his apartment, he poured himself a whisky and sat in the armchair by the window, looking out over the sleeping city. A heavy mist had descended, diffusing what little light was left. It reminded Nic of a moody closing shot from an old black-and-white spy film—except that this was Nic's new reality, and it was in glorious Technicolor.

As the whisky took hold, he began to feel melancholy. He had been distracted by Irina's looks and personality and allowed her to dictate the course of the evening. He needed to better control his emotions. Sighing, he drained the last of the whisky and climbed into bed.

He picked up a paperback book that Ranger had given him. It had not yet been published in the UK. The title was Last Exit to Brooklyn, a graphic and depressing view of life in New York in the 1950s. As he read the vivid depictions of drug use, gang rape, and homosexuality, he wondered whether the Soviet view of the West's moral decline was so far from the truth. It was not long before he fell asleep. He dreamed of Irina's disarming smile, the gentle teasing, and the feel of her lips on his cheek. He hoped it wasn't all an act.

18

Three weeks had passed since his dinner with Irina, and Nic wondered whether he had read the signs correctly. He had been convinced Irina was evaluating him as a potential KGB double agent. However, SirRod urged caution. There could be many reasons for her approach, from genuine interest as a member of the A-SECS delegation to an attempt to compromise him sexually. He advised Nic to move slowly but play along if she contacted him again. 'She may well try and seduce you,' he cautioned. 'If she does, there will be a camera somewhere. Do not let your personal feelings cloud your professional judgement.'

Seb had put it more bluntly, 'Make sure your balls don't rule your brain.'

The more he thought about the evening, the more intrigued he became. Irina had been candid in expressing her fears about nuclear war and had not shied away from criticising the Soviet regime; that did not seem like typical behaviour for a loyal KGB operative.

SirRod suggested he work with Simon and Charlotte to assemble a package mixing real and fake information he could pass on to Irina if she approached him about working for the KGB. He emphasised that any exchange needed to be a two-way process.

Nic needed to intrigue Irina, or more accurately, her superiors. But first, he needed to advance the relationship. One dinner and a kiss on the cheek did not constitute a basis for double agency.

He had no way of contacting her, so he was forced to wait for her to reach out to him. A few days before the next A-SECS meeting, he returned to his office after lunch to find an envelope on his desk. He slit it open using a very ornate Embassy paper knife, noting that it had already been opened once. He took out the piece of paper inside; it read, 'Sunday, noon, VDNKh, I.'

This was bold, Irina sending him a note directly at the Embassy. She knew it would be opened and read before it got to him. Looking again at the note, he was both nervous and excited. She had not waited for the next A-SECS meeting to make contact. It was also clever. By contacting him at the Embassy, she was effectively telling MI6 that she was pursuing one of their agents, which may be a cover for signalling that she was recruitable.

Before he had time to fully digest the implications, the phone rang. He picked up the receiver, and SirRod's voice bellowed from the handset, 'Excellent work, my boy. She is on the hook. Do not screw this up.'

'Yes, Sir,' Nic stammered in reply.

VDNKh was a Russian acronym for the Exhibition of Achievements of the National Economy, a combination trade show and amusement park in northeast Moscow. The nearby Metro station had the same name.

19

5th July 1964

Nic made sure he arrived in good time. As he walked up the steps from the platform, it was clear why she had chosen this location. Signs announced that a ceremony was being held in the park next door to the exhibition site to officially open a new monument celebrating the Soviet Union's achievements in space. Seven years ago to the day, the Soviets launched the first satellite to orbit the earth, Sputnik I. They followed this with the first man in space, Yuri Gagarin; the first woman in space, Valentina Tereshkova; and the first manmade object to land on the moon, Luna 2. The Americans had been struggling ever since to catch up.

Hordes of people were streaming out of the station towards the park. Parents guided excitable children along the pavement, and old couples shuffled along with smiles on their faces. Everyone looked happy. It was a shrewd propaganda play by the Russians. Celebrate Soviet successes while also emphasising the nation's dominance over America. The people could be proud of their great nation despite the problems they faced every day. Cynically, Nic wondered about the timing. Were the Russians celebrating now because they were beginning to fall behind the Americans in the space race? After all, Kennedy had promised to get an American to the moon and back before the decade was out.

He was jolted from his thoughts by a sharp poke in the ribs. He turned and saw Irina standing next to him. 'You really are the worst spy in the world. I could have walked up and stabbed you before you knew anything about it.'

'But I knew you wouldn't,' he said.

She smiled, grabbed his arm, and guided him through the crowds. It felt natural, but he was sure this was all part of her act; after all, it was only their second meeting.

Everyone looked skyward at the impressive monument, which was over a hundred metres tall and made of titanium. A rocket arced skywards, riding atop its exhaust plume, with the sun glinting off the metal, creating the illusion of sparks flying from the rocket's exhaust.

Irina leaned close and whispered, 'Surely you must see now that the Soviet Union is the greatest nation in the world?'

Nic nodded, 'If technological leadership is evidenced by self-aggrandising monuments, then you are running a close second to the French!'

'The French! How dare you compare us to the French. Napoleon only got to spend a month in Moscow before we kicked him out.'

A viewing platform had been set up at the base of the monument. Various dignitaries were making long, boring speeches that were being ignored by everyone in the park. Nic and Irina spent an hour wandering aimlessly around the park. It felt like a date to Nic, except for Irina's pointed questioning.

'Do you think capitalism is superior to socialism?'

'That is the wrong question,' he replied. 'You should be asking whether democracy is preferable to a totalitarian state where all opposition is banned. My answer would be to quote Churchill, "Democracy is the worst form of government, except for all those others that have been tried".'

Irina nodded thoughtfully before asking, 'But it was a so-called democracy that was the first to use nuclear weapons. How can it ever be justifiable to use such abominable weapons?'

'You can make a case that bombing Hiroshima and Nagasaki ultimately saved lives. An American invasion of mainland Japan would have been a bloody affair, given the Japanese vow to fight to the death. As America was the only nation to have such a weapon, there was no real threat of an escalation that could lead to nuclear Armageddon. That is not true now. You must look at nuclear weapons in the same context as chemical weapons. Their impact can be so broad and indiscriminate that it would be better if they did not exist. Still, given that they do exist, the key is that they remain a deterrent to their use.'

'Do you think there will be another world war?'

'Unfortunately, yes. The Cold War is a phoney peace. We nearly had a nuclear war break out over Korea and again over Cuba. It could happen over Vietnam or over Europe.'

Irina nodded, 'That is what I fear.'

Nic looked at her. Her concern seemed genuine. She changed the subject, 'Let's find somewhere to get a drink.'

'I think I've earned one,' Nic replied. They walked back through the crowds and found a café near the park entrance on Prospekt Mira. The place was packed, but they found a table in a corner by the window. The noise level was such that there was no chance of being overheard. Irina ordered tea and slices of Russian Napoleon cake, a crispy pastry filled with sweet, creamy custard.

As the waitress set the cups and plates down, Irina looked at Nic and said, 'As you seemed to answer my questions honestly, there are some things I want to tell you.'

'Okay,' Nic replied, wondering whether this was the beginning of the next act of the play they were performing. He wished he had seen the script in advance.

Irina took a bite of cake, washing it down with some tea, 'Almost everything I told you at Anatoly's was true.'

'I bet I can guess which part was a lie!' Nic said.

She smiled, 'I am sure you can, but let me tell it my way.' He nodded. 'When I was thirteen, I was identified as a future KGB recruit because of my fluency in English, excellent academic scores, and my mother's service in the NKVD. The day after my fourteenth birthday, I was sent away from home to a specialised academy for gifted children. It was really a sort of prep school for future KGB operatives. My education in the traditional sense ceased at that point. For the next four years, the focus was on two things: indoctrination in Marxist-Leninist philosophy and training to be a KGB agent.'

'That started when you were fourteen?' Nic said in astonishment.

'Yes. I was only allowed to see my parents twice a year. Seven days a week, we were schooled, or maybe brainwashed, is a better word as to why Soviet socialism is the only viable model for the world. We also learned a myriad of different skills. By age eighteen, I could kill someone in a dozen different ways, fire everything from a pistol to a rocket launcher, concoct various poisons, torture someone to the verge of death, fly a light aircraft, and speak three languages fluently. I was told that my life was solely dedicated to our leaders' service.'

'What does that mean?'

Her cheeks coloured. 'In Russia, women exist for only one purpose—to serve men.'

Nic was shocked but not completely surprised. He had heard about the almost slavish exploitation of women in the Soviet Union. 'We're you abused?' he asked angrily.

Seeing his anger flare, she said, 'Don't worry. I can handle myself. Quite a few men got very sore balls after trying to corner me in a dark corridor or broom cupboard.'

Nic couldn't help but smile.

'It's an occupational hazard for a woman in Russia.'

Nic nodded; he was not sure things were much better at home. Sexism was rampant in the security services.

She continued, 'I would rather do this than work in a munitions factory in Irkutsk. Smart women have a lot of leverage. Men underestimate our abilities. Their ego demands they boast about their power, which is their biggest weakness. Empires have been won and lost through loose talk in the bedroom.'

'I hope I never get on the wrong side of you.'

'Smart man,' she said. 'There is one other thing I learnt. Everything I was taught about the superiority of the Soviet Union's political and economic model was a lie.'

Nic was again surprised by her candour. This was not how he thought his recruitment would go.

'How did you work that out?' he asked.

'My stepfather…'

'The university professor?' Nic interrupted.

'Yes. He is one of the few academics allowed to travel overseas. He has taught classes at Harvard, spent time in Paris and Zurich, and corresponds with some of the capitalist world's most distinguished economists. He is under no illusions about the reality of the failed Soviet economic system. Over the years, he explained it all to me.'

'How has he managed to get away with it? Surely people who express that type of sentiment disappear?'

'They do, but he happens to be one of the principal architects of Russia's industrial revolution. After the failure of the collectivisation of agriculture after the revolution, the Soviet Union needed to rapidly develop its industrial base to buy food and fund the military. He was instrumental in directing investment towards mineral extraction and heavy industry. He is indispensable to the Politburo and therefore given much more freedom than his peers.'

'Why are you telling me this?' Nic asked.

'I am trying to recruit you.'

By now, her directness did not surprise him. 'Recruit me to do what?'

'Most of our high-placed sources in the UK intelligence services have defected. My mission is to replace them.'

She was so confident and self-assured. Nic nodded slowly, not sure what to say next. Things were moving quickly; this was only their second meeting. How could he be certain she would accept his approach out of hand? He needed time to think. 'This seems a bit odd. First, you denounce the Soviet system as a failure, then you suggest I work for it.'

She smiled, 'It's unconventional, certainly. We are taught to develop a specific recruitment strategy based on the person they are targeting. I decided you probably would not respond to an all-out denunciation of bourgeois capitalism. So, Yuri and I decided on a different approach.'

'Yuri? You are working together?'

She nodded, 'Yuri is the only person who knows what I am doing.'

Nic slowly nodded, 'You had Yuri check me out at the A-SECS meetings before you showed up?'

'Yes.'

'I cannot work him out. He doesn't seem very Russian to me.'

'He is not. He is from Siberia. They are a bit different up there.'

'You mean he has a personality!' Nic replied.

Irina laughed. 'Yuri is the only person I trust enough to share my real views about our glorious country. Do not underestimate him. He is one of the smartest people I know. We met twelve years ago at the academy and moved on to the same KGB training class. We have a special relationship.'

Nic felt a stab of completely irrational jealousy.

Irina saw Nic's expression.

'No, not like that! We protect each other. Being a woman in the KGB is not easy. Yuri helps me deal with the rampant misogyny. I help him with a couple of his weaknesses.'

'What weaknesses?'

Irina sighed, 'That is between him and me.'

Nic was trying to process what she had told him, 'This is a lot to take in,' he said.

She nodded, 'I know. You do not need to decide now. Think about what I have said. I am asking you to betray your country. Even in your country, treason still carries the death penalty. I will contact you in a few days. If you want to continue this conversation, follow the instructions in the message. If not, ignore it, and we'll never see each other again.'

She stood and left the café, leaving Nic staring blankly at his cold tea.

20

Irina had not made contact or attended the August A-SECS meeting. Nic wondered if her proposition had been real. He analysed everything that had happened at their meeting over and over. From a professional perspective, it could be good news. A KGB agent had approached him about becoming a double agent. Everything else was complicated. His thinking was muddled by his emotions. She was beautiful and intelligent and had flirted openly with him, but it could all be an act. He needed to be dispassionate, but that was impossible.

When he wrote his contact report, he wondered how much he should disclose. He sat staring at a blank piece of paper for a long time. It was a slow process. He cursed often; his two-fingered pecking at the keyboard was tortuously slow and error-prone. Soon, the floor was littered with discarded paper.

After an hour, he pulled the finished report and two carbon copies from the typewriter. He put the top copy in a sealed envelope marked for Sir Roderick's attention. He filed one of the carbon copies in a folder, which he put in a locked drawer in his filing cabinet. He had twenty minutes before he met with SirRod—just enough time to take the other copy down to the telex room for encoding and transmission to Seb in London.

As he got up, Webbe's squat frame appeared in his office doorway. He looked disdainfully at the discarded drafts that littered the floor.

'How did you ever get into the service? You can't even type!'

Nic ignored the jibe and said, 'Can I help you, Sir?'

'I have read the contact report of your meeting with Rosa Klein. Why are you wasting time on her? Are you trying to get laid? If so, forget it. You have one job here. If I do not see any progress soon, I will be recommending to Sir Roderick that you be replaced. Understand?'

'Yes, Sir,' replied Nic. He decided not to share the report he held in his hand. There was no point engaging with the little shit. Seb had warned him about Webbe. He had a Napoleon complex and an inflated sense of his own abilities.

SirRod was delighted to hear of Irina's approach. 'Excellent, play along with her,' he advised. 'What story are you going to use?'

'I will tell her that I am disillusioned with Britain. The working class continues to be exploited by the capitalist class. The Labour Party has lost its way, failing to build on the progress made by Atlee in building a socialist state after the war. Overseas, Britain is too dependent on an America determined to fight wars everywhere and drag Britain along with them.'

'Very good,' SirRod said. 'You almost sound as if you believe it.'

Nic thought he detected a hint of suspicion in his voice.

'Make sure she understands it must be a two-way exchange. She must give you credible information to maintain your cover.'

Nic nodded. SirRod was a devious bugger.

21

31st August 1964

Nic woke with a start and glanced at the clock. It read 04:00. He had managed only four hours of sleep. Cursing, he rolled out of bed, put on his dressing gown and slippers, padded to the kitchen, and put the kettle on.

It was always freezing in the mornings. The heating in Kandinsky House was temperamental, taking forever to get going in the morning. Maybe the Soviets purposely limited the gas supply to keep everyone chilled.

He was fed up. After the initial excitement of Irina's attempt to recruit him, weeks had passed with no contact. She had not attended the last two A-SECS meetings. He tried to talk to Yuri but got nowhere.

The more time passed, the more Webbe berated him for lack of progress. He even threatened to have Nic posted to the Falkland Islands! Thankfully, SirRod was more sanguine. He reiterated that they were playing a long game.

Nic had thought about contacting Irina, but he couldn't really walk up to the Lubyanka and leave a message. He was worried. Something had gone wrong. Had it all been a tease?

After making his tea, he walked to the living room and saw an envelope lying on the floor by the front door. That was strange. Entry to Kandinsky House was limited to Embassy personnel only. All mail was placed in individual mailboxes on the ground floor.

He bent down and picked up the envelope. He recognised the hint of perfume. At last, he thought, ripping open the envelope. The note read, 'Gorky Park Museum, 15:00, I.'

He breathed a sigh of relief. As time passed, he began to wonder if any of it had been real. Now, in typical Irina fashion, she had defied tradecraft rules and sent a note to him at the residence. How had she managed to get it delivered directly to his doormat?

His emotions were a mess, but he smiled as he entered the shower. He found himself singing the refrain to The Beatles, "She Loves You", complete with all yeah, yeah, yeahs.'

As he walked to the Embassy, he considered different scenarios for the upcoming meeting. He needed to be prepared to respond to whatever Irina suggested. Upon arrival at the Embassy, he left a note for Vera to give to SirRod and sent a telex to Seb in London. His brain was a jumble of disorganised thoughts. Armed with a pot of coffee prepared by his newly appointed secretary, Penny, he sat at his desk, trying to structure his thinking.

Just before noon, Penny put her head around the door and said, 'Meet SirRod at 12:30 by the front gate.'

Penny was a typical Foreign Service secretary—posh, pretty, and proficient at everything. He liked her but suspected he was a bit of a disappointment to her. She disapproved of what she called his slovenly approach and lack of respect for the traditions of the Foreign Service. She was probably hoping to find an aristocratic undersecretary for a husband and found working for an uncouth, working-class oik a big disappointment. He considered introducing her to Seb but could not bring himself to do that to the poor girl.

Needing to calm his nerves, he took a cigarette from the packet he kept in his desk drawer.

'Penny, have you got any matches?'

She appeared at the door frowning. 'You're pretty hopeless, aren't you?'

She said, tossing a box of Swan Vesta's in his direction.

'Sorry and thanks,' he replied sheepishly.

He struck the match and placed the cigarette's tip just above the blue centre of the flame. The tobacco emitted a slight crackling sound as it ignited. Two puffs and a cloud of bluish smoke spiralled towards the ceiling. He was getting better at this smoking thing. Perhaps not Bogart cool, but passable.

SirRod ambled through the Embassy gates and crossed the road to where Nic stood. He seemed oblivious to the traffic, which miraculously avoided him as he concentrated on relighting his pipe.

'I hear your fish is back on the hook,' SirRod said.

'Yes, Sir. Although, I am not sure who is on whose hook.'

'Don't worry about that. You are back in contact. Remember, it's a marathon, not a sprint. If Irina takes the lead at first, that is fine. It will give her a sense of control. The important thing is who wins the race. Continue developing the relationship, but do not push it. We have not had a decent source in Moscow for years—Philby betrayed them all. Do whatever it takes, understand?'

Nic nodded. The thought of doing whatever it took to develop the relationship sounded good. 'Yes, Sir,' he said

'Walk with me,' SirRod said. I hate using that bloody greenhouse inside. It's much easier to avoid the bugs with a brisk walk.' SirRod was referring to the purpose-built glass cube that had been constructed inside the Embassy to provide a sound and bug-proof environment for sensitive conversations.

Across the river, Nic noticed a man in an ill-fitting dark grey suit take a parallel path along the opposite riverbank.

'I assume you have noticed the two Borises following us?' SirRod asked.

'Two?' Nic queried. 'I see one on the other side of the river.'

'Boris II is about a hundred yards in front of us,' said SirRod, indicating another grey-suited man. Nic saw and silently cursed himself. Front and follow was one of the most basic surveillance techniques. One team member walked in front of the target, anticipating their route, while the second team member followed to the rear. It was a risky strategy unless the target's destination was known.

'Why do you call them Boris, Sir?'

SirRod chuckled, 'During the war, we called all Russians Boris; the Americans are Chuck; and the French, Pierre. Refresh my memory about your previous meetings with Sashkaya.'

Nic recapped the first two meetings, sticking to what he had written in his contact report. He was so engrossed in what he was saying that he had to quickly sidestep a lamppost that appeared out of nowhere. SirRod smirked but said nothing. When he had finished, SirRod asked, 'When is your next meeting with her?'

'Tomorrow in Gorky Park.'

'Good, make sure you do more listening than talking. Irina set up the meeting, so it's her agenda. There's a lesson I learnt during the war you might find useful. Don't just listen to what she is saying; pay particular attention to how she says it. What words and tone does she use? What does her body language tell you? For example, if she apologises for the delay in getting back in touch but gives a long, drawn-out, overly complicated explanation while failing to maintain eye contact, she is probably lying. If she gives a succinct and rational answer while looking directly at you, it is more likely to be the truth.'

Nic nodded, 'Good advice, Sir.'

'Your job is to discern the reality from the role. These Russian Lolita's are cunning. Many times, a naive agent has succumbed to their charms only to end up in the Lubyanka or mysteriously disappear into the gulags. I do not want to be arranging a spy swap to get you home. Tease her with some low-grade intelligence, but do not share anything meaningful until you know we will get something in return.'

'Understood. I have been assembling a few stories with Simon and Charlotte.

'Good. Just don't give the whole bloody lot away at once.'

They crossed the river using the bridge where the Yauza River flows into the Moskva and turned back towards the Embassy. This caused a problem for their tails. Boris I had not anticipated the turn onto the bridge, so he walked away from them. In contrast, Boris II walked straight towards them.

SirRod whispered, 'He is flummoxed now! Watch this.'

Boris II executed a swift about-turn, effectively switching places with Boris I. He was ahead of them while Boris and I hurried across the bridge to take the rear position.

'It is all a big game,' said SirRod. 'Occasionally, we can win a small skirmish.

Nic had heard stories about SirRod. At the outbreak of World War Two, he had been transferred from the Foreign Office to the SIS, more commonly known as MI6 or just Six. He quickly rose through the ranks as the service became ever more instrumental in the war effort. In the run-up to D-Day, he had been responsible for coordinating numerous clandestine operations conducted jointly by Six and the French Resistance. Churchill himself had commented that SirRod had been instrumental in ensuring the success of the Allied landings.

Towards the end of the war, he transferred to Berlin to root out the Nazis. Once there, he soon realised that former Nazis were far less of a threat than the Soviets. According to Seb, SirRod was among the few to alert London to Stalin's true ambition to dominate Eastern Europe.

'I know I look like an old fart,' SirRod said, 'but I did my fair share of fieldwork. Berlin was a hive of espionage, counterespionage, blackmail, and subterfuge after the war. It was great fun. Everyone watched everyone else. No one knew who the real enemies were. Turned out it was the Russians who, despite being our allies, were already working to secure as much territory as quickly as possible. After the dust settled, they controlled most of Eastern Europe, and we have been paying the price ever since.'

They had arrived back at the Embassy. SirRod looked at Nic and said, 'Good luck. Remember, don't fall in love with her.'

22

1st September 1964

1ˢᵗ September 1964

Before leaving for Gorky Park, Nic read Seb's reply to his message. His advice was consistent with SirRod's. Irina's re-establishing contact was positive. However, the long delay did raise suspicions. He recommended caution and suggested he ask her what caused the delay to see if it made sense.

It was a forty-minute walk to Gorky Park. As he passed through the Embassy gates, he saw Boris I sitting on a bench by the river and Boris II leaning against a wall about 100 metres further along. Should he try to lose them? Probably not; it would look suspicious.

The British Embassy sat on a big bend in the Moskva River. He had to cross the isthmus and use the Krymsky Bridge to reach Gorky Park. The museum was just inside the entrance. He sat on a bench in front of the entrance. The warm weather had encouraged a few Muscovites to venture out. A harried mother tried to corral two small children; a couple walked arm in arm, staring intently into each other's eyes, and a drunk lay asleep by the museum wall, an empty bottle of vodka lying by his side. Nic watched as two policemen approached. Alcoholism was endemic in the Soviet Union, often encouraged by the government, which needed the tax revenue. Kiosks selling cheap vodka adorned every street corner in much the same way as newsstands did in London.

As the police officers reached the man, a van pulled up beside them. They dragged the drunk to his feet and bundled him into the back of the van. After a night in the cells, he would be released, and no doubt make his way to the nearest kiosk, replenish his vodka supply, and the cycle would begin again. At least he would have a warm, dry bed for the night.

As the van's rear door slammed shut, Nic jumped as his hat was pulled off his head. He turned and saw a laughing Irina standing behind him, 'You really are a terrible spy!'

Nic felt his face colouring. She sat down next to him. Her behaviour continued to bewilder him. He expected everything to be clandestine, discreet, and covert. Still, she openly flirted and teased him about being a spy. He decided that two could play at that game, 'I heard you ages ago. I have memorised the rhythm of your heels as you walk. I just feigned surprise for Boris I's sake.'

She looked confused, 'Boris I?'

Nic nodded to where Boris I was standing, smoking yet another cigarette.

Irina laughed, 'His name is Timur,'

'I prefer Boris. Does he work for you?' Nic said.

'Not exactly, but he occasionally does favours for me.'

'Like following me?'

'Of course. You are a foreign agent who cannot be trusted.'

'I suppose Boris II is one of yours as well?'

'You must be talking about Lev, Timur's partner?' Irina replied.

Nic nodded, 'They are not exactly stealthy.'

'They can be when necessary. We want you to know you are being followed. It keeps you on your toes.'

Nic smiled, 'So why are we here? It's been almost three months.'

'You missed me! How sweet,' she teased.

'Why has it taken so long for you to get back in touch?'

Her expression turned serious, 'Things have been a bit complicated of late.' She did not elaborate, simply saying, 'Have you thought about what we discussed last time?

Nic looked directly at her. 'I have thought about little else.'

It was time for him to take the initiative. 'It is a ruse to compromise me. It makes no sense for a KGB agent to make such an overt approach so soon after meeting a target.'

To Nic's surprise, her enigmatic smile reappeared, and she said, 'That is exactly what I would think in your position.'

Nic was taken aback. What game was she really playing? She stood up and said, 'Walk with me.'

He was pleasantly surprised when she took his hand as they strolled through the park; it felt soft and warm. They walked in silence until Irina said, 'I am going to give you a history lesson. The Tsars ruled Russia heartlessly and ruthlessly for centuries, much like your medieval kings in England. The difference was that Russia was isolated from the rest of the world and had few moderating influences.

'In Britain, the church was a powerful counterbalance to the monarchy. When one of your kings got above himself, you chopped his head off. Later, the Industrial Revolution raised living standards and created much wealth, but only for a few. Eventually, a combination of social concern, trade union action, and government policy improved the lot of the proletariat through improved education, housing, and healthcare. It was far from perfect but represented progress and probably prevented a revolution.'

Nic was impressed by her knowledge. 'None of that happened in Russia. The Tsars and their cronies shared nothing. They exercised brutal, autocratic control over the Russian people and suppressed political debate. It took a revolution to trigger change. The new regime promised to free the exploited masses in a worker-led state. But the Soviet Union is a little harder to manage. It is seventy times larger than Britain, covers eleven time zones, and comprises 120 ethnic groups speaking over a hundred languages. The only way the communist party can exert control is through a rigid, and frequently brutal, centralised command and control structure.'

Nic wondered what point she was trying to make. Looking at him, she said, 'You have no idea why I am telling you this, do you?'

'I was wondering,' he admitted.

'Understanding our history is essential to understanding why the Soviet Union behaves as it does. We are paranoid about two things: first, that other nations want to destroy us. Napoleon and Hitler both tried and failed—but only just. Now, America is trying to do the same thing. What you see as offensive actions, we see as defensive.

'And second?'

'Destruction from within—another revolution. With so many different ethnic groups, religions, and other constituencies, it is impossible to please everyone—some would say the current regime pleases no one. Soviet leaders use external threats to unite disparate groups. By casting foreign powers as out to destroy us, they unify the nation against a common enemy. It worked for Stalin during the Great Patriotic War and is now working with the United States.'

Nic nodded. It made sense. Some commentators argued that World War I had prevented a revolution in the UK, and no one could doubt that World War II had moved the US from economic depression to global economic supremacy.

Irina continued, 'The situation in Russia is deteriorating. The economy is failing, and people are becoming more aware that the standard of living and quality of life are lagging far behind the West. China is approaching superpower status and sits right on our eastern border. Our leadership feels cornered, and that makes them dangerous. They are surrounded by sycophants who constantly goad them to take military action to distract from domestic issues.'

'What sort of action?' Nic asked.

'Invade West Germany, attack China, arm North Vietnam, prop up Cuba; it is a long list. There is a hard-line group in the Politburo that believes America has no appetite for a major conflict and will never resort to using nuclear weapons because they fear mutually assured destruction. They want to exploit what they see as American weakness to expand Soviet influence—that logic is flawed. America will not just stand by and let that happen. The world will be plunged into another, much more deadly, war.'

They had stopped walking and leaned on a wall overlooking the Moskva River. Irina's expression was one of genuine concern.

'Are the Politburo really that stupid?' Nic asked.

'It is not stupidity; it is a calculated gamble.'

'With huge consequences if they are wrong.'

Irina nodded, 'They have convinced themselves that the United States would never use nuclear weapons again. Plans are already in place for future attacks.'

Nic was shocked, 'Seriously? Where and when?'

'Before I tell you, you have to make a decision.'

'What?'

'If you believe what I am saying, I want us to work together to try and prevent war. We will tell our respective masters we have successfully turned the other into a double agent. In reality, we will be working toward our own agenda. We will both be traitors to our countries but for good reasons. If you think I am trying to deceive or entrap you, you should walk away and forget we met.'

Nic stared across the river, not saying anything. This was the point of no return. Irina was proposing something far beyond the scope of his mission. Could he trust her? He was conflicted. He wanted to believe her, but it all sounded a bit surreal.

His mind went back to a conversation with Seb during his training. Seb had said that the Soviet Union believed that NATO was not a defensive alliance but a US-led vehicle to destroy the Warsaw Pact. That correlated with what Irina was suggesting.

He looked at Irina and said, 'I don't know if you are telling the truth, but if you are, I cannot sit by and do nothing. Do you really think we can stop a war from breaking out?'

'I don't know—but I have to try.'

'Then I am with you,' Nic said somewhat hesitantly.

'Don't sound so excited,' she said, smirking. 'You can always betray me if you wish.'

'And you me,' he replied.

'That should keep us both honest,' she replied.

They started walking again.

'Why did you approach me?' Nic asked

'I have been looking for a candidate for months. At first, I thought it needed to be an American, but they have such a black-

and-white view of the world—USA good, USSR bad. I was beginning to despair of finding anyone, then your profile came across my desk last November.'

'So, I was the last resort?'

'Pretty much.'

'Wait a minute, November? That was before I knew I was coming to Moscow.'

She smiled, 'We still have a few sources in London.'

'How did you decide I was the right person after only two meetings?'

'I did my homework. I knew all about Dominic Slater before we even met. Remember that incident in Manchester when you were sixteen?'

Nic was gob-struck. He and two friends had stupidly stolen some records from a shop in Manchester. They thought they had got away with it until a policeman apprehended them as they ran towards the station. They were hauled into court, where the judge gave them a severe telling-off, accusing them of being delinquent teenagers. Each was fined five pounds and made to pay for the records.

The formal punishment paled in comparison to the telling off they received at home. The only good thing about the episode was that he got to keep the records. "Hound Dog," "Rock Around the Clock," and "Be Bop a Lula" became the foundation of his record collection.

'What else do you know about me?'

'The one thing that convinced me to target you was that while you were being recruited by Viscount Weston, you said your motivation for joining the service was less about destroying the Soviet Union than ensuring there was never another world war.'

Nic was astonished. The KGB must have a source inside MI6. Could it be Seb? Surely not.

They had reached the rose garden; water was tumbling over a delicately carved fountain. A few late-season roses were still in bloom.

'Is there anything you don't know about me?'

'Probably not. Remember, my mission is to recruit foreign agents. We conduct extensive background checks on every diplomat posted to the Soviet Union. Your working-class background, fluency in the language, and family links to Russia made you a candidate.'

He was beginning to understand. Irina was not recruiting him to work for the KGB but to work with her. She was staring at him, 'If I am wrong, you will share what I have said with your superiors, and this will be over. But I think I have guessed right.'

She was perceptive; Nic was genuinely concerned about the world's future. Even after two world wars, there was still an appetite for conflict. The current peace was fragile, and too few people appreciated the deadly power at the disposal of world leaders. If one side or the other believed they had an advantage, it could easily lead to a pre-emptive attack.

They were back at the museum. As they parted company, Irina said, 'Think about what I have said and give me your answer at the next A-SECS meeting. We don't have much time.'

Back at the Embassy, he thought about his burgeoning relationship with Irina. He realised he was operating at a considerable disadvantage to Irina; she knew so much more about him than he knew about her. He went to see Charlotte and Simon and asked them to dig into Irina's background. Charlotte sighed, 'You know it is a terrible waste of our talents to have us vet your potential girlfriends? But don't worry, I'll wander over to the Lubyanka and ask for her personnel file.'

'Ignore her ladyship,' Simon said, 'she broke a nail this morning and has been grumpy ever since.'

Nic laughed while Charlotte rewarded Simon with a kick under the table.

Despite Charlotte's protestations, within two days, they had confirmed much of what Irina had told him. She graduated from Moscow State University in 1961. Her student record noted her birth in Kaluga, about two hours south of Moscow, on 18 October 1941.

A search of Soviet war records confirmed that her father had died in the Battle of Stalingrad in January 1943. Irina was primarily brought up by her maternal grandparents. Charlotte confirmed they were Scottish and had emigrated to the USSR after 1922. They had been members of the Communist Party while living in Glasgow.

After the death of Irina's father, her mother served as an interpreter for senior Soviet officials and attended the Potsdam Peace Conference in 1945 as part of Stalin's delegation. Then, she married Irina's stepfather, cited as one of the authors of the Soviet Union's fourth and fifth five-year economic development plans. Irina was telling the truth, or at least what she was telling Nic matched the official records. Of course, it could all have been faked as part of her cover story.

Nic exchanged a series of coded telexes with Seb in London. He shared Irina's comments about the KGB still having well-placed sources within MI5 and MI6. Seb's response was anger but not surprise. Everyone suspected that Philby had left some sort of network behind when he defected. All personnel in the security services were being re-vetted to try to root out any remaining moles.

He didn't share any details of the collaboration Irina had proposed. He liked to think Seb would understand, but he could not risk Seb feeling honour bound to report Nic's treachery. Nor did he tell Seb about his growing personal feelings for Irina. It did not stop Seb from offering his advice, 'Stay focused on your mission.'

Easier said than done, Nic thought.

23

13th October 1964

Neither Irina nor Yuri attended the September A-SECS meeting. Again, Nic wondered if he was being played. A pattern seemed to be emerging: an intense meeting followed by a long silence. Twice now, Irina had committed to follow-up meetings that had not materialised. Perhaps she was testing him to see if he was serious.

The next meeting was being held at the Lenin State Library. Nic had decided how to respond to her approach but was still conflicted by his personal and professional feelings.

The library was only a short walk from the Embassy. Boris II shadowed him from his usual position on the far side of the river. He wondered if he was there at Irina's behest or whether it was a random assignment. SirRod said the Soviets knew who the spies were and would randomly assign a tail to keep them on their toes.

The library had opened in 1862 and was renamed for Lenin after he died in 1924. He climbed the library steps, passing between the columns that supported the vaulted entrance. Before going to the meeting room, he stopped by the cloakroom, checked his reflection in the mirror, made sure no food was stuck in his teeth, retied his tie, and brushed the hint of dandruff off his shoulders. He felt surprisingly good, not quite Sean Connery, but good enough.

As he walked inside, he heard a voice shout, 'Privyet,' the Russian equivalent of 'Hi' across the foyer. Nic raised his hand in acknowledgement as Yuri walked over and said with a big smile, 'Good to see you, Mr. Bond. Seduced any SPECTRE agents recently?'

Nic smiled. Ian Fleming's books were popular in Russia. The rumour at Six was that the KGB made all their agents read the complete series as part of their training.

'No, but I hear SPECTRE has penetrated the KGB, so you better watch out.'

Yuri laughed. Nic wondered how much Irina had told him. They chatted easily in Russian and English as they climbed the marble staircase and followed signs to the meeting room. About half the delegates were already there. Nic scanned the room but could not see Irina. He glanced at his watch. There were still five minutes until the scheduled start time. He wanted to ensure that he sat beside her, so he was loath to choose a seat. He ambled over to the refreshment table and poured himself some tea.

The other delegates were taking their seats around the table. Nic moved to study the spines of some of the books on the shelves. Judging by the titles, the room housed 17th-century romantic Russian fiction, a genre Nic did not know existed.

Just then, the door opened, and Irina strode into the room, waving hello to the assembled group. Every set of eyes appraised her as she slid off her hat and coat, throwing them carelessly over one of the empty chairs lining the outside of the room. She looked stunning. Her cream dress was more Parisian than Russian, and Nic had no objection to her black-seamed stockings and high-heeled shoes.

She barely glanced at Nic before moving straight to an empty seat on the far side of the room, facing the large window that overlooked the courtyard below. Nic reacted quickly enough to head off at least three other delegates and grab the seat next to her. As casually as he could, he said, 'Hello. It's good to see you again.'

Irina turned towards him, her head lowered, eyes peering over the top of her glasses, and said, 'Ah yes, Slater, isn't it?'

She was playing it very cool. However, a flicker of her trademark smile creased her lips. The topic for the meeting was the impact of the newly emerging data processing technology on international trade. Nic thought it sounded incredibly dull. His knowledge of the new-fangled computers that occupied whole rooms in office buildings was minimal. Before leaving the Embassy, he had asked Vera what she knew about data processing. Her answer had been cryptic, hinting that the forerunner of today's computers had significantly impacted her wartime work, so he should pay attention.

The agenda called for each delegation to make a short presentation, setting out their perspective, followed by a discussion of computers' possible future economic impact.

Vasily Fischukova, an engineer at the Soviet Academy of Sciences, was the first presenter. To Nic's surprise, his presentation was fascinating. Not so much for the technical content, which he barely understood, but for the central role science and technology played in Soviet ethos. Fischukova touted the centralised planning and control system as providing the Soviet Union with a key advantage in research and development. He explained that the Soviet approach to science was rooted in developing technologies to help the workers while the driving force was making a profit in the West. Vasily proudly cited recent Nobel Prize wins in Physics and Chemistry as proof of Soviet leadership. He argued that the same research-driven approach was being applied to computing. Starting with the space program, the Soviet Union developed advanced computing applications to operate telemetry, life support, and engine management systems. That knowledge was being applied to improve electricity distribution networks and public transportation systems and optimise the distribution of welfare services.

As he was wrapping up his talk, Nic glanced at Irina. She had been making copious notes in a small notebook. He could not read them as they were in shorthand, but it looked like she had drawn a seating plan of the room and made notes beside each British delegate.

The next speaker was Nigel Farthington-Worth, who, like Fischukova, was a real scientist. He was on secondment to the British Embassy from Imperial College, London. He looked like the archetypal English academic: tall, thin, slightly balding, with thick, round, black-rimmed glasses. He wore a tailored three-piece tweed suit with a pocket watch and chain. A bright red and yellow bow tie with a matching pocket square completed the ensemble. Given his gaunt frame, the look was more scarecrow than sophisticate. His hair needed the attention of a comb, the suit needed pressing, and the pocket watch had fallen out of its home and swung pendulum-like across his groin.

He fumbled through a pile of papers and began his presentation by saying, 'Great Britain has a proud history of technological innovation, most notably as the cradle of the Industrial Revolution.'

He highlighted some of Britain's technological advances, from the Spinning Jenny to early computers such as the

Manchester Baby and LEO-1. Britain, he said, remained at the forefront of technological innovation, as was shown by the new Labour government's commitment to "harness the white heat of the technology revolution."

Nic glanced again at Irina, who was still making notes. She turned towards him and whispered, 'No copying,' making a show of covering her notes with her hand,

Nic whispered, 'I haven't deciphered your code yet, but I am working on it.'

Farthington-Worth peered over his glasses with a disapproving look. Nic sheepishly turned his attention back to the presentation, feeling like he had been caught cheating on a school test.

After Nigel finished his presentation, more polite applause followed. There was a fifteen-minute break before the discussion session. Nic leaned over to Irina and said, 'I have been thinking a lot about what you said.'

'Good. Have you made a decision?

'Yes, and it is yes,' he replied.

He was rewarded with a broad smile, 'Good. Things are about to get very interesting here in Moscow. I cannot stay after the meeting, but we should meet soon.'

'How about at the Bolshoi on Sunday? They are doing Swan Lake,' Nic asked hopefully.

'What an interesting idea,' she said. The chairman called the room to order, and the discussion session began. His invitation went unanswered.

The discussion was lively, but Nic was not really paying attention. He wondered what she had meant about things getting very interesting. Was it good or bad news for them?

He tuned back into the discussion around the table. The essence was that technology was changing the world and that computing was the next big wave. There was the usual ideological disagreement about whether state-controlled research and development or state-sponsorship of private-sector innovation was the best approach. Nic did not think this was an either/or question. Some combination of the two would probably be most effective. The Government should help set the agenda and fund basic research, while the private sector focuses on commercialisation.

He felt a slight tap on his ankle and glanced at Irina. She was still making notes. Amid the hieroglyphics, she had written one word in English—Yes'

He picked up his pen and wrote on his notepad, '14.00, fountain, Bolshoi.'

Irina glanced over and nodded. That smile was there again. It really was most disarming.

When the meeting wrapped up. Irina apologised that she could not stay for the social as she had to visit her mother. As she left, she tapped Nic on the shoulder and whispered, 'See you on Sunday. It will be a nice way to celebrate my birthday!'

Of course, Nic thought the 18th of October was her birthday. He stayed and talked to Yuri, trying to subtly fish for more information, but Yuri did not take the bait. After a few minutes of fruitless probing, he excused himself.

It was raining outside. Nic crossed the road to seek shelter in the lee of the Kremlin walls. Irina had put on another accomplished performance. Everything she did seemed choreographed to beguile him while affirming her total control of the situation.

He was delighted that she had accepted his invitation to the ballet. More for personal than professional reasons. Now, he only needed to think of a suitable birthday present.

As he crossed Red Square, the cobbles glistened under the lights as the rain continued to fall. There were few people about as darkness fell over the city. The Kremlin walls and domes of St. Basil's cast long shadows in the fading light. A solitary police car sat in front of the Lenin Mausoleum—its occupant fast asleep. He turned down Ulitsa Il'inka by the side of GUUM. Feeling happier than he had for a long time, he decided to treat himself to dinner. He would try a restaurant nearby that Rosa had recommended to him.

24

15th October 1964

As Nic walked across the Embassy lobby, he heard a voice shout, 'Oi Slater. Have you heard about Khrushchev?'

He looked round to see Barry Finnis beckoning him over, 'What about him?' Nic responded.

'The Russkies have only gone and foot-pumped him!'

Nic had no idea what he was saying, 'Speak English, will you.'

'Foot-pumped, dumped—Cockney rhyming slang mate. There's been a Palace coup, Khrushchev's out, Kosygin's, Premier and Brezhnev, First Secretary.'

'Seriously?' Nic exclaimed. Khrushchev had been in power for eleven years after winning the battle to replace Stalin. His authority had seemed absolute. Is this what Irina's cryptic comment at the meeting had meant? Had she known of Khrushchev's demise in advance?

He took the stairs two at a time as he hurried to his office. He needed to gather his thoughts before reporting to SirRod. Penny appeared with a cup of coffee. She shook her head in disapproval at the sight of his legs resting on the desk.

He took a sip of coffee and scanned Pravda's front page. There was no mention of any change in leadership. He picked up the phone and called Charlotte's number. In a poor imitation of a plummy, upper-class accent, Simon answered and said, 'Her ladyship's residence, whom may I say is calling?'

'Bond, James Bond,' Nic replied.

'Charlie, I have Mr Bond on the line for you.'

Nic heard a string of expletives in the background before Charlotte came on the line, 'What do you want?' she barked.

'What's your take on the news about Khrushchev?' he asked.

'He is paying the price for Cuba,' she said. 'When he backed down, he lost a lot of support amongst the hardliners. They thought he made the USSR look weak. Since then, he has been trying to rebuild support, but he obviously ran out of time. Russians are always looking for an excuse to stab their leaders in the back.'

'What will happen now?'

'Whenever the leadership changes hands, be it Lenin to Stalin or Stalin to Khrushchev, there is a period of instability while the new leader tries to consolidate power. I suspect Kosygin and Brezhnev are already trying to rally support so that one of them becomes the clear leader. They will be susceptible to taking risks to establish their authority. We are entering a perilous time.'

After hanging up, he shouted through to the outer office, 'Penny, get me five minutes with Sir Roderick, please. It's urgent.'

He heard Penny rise from her desk and walk over to his office. ' There's no need to shout,' she chastised. 'If you are too lazy to come through and ask politely, you can always dial my extension.'

That was two admonishments already, and it wasn't even 08:00.

He sat back and continued to think about Irina. Suppose she had advanced knowledge of Khrushchev's ouster. In that case, she must be very well connected, so why was she spending time at A-SECS meetings trying to recruit him?

His thoughts were interrupted by Penny gently tapping on the door, 'Sir Roderick will stop by on his way to the department heads meeting,'

'I am already here,' bellowed SirRod's deep baritone behind her.

Penny stepped back, and Sir Roderick strode through the door, closing it behind him. Nic quickly removed his feet from the desk.

'Morning, young man, everything is going bonkers around here with the news about Khrushchev.'

'Yes, Sir. That is what I wanted to talk to you about. I believe Sashkaya knew about Khrushchev's impending demise before it happened.'

SirRod abruptly sat on the chair in front of Nic's desk. It groaned as his ample frame touched down. 'Really?' he said.

'I think she may have connections at quite a senior level inside the Kremlin,' Nic added.

'Interesting. It seems like you have a big fish on the hook. Now, all you need to do is reel her in. Keep me posted.'

'Yes, Sir,' replied Nic, conscious that he was already beginning to withhold information from his boss.

25

16th October 1964

Nic agonised over whether to give Irina a birthday present. Would it be presumptuous? What was the protocol regarding buying presents for the enemy? Unfortunately, there was no handbook for spies, and it wasn't something he felt comfortable asking Seb or SirRod about.

As he pondered his dilemma, a thought popped into his head. He opened his desk drawer and took out the business card Rosa Klein had given him. He picked up the phone and asked to be connected to Rosa Klein at the Brazilian Embassy. A few seconds later, he heard the operator say, 'Miss Klein, I have Mr Slater from the British Embassy for you.'

'Klein here. How can I help you?' said Rosa in her most professional voice.

Aware that the line was probably tapped, Nic improvised, 'Hello, this is Dominic Slater from the British Embassy. We are planning a reception for some visiting South American diplomats. I wondered if you could advise on the correct protocol for such occasions.'

'Certainly,' she replied. She was clearly trying to suppress a giggle.

'Thank you. Would you be available this afternoon?'

'You are lucky. One of my meetings has just been cancelled. I will meet you outside St. Basils at two.'

'Yes, ma'am, thank you.'

'My pleasure,' Rosa replied.

Nic wondered if he was doing the right thing. How would Rosa react to being asked for advice on buying a present for another woman after he rejected her earlier overture?

He spotted her from the other side of Red Square. In her bright red coat, she was a beacon of colour amidst the grey crowds. She smiled as he approached, and they exchanged cheek kisses. He was beginning to get quite good at it.

She took his arm, and they started walking across the square. 'So, what is so urgent that my English spy requires an immediate meeting? Surely, it is not advice on diplomatic protocol.'

Like Irina, Rosa was assured and self-confident. When Nic said nothing, she stared at him and said, 'Well?'

'I am sorry,' he stammered, 'I think this may be a bad idea.'

'Stop being pathetic. What do you want?'

'I need your advice on what to get a woman as a birthday present.'

Rosa's expression hardened, 'Well, you certainly know how to make a girl feel special. Here, I think a handsome English gentleman will take me up on my offer, and all he wants is advice on what present to buy for his Commie girlfriend. I bet she works for the KGB too!'

Nic could feel himself blushing. Rosa burst out laughing. 'I am teasing. Tell me all about her?'

Nic described Irina as a Russian translator who had been assigned to the embassy. He knew Rosa didn't believe a word, but he could not tell her the truth. When he finished, she looked serious, 'You've fallen in love, haven't you?'

He didn't respond. Rosa smiled and said, 'Don't worry. I am only a little bit jealous. I know the perfect place—we are going to a Beryozka shop.'

'What is a Beryozka shop?'

'They are government-run shops that sell luxury goods unavailable to ordinary Russians. You can only use foreign currency to buy things; it is a rather pathetic attempt by the government to acquire more foreign currency. There's one behind GUUM. We will find something nice to ensure her knickers fall off easily!'

Not for the first time, Nic blushed.

26

18th October 1964

Winter had arrived in style. The temperature was freezing, and snowflakes drifted down from heavy grey clouds. Thankfully, the cold Siberian winds had not yet arrived. Nic was still happy to have swapped his trilby for an ushanka, a traditional Russian fur hat he had purchased at the Beryozka shop on Rosa's recommendation. He had not yet deployed the rather stylish ear flaps.

The Bolshoi Theatre looked to be encased in a snow globe. People were converging from all directions. Nic scanned the crowd, looking for Irina. The emergence of everyone's winter wardrobe made identification challenging. A statuesque beauty like Irina would likely be swathed in hat, coat, and fur-lined boots.

'Hi, handsome,' said a sultry voice in a perfect American accent. Nic spun on his heels and immediately sensed his mistake. The leather soles of his Oxford brogues lost traction on the icy surface, propelling him forward into Irina's arms.

'Woah, steady on, big boy. You need some proper boots,' she chided.

'You're right,' he said, 'I did get a hat,' he said, pointing to the ushanka.

'Yes—very Cossack!'

'Just trying to blend in with the locals.'

Irina laughed. One of those laughs engaged the whole face, eyes sparkling, lips parted, cheeks glowing.

'It is a start, I suppose. We must work on the rest of your wardrobe and fix your haircut!'

'What's wrong with my haircut?'

'You are not the fifth Beatle!' she replied, flicking at his bushy sideburns. Slipping her arm through his, they walked towards the theatre entrance. The Bolshoi was a relic of Tsarist Russia that opened in 1825. It had an impressive frontage supported by eight neoclassical columns; four horses galloped across the pediment. As they entered the lobby, an usher checked their tickets and led them up a grand curling staircase to their seats in a box to the right of the stage. Nic had prevailed upon the Embassy's cultural attaché to secure the best tickets available. Apparently, a relatively small bribe in foreign currency was all that was needed.

Irina nodded approvingly as they took their seats. The theatre certainly lived up to its name, Bolshoi, which means "big" in Russian. Below their box, there were rows and rows of stalls; layered around the sides were five tiers of boxes stacked one on top of another in a giant horseshoe. Their box was on the second tier, with a wonderful view of the stage. Nic thought it looked like an indoor version of the Colosseum.

'This is amazing,' he said to Irina.

'It is very decadent,' she replied. 'Thankfully, it represents a tribute to the craftsmanship of the working man more than the excesses of bloated plutocrats; therefore, it is ideologically acceptable.'

After they had settled down, Nic said, 'Can I ask you a question?'

'Go ahead. I cannot promise I will answer, though.'

'How did you persuade the KGB to let you try and recruit foreign agents, given your less than patriotic agenda?'

'That is an easy one. Beauty, brains, and personality,' she said with a hint of a smile.

'Be serious,' Nic replied.

'I am, sort of. Yuri and I graduated at the top of our training class, and both speak fluent English. He shares very similar views to me. We have been able to successfully hide our true goal. Semichastny, the head of the KGB, thinks he controls us. When he briefed us, he told us to use all means at our disposal to entice foreign agents into the fold. What he meant was sex. Yuri is supposed to target the secretaries, and I get the rest!' she said.

'How do you feel about being used?'

'We are not the ones being used. We are praying on our leaders' assumptions. They assume the years of brainwashing have convinced us that our brains and bodies are the property of the state and that we will obey orders without question. They have also threatened our families if we do not follow orders.'

'That is blackmail,' Nic exclaimed.

Irina nodded, 'It is standard operating procedure in the Soviet Union, but it also provides great cover. No one expects us to risk so much.'

'Aren't you scared of being found out?'

'Of course, but you are the only one who knows, so you hold our lives in your hands. The risk is worth it. The greatest threat to the world is the Cold War, escalating into a nuclear war. No one wins that war, but some in the Politburo do not see it that way.

'Seriously?' Nic exclaimed.

Irina nodded, 'They think Khrushchev should not have backed down over Cuba; it is one of the main reasons he was replaced. They believe he should have called JFK's bluff.'

This confirmed what Charlotte had told him. 'That is scary. What do you need me for?'

'We must get NATO, and more importantly, the Americans, to wake up the threat.'

'Sounds simple when you put it like that,' Nic said.

The auditorium was filling up; it was going to be a sold-out performance. Nic studied the patrons. Despite the Soviet mantra of equality, this was not a working-class crowd. Men wore suits and ties; women were in their finest dresses, complete with appropriate jewellery. Moscow was in the thrall of Parisian couture, and while that was beyond the means of all but a few, it was clear that seamstresses across the capital had been busy.

Irina nudged Nic and pointed at the bag by his side, 'What are you hiding in there?'

Here goes nothing, he thought, picking up the bag and handing it over while saying 'Happy Birthday.'

She smiled, 'Are you trying to get me into bed?'

There was no good answer to that question. Rosa had asked him the same thing while they were shopping. His answer was that he wanted something romantic but not desperate. They had settled on Swiss chocolates filled with French liqueurs.

She took the box out of the bag and said, 'Chocolates! We can eat them during the performance.' Her reaction seemed genuine, which made him feel good.

The lights dimmed, and the orchestra started playing the opening movement. Irina whispered, 'Swan Lake was performed here for the first time in 1877.'

They sat back to enjoy the performance. It was stunning. The music, choreography, and dancers were perfectly synchronised. Occasionally, Irina hummed along to the score. Nic was mesmerised by both the performance and his companion. He could not help sneaking frequent glances at Irina. She was consumed by the performance.

The first half seemed to fly by. As the curtain came down, Irina said, 'Not bad for a third-rate socialist state.'

Nic laughed. Indeed, communism had not diminished the artistic excellence of the Bolshoi. He found it all a bit confusing. In Britain, ballet was seen as elitist and decadent, just the sort of thing communism railed against. Yet here, it thrived under a system that ought to abhor such bourgeois pastimes, one of the many contradictions inherent in the Soviet system. Decadence and elitism were perfectly acceptable so long as it was done in the name of the proletariat.

Nic took Irina's hand and led her out of the box to the refreshment area, where they enjoyed tea and biscuits. They spoke English to each other, attracting quizzical looks from their fellow patrons.

'Should we change to Russian?' he asked.

'It is fine. Very few people here speak English. Muscovites are used to seeing foreigners from the various embassies and missions at the ballet. If we were anywhere else, they would probably call the police.'

The bell rang to signal that the performance was about to recommence. They took their seats just as the curtain was rising. The second half was, if anything, more impressive than the first, but Nic was distracted. He was trying to think through the implications of everything Irina had told him. Her plan might work if the information they exchanged was credible. The big question was how each side would react. Would NATO stand up to the threat of Soviet aggression? Would the Soviets back down?

The performance ended with the lovers committing suicide so they could be together for eternity—was there a message somewhere? As the curtain fell for the fifth time, the audience was still standing and applauding energetically.

Nic and Irina slipped out of the box and headed for the exit. Outside, the chill November air made them both shiver. Nic considered deploying his ear flaps but did not want to look like a total Wally. They walked down the steps in front of the theatre towards the river. Irina turned and said, 'So do you think World War III will break out?'

Nic looked bemused, 'Not today, I hope.'

'I'm serious,' she said, 'haven't you heard? The Chinese tested their first atom bomb yesterday.'

'They did?' Nic exclaimed. 'That makes things interesting.'

'The Politburo is getting nervous. Tensions between Moscow and Beijing have been building ever since Cuba. The one thing Russian leaders, be they Tsars or apparatchiks, fear is border threats.'

'What do you think they will do?'

'I don't know. Four of the five countries with nuclear weapons, the US, UK, France, and now China, are not exactly our friends at the moment. If our leaders feel isolated, it is dangerous.'

They continued walking in silence. Nic found it hard to focus on the big picture. His head was full of the minutiae of the partnership Irina was proposing.

'There is something else I need to ask you,' he said.

Irina looked at him quizzically.

'Ever since we first met, I have felt you are following a script I have not seen. Am I being set up?'

That sly smile appeared again, 'Of course, you are. But isn't it the same script you are following? We both have the same goal.'

She was right—except she was word-perfect, but he needed a prompt at every stage.

'Remember, in any good performance, there is room for improvisation,' she said, gently kissing him.

'Was that in the script?'

'What do you think?' she replied.

'I don't know, you are an outstanding actor.'

'Yes, I am,' she said, kissing him again. This time, it was long and passionate as her tongue probed his lips.

As they separated, she whispered, 'That was not acting.' He wanted desperately to believe her.

He had booked a table at a restaurant in the Metropole Hotel, a short walk from the Bolshoi that SirRod had recommended. Once seated, he said, 'I have been thinking about what you said. You are right; atom and hydrogen bombs are making the world a much more dangerous place. War no longer has boundaries. A few targeted missiles and a whole country can be destroyed in minutes with effects lasting for decades.'

Irina nodded, 'Agreed.'

'Do the Politburo warmongers believe they can win a conventional war without it turning nuclear?'

'Yes,' she said bluntly. 'NATO depends upon the Americans to maintain an effective fighting force. Since 1962, US troop numbers in Europe have steadily declined. As they become more embroiled in Indochina, it will only continue. Without full American support, the Soviet Union has a significant numerical advantage over the rest of NATO in conventional forces. The Politburo is convinced NATO won't use nuclear weapons under any circumstances. After Cuba and the test ban treaty, the prevailing wisdom is that the West is only interested in further de-escalation.'

'That is a big assumption.'

'I think it is realistic, don't you?'

Nic thought for a moment. 'You are probably right. Wasn't it US Defence Secretary Robert McNamara who talked about mutually assured destruction? The ability of one nation to be able to fully respond to a nuclear first strike by another nation means there would be no winner of a nuclear war.'

'Exactly. One other thing gives our leaders the confidence they can win.'

'What is that?'

'I can't go into detail. But over the last five years, we have conducted successful operations across Europe and the US that have gone undetected by your intelligence agencies. More are planned soon.'

'Surely not, I have never heard of any such operations,' Nic responded.

'That is sort of the point. Anyway, I can prove it.'

Nic's head was spinning. She sounded so convincing.

The waiter appeared to take their order. 'SirRod recommended the pelmeni,' Nic said.

'Good choice. I love dumplings.'

After the waiter left, Nic asked, 'What are you proposing we do?'

'The first step is to convince our superiors that we have successfully recruited the other as a double agent. We set up a two-way flow of information and pass along a mix of real and fake intelligence that is all plausible. I will give you information proving the strategy of 'peaceful co-existence' was a cover for a series of past and planned operations to weaken the NATO alliance.'

'What do you need in return?

'The most effective way to deter the hard-liners is to convince them NATO knows about our plans and will respond accordingly.'

'Sounds like a piece of cake,' Nic said nonchalantly. Irina's smile moved from her lips to her whole face this time. Nic couldn't help but be distracted; she was very beautiful.

Her next comment snapped him back to reality, 'Of course, that is when we both become traitors.'

'Traitors and triple agents,' he added. 'We share secrets with each other, giving the impression we are double agents, thereby making us triple agents.'

Irina burst out laughing, 'I think I follow your logic! The key is to restore some semblance of a balance of power between East and West, even if it is only in the minds of our leaders.'

'Agreed, but surely any balance will only be temporary?'

Irina sighed, 'True. We must hope the world comes to its senses at some point.'

'Not much chance of that happening.'

'Don't be so pessimistic. We have to try!'

She was right. It was the reason Nic had joined MI6 in the first place.

'Okay, I'm in,' he said emphatically.

'Great. It's exciting, isn't it?'

'Terrifying might be a better description.'

'Enough shop talk. I want to enjoy my birthday dinner.'

The food was excellent and the vodka chilled. After the table was cleared, they drank Ararat cognac and Armenian brandy. Irina reached into her coat pocket and took out four chocolates she had saved from her birthday present.

'Chocolate is the perfect accompaniment to cognac,' she said, slipping one into Nic's mouth before taking one for herself. Nic watched as she ate—it was a sensual act, and she knew it.

Upon leaving the restaurant, they walked arm in arm by the Moskva to the subway station, where they kissed, bodies meshing through their thick winter coats. It felt good. As they separated, Irina said, 'That should look good in the photographs our bosses get to see tomorrow.'

Nic smiled and said, 'It felt pretty good as well. I would happily give you another birthday present.'

Irina sighed and whispered, 'Not tonight,' she said. 'But maybe on Friday. Meet me at Sokol station at seven.' The smile was there again.

'That will be nice,' he replied.

'It will be better than nice,' she said with a wink. As she got on the escalator, she turned and blew him a kiss.

Back in Kandinsky House, he tried to process the evening's events. Should he be elated or scared? If what Irina had told him was true, the world was on the verge of war. The news that

China was now a nuclear power only raised the stakes. Both the US and USSR could soon be threatened by a third superpower.

Was it realistic to expect that he and Irina could do anything to restore the balance of power? He still had a nagging feeling that he was being set up. It had been drilled into him that Russians were brainwashed from birth to hate capitalism and laud communism. Had Irina really been able to resist such indoctrination?

He wanted to believe she was genuine but knew he was not the most objective arbiter.

27

19th October 1964

SirRod stared intently through a cloud of pipe smoke as Nic recounted his date with Irina. He did not lie; he just did not share everything. SirRod did not interrupt. When Nic finished, SirRod set his pipe down on the heavy crystal glass ashtray on his desk and leaned back in his chair. Nic could almost see the cogs whirring as he processed what he had heard.

'Interesting, very interesting,' he said, 'the Soviets seem to be getting quite creative. Normally, they stick to tried and true methods like blackmail, bribery, or sex. Creating the illusion that each of you is a double agent working for the other side is clever but complicated. Instead of being a clandestine one-way relationship, you must both maintain the illusion that you are working for the other side.'

Nic wondered how SirRod would react if he knew the truth.

'You need to proceed very carefully. Sashkaya is more experienced, and she is making you play her game. We can help you try to anticipate her moves, but most of the time, you will be on your own. You must make split-second decisions based on your reading of the situation. How do you feel about that?'

'I have given it a lot of thought, Sir. I agree it isn't very easy, but it demonstrates a level of creativity on Sashkaya's part. It tells me she is serious about working with us. If the KGB believes she is running a valuable double agent inside MI6, it gives her the perfect cover.'

SirRod nodded, 'Good point. You must do your homework— run through all possible scenarios so you are prepared.'

'Agreed. I do have a couple of questions?'

'Fire away.'

'What type of intelligence is most valuable to us?'

'We must understand Soviet plans for Europe, Vietnam, and China. Since the Wall went up, things have gone very quiet in Europe. We assume Moscow is comfortable with the status quo as part of Khrushchev's "peaceful coexistence" strategy.'

Irina was right, Nic thought. The West was severely underestimating Soviet intentions in Europe.

SirRod continued, 'The Soviets and Chinese are both supporting the communists in Vietnam; however, we have picked up signs of growing tension between them. Mao was furious the Soviets did not go to war with the US over Cuba. We suspect there is a divergence in philosophy which we may be able to exploit. With China getting the bomb, we could soon see a three-superpower world. The Americans think they can play China off against Russia as they compete for Asian influence.

'My second question is more personal,' Nic said hesitantly.

'Spit it out, boy,' said SirRod.

'On occasion, Sashkaya has been, how should I say it, forward.'

SirRod smirked, picked up his pipe and relit it using the lighter on the desk. He inhaled deeply, smoke billowing up over his head. 'You mean she is trying to seduce you?'

Nic wished he'd never asked.

'Well, my boy. Remember, you work for Her Majesty. Your actions should be governed solely by the objectives of your mission and your oath to the crown. Do not let your heart rule your head. She is an attractive woman, but she is also a highly trained Soviet agent. You must use your professional judgment. Remember what Molly taught you,' he said, smiling.

'Yes, Sir.'

'When is your next meeting?'

'Tomorrow, Sir.'

'Good luck,' he said with a wink.

As he passed through the outer office, Vera said, 'I hear you have her on the hook.'

'It's early days,' he replied.

'Be careful. You know what attractive Soviet spies are called?'

Nic shook his head.

'Black widows. They are notorious for mating and then destroying their lovers. She will probably eat you alive.'

'What a way to go,' Nic said, smiling.

Vera's laugh still rang in his ears as he walked down the corridor.

28

23rd October 1964

Nic emerged from Sokol station in the northern suburbs of Moscow. The temperature had dropped well below freezing, and the Siberian wind had arrived, making it feel much colder. Every breath hurt. He was grateful for his new fur-lined boots and quickly deployed the Ushanka's earflaps. Irina was standing by the station entrance, sheltering from the wind.

'Maybe, just once, can we meet indoors?' he asked.

'Too cold for you?' she replied.

'Just a bit. Where are we going?'

'My apartment,' she replied.

'I hope it's warm.'

'It will be once we get there,' she said, striding down the street.

Irina's apartment was in a typical post-war Soviet concrete block devoid of any architectural merit. Eight storeys high, it looked like a giant shoebox with square holes cut along the sides for windows. The concrete was stained and cracked, and the windows were coated in layers of soot. A tattered Soviet flag fluttered from a pole on the roof, frayed from the constant attack of the wind.

Irina used her key to open the front door of the building. Once inside, it was not noticeably warmer. The lift was out of order, so they climbed the stairs to the third floor. Irina unlocked the door of apartment 307 and ushered Nic inside. The entrance hall was sparsely furnished, just a small table with a telephone and lamp. The phone was a luxury afforded to very few Muscovites.

The floor was not carpeted. Cracked, shiny blue linoleum had been glued down onto the bare concrete. A single, bare bulb hung from the ceiling, casting a shadowy light down the short corridor.

Irina led Nic through to the open-plan living area. It was spacious by Soviet standards, another perk of being a KGB agent. Three steel-framed windows lined the far wall. The heavy black curtains were drawn, no doubt in a vain attempt to keep the heat in and cold out. At the far end of the room, a screen separated the sleeping area from the rest of the room. For some reason, Nic noted the large double bed.

The living area comprised two threadbare armchairs, a battered chaise longue, and a large sheepskin rug laid out in front of an electric fire mounted on the wall. In the corner was a small kitchenette and a door that presumably led to the bathroom. Irina bent down and flicked the switch to turn on the electric fire before shedding her hat and coat.

'Welcome to my palace,' she said laughing. 'I have only been here a few weeks. The rug is the only item I own.'

'Very cosy,' he said.

She smirked, 'You are joking. It is freezing, and the furniture is only fit for a bonfire.'

Nic laughed, 'My flat in London isn't much better.'

'I thought all Englishmen lived in castles with servants to wait on them hand and foot,' she teased.

'You are confusing me with Viscount Weston!'

She moved to the kitchen and took a bottle of vodka and two glasses out of one of the cupboards.

'The good thing is that you don't need to chill the vodka.'

She filled the glasses to the brim. Nic was still adjusting to the Soviet custom of drinking vodka anywhere, at any time. He must pace himself; he did not want his senses dulled tonight.

He walked over to the windows, partially drew the curtain, and peered through the grime. Ice was forming on the inside of the glass. He could see a few lights in the distance, but nothing like the orange glow that shrouded London at night. Black smoke spewed out of numerous factory chimneys, blocking any view of the night sky.

'Why am I here?' he asked.

'Can't you guess?' she said with a wicked grin. 'It is standard operating procedure for female agents to seduce their targets.'

'Oh goody, I've been looking forward to that bit,' he replied.

'Sit down,' she said, pointing to the slightly less worn of the two armchairs. She handed him a glass, and they both took generous slugs. The immediate warmth felt like a fire igniting in his throat.

'Wow, that's strong,' he said hoarsely.

She laughed, 'It is made at an illegal distillery in my hometown.'

'Illegal?'

'Most Russian vodka is produced illegally. Legal distilleries can only meet about a third of the demand. The average Russian consumes a bottle every two days. If the government restricted the supply, there would be another revolution. As an economist, you should know the black market is an essential lubricant of the Soviet economy. While technically illegal, it is unofficially sanctioned. It is the only way to supply the country's needs.'

'So much for the Soviet economic miracle.'

'Touché,' she said, refilling their glasses.

'Don't you have black markets in the UK?' she asked.

'Of course, we do,' Nic replied, 'but they're limited to things like pornography, drugs, and dodgy electronics. If the demand is there and the price is right, someone will make a market.'

'You are not so different to us.'

'If you say so.'

The vodka was working. Nic felt a warm glow spreading through his body. He looked at Irina and said, 'Is it safe to talk here?'

'Yes. We do not bug our agents unless they are suspected of being traitors,' she said, smiling wryly. Nic hoped that would not prove prophetic.

'Talking about treachery. Are you serious about betraying your country in pursuit of world peace?'

Irina smiled, 'It sounds naive when you say it like that, but I don't see it as a betrayal. I am a proud Russian, but I am not blind to the flaws of the Soviet system. We have strayed far from the Marxist-Leninist doctrine. We eliminated the monarchy and aristocracy but replaced it with a new political elite that still suppresses the average citizen. The Soviet apparatchiks are the new royalty. They are just as decadent in their own way. We struggle to feed our people, are falling ever further behind in so many areas, and spend what little wealth is created on bombs and guns. Khrushchev was stupid to taunt the US over Cuba, but that was just the latest in a series of pointless provocations: Berlin, Korea, Hungary, and now Vietnam. It is stupid. The only way to maintain peace is to maintain some balance between the superpowers. If I can help do that, I am serving my family and my compatriots.'

She looked at Nic, 'You think I'm crazy, don't you?'

'Yes,' he replied, 'but in a good way. The US and USSR are like two supertankers on a collision course. Getting them to change direction will not be easy.'

'You are right, but I must try. What is the Latin proverb? Praemonitus, praemunitus—forewarned is forearmed. If we can neutralise any advantage one side may gain, we can make an impact.'

She was not only beautiful but also smart. 'You are right, and what have we got to lose?' he said.

'Only our lives,' she said, smiling.

Nic laughed, 'Let's drink to that,' he said, refilling their glasses.

She peeled off her sweater, tossing it over the chaise-langue. Underneath, she was wearing a very clingy white blouse. She moved over and sat on his knee, putting her arms around his neck and kissing him on the lips. He hugged her close, knowing she could feel more than his embrace. Soon, they moved awkwardly towards the bed, discarding their clothes along the way.

Sometime later, they lay side by side, neither feeling the cold anymore.

'You are amazing', Nic said as he gently kissed her breast.

'I am, aren't I?'

'This is all a bit surreal. Not long ago, I was at university thinking about becoming an accountant. Now I am in bed with a KGB agent in Moscow plotting to betray my country.'

Irina stroked his hair and laughed, 'You must admit this is a bit more exciting. Now stop talking and get back to work,' she said as her hand reached beneath the sheets.

By morning, they were exhausted. Irina stepped naked from the bed, shuddered in the cold air, and put on a thick woollen dressing gown and slippers before padding to the kitchen. She returned with two steaming mugs of tea, slipped off the gown, and slid back under the covers.

As they lay in bed, Nic performed his first act of treachery. 'I have a tasty morsel of information for you in return for your Khrushchev tip.'

'Go on,' she said.

'France is about to withdraw from NATO.'

'Why?'

'De Gaulle is convinced the US will not come to Europe's aid in the event of a Soviet attack. He is insisting France develops its own independent nuclear deterrent. By 1968, he plans to have the capability to kill eighty million Russians.'

'He would launch a first strike?'

'He says no.'

'This is most interesting. It may cause the Politburo to accelerate their plans.'

'What plans?' Nic asked.

Irina said nothing. For the first time, Nic sensed he had thrown her off balance. She picked up her mug and drained it before saying, 'Plans are being developed for invasions of Finland and Iran later this year.'

'Seriously?' Nic said.

'Yes.'

'I think we just crossed the point of no return,' Nic said, leaning over and nibbling her earlobe. She looked at the clock and said, 'We can't stay here forever.'

'Why not?'

She smiled, stepped out of bed, and headed for the bathroom. When Nic got back to Kandinsky House, it was almost noon. He needed to shower, change, and get to the Embassy for a call with Seb in London.

29

23rd October 1964

'I hear you have caught your first fish,' said Seb.

'Not quite, but I have one on the hook, and I'm trying to reel it in. The water is pretty murky, though.'

'Time to use what you learnt in Bermondsey.'

Nic and Seb had developed their own code, assuming that the Soviets would be listening to their phone calls.

Bermondsey referred to an exercise during Nic's training that involved setting up an information exchange protocol with an informant. The protocol involved deaddrops, codes, and covert communications to enable the exchange of messages.

Seb continued: 'I will send you a copy of Maurice Wiggins' Guide to Fly Fishing.'

The mention of the book told Nic that Seb would be sending new instructions in the diplomatic pouch.

'Thanks, I will keep practising and try to find the right bait. I might end up using caviar!'

'Don't put that on your expenses!' Seb responded.

Irina was waiting at their usual spot in Gorky Park. They had agreed to start exchanging information to convince their respective masters that they had successfully turned a foreign agent. Nic worked with Simon and Charlotte to assemble an intriguing mix of real and fake intelligence to whet the KGB's appetite.

An icy wind was blowing through Moscow as he walked towards the park. Thankfully, the ushanka's ear flaps were working well.

Nic saw Irina's silhouette through the partially steamed-up windows of the museum café. He pushed open the door, slipped off his gloves, and walked over to where she was sitting. She stood up, and they exchanged kisses. There were only three other people in the café; any one of them could be watching and trying to listen. The Soviets trusted no one, not even their own agents.

Irina had a copy of Izvestia on the table in front of her. As he sat down, Nic placed his own copy on top.

'I have ordered you coffee,' she said, 'This is one of the few places in Moscow where they make it properly.'

'Good, I could use a jolt of caffeine.'

'Late night?' she asked.

'All nights are late,' he replied.

The waitress arrived with their drinks and two slices of medovik, a Russian honey cake. They sat in silence as they ate.

After finishing their coffee and cake, they stood up to leave; each now carried the other's newspaper.

Once outside, Irina asked, 'What information is in here?' she asked, nodding towards the newspaper.

'Details of upcoming NATO exercises in West Germany; planned clandestine operations in Eastern Europe; and a list of Soviet agents turned by British intelligence.'

'Excellent,' she said.

'What about you?' Nic asked.

'A very long list of British politicians, trade union members, and academics on our payroll.'

'Excellent. That has been a source of much speculation back in London.'

They parted company with another kiss. Irina whispered, 'No turning back, now, lover boy.'

'Good,' Nic said.

30

10th November 1964

They met regularly over the next few weeks, establishing a pattern of exchanges designed to build their cover.

Charlotte and Simon ensured Nic had coherent materials to pass to Irina. Some of it was real, some fake, but all plausible. They varied meeting locations, using cafes, hotel bars, and restaurants. Sometimes, a Boris would make an appearance.

One evening, they returned to Anatoly's. Nic arrived first and was greeted like an old friend. Anatoly insisted they have a drink together. He peppered Nic with questions about his latest passion—pop music. The Soviet authorities had recently stopped jamming Western radio stations, allowing young people to be exposed to the new wave of pop music sweeping the world. Young Russians were quickly becoming fans of The Beatles, Stones, or some other group. Anatoly quizzed Nic about "The Girl from Ipanema" and what was meant by "A Hard Day's Night"? As Nic tried to explain, an old lady approached the table and said sternly, 'Anatoly, get back to work.'

'Nic, meet my mother, Mila,' Anatoly said.

'Delighted to meet you,' Nic said.

Mila nodded in acknowledgement but was more interested in directing Anatoly towards the kitchen.

When Irina arrived, Mila rushed over and gave her a big hug. When she sat down at Nic's table, Mila looked disapprovingly at Nic and said to Irina, 'What are you doing with this young man?'

'He is my new boyfriend,' Irina said, smiling.

Mila fixed Nic with a stare, or was it a glare?

'Young man, I trust you will treat my darling Irina like a princess.'

Nic smiled and said, 'Of course, Babushka. You have my word as an honourable Englishman.'

Mila gasped, 'You are English?'

Nic nodded.

'I love English men—Leslie Howard, Cary Grant, Prince Philip. They are such gentlemen and handsome, too,' she said, smiling broadly.

'Behave yourself, Mama,' said Anatoly as he set down two glasses of Medovukha, a traditional Russian aperitif, on the table. Mila smirked and retreated to the kitchen.

'Well done,' said Irina, 'winning over a babushka is no easy feat.'

She waited for Anatoly to move away from their table before saying, 'I met with Semichastny this morning. He is delighted with the information you are supplying. He thinks you could become an adequate replacement for Philby or Blake. According to Yuri, you are seen as a rising star of British intelligence.'

Nic couldn't help laughing. 'MI6 thinks the same about you.'

'Good. Has anyone voiced any suspicions?'

'No. One jerk at the Embassy is giving me a hard time, but it has nothing to do with us. He just has it in for me.'

'Let me guess,' she said. 'Jeremy Webbe?'

'How do you know?'

'Let's just say his reputation precedes him.'

Nic wanted to know more, but Mila arrived with their food.

'What's this?' he asked.

'Poharsky cutlets and dumplings.'

'It looks delicious.' Nic said. Mila smiled at the compliment.

They ate in silence, enjoying the food and each other's company. When they finished, Nic said, 'Don't you wish this was just a regular date?'

'Don't be stupid. We would never have met if it wasn't for our jobs.'

'I'm not complaining, but it feels odd.'

'Weren't you trained to avoid personal attachments?'

He nodded before saying, 'I am finding that hard.'

'Then, I must be doing my job!' she said, laughing.

He was getting nowhere, so he changed the subject.

'I have to go to Leningrad next week,' he said,

'Why?' she asked.

'London wants me to test a fallback route for sending information using a British businessman who regularly visits Leningrad.'

'Is he MI6?'

'Not exactly. He occasionally works for us as a courier.'

'Be careful. Being a port city close to the Finnish border, the local KGB office is very sensitive to foreigners on their turf.'

Mila appeared and interrupted their conversation. 'Time for dessert,' she said. 'This is my homemade pryanik, jam-filled dough stuffed with honey and cinnamon.'

Nic took a bite. It was the sweetest thing he had ever tasted, 'Wow, that is amazing,' he said. Mila smiled broadly.

As usual, they were the last two people in the restaurant. Mila had left for the evening, so Anatoly locked up after them. Stepping onto the street, Irina slipped her arm through Nic's, 'When do you leave for Leningrad?'

'I am on the overnight sleeper on Thursday, I should be back on Friday,' Nic replied.

'Come over to my apartment when you get back.'

He liked the sound of that. They exchanged kisses and parted ways. Nic watched as she walked down the street. Should he have told her about Leningrad? If she was setting him up, he had given her everything she needed to arrange for him to be captured, trying to smuggle secrets out of the country.

31

12th November 1964

Before heading to the station, Nic returned to Kandinsky House and packed an overnight bag. He did not want to draw unnecessary attention to himself, so he changed into his most nondescript suit. He had never been to Leningrad, a port city of 3.5 million people on the Baltic. Given its proximity to Finland and easy access to the sea, it was a popular route for the clandestine extraction of people and secrets out of the USSR.

As darkness fell, he left for Leningradsky Station. A persistent drizzle was finally melting some of the accumulated snow. The streets were crowded as workers splashed their way home, most hunched under umbrellas.

Nic carried his overnight bag in one hand and a small briefcase with the papers he was to hand over in the other. Boris II followed behind. No doubt Irina had told him where Nic was going, negating the need for full surveillance team.

Armed soldiers patrolled the streets around the station. Nic was convinced they were all looking at him. He tried to keep a neutral expression on his face as he crossed the concourse. Spycraft was not yet instinctive; every action had to be performed consciously.

He was booked in a sleeper berth on the Krasnaya Strala (Red Arrow), leaving Moscow at 23:55 and arriving in Leningrad at 07:55 the next morning. He stopped at the station bar for a couple of drinks to calm his nerves. The usual cross-section of humanity was on show. A noisy group of soldiers were drinking at the bar; an elderly couple sat staring blankly at one another over half-drunk cups of tea; and a young couple were engaged in a heavy petting session, oblivious to the world around them. At the end of the bar stood a tall man in a grey raincoat scanning the room. He was almost certainly Boris II's replacement.

Twenty minutes before the scheduled departure time, Nic picked up his bags and made his way to the ticket barrier. Grey raincoat man made no attempt to hide that he was following. Nic had his ticket punched at the barrier and walked down the platform. Upon reaching coach nine, a steward stepped down from the train and offered to take Nic's bags. He handed over his overnight bag but kept a tight grip on the briefcase.

The steward showed him to his berth and placed his bag on the luggage rack. It was a four-berth compartment. His three travel companions, all male, were already seated. Two looked to be standard issue KGB, resplendent in dark grey suits and sunglasses. Irina had said surveillance would probably be handed over to agents in the KGB transport section. Both men eyed him warily as he took his seat. The third occupant wore the uniform of an army colonel. He was engrossed in the evening paper.

Nic rested his briefcase on his lap and took in his surroundings. The compartment has once been quite grand. Rich, dark wood panels lined the walls above the seats. The light fixtures were tarnished brass, and the thickly woven cloth on the seats was badly faded.

The steward returned and served tea. The two suits were engaged in a heated discussion about the Spartak Moscow football team's dismal form. The Colonel was still engrossed in his paper.

At 23:50, a loud blast of the train's whistle signalled their departure. As the engine slowly started moving, clouds of smoke were funnelled into the compartment through the open window.

Nic was tired, but he needed to stay awake for a while longer. He leaned his head against the window and watched the buildings scoot past it as the train navigated through the Moscow suburbs.

The steward served a light meal consisting of pirozhki, a small pie stuffed with meat and cabbage, and a strawberry varenye. The Colonel set down his paper, looked up at Nic and nodded a greeting. Nic reciprocated. The Colonel said in Russian, 'Where are you from?'

There was no point in lying, 'I am from England. I work at the British Embassy,' he replied in Russian.

The Colonel smiled and said, 'You must be a spy!'

Nic laughed, 'I am. So be careful what you say.'

The Colonel laughed. Nic could see the two men listening intently to the exchange out of the corner of his eye. One looked distinctly uncomfortable, and the other sat stony-faced. Rumbled you, he thought.

'What takes you to Leningrad?' the Colonel asked.

'To help some British citizens with their visa renewals.'

The Colonel nodded, 'I am going home,' he said excitedly, 'I have not seen my wife or son for two years.'

'That is wonderful,' Nic replied, 'I am sure they will be pleased to see you.'

The Colonel smiled broadly, 'I just hope she has kicked her lover out before I arrive!' Nic was not sure if he was joking.

When they finished eating, the steward cleared away the trays and suggested they move to the bar in the next carriage while he made up their berths. The train was thundering through the countryside at its top speed of almost 160kph. The coaches were swaying from side to side, so they had to steady themselves as they walked down the corridor.

The Colonel was in an expansive mood and insisted on buying the drinks. 'I hope my son is going to school tomorrow. My wife and I have a lot of catching up to do,' he said while making an obscene gesture with his hands.

Once back in the compartment, they prepared for bed. Nic lay down on his bunk and placed the briefcase in the luggage rack directly above him. Below, the Colonel was reading a book, probably too excited to sleep. The man in the other bottom bunk was either asleep or feigning sleep. His companion lay in the bunk across from Nic, staring at the ceiling.

The train rumbled through the night. Nic tried to stay awake but found the rhythmic clatter of the wheels on the rails soporific and soon fell asleep. He woke sometime later and saw a shadow looming over him. The opposite bunk was empty; the occupant was standing beside Nic with his arm raised as if trying to reach Nic's briefcase. Nic just stared at him. The man pulled his arm down before sliding open the compartment door and stepping out. He had been caught, and he knew it.

A few minutes later, his colleague rolled out of his bunk, gathered his things, and left the compartment. Neither of them returned. Nic made sure to stay awake for the rest of the journey. He was surprised at the clumsy attempt; the transport section was obviously not staffed by the most talented agents.

It was not long before shafts of light slanted through the tears in the window blind. Nic swung his legs over the side of the bunk and climbed down. The train was beginning to slow as it rumbled through the outer suburbs of Leningrad.

There was a knock at the door, and the steward announced they would arrive in half an hour. He left behind two breakfast trays of hot tea and black bread with honey.

The Colonel sat up, looked around the compartment and said, 'What happened to our friends?'

'I am not sure,' Nic said, 'Maybe they got lucky!"

The Colonel laughed, 'I hope I will be lucky soon!'

Nic smiled. He raised the window blind and looked out at another grey landscape. The devastation caused during the thirty-month German siege of the city during the war was still evident. Few buildings had been spared, and reconstruction work looked to be moving slowly.

When the train pulled to a halt at Moskovsky Station, the Colonel said goodbye and jumped off. Nic saw him running down the platform, such was his eagerness to reunite with his wife and maybe even his son. There was no sign of the other two men.

The station was busy, as morning commuters scurried in all directions. Nic checked his map; the hotel was less than a kilometre away. As he crossed the concourse, he noted that he had acquired a new follower. This one was better equipped for the weather—army boots, a greatcoat, and a ushanka. Nic paused to button up his coat and deploy his ear flaps before leaving the station.

The icy wind blowing in off the Baltic hit him full in the face. It was colder than Moscow but felt refreshing after the train compartment, where sweaty body odours, alcohol fumes, and cigarette smoke had created an unpleasant fug.

32

13th November 1964 – Leningrad

His hotel was more of a rundown guest house than the Ritz. Nic wondered if they rented rooms by the hour. It sat beside the Moyka River, a tributary of the much larger Neva River. An elderly lady, cigarette dangling from the corner of her mouth, sat at the small reception desk. She baulked when Nic asked if he could check in early until a ten rouble note did the trick.

His room was not much larger than a broom cupboard. There was enough room for a wire-framed metal bed jammed under the window and a solitary chair that appeared to also serve as the bedside table. The toilet and bathroom were shared with the other rooms and were down the corridor. Nic glanced out of the window. His new tail was leaning against the river wall, smoking a cigarette. Nic had time for a shower and change of clothes before heading out for his rendezvous.

When he left the hotel, he saw that his tail had been joined by a second, identically dressed man standing on the far side of the river. He would have to lose them both before handing over the documents in his briefcase.

He crossed the Moyka and walked down to the banks of the Neva, which, at this point, was over seven hundred meters wide. Lumps of ice drifted silently by, and flurries of snow bounced around in the air. He stopped to light a cigarette and check on the position of his tails. They were about 100 metres behind, walking on opposite sides of the street. They had both stopped to light cigarettes as well. Nic chuckled; it was all a big game.

He picked up his pace as the road arced gently to the left. For a moment, he was out of sight of both tails. He ducked into a side street, started jogging, and then turned left into another road. He was now walking parallel to his tails but in the opposite direction. He made another left turn, which took him back towards the river.

At the next junction, he stopped and peered round the corner. One of his tails stood 100 metres up the street, looking bewildered. Seconds later, his colleague emerged from a side street, shaking his head. He had lost them. Turning around, he walked quickly in the opposite direction.

Five minutes later, he reached the Church of the Saviour on Spilled Blood, so named as it was on the spot where Tsar Alexander II had been killed by an assassin's bomb in 1881. It was now a vegetable warehouse. Nic saw his contact sitting on a bench outside the church reading The Daily Telegraph. A briefcase, identical to Nic's, sat beside him. Nic sat down and put his briefcase on the bench between them. He muttered the code words, 'Up the Potters,' referring to the English football club Stoke City.

The man responded with, 'Bugger the Potters, it's the Valiants for me.' A reference to Stoke's local rivals, Port Vale. Nic nodded, and the man stood, picked up Nic's briefcase, and walked away, leaving his newspaper behind. Nic picked up the paper and started reading. A few minutes later, his two tails, looking angry, emerged from behind the church. Nic opened the briefcase the man had left behind and put the newspaper inside. The men glared at Nic as they walked past. Nic grinned back at them, stood up and started walking in the opposite direction.

He paused before a shop window and checked the street behind him. One of the men had turned around and was now following him; he couldn't see the other. He was almost back at the hotel when someone stepped out of a doorway, grabbed hold of his arm, and twisted it behind his back. With a look of barely controlled rage, he spat out the words, 'You are coming with us.'

The second man now grabbed his other arm. Nic calmly said in fluent Russian, 'I should warn you that I have diplomatic immunity as a member of the British Ambassador's staff.'

The men just laughed. A small black van drew up, and Nic was bundled into the back, getting a nasty bump on his head. One of the men got in beside him while the other got into the passenger seat. A hood was placed over his head, and his wrists were tied together. A shiver of fear passed through his body. Foreign spies had a nasty habit of disappearing in the Soviet Union.

The journey seemed to last about twenty minutes. Once they had stopped, the rear doors opened, and Nic was roughly pushed out, almost falling to the ground. Two pairs of hands hauled him up a flight of metal steps. He heard a door open and was guided forward before being made to sit on a chair. He heard footsteps receding and a door closing. The only sound he could hear was the distant rumble of machinery.

He tried to gather his thoughts. He had no incriminating information on his person, was unarmed, and had his diplomatic passport in his pocket. There were no grounds for his abduction unless Irina had betrayed him. That was the most obvious explanation. Had he fallen for the oldest trick in the book? Attractive enemy agent seduces naïve operative and turns him in.

He had no idea how much time passed before he heard the door open. He counted three sets of feet entering the room. The hood was removed, but he could see nothing.

'Why am I here?' Nic growled, 'I am here on official Embassy business. You have violated international law by apprehending me.'

A hollow laugh filled the room. Nic heard a switch being flicked, and a bright light momentarily blinded him. As his eyes slowly adjusted, the silhouettes of two men took shape. One was tall and thin, the other short and fat. Nic was reminded of Laurel and Hardy.

'Now, now,' said Laurel in an impeccable upper-class English accent. 'This is just a friendly chat. I must apologise for your treatment, but we were not sure you would come willingly.'

Nic blinked as he tried to focus before he almost gasped out loud. He recognised Laurel. It was Kim Philby, Britain's most notorious traitor. He looked older than in the photographs Nic had seen and had the wrinkled, spotted, dry skin of a lifelong drinker, but it was definitely him.

'I see you recognise me,' the man said with a hint of a stammer. 'I suppose they are still frightfully angry with me in London,' he said

'Are you surprised?' Nic replied.

He thought he saw a slight flicker of satisfaction flit across Philby's face. 'No. Although, they should really be asking themselves how I could operate under their noses for almost thirty years undetected.'

He may be a communist, Nic thought, but he had not lost any of the smug arrogance so typical of the English upper class.

'It may have something to do with the dozens of agents who lost their lives when you betrayed them,' he retorted.

'Yes, well, that is as may be, Mr Slater. I would advise you to take note of the adage about people in glass houses. We know that you, like me, are a traitor. You have been passing confidential information to Comrade Sashkaya. I am here to warn you not to try and trick us. If we find out you are using Sashkaya to spread disinformation, you will meet my colleagues again,' he said, nodding towards Hardy and the unseen third man. 'You can be sure they will be much less hospitable next time.'

Nic just stared at Philby, saying nothing. The man was despicable. Philby smiled and, adopting the tone of a patronising parent, said, 'Now run off back to Moscow and remember what I have told you. Oh, and give my regards to SirRod. We used to have some splendid dinner parties—lots of naughtiness! I am not sure he ever found out about the time I rogered a very tipsy Lady Barker during a game of hide and seek at Chartwell. I am certain Winston found out, though.'

Nic wanted to fight back in some way but resisted the temptation. Philby moved out of his sight line. Hardy stepped forward and put the hood back on. He was soon back in the van.

The return journey seemed a little shorter. Nic felt his hands being untied, and the hood was taken off. The van had slowed but did not stop. Hardy opened the back door and roughly pushed Nic out. He landed on a cobbled street and bounced into a gutter filled with slush.

He lay still for a few seconds, checking his limbs for damage, before slowly getting to his feet. There was a warm, damp patch on his cheek. Blood was flowing from a wound just above his left eye. He took a handkerchief from his pocket to staunch the flow.

He had been dumped in a dark, narrow street where the only illumination was provided by the crescent moon. In the distance, a clock chimed two a.m. He had been held captive for thirteen hours.

He started walking through the deserted streets, trying to orient himself. It took him an hour to find his way back to the hotel; fortunately, he still had his key. He stopped off in the bathroom to survey the damage to his face in the mirror. Thankfully, the bleeding had stopped, but he had a nasty gash on the side of his head and a splitting headache. He washed his face and hands, returned to his room, and collapsed on the bed.

He woke up to find the sun streaming through the window. For a moment, he thought he was back with Philby with the light shining in his face. As he slowly came to, the dull thud in his head reappeared. He rolled off the bed, opened the bedroom door and was pleased to see that the bathroom was unoccupied. He grabbed a towel, headed down the corridor, and took a long shower that went some way to soothing his aches and pains. Returning to his room, he dressed, packed his bag, and gingerly walked down the stairs. The old lady sitting behind the reception looked at him. She shook her head while muttering something in a language he did not understand. She probably thought he had been out on the tiles until the early hours and was nursing a hangover.

He tried to piece together the events of the last twenty-four hours. What had just happened, and more importantly, why? He had been lucky to complete the handoff before the KGB abducted him. Whatever they suspected, they had no evidence he had done anything wrong.

Rolling out Philby had been an audacious move. London would be livid when they found out. What he could not work out was why the KGB would go to all that effort if, as Irina had told him, they already valued him as a double agent. Something else must be going on. Were they trying to intimidate him? If so, it had worked.

When he reached the station, he bought a ticket for the mid-morning train back to Moscow. Three cups of strong tea helped clear his head. Thankfully, he found an empty compartment, lay down across three seats, and immediately fell asleep.

When he woke, he saw a mother with two children sitting opposite. The mother shyly lowered her eyes, but the children stared directly at him. The younger of the two, a boy of about six, said in Russian, 'Have you been fighting? My mother says only naughty boys fight.'

The woman tried to shush him and started to blush. Nic just smiled and said, 'No, I have not been fighting. I tripped, fell over, and banged my head.'

The boy looked disappointed. Nic caught the mother's eye and winked. She smiled back. He sat up and stretched, trying to get the kinks out of his bruised body.

33

15th November 1964 – Moscow

The next morning, Nic arrived early to update SirRod on his Philby encounter. He was making his first cup of coffee when the phone rang. He ran back into his office and picked it up. 'Slater, good, you are in. Come to my office immediately,' thundered Sir Roderick.

Vera nodded for him to go straight in. She followed and sat in the corner, notepad and pencil in hand. SirRod motioned for Nic to take one of the chairs before his desk and said, 'Tell me about Leningrad.'

'It did not go quite as expected,' Nic said. SirRod's brow furrowed, 'In what way?'

'The exchange went smoothly, but immediately after the handover, I was picked up by the KGB.'

SirRod raised his eyebrows.

'I suppose that explains your bruises?' Vera asked.

Nic nodded, 'They were a little rough on me.'

What happened?' asked SirRod.

'I lost the two tails before completing the exchange. I'm sure it was not observed. However, as I was walking back to the hotel, they reappeared. I was bundled into the back of a van, my hands were tied, and a hood was put over my head. We drove for about twenty minutes, and then I was taken into a building and tied to a chair.

'Any idea where?' SirRod asked.

'Not really. I could hear the distant sound of machinery. It might have been a warehouse near a factory. When they removed the hood, all I could see was broken windows, indicating it may have been derelict.'

'Did you hear anything?' asked Vera.

'Apart from the hum of the machinery, no. It was very disorienting. My abductors left me in the room with the hood still on for quite a long time.'

'How long?' Vera probed.

'I don't know a few hours at least. It was bitterly cold. By the time they returned, my teeth were chattering. When the door opened again, I could tell by the footsteps that three people entered. The hood was removed, and a single light was switched on, which shone directly into my face. Two men stood in front of me, but I could only see their silhouettes because of the light. One was tall and thin, the other short and fat. He was one of the men tailing me. The other one must have been behind me.'

'I told them I worked at the British Embassy and had diplomatic immunity, but they just laughed.'

'We will be filing a complaint about that,' SirRod said indignantly, 'What happened next?'

Nic heard Vera say under her breath, 'Fat lot of good that will do.' Nic almost laughed.

'By now, my eyes had adjusted to the light, and I recognised the tall, thin man.'

'Are you sure?' exclaimed SirRod.

'No doubt, Sir. It was Philby.'

Nic heard Vera gasp, SirRod simply said, 'Bloody hell.'

'My thoughts exactly, Sir. He stood there smiling at me.'

'What did he say?' asked SirRod

'He warned me not to try and use Sashkaya to spread disinformation.'

'How did you respond?' asked Vera.

'I didn't. I just stared at him.'

'How did he react to that?' asked SirRod.

'He threatened me. He said if they found out I was using Sashkaya to pass disinformation, I would quietly disappear.'

'They are just trying to frighten you.'

'I understand, Sir, and it worked.'

SirRod grunted, 'Did Philby say anything else?'

'Yes, Sir. He sends you his regards and fondly remembers the dinner parties you both used to attend.' He decided not to mention Lady Barker.

'That is Philby,' said SirRod. 'Cheeky bastard.'

'What happened next?' prompted Vera.

'The hood was put back on, and I was returned to the van. After what seemed to be a shorter drive, they dumped me on a side street. They didn't even bother to stop when they threw me out.'

'Ouch,' said Vera.

'You were lucky,' SirRod said, 'Not many agents get to walk out of a KGB interrogation. What do you think, Vera?'

'There are three possible explanations. The most obvious is that Sashkaya organised this to shake you up.'

'I am certain she didn't,' Nic interjected.

Vera sighed, 'My dear, you are not exactly objective regarding Sashkaya. Another alternative could be they suspect Sashkaya is the real double agent, not you, and they wanted to see if you would blow her cover. The third option is that they simply wanted to use Philby to remind us of our own incompetence. We need to plan our next steps very carefully.'

'I agree,' said SirRod, looking at Nic, 'I am sending you back to London. We need to develop a comprehensive plan for managing Sashkaya. The Soviets know something is going on. We need to make sure they don't discover the truth.'

Nic considered the irony of Sir Rod's statement. He started to object, but Vera simply said, 'Don't. The KGB will expect you to be sent back to London to brief C in person after your encounter with Philby.'

Nic's mind was racing. Was his partnership with Irina over before it really got started? Would he ever see her again? Despite Vera's words, he was convinced she had not betrayed him.

Nic met with SirRod and Vera the next morning to get his instructions. 'You will report everything to C. The reappearance of Philby is no accident. There will be a reason they rolled him out, and it was not just to scare you. Work with Harmes to complete a full risk assessment regarding Sashkaya. Did she blow your cover? Can we trust her going forward? How do we best use her? Any questions?'

Nic shook his head. He had many questions, but now was not the time to ask them.

'You are booked on the seven o'clock out of Sheremetyevo,' Vera said. 'Go and pack. I will arrange for Anna to take you to the airport,'

'Yes, ma'am,' he replied. This earned him a withering look. He stopped by his office and told Jenny he was going to London for a few days.

'More like permanently,' said a voice from the corridor. Webbe appeared in the doorway, 'Looks like you have blown it already. What did I tell you? Your sort is not cut out for this game.'

Nic wanted to punch him in the face. Instead, he picked up his briefcase, saying, 'You would know all about failure, wouldn't you?' as he walked past.

Jenny tried to suppress a laugh. Webbe's expression was priceless. As he walked down the stairs, he did wonder whether Webbe was right.

He needed to get word of his departure to Irina. They had established a system for setting up meetings or exchanging messages using a lamppost behind St. Basil's Cathedral. It had the benefit of being hidden around a corner, allowing a mark to be left without being observed. Anytime one needed to meet urgently, they would leave a chalk mark on the lamppost. Different symbols meant different meeting times or message locations. They agreed to check the post at least daily.

It was time to put the system into operation. Nic took a piece of chalk from his pocket and scrawled two parallel lines on the lamppost. This would tell Irina he was going to leave her a message at an agreed-upon location, in this case, the Russo-Bolt Hotel. After packing, he headed across the city to the hotel. As he left Kandinsky House, he saw Boris I waiting outside.

The Russo-Bolt was a grand art nouveau building halfway between Red Square and the Embassy. Nic pushed through the revolving door and crossed the lobby to the small bar, where he occasionally stopped for a drink.

Taking a seat by the window, he ordered a vodka and tonic. Through the window, he could see Boris standing under the awning of a flower shop, smoking a cigarette.

After meeting with SirRod and Vera, he had come up with another possible explanation for his hasty trip back to London. MI6 might suspect he was a traitor and they were getting him out of harm's way. He had heard stories of agents being recalled from the field for some spurious reason so that they could be interrogated. It had happened to Philby in the early fifties. MI5 were convinced he was a Soviet agent. He was summoned to London and interrogated, but they could not find any hard evidence. With the backing of the Foreign Secretary and future Prime Minister, Harold Macmillan, and most of his colleagues in MI6, Philby had been reinstated and continued spying for the Soviets for another decade. Nic did not think he was under suspicion; however, he did work for an agency full of professional liars.

He finished his drink, leaving a few coins on the table. As he stood up to leave, he feigned accidentally dropping his hat on the floor. As he bent to pick it up, he slipped a note he had written before leaving his apartment from his pocket and affixed it to the underside of the table using a pre-attached piece of Sellotape. Walking out of the bar, he nodded to the barman and said, 'Dasvidaniya.'

Boris I was still outside. Nic nodded and received a nod back. Sometimes, the spy game could be almost civilised.

Anna was waiting at the Embassy when Nic returned. 'You going to London?' he asked as Nic climbed into the front seat.

'Yes—just a flying visit, I hope.'

'Do not forget my whisky.'

Nic laughed, 'I won't.'

Another section of the Moscow ring road had recently opened, shaving a few minutes off the trip to the airport. Anna dropped Nic off at the newly opened international terminal, which BEA now used. Nic walked to the check-in desk and showed his diplomatic passport to the agent.

'Mr. Slater, welcome,' she said, 'please follow me to the VIP lounge.'

She escorted him through the diplomatic channel, bypassing all the security and immigration checks. Nic reflected that it was much easier to leave the USSR than enter—unless you were a Soviet citizen.

There were only four other people in the lounge. Nic was dismayed to see that one of them was Jeremy Webbe. He silently prayed that they would not be sitting next to each other. As Nic walked by, Webbe smirked, 'I hear Kim Philby gave you a personal welcome to the Soviet Union. That's another nail in the coffin of your career.'

Nic managed to keep his temper in check and ignore the taunt. He poured himself a glass of wine and sat down to wait for the flight to be called. He wondered if Irina had retrieved his note yet. In addition to informing her of his trip to London, he asked her to try to find out the real reason behind his abduction and meeting with Philby in Leningrad. He hoped he would be back soon to find out the truth.

He had just finished a second glass of wine when the flight was called. He and Webbe were the only people in the lounge traveling to London. Thankfully, Webbe was seated two rows in front of Nic for the six-hour flight, which included a refuelling stop in Frankfurt.

Nic made sure to enjoy the in-flight meal: caviar and toast, followed by roast duck accompanied by a few glasses of Chateau Ausone, a very pleasant St. Emilion. All of this was served by a delightful, blonde stewardess named Mary, who openly flirted with him. He would have enjoyed the frivolous banter in different circumstances, but Webbe's presence made him uneasy.

It was after midnight when they landed at London Airport and taxied to a gate at the Britannic terminal building. Nic had read that the airport would soon be renamed Heathrow to better distinguish it from London's other airports, Gatwick and Stansted.

He took his time retrieving his bag and leaving the plane. He did not want to see Webbe again. Given the late hour, the terminal was deserted, and he passed quickly through the diplomatic channel, where a barely awake immigration officer did not even bother looking at his passport.

Exiting the terminal, he was pleased to see that despite the late hour, there was a plentiful supply of black cabs. He climbed into the first in line and asked the driver to take him to Edith Grove. Half an hour later, he unlocked the door to his flat for the first time in almost a year.

Before leaving Moscow, he had sent Mags a telegram, and she had thoughtfully stocked the fridge with essentials. He was delighted to see she had also placed a bottle of Talisker on his bedside table.

After showering, he lay on his bed, staring at the ceiling with a large tumbler of the rich, smoky liquid by his side. A spider's web was forming below the coving.

He tried to remember Irina's Mona Lisa-like smile, the soft touch of her lips, and the smoothness of her skin. Thanks to the combination of exhaustion, alcohol, and pleasant thoughts, he soon drifted off to sleep.

34

16th November 1964 – London

The alarm clock shattered a very pleasant dream. For a few seconds, he thought he was in Kandinsky House. Slowly, his eyes adjusted, and the shapes of familiar objects confirmed that he was back in London.

An hour later, he exited his flat and headed down the stairs. As he reached the ground floor, the door of flat two opened, and his neighbour, Mrs Grimes, poked her head out. She was at least eighty but still sharp as a tack.

'I thought it was you, Mr Slater. Are you back from Scotland?' That was his cover story to explain his long absences.

'Just a flying visit, Mrs. G. How is everything with you?'

'Oh, I can't complain. At least those long-haired young men from next door have moved on, so it's quieter at night. How long are you staying? She asked.

'Just a few days.'

'You are never here! Well, stay warm up there, duck. It gets proper chilly in the Highlands.'

He smiled and assured her he would. He opened the front door and walked down the steps to the street with his arm raised. Almost immediately, a cab swerved to the kerb.

'Century House, Westminster Bridge Road, please,' Nic said through the cab's open window as he climbed into the back.

'Okay, mate,' the cabbie responded. 'Do you want to go along the river or through Victoria? At this time of day, it will be the same difference.'

'By the river, I think.'

'All right, mate.'

Nic sat back as the cab navigated Worlds End and crossed Battersea Bridge towards Westminster. Under the dark skies, the Thames looked cold and grey, but at least it wasn't raining.

They passed St. Thomas' Hospital and turned onto Westminster Bridge Road. The driver pulled up in front of Century House. Nic passed a ten-shilling note through the screen and said, 'Thanks, keep the change.'

'Cheers, mate, happy spying,' said the cabbie, chuckling as he pulled away.

This was the first time Nic had been to the security services' new headquarters. MI5 and MI6 had relocated from the Broadway offices next to St. James Park tube station just after he had left for Moscow. The new location was supposed to be top secret. Nevertheless, it was already part of the Knowledge, every London cabbie's encyclopaedic understanding of the city.

There was no outward indication that this was the home of the Intelligence Services. A nondescript sign listed the tenants as: Sinclair Haulage, Cumming Enterprises, and Menzies Import-Export. Nic smiled; Sinclair, Cumming, and Menzies were all former SIS chiefs.

He showed his identification card to the guard, walked over to the reception desk, and said, 'Nic Slater, I have an appointment with Viscount Weston.'

The receptionist consulted a list and replied, 'Welcome, Mr. Slater. Viscount Weston is in room 407 on the fourth floor. The lifts are down the corridor on the left. I will call and let him know you are on your way up.'

He thanked her and walked towards the lifts. The walls were painted an institutional grey, which, when combined with the stark lighting, made the building feel very cold. Two other people stepped into the lift with him. One had a copy of the Times tucked under his arm. The front-page headline reported that last night, the House of Commons had voted to abolish the death penalty for murder. Nic shivered slightly at the thought that treason was now the only crime which still carried the death penalty.

The lift bell chimed, and the doors slid open. Nic stepped out while his fellow travellers stayed behind, heading for loftier destinations. A sign on the wall indicated that rooms 401-410 were to the left, but Nic needed no directions. He could hear Seb's voice echoing down the hallway, accompanied by the unmistakable aroma of his foul-smelling Mexican cigars.

The office door was ajar. Seb and another man were sitting in plush leather armchairs set in front of the desk. They were discussing a recent rugby match through a fog of dense smoke. Seb looked up and saw Nic. Levering himself out of his chair, he loudly said, 'Well, if it isn't our very own Rasputin, seducer of the Russian Queen.'

Nic grimaced and was engulfed in a bear hug. There was no upper-class British reserve with Seb. Nic flinched; his working-class roots made any physical sign of affection between men uncomfortable. He could not ever remember his own father ever hugging him. After releasing Nic, Seb turned to his visitor and said, 'Good seeing you, James. Let's catch up for a drink at the club.'

James nodded before turning and shaking Nic's hand, 'Welcome back,' he said before stepping out into the corridor.

'C wants us in his office in twenty minutes, but I want to talk to you about something first. You have certainly created a stir here.'

Nic took the seat James had just vacated, 'Go on,' he said.

'We did some digging into Miss Sashkaya's background and found some interesting information about her mother, Luda.'

'Okay.'

Seb picked a piece of paper from his desk and started scanning it. 'She was born in Krasnoyarsk, the third largest city in Siberia, in 1919; the result of a brief affair between two revolutionaries who abandoned her soon after birth. She was sent to an orphanage near Moscow. When she was fourteen, she joined the Communist Youth League and met Sashkaya's father. She got pregnant at seventeen, and Irina was born in 1941. Her father was killed at Stalingrad without ever seeing his daughter.'

'Irina told me all that,' said Nic, 'she said that Luda worked as an interpreter and even attended the Potsdam conference.'

Seb nodded, 'Did she tell you that Luda had an affair with Konstantin Chernenko?'

Nic looked surprised, 'The same Chernenko recently promoted to Secretary to the Politburo?'

'The very same. Luda and Chernenko appear to have remained on good terms with each other even after they married other people. Chernenko appears to have been an unofficial godfather to Irina.'

'Interesting. That might explain the hints Irain gave about having connections in the Kremlin. It would also explain how she knew about the demise of Khrushchev ahead of time.'

Seb nodded, 'It appears you have hooked a whale rather than a minnow.'

Nic was unsure whether he liked the analogy, but he got the point.

Seb continued, 'This could be a goldmine—Chernenko is a rising star. If we can persuade Irina to use her relationship with Chernenko, we can get information to and from the Politburo. We will talk more later; we better go and see C.'

They were ushered directly into C's office.

'Good morning, Sir,' said Seb.

'Ah, Harmes, Slater, take a seat.' He didn't waste any time. Looking at Nic, he said, 'I understand you had an encounter with Mr. Philby.'

'Yes, Sir,' Nic replied before recounting all the details. C listened intently, his expression stern. When Nic had finished, C slowly shook his head.

'It seems like his new masters are making him earn his keep. They will have to work him hard simply to pay his bar bills! Do you think Sashkaya set you up?'

'I do not, Sir,' Nic replied. 'I sense that she and Kovlev operate somewhat independently of the KGB leadership. They both commented about senior KGB leaders fouling up operations through excessive interference.'

'Why do you think they are being given such freedom? That is not the KGB's normal modus operandi. Agents normally need approval in triplicate to take a piss.'

'We think she has the support of Chernenko, the new Politburo secretary,' said Seb. 'He has known Sashkaya all her life and seems to be her mentor and protector.'

'Interesting,' C said, 'So what triggered the Philby meeting?'

'We are not certain,' Nic said, 'I have asked Sashkaya to try and find out, but our best guess is that it was a clumsy attempt to find out what she is up to. The Head of KGB, Vladimir

Semichastny, is not a fan of female agents and does not get on well with Chernenko.'

'Plausible,' said C, 'Soviet bureaucrats hate not being in total control. We can use this to our advantage.'

'I agree, Sir,' said Seb.

Looking at Nic, C said, 'Before you return to Moscow, we need a plan that convinces the KGB they have successfully recruited a valuable double agent. We can use Sashkaya as a conduit to feed disinformation to the Soviets.'

'What about Philby's threat?' Nic asked.

'He was just fishing. If Sashkaya really does have a direct line to Chernenko, she will be untouchable unless concrete evidence emerges. You two must make sure that does not happen.'

'Yes, Sir,' Nic and Seb said in unison.

'Good. Set up a briefing with me before heading back to Moscow.'

'Yes, Sir,' Nic replied.

When they got back to the office, Seb's first question was, 'Tell me all about the sultry Irina. Is she a real femme fatale?'

'You are turning into a dirty old man.'

'As your handler, I am entitled to know everything about your operation,' Seb said indignantly.

'Well then, we had better go and get a drink.'

'I like your style,' Seb replied.

After leaving Century House, they walked along York Road towards Waterloo Station. It was cold and damp, a typical December day. A constant stream of taxis and red double-decker buses crawled along Waterloo Road. Nic narrowly avoided a young man who jumped from the kerb onto the rear platform of a moving 34 bus.

The White Hart sat on a quiet back street behind the former King George Military Hospital. As usual, Seb had timed his arrival perfectly. The landlord was unlocking the front door. Upon seeing Seb, he said, 'Perfect timing, as usual, Milord,' failing to hide the sarcasm in his tone.

'Good morning, George,' Seb replied. Turning to Nic, he said, 'George is a hard-line communist. If we ever have a revolution, I will be one of the first he puts up against the wall.'

'Only if your tab is fully paid up,' George replied as he walked to the bar. 'What can I get you two gentlemen to drink? Your usual, Milord?'

'Yes, George, and a pint of Fullers for my friend.'

George poured a large gin and dry vermouth, added a lemon, and handed it to Seb. Then he took a pint jug off the hook above the bar and pulled Nic's pint from one of the pumps on the bar. Seb made no attempt to pay and headed for a table in the far corner of the pub. Seeing Nic's quizzical expression, he said, 'Daddy owns the place.'

'And you are clearly a local,' Nic said.

'Not really. I only come here three or four times a week.'

Once seated, Nic spent the next hour sharing almost everything that had happened since he had arrived in Moscow, only omitting details of his night of passion with Irina and their mutual 'off the books' arrangement.

When he finished, Seb said, 'Well done, old chap. I hope you have not gone and fallen in love with her.'

Nic hoped it wasn't that obvious; SirRod had implied the same thing. He decided to laugh it off, 'No, of course not. She is a great lay, though!'

'Lucky bugger,' Seb exclaimed.

It was time to change the subject. 'Let's talk about the plan C wants us to develop.'

Seb nodded, 'If Irina has been telling the truth, our intelligence is woeful. None of our scenarios envision a Soviet attack in Europe or the Middle East. The consensus is that the idea died with Stalin. All the indications are that Khrushchev was running down in investment conventional forces and replacing them with nukes to try and achieve parity with the Americans.'

'Do we think they will use them?'

'We don't think so. They have had three chances so far: Korea, Taiwan, and Cuba, he baulked each time.'

'But we are not dealing with him anymore,' Nic replied, 'the hardliners used Khrushchev's humiliation over Cuba to force him out.'

'True, but the Americans still have a massive numerical advantage in nukes, and Moscow has other problems. They need to shore up the Warsaw Pact. With Tito going rogue and Albania splitting with Moscow, other Warsaw Pact countries are trying to loosen the Soviet yoke. In Indochina, the Soviets and Chinese are both supplying arms to the North Vietnamese and Viet Cong. However, recent intelligence reports suggest they have started competing to curry favour with Ho Chi Minh. They will have their hands full for quite some time as Brezhnev and Kosygin battle for supremacy. Elsewhere, all we see them doing is providing financial support to local communist parties and bribing left-leaning politicians to back Soviet-friendly policies.'

Listening to Seb, Nic realised that MI6's, and therefore, the CIA's assessment of Soviet intent, was fatally flawed.

Their conversation was interrupted by the pub door swinging open. Three railway workers coming off shift entered. Nic saw there were already three pints sitting on the bar. One of the men nodded to Seb and said, 'Nice to see the toffs working hard. Still sticking it to the working man, are you?'

'Got to keep the plebians in line, Sam,' Seb replied.

'Not for long,' replied Sam. 'Come the revolution...'

Seb laughed, turning to Nic, he said, 'The bloody reds are everywhere.'

The men grabbed their pints and sat at a table on the far side of the pub. Smoke from their cigarettes rose vertically before being redirected by the heat from the overhead lights. The pungent smell of unfiltered Woodbines began to fill the air.

Seb looked at his empty glass, 'Your round, I think. Get a couple of George's famous pasties while you're at it,'

Nic walked up to the bar. The landlord looked up, 'Same again?'

'Just a half for me, and can we get a couple of pasties, please?'

'Don't forget the chips and gravy,' Seb shouted across the room.

When Nic returned with drinks, Seb said, 'Lightweight!' on seeing Nic's half a pint.

'You drink enough for both of us,' Nic replied.

'Alcohol lubricates the brain!' Seb replied.

'Pickles it more like,' Nic retorted

'Do you believe Sashkaya?' Seb asked. 'She could be running her own disinformation campaign through you to provoke us into making a pre-emptive move.'

'I don't know,' Nic said, 'she is very convincing, but I have no proof. She says there is a power struggle going on in the Kremlin. Kosygin and Brezhnev are not the best of friends. If one of them aligns with the warmongers in the Kremlin to curry favour, it could tip the balance.'

'We need to use her access to Chernenko to find out what's happening?'

'She will need something pretty compelling in return. We must ensure her superiors believe I have been turned,' Nic said.

'I have been thinking about that,' Seb said. 'Do you remember Wilson's white heat of technology speech at last year's Labour Party conference?' Nic nodded. 'Wilson said the next decade will be all about technology. Computers, communications, and advanced electronics will transform everything from accounting to weapons systems. It's an area we know the Soviets are way behind. So how are they going to catch up?'

'By stealing stuff?'

'Exactly. After all, that's how the Soviets got the bomb. Instead of Klaus Fuchs, they will have Nic Slater.'

Nic wasn't sure he liked the comparison. Although born in Germany, Fuchs was part of the British delegation working on the Manhattan Project while passing secrets to the Soviets. His treachery took years off the development cycle of the Soviet atom bomb.

'You can feed information through Irina. We will tweak it so it doesn't give the whole game away.'

Nic nodded. 'It might work, but she hinted that Moscow fears falling behind technologically. What are you thinking about?'

'Two things come to mind. The government recently approved a program to develop a vertical take-off and landing (VTOL) fighter. It doesn't need a runway, so it can operate from almost anywhere.

'Seriously?' Nic asked.

'Oh yes. The boffins are also developing computers that can calculate precise missile trajectories, allowing for more accurate bombing, telecommunications systems that provide instantaneous end-to-end encryption, and spy satellites that will replace spy planes. The Soviets will be desperate to get hold of these technologies.'

George arrived with two plates, each containing a steaming, well-stuffed Cornish pasty and a generous portion of chips covered with thick gravy.

'Don't forget the HP and Worcestershire, my good man,' Seb said.

'Yes, Milord,' said George as he mimed tugging his forelock.

Once Seb had liberally sauced his pasty, Nic asked, 'How will we handle the Americans?'

Seb picked up his knife and fork and cut into the pasty— steam poured out. 'Very carefully!' he said, 'If they find out what we are up to, they will try to take over. C wants this kept hush-hush. Only you, me, SirRod, and C will know about your mission.'

'Then we need to do something about Webbe,' Nic said.

Seb groaned, 'Not that little twerp. He was in the same year as my brother at prep school. He was a nasty piece of work even then. I have no idea how he managed to get into SIS. Leave it with me.'

Nic took a bite of his pasty; it was excellent. He missed good, stodgy English food. Borscht was fine, but you could not beat a good pasty, chips, and gravy.

Seb inhaled his food, 'Bloody good as always,' he said, putting down his knife and fork; Nic was still eating.

He slipped a leather cigar case out of his jacket pocket and went through the ritual of clipping and lighting one of his foul-smelling cigars. The combination of acrid cigar smoke and unfiltered Woodbines cast a pall over the whole pub. It was so dense you could barely see across the room. The Clean Air Act may have eliminated London's notorious smog, but it had not improved the air quality inside pubs one jot.

What is the scoop on the new government?' Nic asked.

'Not sure. You can never tell with bloody socialists,' Seb replied. 'Their manifesto harps on about a new era in Anglo-Soviet relations, whatever that means. They want to scrap our own nuclear weapons and rely on the Yanks.'

'Like everyone except the French,' Nic said. He had followed the rise of the Campaign for Nuclear Disarmament and its influence on Labour Party policy. Personally, he agreed with nuclear disarmament but was not convinced a unilateral approach was viable.

'The Cabinet is a mix of middle-of-the-road social democrats and ex-communists. If the list you got from Irina is accurate, quite a few are on Moscow's payroll. As for Wilson, he is an odd sort, smart but tough to read. There were rumours he was on Moscow's payroll at one time, but no concrete evidence was found, and he was not on Irina's list. I am not sure our standing in the world will improve.'

'We look pretty weak at the moment,' Nic replied. 'It was only a couple of years ago that the Tory Minister of War was caught shagging a Soviet spy's mistress!'

Seb smiled, 'Good point. Blake and Philby haven't helped either. The Yanks don't trust us. Some people already believe the Cold War is not the Warsaw Pact versus NATO but the Soviets against the Yanks.'

'Everything I heard in Moscow confirms that,' Nic said. 'The Soviet leadership is scared stiff of the Russian people finding out how much higher the standard of living is in the West. Irina hinted that some members of the Politburo want to pursue an aggressive military strategy to distract the populous from the problems at home.'

Seb sighed, 'That tactic has been used for centuries. Given all the other distractions, they probably want you to test America's commitment to NATO. I bet it's the real reason she is screwing you! You are a backdoor conduit into the CIA.'

Nic hoped there was more to it than that but saw Seb's point: 'We can exploit that, can't we?'

'Most definitely, but we must tread carefully. The Americans are very sensitive. Anyway, enough shop talk. Why don't you get together with the research johnnies this afternoon and work up the disinformation plan?'

'Sounds good,' Nic replied.

'I will see you in my office tomorrow at ten. I have a dinner at the Mansion House tonight and may need to sleep it off. The Lord Mayor always serves the most excellent port.'

The next couple of weeks followed a similar pattern for Nic. In the morning, he met with the research team, enjoyed a boozy lunch with Seb, and spent the afternoon trying to focus on his own work. On one occasion, he overindulged at lunch and had to head straight back to his flat to sleep it off.

Despite the excessive alcohol consumption, it was a productive week. He assembled a potent mix of material to pass on to Irina, including the initial design blueprints for the VTOL jet, a joint Anglo-American research paper on the use of computers to develop rocket guidance systems, a design document on a protocol for linking computers together in a network, and a Pentagon-produced position paper on the future of NATO.

Unbeknownst to anyone else, he also gathered some additional materials to share with Irina. He attended internal briefings and read every top-secret report he could. His official mission gave him wonderful cover for such activities.

Each evening, back at his flat, he made comprehensive notes. He documented clandestine plans to support dissident groups in Poland and Czechoslovakia; joint CIA/MI6 missions to infiltrate the French, Italian, and Greek communist parties; Anglo-French plans to combat communist influence in Africa; and long-range plans to use the 1966 World Cup, to be held in England, as cover for a series of sting operations against senior Soviet officials who were expected to attend.

It made for an attractive package that he hoped would intrigue, confuse, and distract Moscow.

35

On his final night before returning to Moscow, Nic was summoned to attend a dinner with C and the Foreign Secretary at one of Seb's clubs. This was far out of his comfort zone. Yorkshire lads did not dine at private members' clubs in Pall Mall.

Seb ordered Nic to get a haircut and shave at his barbers on Jermyn Street and buy a decent dress shirt while in the area. He returned twelve guineas poorer. Thankfully, Seb lent him a set of cuff links.

Standing in front of the mirror, he was not sure his investment would pay dividends. The new shirt simply highlighted the shabbiness of his suit.

He left in good time to allow for any travel delays, walking to the bus stop on Kings Road. He suspected he would be the only person at the club who had arrived on the number 9 bus. Three girls wearing impossibly short skirts giggled as he said good evening. One carried a bag from The Shop, a recently opened Kings Road boutique part-owned by photographer Terrence Donovan.

When the bus arrived, he grabbed his favourite seat—top deck, front row, left-hand side. From there, he had an unobstructed one-hundred-and-eighty-degree view of the road ahead and both footpaths. He could peer into shops, study pedestrians from above, and gaze into first-floor bedrooms and living rooms. It was amazing how many people left their curtains open.

The conductor swayed down the centre aisle of the bus, and Nic paid the four-penny fare. The bus made its way through Eaton Square, around the back of Buckingham Palace, past Hyde Park Corner, and on to Piccadilly. He got off opposite The Ritz and walked down St. James Street to Pall Mall.

The Chevening Club was one of many private members clubs that lined both sides of Pall Mall and served as a London outpost for the landed gentry. It was variously described as elitist, stuffy, and anachronistic. A liveried doorman opened the door for Nic and said, 'Good evening, Sir. May I enquire as to who you are meeting with this evening?'

'Viscount Weston,' replied Nic.

'Thank you, Sir. May I take your coat?'

Nic slipped it off, and it was deftly handed over to a young girl sitting in the coat room. In exchange, he received a numbered ticket and was led down a thickly carpeted corridor. Large oil paintings of notable club members lined the walls. Nic recognised Lords Wellington and Kitchener and a more recent painting of Churchill.

He was shown into an elegant, high-ceilinged room. Leather-backed armchairs were grouped around mahogany tables. Clouds of smoke hung in the air, and ice clinked in tumblers as the great and good solved the world's problems over pre-dinner cocktails.

Nic was still bemused by the dress code of the English upper classes. Seb had tried to explain that the nouveau riche tried hard to wear just the right clothes for every occasion. They had wardrobes full of finely tailored outfits suitable for dining at one's club, attending Royal Ascot, or a weekend of grouse shooting. On the other hand, old money could not care less about such norms. They were comfortable in their superiority over the masses and wore whatever they damn well wanted.

The Chevening was an old money haunt. Smartly tailored, fashionably cut suits were conspicuous by their absence. Seb sat beside an ornate marble fireplace in the far corner of the room. He wore olive-green corduroy trousers, a white shirt, bright red waistcoat, yellow bow tie, and a tweed jacket that had seen better days.

'You certainly stand out from the crowd,' Nic said.

Seb looked up from the paper he was reading, peering over the top of his half-moon glasses. 'Dear chap, my father told me that you have already failed if you have to dress to impress.'

Nic shook his head and sat down. He and Seb were easily the youngest men in the room. There were no women.

A large gin and tonic appeared on the table at Nic's side. While they waited, Seb gave Nic some background on the Foreign Secretary. Patrick Gordon-Walker was the son of a Scotsman who had served as a judge in the Indian Civil Service. He had got the socialist religion at Oxford before the war and joined the Labour Party. Nic wondered whether the Soviets had penetrated Oxford as successfully as Cambridge.

While most members of the new government came from working-class backgrounds, there were a few champagne socialists and members of the upper class who had adopted socialist ideals. Gordon-Walker was from the latter group, along with socialist firebrand Tony Benn, formerly Viscount Stansgate, until renouncing his title in 1963.

Gordon-Walker was in a rather invidious position. He had lost his seat in parliament at the recent election, despite his party sweeping into power. He should not really be serving in the government. However, Wilson appointed him as Foreign Secretary anyway. The plan was for him to stand in an upcoming by-election in the hope of returning to parliament and continuing to serve as Foreign Secretary.

Seb was interrupted by a gruff voice saying, 'Ah, Sebastian, how are you?'

Seb and Nic both stood up.

'Very well, Foreign Secretary. I am glad to see that your socialist colleagues have not banned you from mixing with the idle rich.'

The Foreign Secretary smiled, 'Not yet. But don't worry, we will tax you all into penury soon enough.'

Seb chuckled, 'Sir, let me introduce you to Dominic Slater, a proud member of the working-class proletariat.'

Nic stood and shook the proffered hand. C arrived moments later, and they moved to the dining room. Over dinner, Gordon-Walker asked Nic about his impressions of the Soviet Union. Nic described his experiences and ended by saying, 'We should not underestimate the resolve of the Soviet leadership to maintain and expand their global influence.'

'That could be complicated by China.'

'Yes, Sir,' Nic replied, 'There are already signs of tension on the Sino-Soviet border and in Vietnam.'

'Our stance is to continue supporting NATO and maintaining the special relationship with the United States. Government policy will not change much.'

'What about nuclear weapons?' Seb asked.

'We are committed to unilateral disarmament.'

'Would that policy hold if there was evidence of Soviet intent to launch a pre-emptive first strike?' Nic asked

Nic saw Seb smirking in the background. Gordon-Walker looked surprised and asked, 'Do you really think that could happen?'

'It is a possibility, Sir,' Nic replied bluntly, 'Even though the Soviet Union signed the test ban treaty, they have been ramping up investment in their nuclear arsenal.'

Gordon-Walker looked concerned. 'If that proves to be the case, it may change the calculation, but I have not seen any evidence yet.'

Nic saw Seb gently shake his head. Nic got the message and changed the subject.

'Sir Roderick Barker sends his best wishes,' Nic said, 'I understand the two of you were in Germany at the war's end.'

Gordon-Walker smiled, 'Yes, I was in Berlin with the BBC while he was chasing down Nazis. It was a strange time. Everyone was relieved the war was over, but we were only just learning about the true horrors of Hitler's reign. SirRod and I were at the liberation of Bergen-Belsen. It was the most shocking experience of my life. Thirty thousand people died in that camp in the two months before we arrived. Those that were still alive were nothing but skin and bones. SirRod was fuming. His mother was Jewish, and many of her family perished in the camps. Everyone who saw such scenes vowed that it should never be allowed to happen again.'

Fine words, Nic thought, but that was precisely what had been said at the end of World War I.

The conversation moved to Nic's role in Moscow. Gordon-Walker definitely supported any effort that improved the flow of intelligence to Britain and her allies. He assured Nic that his mission was endorsed at the highest levels.

Nic was not sure he felt reassured. He knew that if he screwed up, the government would disavow any knowledge of him.

The dinner ended with Gordon-Walker wishing Nic good luck. After he and C had left, Seb asked for his thoughts on the evening.

'He is delusional. How can he think unilateral disarmament is compatible with blunting Soviet ambitions? If the Soviets sense any weakness, they will exploit it.'

Seb nodded in agreement. 'It makes your work with Irina even more important.'

Nic pondered the implications. Seb was right. His work with Irina was vital, but not in the way Seb thought. It seemed that neither the government nor MI6 were willing to recognise the true threat posed by the Soviet Union.

They parted company outside the club. As Seb climbed into a chauffeur-driven Rolls-Royce, he said, 'One final thing. You will be pleased to know that our mutual friend, Jeremy Webbe, will not be returning to Moscow. SirRod has had enough of him. Apparently, he went behind SirRod's back and directly raised concerns about your mission with C. That was a big mistake. C and SirRod go back a long way. I think Mr Webbe is due for a plum posting to either Haiti or Honduras.'

Nic couldn't help but smile. It was the first good news he had received in a while.

36

6th December 1964 – Moscow

Two days later, Nic was back in Moscow. Anna met him at the airport and gratefully accepted the two bottles of fourteen-year-old Oban malt. On the drive into the city, Nic felt he was coming home, and it was not just the prospect of seeing Irina. Since joining MI6, he had spent more time in Kandinsky House than in his flat in London. The high ceilings, heavy curtains, and faded upholstery of the mansion were familiar. Even the vagaries of the heating system felt comforting.

The next morning, he slipped out of bed, put on his luxurious Derek Rose dressing gown, a graduation gift from Mags, and padded barefoot to the bathroom. He splashed cold water on his face and turned on the shower. It would be a few minutes before any warm water emerged.

It was another cold, crisp morning. Given the early hour, the street was deserted, save for a dustbin truck navigating down it. Periodically, one of the crew would jump down, scoop up a bin, and empty its contents. There was no sign of a Boris.

He took his usual route through Red Square to the Embassy. In contrast to London, there were no signs of Christmas; the Soviets had effectively banned it in 1929.

He checked the lamppost. There was a simple tick mark indicating that Irina had got the message he had left before leaving for London. The absence of any other mark was a good sign—their cover had not been blown—yet.

He quickly chalked the Greek letter alpha. He was becoming adept at lighting a cigarette with one hand while scratching a chalk mark with the other. The symbol indicated he wanted to meet Irina in the bar of the Metropole Hotel at 18:00. He wondered if Irina had found out any more about his encounter with Philby in Leningrad while he had been back in London.

Walking through the wrought iron gates that fronted the Embassy, the officer standing guard nodded and said, 'Welcome back, Sir,'

'Thank you, Braithwaite. Leeds is on a roll this season. That 5-1 win over Burnley was impressive.'

'Yes, Sir. Shame about your Blades. At least they hammered Arsenal.'

'There is always next season,' Nic said as he climbed the front steps.

Jenny was already at her desk, 'Welcome back, Sir. Good trip?'

'Yes, thank you,' he replied.

'Coffee is made. Sir Roderick said to go straight up.'

Nic poured himself a cup and headed upstairs. Vera greeted him with a smile and said, 'I hear you were dining with the Foreign Secretary; no doubt a knighthood is in your future!' she said, chuckling, 'Go straight in.'

SirRod looked up from the file he was reading and said, 'Welcome back, Slater. How was London?'

'Wet!' replied Nic.

SirRod smiled, 'Some things never change. What did C have to say?'

Nic updated SirRod on his meetings with C, Seb, and the Foreign Secretary.

'I agree with you. We seem to have badly underestimated the Soviets again. We did that after the war, and it cost us half of Europe. Your mission just became that much more important.

We need Sashkaya to provide intelligence to convince London and Washington that the Soviet threat in Western Europe is real. The Russians can be devious buggers. You need to make sure Sashkaya delivers.'

'I will, Sir,' Nic said with more confidence than he felt. The good news was that C, SirRod and a few others were beginning to wake up to the threat.

Nic spent the rest of the morning clearing his intray and catching up on recent intelligence reports. Just before lunch, he heard the distinctive voice of Barry Finnis in the outer office. Assuming he had come to see him, Nic got up from his desk and moved to his office door. He saw Barry sitting on the edge of Penny's desk. He was in full cockney charmer mode.

'So darling, you up for a night out?' he said.

Nic could see Penny's face. She was both smiling and blushing. Nic could not hear her whispered reply, but her demeanour made it clear she enjoyed being chatted up. He had clearly misjudged her preference for suitors! He retreated, leaving them to their flirtation.

At lunchtime, he checked the lamppost. The letter 'X' was scrawled on top of his mark. Irina could not meet tonight; had something happened?

37

24ᵗʰ December 1964

He checked the lamppost every day for almost three weeks, becoming increasingly agitated as time passed. Finally, on Christmas Eve, there was a mark. Irina would meet him at 14:00 in Sokolniki Park. He breathed a sigh of relief, tinged with concern about the cause of the delay. Did it have something to do with his Philby encounter? Was he walking into a trap?

Sokolniki Park was about five miles northeast of the city centre. It had once been home to the Tsar's falconers, Sokol being the Russian for falcon. Nic wondered whether he was today's prey.

Vera shared the recent historical significance of the park; it had been the scene of an impromptu meeting between Vice-President Nixon and Khrushchev at the opening of the American National Exhibition in 1959 during a short-lived Cold War thaw. Less than a year later, after a delegate at the United Nations accused the Soviet Union of depriving the peoples of Eastern Europe of their civil and political rights, Khrushchev had theatrically banged his shoe on his desk in protest before launching into a lengthy denunciation of the delegate, branding him "a jerk, a stooge, a lackey", and a "toady of American imperialism". The thaw in relations had ended instantly.

Irina was leaning on a fence surrounding the park's ice-skating rink. She smiled when she saw Nic. He relaxed, then saw she was holding two pairs of ice skates.

'You expect me to skate?' he asked.

'Don't tell me you can't skate?'

'I have never tried.'

'This should be fun,' she said as she sat on a bench and strapped on her skates. Nic reluctantly followed suit.

There were only a few people on the rink. To Nic, all the men looked like expert ice hockey players, and the women accomplished figure skaters. This was not going to end well.

Irina guided him onto the ice. He grabbed onto the fence for support as his legs started to move in opposite directions. Irina stood laughing before pushing off and gliding effortlessly around the ice. He managed to relocate his feet under his body and slowly edged along the rink's perimeter while trying to work out how to stay vertical.

Irina swept around the rink towards him at great speed. He braced for the inevitable collision. However, when she got to within a metre of him, she flipped her skates sideways and slid to a perfect stop, creating a spray of ice crystals as the edges of her skates carved through the ice.

'Put your arm round my waist,' she ordered.

He did as she instructed, reluctantly releasing his grip on the fence. He wobbled, but Irina stabilised him. After a few minutes of instruction, he was amazed that he could propel himself forward without falling over. He slowly navigated his way around the rink, never straying far from the fence. Irina slowly quickened her pace. Nic tried to keep up, but that was when it all went wrong. He caught his left skate on the back of the right, and before he knew what had happened, he was sprawled face down on the ice. Irina stood over him, laughing.

'Can we sit down?' Nic pleaded, 'My head hurts, my arms are bruised, and my calves are burning.'

Irina laughed, saying, 'Skating is supposed to be a relaxed, flowing motion.'

'For you, maybe,' he replied.

She relented, and they left the ice. After removing their skates, they walked to the café and bought cups of hot tea. Nic could no longer contain himself, 'What did you find out about the Philby meeting?'

'The good news is they do not suspect you of playing me.'

'Why did they have Philby meet me?'

'I think it was more about me than you. Semichastny suspects that Yuri and I are doing our own thing. We only share the bare minimum with him about our operations. He wanted to rattle your cage and see how you reacted.'

'I was too stunned to react at all.'

'I am not surprised. The good news is that your interrogators took your muted reaction as a sign you were genuine. If you had loudly denounced Philby, it could have signalled you were lying about being willing to work for us.'

'I am glad I didn't screw things up.'

'You passed with flying colours. So, what happened in London? I was worried you would not come back.'

'So was I, but it went well. MI6 is excited about having you as a source, and I am excited about exploiting you!'

A smile crossed her face, 'And I am ready to be exploited,' she said, gently stroking his cheek. He leaned forward, and they kissed. After a few seconds, she leaned back and started laughing, 'You are pleased to see me! Get up while you still can.'

They linked arms and headed back towards the park entrance. 'I did learn something else while in London,' Nic said.

'What?'

'You are right. London and Washington are seriously underestimating the Soviet threat in Europe. They are convinced no attack will take place in the foreseeable future.'

Her expression turned serious. 'If the Politburo hawks find out, they might get their way. Did you tell them they are mistaken?'

'I did, but without hard evidence, it is just my opinion.'

'We can fix that,' she said. 'You realise what this means?'

'I think so.'

'From now on, our fates will be inextricably linked.' Her eyes seemed to be searching his for any sign of doubt.

'I'm ready.'

'Good! The Soviet Union is not weak. We have been investing vast sums in both conventional and nuclear capabilities. That is the main reason the economy is such a mess. Khrushchev used his "peaceful co-existence" doctrine to convince NATO the Soviet Union was not interested in military conflict and wanted nuclear de-escalation. The reality is very different; the West is not winning the Cold War—it is losing it. Over the last four years, our leaders have masterminded a series of operations that have progressively undermined the US, the UK, and the rest of NATO. The Politburo is about to approve a significant expansion of that campaign. It goes far beyond Indochina to Europe, Africa, and South America. It will make Cuba look like a garden party.'

Nic was dumbfounded. If true, the world was sleepwalking towards another war. It sounded like a rerun of the 1930s. The world chose to appease Hitler despite evidence of the horrors that lay ahead. NATO had bought into Khrushchev's peace overtures, celebrating nuclear test ban treaties while being simultaneously blindsided by the Soviet Union's clandestine military build-up.'

'What operations are you talking about?'

'Big ones,' she said with a wry smile. 'Yuri and I have been summoned to a meeting in Minsk to discuss the plan. I will be able to tell you more when I get back.'

'Can you give me some idea?'

'Let's just say you should look for a common thread linking the biggest global events of the last few years.'

Nic tried to digest the meaning of what she said. He needed more information. 'You can't say that and walk away. Let's go back to your flat and talk about it,' she said.

That smile reappeared, 'Talk? Nice try, lover boy. You forget I am only supposed to screw you when absolutely necessary.'

'That is not what I meant,' he stammered.

'I know,' she said. 'You must be patient.'

38

25ᵗʰ December 1964

Rolling out of bed, Nic realised it was Christmas morning. He opened the curtains. It was snowing, but few in Moscow would be celebrating a white Christmas. One small part that would be celebrating was the British Embassy. The Ambassador was hosting a Christmas dinner for all staff.

Nic had been shaken by what Irina had told him. He wondered if he should tell SirRod or wait until she returned from Minsk. He thought it better to wait until he had something concrete to report.

The Embassy staff had done a fine job trying to replicate a traditional English Christmas. A tall yolka tree stood in the entrance hall, decorated with handmade baubles and lit with multiple strings of white lights. A nativity scene carved by a former Embassy security chief sat to the side. The staff choir sang carols as guests arrived.

After cocktails, dinner was served in the grand ballroom. It started off as a rather formal affair. Still, as alcohol consumption increased, crackers were popped, presents opened, toasts made, and tables pushed back to allow for dancing. Someone had connected a pair of large loudspeakers to a radiogram that had been moved down from the Ambassador's private rooms. A collection of records had been acquired, and Barry Finnis assumed the role of disc jockey. Penny spent the whole evening by Barry's side.

Nic enjoyed seeing the usually staid diplomatic staff let their hair down as they danced the night away. Even SirRod and his wife managed to adapt their unique waltz interpretation to an eclectic mix of sounds from Handel's Hallelujah Chorus to The Dave Clark Five's "Glad All Over". Nic could not get the image of Lady SirRod and Philby out of his head.

Vera insisted on dancing with him and revealed a previously unseen talent for the jive. All he needed to do was be in the right place at the right time to catch her as she whirled around to "Please Mr. Postman" and "Jailhouse Rock". She also trapped him under the mistletoe and gave him a very passionate kiss. He was beginning to understand why Barry had taken to calling her Miss Moneypenny.

When the party broke up, it was approaching midnight. Nic walked Vera back to her apartment. The cold night air was refreshing. They sang carols as they weaved their way through the streets. Upon arrival, he was rewarded with a very sloppy kiss.

Walking back to Kandinsky House, his thoughts were eighteen hundred miles away. For the first time since arriving in Moscow, he felt homesick. The holidays were a special time for the Slater family. Christmas Eve meant drinks in the pub, followed by the midnight carol service. Christmas Day started with present opening, followed by turkey and all the trimmings, listening to the BBC broadcast of the Queen's Speech, and endless games of charades. On Boxing Day, Nic and his dad would head off to Bramall Lane to watch Sheffield United. New Year's Eve was spent at the local working men's club, listening to a local comedian tell jokes his mother found rude and his father hilarious and having a sing-along accompanied by Mrs Shacklady on the piano. His parents would get slightly drunk before everyone stood to sing Auld Lang Syne at midnight.

This year, he suspected Dad would be asleep in his armchair, an empty whisky glass by his side. Mum would still be in the kitchen, clearing up the detritus of Christmas dinner and preparing a buffet for Boxing Day, when Mags and her family would arrive.

39

31ˢᵗ December 1964

The Embassy operated with a skeleton staff over the holiday period. Nic took advantage of the peace and quiet to read every intelligence report he could find. He looked for any hint of Soviet involvement in significant Cold War events. The only two hints he found were speculations about JFK's assassin, Lee Harvey Oswald, based upon his time spent in Russia and the involvement of the Russian naval attaché in the Profumo affair.

Back in his room, he sat with a notepad open on his lap and a whisky by his side. He wrote down every significant Cold War event, starting with the Berlin blockade in 1948, Soviet atom bomb testing, Korean War, Hungarian uprising, space race, Taiwan Straits, Berlin Wall, Bay of Pigs, Cuban missile crisis, and Vietnam. The scope was global, the focus, the fault line between capitalism and communism. Beyond that, he could see no common thread. Frustrated, he threw the pad on the floor and refilled his glass.

As days passed with no word from Irina, he began to worry he was being used. He went so far as to set up a meeting with SirRod to share his suspicions. Finally, a mark appeared on the lamppost. Irina wanted to meet the next day, New Year's Eve, at the Lenin Hills observation deck overlooking the city.

After another restless night, he woke early. Even though it was going to be a cold and snowy end to 1964, he decided to walk to the Lenin Hills. There was something about the crunch of fresh snow underfoot that felt very satisfying. His route took him along the north bank of the Moskva to Vorobyvoy Gory station. There, he crossed the river and climbed up into the

Lenin Hills. No Borises were on duty; maybe they had the day off.

He reflected on his year. It started at home with his family and ended with him betraying his country. It would be difficult for 1965 to top that.

The cold air and steep climb exercised his lungs, and he was panting when he saw Irina sitting on a bench. Despite the cold, she had dispensed with her fur hat. Wisps of light brown hair escaped from beneath a very French-looking beret. As he approached, she turned, and he saw a flash of her enigmatic half-smile. She stood up and walked towards him. He tilted his head, hoping for a kiss, but she grabbed his arm and said brusquely, 'Walk.'

'Why?' he asked.

'Just shut up and walk,' she commanded.

Confusion gave way to anxiety.

'What is going on?' he asked.

'Are you deaf?'

Finally, he got the message. They walked briskly down the hill in silence. Irina steered him across the grass to a gazebo beside a pond just before reaching the park exit.

'Sit,' she ordered before leaning forward and kissing him passionately.

'Sorry about that. We were being watched.'

'I didn't see anyone.'

'They followed me and hid in the woods above the observation deck. They were American.'

'How do you know?'

She laughed, 'They are not exactly inconspicuous.'

'Why are they following you?'

'I think they must know about us. Probably another leak from the sieve that is MI6!'

'I think it may be my fault. I told my CIA contact I was trying to recruit someone inside the KGB.'

'Why?' she said angrily.

'I was trying to get them to back off. Since Philby's defection, they have tried to muscle in on every operation. I hoped they would not come barging in and screw things up.'

'Well, it is not working!' she said.

'I'll sort it out. Now tell me about Minsk.'

'Yuri and I had to stay in Minsk for three extra days, so I could not meet with you before today. Detailed plans have been developed for the next phase of a long-term strategy called Pobezhdat.'

'Vanquish?'

She nodded, 'Yes, Vanquish is the umbrella name for all operations designed to destabilise the West. It started four years ago.'

'Four years?' Nic exclaimed.

'Yes. The program started after Kennedy was elected. The Politburo saw an opportunity to take advantage of his youth and inexperience to undermine America's leadership of the anti-Soviet coalition using Khrushchev's peaceful co-existence doctrine as cover. That view was reinforced after Khrushchev bullied Kennedy at the 1961 Vienna summit. Operation Vanquish was the result.'

'I have combed through all our intelligence reports, and no such operation is mentioned.'

'That shows how successful it has been.'

'What operations are you talking about?'

'How about the Berlin Wall and Profumo in 1961, Cuba in '62, JFK's assassination in '63, and now Vietnam?'

Nic blanched. 'Are you serious? Those were all part of a coordinated Soviet strategy?'

'Yes. It started with the building of the Berlin Wall. Khrushchev wanted to see if he could get away with it, and he did. At the same time, another opportunity fell into our lap in London. Our naval attaché, Yvegeny Ivanov, was screwing a young English girl he had met. He noticed your Minister of War, John Profumo, eying her up at a couple of parties and got an idea. He persuaded a friend who also knew Profumo to introduce the girl, Christine Keeler, to Profumo. It did not take long for them to start an affair. The KGB in London slowly leaked details of the affair. After initially denying it, Profumo admitted the truth and had to resign. Not long after, a socialist government won the election.'

Nic nodded, thinking back to Seb's walk-on part in the affair.

'What about JFK? Are you saying the rumours about Lee Harvey Oswald were true?'

'Yes. The Americans should have worked it out; all the clues were there. Oswald lived in Minsk in the 1950s, married a Russian, and was recruited by the KGB. The KGB promised him a new life with his wife in Russia. However, he bungled his escape after the assassination and was arrested. Moscow knew Oswald would talk. The KGB ordered the Mafia to kill Oswald. Jack Ruby, a Texas nightclub owner who was on the Mafia's payroll, shot Oswald outside the Dallas Police Headquarters.'

'But why assassinate Kennedy if they thought he was weak?'

'He turned out to be anything but weak. He humiliated Khrushchev over Cuba. That rattled the Politburo. They thought

Johnson would be easier to manipulate. So far, they seem to be right.'

'No one has connected the dots between these events.'

'Frankly, we are surprised. All the clues are there, but the Americans are so convinced of their superiority that they can't or won't see what is happening. And those are just the major operations. Recently, we have successfully driven a wedge between Turkey and Greece over their competing claims to Cyprus. Greece has already withdrawn its forces from NATO. We are also making headway in seeding unrest in France, Italy and elsewhere.'

Nic tried to comprehend what she was saying. If true, Moscow had orchestrated every major Western crisis of the last few years.

'If the Americans find out about JFK, it could galvanise American public opinion, just like Pearl Harbor did.'

Irina nodded, 'I know. We have to try and prevent that from happening.'

'What should we do?'

'In Minsk, Yuri and I worked with our military commanders to develop plans to invade Finland and Iran next year. All the successes to date have emboldened the warmongers in the Kremlin. There is growing confidence, bordering on arrogance. They now want to move to more direct conflict. Finland and Iran will be a test. If successful, the plan is to directly attack Western Europe.'

'Shit,' Nic exclaimed. The Soviets had completely blindsided NATO. A seemingly unconnected series of events was weakening the alliance. It pointed to a scale of organisation, intelligence, and execution that dwarfed any western assessment of Soviet capability.

'Tell me about Finland and Iran.'

'The invasions are planned for June or July. False flag attacks will be used as the justification. Yuri and I have been ordered to develop a disinformation program to mask the true objectives. Part of that involves me passing fake intelligence to you.'

Nic nodded, 'How do we disrupt those operations without getting discovered? It is a dangerous game.'

'Everything we do is dangerous, but think about it, misdirection is one of a spy's most powerful tools. You British mastered it during World War II. You convinced Hitler that Pas de Calais, not Normandy, was the target of D-Day. Suppose we can shake NATO from its complacency and divert some of America's focus back to Europe from Indochina. In that case, we may be able to trigger a response to the invasions that is more than the usual angry words and public denunciations.'

He thought about what Irina was saying. 'We need to know when and where the invasions will take place. Then we may be able to prompt a response that goes some way to restoring the status quo.'

Irina nodded, 'The exact dates and locations have not been finalised. Yuri and I are on the planning team, so we should know as soon as they are finalised.'

'I hope it gives us enough time to respond appropriately.'

'You need to start doing that now. Use what I have told you to wake NATO from its slumber.'

Nic nodded, 'Let me see what I can do. Let's meet ¬¬at the Metropole next Thursday and see where we are. ¬

'See you then,' she replied, leaning in to give him a kiss. She whispered, 'Happy New Year,' in his ear.

'Let's hope it is not our last one,' he replied.

Nic went straight to SirRod's residence. He would be interrupting his boss's New Year's Eve but felt it was justified. He rang the bell and waited. After two more rings, a maid opened the door.

'I need to speak with Sir Roderick. It is urgent.'

She frowned but allowed him to enter, showing him into a formal sitting room that looked more like Mayfair than Moscow.

Nic could hear muffled laughter in the distance. The party was in full swing. After a few minutes, the door opened, and SirRod entered the room.

'This better be good, young man,' Sir Roderick said grumpily. His pipe was wedged into the side of this mouth, and he had a large brandy snifter in one hand.

'It is, Sir.'

He gave SirRod a detailed account of his meeting with Irina. He only omitted mention of JFK, which was too incendiary to share.

When he finished, SirRod said, 'We suspected they were up to something, but not on this scale.'

He sat puffing on his pipe. Concentric circles of smoke rose towards the ceiling. Nic was impressed. He still had not mastered smoking, never mind-blowing smoke rings. He waited for SirRod to speak. After a long pause, he said, 'I need to talk to London, but I think this may warrant accelerating our plan for you.'

'What plan is that?' Nic said, unable to keep the irritation out of his voice.

SirRod ignored his tone, saying, 'Be in my office at noon tomorrow. Now, let me get back to my guests. Happy New Year.'

40

1ˢᵗ January 1965

Nic presented himself right at noon, 'Happy New Year,' said Vera, 'Go straight in.' Again, she followed him into the office.

'Sit down, we have a lot to cover,' said SirRod

Nic did as instructed. SirRod went through the ritual of lighting his pipe before saying, 'We are transferring you back to London.'

Nic was flabbergasted. 'But Sir, I am close to turning Sashkaya. Given her connections, she can be a wonderful intelligence source.'

'I know, and that is part of the rationale for sending you back. I spoke with C this morning, and we are agreed. We know the Soviets already see you as a potentially valuable source. The material you gave Sashkaya has been well received in the Lubyanka and Kremlin. The KGB will not want to lose contact with you, especially if they are planning to invade Iran and Finland. We are convinced the KGB will send Sashkaya to London to continue running you.'

Nic nodded, but it made some sense. If the KGB believed he was working for them, they would jump at the opportunity to have a mole on the inside.

SirRod continued, 'It just so happens that the current cultural attaché at the Soviet Embassy in London was caught in a compromising position with an MP in a public toilet near Piccadilly Circus. The government wants it hushed up and is expelling the individual immediately, creating the perfect cover for Sashkaya to be transferred in as his replacement.'

Nic's head was spinning at the possibility of Irina being in

London. 'It would be great if it happened,' he responded, instantly regretting his rather too-obvious enthusiasm.

SirRod smirked, 'I am sure it would, but do not let your personal feelings cloud your judgement. We cannot underestimate the reach of Soviet intelligence. Despite the recent defections, they probably still have some moles in Five and Six. You must guard against the true nature of your relationship with Sashkaya becoming too widely known. If Moscow suspects she, rather than you, is the traitor, things will go sideways very quickly.'

If only he knew the truth, Nic thought.

SirRod continued, 'We need confirmation of the plans for Finland and Iran. I suspect they want Finland to provide an additional buffer to their border. Never mind that they believe it is Russian by right. As for Iran, it would give them direct access to the Persian Gulf and, from there, the Indian Ocean. NATO is not prepared for any threat close to its own borders. The situation is further complicated as neither country is a NATO member. The next few months will be interesting,' he said, taking another puff on his pipe. 'You leave for London in four days.'

Nic was in a daze. He was excited at the prospect of being with Irina in London but worried that C and SirRod were wrong to assume the KGB would have her follow him. He needed to contact her immediately.

Leaving the Embassy, he walked briskly along the river to St. Basil's, grateful that no Boris was on his tail. He chalked two exclamation marks on the lamppost—the signal for an urgent meeting.

41

3ʳᵈ January 1965

Two days passed, and Irina did not respond—no marks on the lamppost or messages under his door. What was going on?

He packed his things in preparation for his return to London, telexed Mags, and wrote a long list of to-dos for Penny. He was becoming increasingly despondent. From both a personal and professional perspective, it felt like failure. Had he misread the signals? Had it all been a charade?

He sought out Vera and asked her advice. As he bemoaned his plight, she looked at him and said, 'Well, we are a lovesick puppy, aren't we? You need to snap out of it. You have a job to do. I agree with SirRod; the Soviets will not pass up the opportunity to place a mole in London. Whether Sashkaya contacts you before you leave is not important; it's what happens next that matters. So, stop feeling sorry for yourself.'

Nic returned to his office suitably humbled. Vera was right. He needed to focus on the job at hand. If that meant sacrificing his personal feelings for Irina, so be it. His thoughts were interrupted when Penny poked her head around his office door.

'Hello, Sir. A belated Happy New Year,' she said with a smile. She had been on leave since Boxing Day. Upon seeing the boxes piled in the corner, she asked, 'What's happening?'

'I am being sent back to London. I leave the day after tomorrow.'

'Why? No, don't tell me, it's probably a secret.'

Nic laughed, 'Did you have a nice break?'

She beamed and thrust her left hand out. A giant diamond sparkled from an ornate gold setting.

'Barry proposed at midnight on New Year's Eve!' she exclaimed.

'Congratulations,' Nic said, smiling. 'When is the big day?'

'We finish our tours in August, so we are looking at October. You will be getting an invitation.'

'I will look forward to it.'

'Reception just called; they have a message for you. I will pop down and get it.'

'Thank you,' Nic replied. It was unusual for anyone to deliver a message by hand to the Embassy. Could it be from Irina? Penny reappeared and handed him an envelope. He opened it and unfolded the piece of paper inside. The message was succinct: "16:00 Kiyevsky, I." He looked at his watch. He had thirty minutes to get to Kiyevsky station.

'I have to go,' he said to Penny as he left his office. She was flipping through a bridal catalogue. Nic suspected she might be a little distracted for the next few months.

Walking through the Embassy gates, he saw Boris II standing fifty metres away. Upon seeing Nic, he nodded before turning and walking away. He must have delivered the message and stayed to make sure Nic acted upon it.

The station was only a ten-minute walk. It was exactly 16:00 when Nic entered the concourse. He walked no more than ten metres before Irina appeared at his side. They did not acknowledge each other.

The combination of noise from the locomotives idling at the platforms and the near continuous announcements over the public address system created a bubble that allowed them to talk without fear of being overheard.

'I am going back to London.'

'When?' she did not sound surprised.

'Day after tomorrow.'

That familiar smile appeared on her face.

'Why are you smiling? We were beginning to make progress.'

'This is perfect,' she said.

'How so?' he said, stepping around a little boy playing with a toy car on the ground.

'I will explain later. Come to my apartment at eight,' she said, winking.

'But...' Nic said. She had already gone.

Irina rested her head on Nic's shoulder. Their clothes lay scattered across the room. In the hour since he had arrived, they had yet to exchange a word.

'Why is my returning to London a good thing?' he asked.

'Because Semichastny will have me follow you.'

'You really think he will do that?'

'Of course. Moscow won't want to lose such a valuable source. Our leaders are paranoid that Vanquish will be discovered. They will want you to alert me if you hear anything and have me feed you disinformation that masks our true agenda. Having you back in London places you much closer to the centre of the action.'

He nodded. C, SirRod and Vera had been correct.

'What will your new job be?' Irina asked.

'SirRod said something about being assigned to the European desk. Specifically, to study Soviet influence over non-Soviet aligned states.'

'Good,' she said as she swung her legs over the side of the bed and stood up—she was completely naked. Nic admired the view as she crossed to the bathroom. She caught him looking and wagged her finger, 'Behave,' she admonished.

'That's not what you were saying a few minutes ago.'

When she returned, she said, 'I have found out there are other Vanquish operations underway. We are helping the communist movements in Turkey, Greece, Italy, and France stir up unrest, funding left-wing trade unions in Britain and blackmailing at least three West German politicians.'

'London knows about most of that, but they have no idea about the bigger operations. What are we going to do?' he asked.

'We have to get the Americans to refocus on Europe. What about your contact at the CIA?'

'What about him?'

'When you get back to London, get in touch with them. Tell them what you told SirRod. Share just enough about Vanquish to convince him that the threat is real. If we can get Washington to show more resilience, it will help reset the balance of power.'

'C doesn't want to engage with them yet.'

'You need to change that.'

She climbed back into bed and said, 'We don't have much time.'

Within seconds, she had his full attention.

42

4th *January 1965*

The next morning, Irina was summoned to a meeting with Semichastny. He did not waste any time getting to the point. 'My sources tell me that you have become intimate with Slater.'

There was no question there, so she said nothing. Irritated, Semichastny said, 'Well, have you?' It was well known that Semichastny had little time for female agents.

'My interactions with Slater have been consistent with my mission. After all, I was trained for almost ten years to use certain skills unique to a woman.'

'Don't patronise me!' he snapped, his face flushing angrily.

'Comrade, that was not my intention. I am sorry if I offended you.' She was enjoying this.

He grunted in annoyance. 'Women are too emotional. They talk too much and cannot keep a secret. You must not let your girlish emotions jeopardise your mission.'

Now, who was being patronised? Irina thought. She refused to rise to the bait. 'Comrade, you can be assured my actions are always in the service of Mother Russia. Slater is like most men. He is vain and easily manipulated.'

Semichastny did not hint that he had picked up on her veiled insult. He simply nodded and said, 'Good.'

He moved on to ask her opinion of the veracity of the information Nic was providing and how well-informed the Western intelligence services were about Soviet operations. He did not mention Vanquish directly, but it was clear to Irina what he was really asking.

She decided to sow the first seeds of doubt in his mind. 'Slater did mention that MI6 suspected Ivanov had not been a passive participant in the entrapment of Profumo. They also suspect we may still have agents operating somewhere in the government, despite Philby's defection.'

This got his attention, and he demanded more details. She kept her comments vague before saying, 'I have just found out Slater has been recalled to London.'

'When? Why?' Semichastny spluttered

'Tomorrow, he is taking up a new post.

His face flushed again with anger. Irina kept her expression neutral, just staring at him. After a long pause, he leaned forward, pointed at her, and said, 'You must go to London. We cannot afford to lose him as a source just as Vanquish enters its most critical phase.'

'I agree, comrade.'

His face relaxed a little, feeling his authority had been somewhat restored.

'Kovlev will be your handler. He will make sure you don't lose focus.'

Irina smiled to herself. He had no inkling of her relationship with Yuri. He assumed that Yuri would be the dominant one in their relationship because she was a woman. How stupid men were. Yuri was a good agent, but she could twist him around her little finger.

The next day, she was summoned to a meeting in the Kremlin. Semichastny was there, but this time, he was joined by Chernenko.

Semichastny looked surprised and irritated at Chernenko's affectionate greeting to Irina. Maybe he was beginning to realise that he needed to be careful around her.

Chernenko opened the meeting by complimenting her on the intelligence she had obtained from Nic, 'The British and Americans are having little success running operations in the Soviet Union and have no knowledge of Vanquish. As the Americans become more involved in Vietnam, NATO is getting weaker by the day.'

Semichastny spoke, 'Comrade Sashkaya informed me yesterday that her MI6 source is being recalled to London.'

'I am aware of that,' Chernenko said. Irina saw Semichastny give her a dirty look before saying, 'I am sending her over there to continue running him.'

'That makes sense,' Chernenko said, 'Are you comfortable doing that, Irina?'

'I am,' she said, smiling.

'Good. You can get me some new shirts from Turnbull and Asser while you are there,'

'Of course, Dyada.'

She enjoyed seeing the shocked expression on Semichastny's face when she used the affectionate term for uncle.

Chernenko moved on to explain the rationale for invading Iran and Finland. 'NATO's weakness provides an opportunity to expand the buffer between Mother Russia and our enemies. In the northwest, Finland sits on our border and has been getting increasingly friendly with NATO. To the south, the British and Americans are using Iran to threaten our comrades in Armenia, Azerbaijan, and Turkmenistan. By adding both countries to the

USSR, we will improve our border security and provide a platform for future missions. We expect NATO to respond only with angry words. You have a crucial role in ensuring success.'

'I will not let you down,' she said, smiling. 'I am honoured by your faith in me.'

'I have complete confidence in you, kotik (kitten),' Chernenko said. Semichastny frowned again.

43

6th *January 1965*

Nic spent his final morning in Moscow meeting with various Embassy staffers to hand over the projects he was working on and briefing his replacement. Nic looked at the fresh-faced young man and wondered if he would be up to the job. Then he remembered that he had arrived at the Embassy fresh out of training school only twelve months before. Had he looked quite so naïve? Probably.

Around lunchtime, Penny delivered another note that had been handed in at reception. Irina had abandoned any pretence of clandestine communication; they were to meet at 14:00 at Moscow Zoo.

It was bitterly cold, yet Irina still insisted on choosing outdoor locations for their meetings. Nic wondered if she did it on purpose. At least he was getting value from his ushanka and fur-lined boots.

She stood by the zoo entrance. After paying the admission fee, they strolled past some of the animal enclosures. The zoo was deserted, and even the animals were hard to spot. They were no doubt sheltering inside from the cold.

They found the only open café. The steamed-up windows promised some respite from the freezing temperatures. Not surprisingly, they were the only customers. After ordering tea, they sat at a table away from the counter. Irina looked at Nic and said, 'Can you get borscht in London?'

Nic stared at her, realisation slowly dawning, 'You are coming to London?'

'Yes. I hope English beds are more comfortable than Russian ones,' she replied.

'Mine is,' he replied.

She told him about her meetings with Semichastny and Chernenko. When she finished, he said, 'If only they knew the truth.'

'There's more,' she said. 'Finland and Iran are viewed as steppingstones towards a full invasion of Western Europe.

'Surely they don't think they can get away with that?'

'Why not? Everything they have tried so far has worked.'

She was right. The Soviets had every right to be confident.

'We need to try and disrupt the invasions,' he said.

She nodded, 'That means convincing the Americans the threat is real.'

'It needs to be compelling. Nothing has provoked the US to take real action, not Hungary, Berlin, or Cuba.'

'But they have no idea about the scope of Vanquish. We can change that.'

'I hope so,' he said

44

3rd February 1965, London

It felt strange to be back in London. After the sombre, greyness of Moscow, the city assaulted every sense. Neon signs flashed atop buildings, music blared out of pubs, clubs, and windows everywhere, and complex aromas emanated from every fish and chip shop, curry house, and Chinese takeaway.

Nic found it ironic that his quality of life declined upon his return. The Edith Grove flat was a definite step down from Kandinsky House, and Century House paled compared to the grandeur of the Embassy. Mags had stocked his fridge before his arrival. Still, he soon found it an adjustment to shop for food, do laundry and ensure an adequate supply of toilet paper after being waited on hand and foot in Moscow.

Each day, he checked the diplomatic immigration records to see if Irina had entered the country. After a month, he became convinced she wasn't coming. Seb urged him to be patient. 'You do not just drop a spy into a foreign country without some preparation,' he cautioned.

Finally, her name appeared on the list. She entered through Harwich on an East German registered cargo vessel carrying cheap furniture for sale in the UK. She registered as the new cultural attaché at the Soviet Embassy, just as SirRod had predicted.

Nic was desperate to see her. He considered taking a casual stroll past the Soviet Embassy in Kensington Palace Gardens in the hope he would run into her, but he dismissed the idea as immature and stupid. She would contact him when the time was right.

45

10th February 1965

Before Nic left Moscow, he and Irina had agreed upon a replacement for their Red Square lamppost—a telephone box outside Queensway tube station. Telephone boxes were essential tools for spies. Their use attracted little suspicion, and calls were difficult to trace or be overheard. They defined a new protocol, set of locations and symbols. They would mark the symbol on the top of the telephone directory page corresponding to the number of the day in the year, so January 1 was page 1, January 2 was page 2, and so on.

Every day after Irina's arrival, Nic checked the directory, varying the time to avoid establishing a pattern. Finally, after two weeks, a symbol appeared at the top of page 41, corresponding to February 10, the 41st day of the year. Irina wanted to meet at 11:30 tomorrow in Trinity Square Gardens next to Tower Hill tube station. Nic placed a slash through her symbol, indicating he would be there.

That evening, he tried to organise his thoughts. Since returning to London, he had worked with Seb to expand the disinformation plan. They had added a storyline about joint Anglo-American espionage operations in Eastern Europe and Southeast Asia that contained just enough truth to be plausible. He needed to maintain the illusion that he was a valuable double agent.

46

11th February 1965

When he woke up, it was still dark. The clock showed it was only 04:00. He got out of bed, wrapped himself in his dressing gown, and sat in the battered old armchair in front of the electric fire. The two horizontal bars glowed orange, taking some of the chill out of the air. The dial on the meter spun rapidly as his supply of shillings diminished.

He went over the plan again. It was solid, but it was enough to give the Soviets pause for thought. He had dropped hints to Seb about a Soviet plan to destabilise NATO. Seb had, like SirRod, not been surprised. However, without knowing the scale of what the Soviets had already accomplished, he did not seem too concerned.

Nic realised that he and Irina were treading a fine line as they balanced their roles as double agents with their own agendas. One misstep would expose their well-meaning treachery.

Finally, it was time for him to shower and get dressed. After leaving the flat, he walked down to the King's Road. A road sweeper was clearing the detritus from the previous night's revelries. Until recently, the street had looked like most other neighbourhood streets, with an assortment of butchers, grocers, dry cleaners, and pubs. However, in the last couple of years, a transformation had begun. Butchers were replaced by hairdressing salons, greengrocers were transformed into boutiques, and the long-established Picasso Coffee Bar had been joined by several new late-night rivals. An influx of young people wearing the latest fashions had prompted the Daily Mail to start discussing a Kings Road scene.

Given the early hour, few people were about. Nic stopped at the only open coffee bar. There were two other customers, a young couple who looked like they had not yet been to bed. Both gazed vacantly at partially drunk cups of tea. Nic ordered a double espresso and two pieces of toast before sitting by the window. He was grateful for the caffeine boost. His mind was swirling with anticipation about seeing Irina again and trepidation about their mission.

He needed to work with Irina to assemble just the right amount of information about Vanquish to persuade C that it was time to engage with the CIA without triggering a massive overreaction. C had an inherent distrust of the CIA, borne of his experience after the War when the Americans reneged on an intelligence-sharing pact. Ever since, the UK had been relegated to junior partner status in the Anglo-American alliance.

He finished his coffee and walked towards Sloane Square tube. As he crossed the road to the station entrance, he caught sight of a man standing in front of Peter Jones. Something about him looked out of place. He was leaning against the wall, reading a newspaper. The headline reported an agreement between the French and British governments to build a tunnel under the English Channel. What was odd was that it was yesterday's edition.

Nic purchased a three-penny ticket from the machine. Looking back, he saw the man dump the paper in a bin and hurriedly cross the street. Nic took the steps down to the westbound Circle Line platform and walked down to the far end. The man appeared at the other end of the platform just as the train arrived.

When the doors opened, Nic did not move, giving the impression that he would wait for the next train. Just as the doors started closing, he stepped forward as if to board the train. He saw the man jump onto the train from the corner of his eye. Nic swiftly pulled his leg back and let the doors close. As the train pulled out of the station, he gave a little wave to his pursuer before heading through the connector passage to the eastbound platform, where he boarded the next train.

Five stops later, he alighted at Temple Station. Emerging into the early morning sunshine, he walked up the hill towards the Strand. Morning commuters crowded the pavement, and he easily blended into the crowd.

He needed to make sure there had not been a full reconnaissance team following him. They often worked in groups of four or five to allow for frequent personnel switches to reduce the risk of detection. He crossed the Strand, walked through Covent Garden to Holborn, took a bus to Marble Arch, walked down Park Lane to Hyde Park Corner, and took another bus to St. Paul's. He stopped at three coffee shops en route and saw no sign of anyone following him. Three hours later, he walked past the Bank of England, through Leadenhall Market towards Trinity Square Gardens.

He could not help thinking about the nature of his relationship with Irina. His training had emphasised the need to be dispassionate. Emotions led to weakness, which led to mistakes. Logic told him that Irina's interest in him was purely professional. She admitted she had been trained for almost a decade to use every means at her disposal in service of the state. Had she any real feelings for him? Surely, she could not have faked everything. He was convinced they had a personal connection. Why else would she have proposed their secret pact?

He cursed himself. He was going around in circles, overanalysing everything. Whatever Irina's motivation, he had committed to a course of action. He could not back out now; he had already betrayed his country.

When he reached Trinity Square, he found a vacant bench in the sunken garden. It was warming up nicely, much more pleasant than the frigid temperatures of Moscow. City office workers sat around eating their lunch. On the bench next to him, a group of young women were comparing notes on the men in their office—who apparently were all sex-crazed Neanderthals. There was no sign of Irina.

As the clock on All Hallows church chimed twelve, he sensed someone about to sit next to him. He turned to inform the intruder he was saving the seat for a friend.

'I see your observation skills have not improved,' Irina said, sitting down. He shrugged and leaned over to kiss her on the lips. She reciprocated.

'It's good to see you,' he said.

'Likewise,' she replied. 'Sorry I am late. I had to lose a tail.'

'You are being followed already?'

'Yes. The Yanks again.'

'They followed me as well. They have been badgering Six for information about the KGB agent we have supposedly turned. They must have taken it upon themselves to check out all new arrivals at the Soviet Embassy.'

'We need to get them off our backs,' Irina said.

'Agreed. As we discussed in Moscow, I am meeting my CIA contact soon.'

He handed her a rather limp cucumber sandwich and a packet of Golden Wonder crisps he had bought at one of his coffee stops. She looked suspiciously at the sandwich, 'You really know how to spoil a girl.'

'Stop complaining. This is the quintessential English-packed lunch.'

'No wonder everyone looks so pale and emaciated. I would rather have a hearty bowl of borscht.'

'You are in England now, no more stew!'

As they ate, she updated him on events since their last meeting in Moscow. The invasion plans were complete, and troops were being trained.

'They expect to be in Helsinki and Tehran within a week of launching the attacks.'

'They are betting there will be no opposition at all.'

She nodded, 'The only reaction they expect is harsh words and empty threats.'

'If we fail, they are probably right.'

After finishing their sandwiches, they walked down the hill to the river. Tower Bridge's bascules were rising to let a boat pass through. Irina leaned her head on Nic's shoulder and said, 'I think I am going to like London.'

'I know I am going to like you being in London,' he replied, kissing her on the cheek.

'Can you come to my flat tomorrow night? We can test the bed,' he whispered. Even he could hear the slightly desperate tone in his voice.

She frowned before that smile appeared. 'I might be able to fit you into my plans. Comrade Gromyko ordered me to do whatever is necessary to ensure you continue supplying high-grade intelligence,' she said, winking.

'He is a smart man. Let's meet in the Fox and Pheasant pub just off the Fulham Road at seven, then we can see where the evening takes us.'

She nodded and gave him a quick kiss on the cheek before she started walking back to the station. He gazed at her legs as she strode along, noting that she had already adopted the trend for shorter hemlines. He hoped to see more tomorrow night.

He knew their relationship was not one of equals. Irina was more experienced, better trained, and oozed self-confidence. She was the dominant party, both professionally and personally. He was not too intimidated, having grown up surrounded by strong women. His mother had endured tremendous hardship and loss before she reached her teenage years. His sister was succeeding in the male-dominated legal profession as one of the youngest and most respected barristers in London.

At Six, he had heard numerous stories of the heroic exploits of female agents, sporting codenames such as Blanche, Simone, and Violet, during the War. In Britain, the post-war years had seen a progressive liberation of women. They were emerging from the kitchen and proving they could be just as, if not more, capable than men in almost any walk of life. Irina had faced a more challenging path in the Soviet Union.

Once back at the office, Nic was not surprised to find that Seb was still out to lunch. Rather than wait, he headed down to the research department. Simon and Charlotte had just returned to London, having completed their two-year postings in Moscow. He had asked them to assess NATO's military strength in

Europe. He wanted to understand how much America's growing involvement in Indochina weakened NATO.

The hallway leading to the research room was lined with metal cabinets containing files recording fifty years of British espionage operations. It would be an author's dream to peruse those files. Seb had told him that Ian Fleming had sourced much of the material he used in his James Bond novels from these files while working for the security services during the War.

The research room was similar to the one in the basement of the Moscow Embassy. It was large and windowless, with shelving on three sides. A huge blackboard and maps of each continent covered the fourth wall.

'Well, if it isn't our very own Rasputin,' came Simon's gruff voice from the other side of the room.

'Very funny,' Nic responded as Simon emerged, smirking from behind a bookshelf. While in Moscow, Simon and Nic had become fast friends, bonding over their northern working-class roots, love of football and warm beer. At six-foot-four, Simon was lanky, uncoordinated, and brilliant. As usual, he was aggressively sucking on his unlit pipe; Charlotte had banned him from smoking in her presence. After taking a first at Cambridge in Natural Sciences, he had been recruited into the service by Kim Philby. Thankfully, his reputation had not been tainted by Philby's defection.

Charlotte sat at her desk, frowning. She was a very different kettle of fish. Born into an aristocratic family with a large estate in Wiltshire and a townhouse on Berkeley Square, she had been presented to the Queen at the debutante ball of 1959. She had been courted by sundry earls, viscounts, and dukes. However, unlike most of her peers, she had no intention of getting married, much to the dismay of her mother and younger sisters. Precociously intelligent, she earned a first-class psychology degree at age nineteen. While undertaking her post-graduate studies, she met Simon, who she termed her "bit of rough."

Her family disapproved of Simon, and she had been banished. She had not cared one bit, completing her PhD at twenty-three, joining Six, and moving into a one-bedroom flat in Holloway with Simon.

She winked at Nic, saying, 'It's nice to see a real man for a change.'

'Stop flirting, you tart,' Simon said, 'You will get your knickers off for anyone!'

Charlotte smiled, 'Who says I am wearing any, darling?'

Simon was beaten again.

'Behave you two, come on, let's get out of this dungeon.'

They walked up the three flights of stairs to the canteen. Simon and Nic added a large slice of cake to their mugs of tea while Charlotte settled for a banana. The lunchtime crowd had dispersed, so they had the room to themselves.

'What have you found out?' Nic asked.

As usual, Charlotte took the lead. 'The Americans are significantly escalating their involvement on the ground in Vietnam. Troop numbers will likely increase from twenty thousand to over two hundred thousand next year.'

Nic whistled, 'That is more like an invasion than a military action. The Soviets think the Americans will get bogged down chasing an enemy they cannot see. Their massive firepower is useless when the enemy hides in tunnels or the jungle.'

'They are right,' said Simon, 'the Viet Cong are giving the South Vietnamese a torrid time. They will do the same to the

Americans. The Soviets and Chinese are shipping weapons down the Ho Chi Minh trail to resupply them. President Johnson thinks Vietnam is another Korea. A place where America must stop the advance of communism.'

'How does it impact Europe?' Nic asked.

'By the end of next year, there will be more US troops in Vietnam than all of Europe. US military personnel in Europe peaked at 400,000 in 1962 and has been declining ever since. Other NATO members cannot fill the gap. The more the Americans are consumed by Vietnam, the less able they are to support Europe.' Charlotte said.

'What is the government's position?' Nic asked.

'Publicly, Wilson supports the US but won't offer any tangible support. Privately, he thinks he can negotiate directly with Moscow and secure a peace deal,' Simon replied.

Nic sighed, 'One of his predecessors tried something like that with Hitler. It did not end well.'

'The Soviets see NATO's weakness and are probably looking to exploit it,' added Charlotte.

Nic grimaced and muttered, 'They already are.'

Charlotte stared at him, 'What do you mean?'

'If I told you, I would have to kill you. Thanks for this. I will read you when I can. In the meantime, try not to kill each other.'

Nic knew the Soviets would be delighted at the US escalation in Vietnam. It strengthened the rationale for invading Finland and Iran. He went back to see if Seb had returned and found him lying on the sofa in his office, snoring loudly.

'Sleeping on the job, are we? What a waste of taxpayer money,' Nic shouted.

'I am just resting my eyes. As for wasting taxpayer money, the Harmes clan makes a significant contribution to the Exchequer, which more than covers my meagre compensation.'

They discussed his meeting with Irina. Seb agreed they needed to make the case to C to brief the Americans.

47

12th February 1965

Unlike most pubs, The Fox and Pheasant was not on a street corner but squeezed in amongst a row of two storey townhouses in the middle of a residential street.

Nic pushed open the door and was met by a cacophony of conversations merging into unintelligible chatter. Deep in the mix was the distinctive voice of Ray Davies, singing "Tired of Waiting for You", the Kinks latest hit record. Looking across the pub, he was surprised to see Irina already sitting at a table in front of the fireplace; a half-drunk pint sat in front of her, and a full pint waited for him. He sidestepped around a noisy darts match to reach the table, slipping off his coat and scarf before bending over and kissing her on the cheek.

'You are early, you are never early,' he said.

'I was just so excited to see you again,' she swooned in a fake girlish voice.

'If you say so,' he said, taking a long pull on his pint, 'We have a lot to discuss.'

'Not here,' she said.

'This is London, not Moscow. We don't bug everywhere.'

'Maybe,' she whispered, 'but those two at the next table are already listening to what we are saying.'

Nic glanced at the couple. They did not look like spies, but then again who did? Taking her cue, they chatted about anything but their mission. A Rolling Stones record came on the jukebox and Nic told her about the three scruffy musicians squatting in the basement next door before he moved to Moscow.

'Are they better than the Beatles?' she asked.

'That is a source of much debate,' he said, 'The Beatles are the clean cut, boy next door band, and the Stones are rough and ready. A music paper recently asked the question, "Would you let your sister go with a Rolling Stone?"'

Irina smiled, 'Then, I am definitely a Stones girl.'

'I suspected you might be. Tell me your first impressions of London.'

'I love it,' she said, 'there is more life and colour than Moscow, and all the streetlights work! There are neon signs everywhere, and those funny orange flashing balls by the side of the road are sweet.'

'Those are Belisha beacons, they mark either end of a Zebra crossing.'

'If you say so. And as for the shops, they are amazing, full of things you can actually buy! I will be doing a lot of shopping.'

'You must have a general allowance.'

'I do.'

Nic felt himself relaxing in her company. The first two pints had slipped down easily, he needed to pace himself.

'Come on, let's go back to my flat. We can grab some fish and chips on the way.'

'Don't you mean castle? I thought all Englishmen lived in castles.'

'Very funny,' Nic said as they left the pub.

As they walked down the Fulham Road, Irina asked, 'What's the fascination with fish and chips?'

'It's our national dish. You have borscht, Americans have burgers, we have fish and chips. Makes sense if you think about it. We are surrounded by water, the Americans have lots of cows, and you grow tons of beetroot!'

The fish and chip shop was on the corner of Edith Grove and Fulham Road. Despite the cool evening air, the door was wide open, and every window was coated in condensation. Inside, large pieces of battered fish sat behind a glass panel on the counter.

'Looks more fat than fish!' Irina commented.

'Exactly how it is supposed to look.'

He ordered two portions of fish, chips, and mushy peas.

'What are mushy peas?'

'The best part. You cannot have fish and chips without mushy peas.'

Irina was none the wiser. She looked on in horror as the server dropped a large piece of fish onto a piece of newspaper, added a portion of chips, scooped dripping with fat from the fryer, and ladled a portion of mushy peas over the top. Then everything was covered with a liberal sprinkling of salt and vinegar before being wrapped up in a neat parcel.

'The vinegar neutralises any harmful effects from the printers' ink,' Nic explained. Irina nodded dubiously.

By the time they reached the flat, fat was seeping through the newspaper making the ink run.

'I think I have lost my appetite,' she said

'Nonsense, wait until you have tried it,' Nic said as he peeled back the newspaper and transferred the steaming contents onto two mismatched plates. 'We should really eat it straight out of the newspaper.'

'No way,' she replied, looking aghast.

Nic took two bottles of Newcastle Brown Ale out of one the cupboards, grabbed a bottle opener, flipped off the caps, and poured the contents into two glasses.

'Oh, you have glasses as well. I am impressed,' she said, looking sceptically at the thick brown liquid sporting a dense white head sitting in the glass.

'I nicked them from the pub,' Nic said proudly.

'I suppose if it doesn't kill me, it will make me stronger,' she said, taking a tentative bite of fish with some peas.

She chewed before saying, 'It's not as bad as it looks.'

'See, I told you,' Nic said triumphantly.

She took a sip of the Brown Ale, 'Interesting,' was her only comment.

As they ate, Irina shared the latest information about Operation Vanquish. 'The plan for 1965 is to move from a series of independent missions to a more coordinated strategy.'

'How did you get the information? Yuri?'

She looked at him and smiled, 'Nice try, but I have my own sources.'

Nic suspected he knew who she was referring to but decided to wait until she was ready to share. 'What is your exact mission here in London?'

'I think you already know,' she said, smiling. 'I am to pass information through you to distract western intelligence from identifying the true goals of the Soviet Union—namely further the spread of Marxist-Leninism across the globe by revolutionary means. Step one is to seize power on behalf of the proletariat and establish a one-party socialist state. Step two calls for state control of the means of production, suppression of opposition, and promotion of collectivism paving the way for a communist society that is classless and stateless.'

'You sound like you are quoting directly from one of Stalin's speeches.'

'I am. Vanguard is our trojan horse strategy for destroying capitalism.'

Nic shook his head in disbelief, 'It is difficult to comprehend how it can all work.'

'I agree, but can we take the risk that it does work?'

'No, but is it realistic to think you, me, and Yuri can stop it?'

'Probably not, but I know I have to try.'

'You are right. I can't knowingly sit back and see millions…'

'Billions,' Irina interrupted.

'Yes, billions of lives potentially lost in a nuclear war.'

He stood up and got them two more beers.

'Do you trust Yuri?' he said as he refilled their glasses.

She smiled, 'Do I detect hint of jealousy?

'No,' Nic said too quickly, 'the two of you work together, so my fate is somewhat in his hands.'

Irina nodded, 'That's fair. Remember when I told you Yuri has some weaknesses?'

'Yes.'

'They are vodka and handsome young men.'

Nic was shocked, 'You mean…?'

'Yes,' Irina said interrupting. 'His vices are not unusual amongst the Soviet elite. Most of the time he keeps his drinking in check and his love life secret, but he occasionally slips.'

'He doesn't sound very reliable.'

'You are going to have to trust me. We all have our weaknesses. He is an exceptional agent and my closest friend. We will not be successful without his help.'

Nic did not feel reassured but had no choice but to trust her judgement. She, in turn, asked about Nic's CIA contact. As he described Ranger, her only comment was, 'I need to meet this man. He sounds gorgeous.'

Seeing Nic's expression, she laughed and said, 'Come on you, time for bed, I think.'

It didn't long to renew their acquaintance. Afterwards, as they lay entwined in bed, Nic stared at the ceiling. He really must get rid of that spider's web.

'What are you thinking about?' she asked.

'I need proof to convince C to bring the Americans on board.'

'I am working on it. I should have something for you soon. But even if you are allowed to talk to Ranger, there is no guarantee the Americans will do anything. Finland and Iran are not NATO members, and their priority seems to Vietnam.'

'Seb and I have talked about that. Current NATO plans are very weak, things like increased funding for opposition groups in countries where anti-Soviet sentiment is high, such as Poland, Czechoslovakia, and Hungary. A partial blockade on Soviet trade routes, and sanctions targeting the Soviet elite—no more Savile Row suits, Mercedes limousines, Spanish villas, Scotch whisky, or Swiss watches.'

Irina nodded and said drily, 'It is not exactly a proportionate response to two invasions and multiple revolutions. We must change the dynamic.'

'How?' he asked.

'The Kremlin is assuming both attacks will come as a surprise. The false flag attacks will muddy any immediate response. However, not all members of the Politburo are on board, some are advocating for a more measured approach. They are worried that launching two invasions simultaneously could trigger a massive over-reaction, perhaps even the use of tactical nuclear weapons, given the weakness of NATO's conventional forces. They are pushing for making small but significant incursions into both countries to test NATO's resolve before embarking upon a full-blown invasion.'

'Which side is winning the debate?'

'According to Yuri, Brezhnev is more moderate while Kosygin is more aggressive, and he is the one running Soviet foreign policy. It is shaping up as a power struggle which will define who becomes the dominant leader. We need to tip the balance in favour of either abandoning the missions all together or limiting them.'

'How do we do that?'

'If we can convince the Kremlin that NATO is aware of the planned attacks and will respond proportionately, it could force them to reconsider. I can make sure that message reaches the Politburo.'

'Using your "special contact",' Nic said sarcastically.

Irina rolled her eyes, 'Your job will be to sound the alarm about Vanquish. Hopefully, the Americans and NATO will wake up and mount some sort of defence.'

Nic smiled, 'You are not just a pretty face, are you?' he said as his hand moved up her thigh.

48

19th February 1965

A week passed before they met again, in a café on Northumberland Avenue near Trafalgar Square. Spring was coming, and London was waking from its winter slumber. The first tourists of the season could be seen gazing up at Nelson's Column. As usual, the Americans stood out, the men in their brightly coloured polyester trousers straining to contain burger-fed bellies, usually paired with plaid shirts and a buzz cut. The female of the species sported Lucille Ball-like hair and lots of make-up. Everything was described as either "quaint" or "cute".

'Americans amaze me,' Irina commented. 'They are loud, gregarious, and always complaining about something.'

Nic smiled, 'Yes, they are. In the run-up to D-Day, tens of thousands of American troops were stationed in Britain. The common complaint was that the GIs were overpaid, oversexed and over here!'

Irina laughed. They sat drinking their coffee, just enjoying each other's company. When they had finished, Irina stood up and walked towards Nelson's column. Nic grabbed her elbow and steered her towards the perimeter of the square.

'What are you doing?' Irina asked.

'We should avoid the pigeons,' Nic said.

'Why?'

'They scare me,' he said sheepishly.

'You're afraid of them?' Irina said incredulously.

'Yes. One day, I was walking to school, and a bird flew out of a hedgerow and smacked into the side of my hood. I ran home crying and never walked that way again. I thought I had grown out of it until I took a girl to see The Birds on a first date. When Suzanne Pleshette gets pecked to death by a murder of crows, I had to leave the cinema. Needless to say, there was no second date.'

Irina laughed, grabbed his arm and said, 'Don't worry. I will protect you.'

Having safely navigated the avian threat, they walked past the National Gallery and headed up St. Martins Lane. Nic saw a tall, thin man looking at them from the steps of St. Martin-in-the-Fields.

He nudged Irina, 'We have company. He doesn't look like a Boris or a Fred; he must be a Chuck.'

'What's a Chuck?'

'According to SirRod, all Americans are Chuck's. Russians are Boris's, French are Pierre's, and Brits are Fred's.'

Irina looked bemused.

'His build and haircut scream, Chuck,' Nic added, 'I will tell Ranger to have them back off.'

At Tottenham Court Road, they parted ways. Nic took the Northern Line to Waterloo, while Irina took the Central Line to Notting Hill Gate, where she could walk to her apartment in Westbourne Grove. Chuck followed Irina.

As she left Notting Hill station, a second man joined the surveillance. Chuck I nodded to Chuck II before turning down a side street. Irina assumed he would move ahead and station himself nearer to her flat.

She decided to have some fun. Lengthening her stride, she slowly increased the gap between herself and Chuck II. When she was momentarily out of his sight, she ducked into an alleyway, stepping into a doorway that shielded her from view.

Seconds later, Chuck II jogged past, trying to work out where she had gone.

She stepped out of the doorway and trotted down to the far end of the alley. Just as she was about to emerge onto the main road, Chuck I ran round the corner and almost knocked her over. A look of horror spread across his face. Irina did not hesitate; she spun and stomped hard on his left foot.

He grunted in pain and muttered, 'Commie Bitch.'

Irina laughed. As he bent down to grab his leg, Irina swung her knee, connecting with his jaw. He staggered back and fell against the wall. Irina looked down and said, 'If you want to talk to me, make an appointment at the Embassy.'

She exited the alley just as Chuck II appeared and saw his stricken colleague. 'Your friend has tripped over,' she said.

Nic had just stepped out of the shower when the doorbell rang. Grabbing a towel, he walked over to the window and peered down—it was Irina. What was she doing here?

He threw on his dressing gown and hurried down the stairs. When he opened the door, Irina looked him up and down and said, 'Am I interrupting something?'

'No. I have just got out of the shower.'

'I suppose she is hiding in the wardrobe or under the bed.'

'Very funny. Why are you here?'

'I just had to beat up Chuck. Are you going to let me in, it's freezing out here?'

He stepped aside to let her pass. 'What did he do to deserve that?'

Once they were settled in his living room, she told the story. When she finished, Nic said, 'Remind me never to get in your way.'

'Clever boy. What do you think the Americans will do?'

'I suspect the Chucks are in for a right bollocking.'

'I will have to report the incident to the London Resident.'

Nic nodded, 'That may cast suspicion on me. He might think I tipped off the Americans.'

'He will, but that is not a bad thing. It is exactly what they would expect you to do. It would be more suspicious if you didn't.'

Nic nodded, 'You are right. Can I tempt you to stay the night?'

'You could try, but some of us must work in the morning.'

Nic looked disappointed as Irina stood up to leave, 'You can tell your girlfriend she can come out now,' she said, closing the door behind her.

49

23ʳᵈ February 1965

Nic sat at a table in The Chanterelle, a French restaurant in South Kensington, sipping a gin and tonic. As usual, Irina was late. When she did arrive, he felt his heart rate increase as she crossed the room. She looked stunning in a dark green wool dress that clung to every curve.

He received a quick peck on the cheek before she sat down. A waiter appeared, and Irina ordered her usual—a straight-up, double Stoli. The waiter did a double take; ladies rarely ordered hard liquor and never doubles, but he said nothing.

As he departed, Irina whispered, 'I have the proof you need.' She handed Nic a piece of paper.

'What is it?'

'A copy of the draft order of battle for Finland and Iran.'

'How did you get that?'

'As I told you, I have my sources.'

Nic quickly read the document. All that was missing was the date the operations would commence,

'Wow,' was all he could say.

'There is more. Kosygin has approved a mission to assassinate an American civil rights leader.'

'Who? King?'

'Probably.'

'Do you know when? I must warn the Americans.'

'I don't think you should.'

'You mean let the assassination go ahead?' Nic asked incredulously.

'Yes.'

'I can't do that.'

'Think about it,' she said sternly, 'if you warn them and they thwart the attack, it will raise suspicions of a leak in Moscow. Guess who will be near the top of the list of suspects? Don't you think it is more important to disrupt the invasions? They carry significantly more risk for the world.'

He could not fault her logic, but her cold calculation was unnerving. She signalled to the waiter for another drink. Instinctively, the waiter looked to Nic for confirmation. Her glare made it clear she was not impressed. He got the message and headed to the bar.

'Now, let's enjoy our dinner.'

The waiter re-appeared with Irina's drink. They both ordered escargots and agreed to share the Chateaubriand. Nic tried to look knowledgeable as he pursued the wine list. He selected a bottle of the 1961 Châteauneuf-du-Pape solely because he had heard Seb eulogising about that vintage.

As they ate, Nic wrestled with whether to warn the Americans. Could he live with the guilt of failing to try and prevent the death of one man, even if it could save many more lives in the future? He had not considered these moral dilemmas when he signed on.

Irina interrupted his thoughts, 'I was watching this silly game on the television called cricket. What is the point of it? One man throws a ball at another man who tries to hit it with a piece of wood. Nearby stands another man also holding a piece of wood. Sometimes they swap places, and sometimes they don't. Occasionally, one of them walks off and is replaced by another man. Only the English could invent something like that.

Then, after hours and hours, the result is usually a draw. Only the English could invent something so pointless.'

Nic tried to explain the nuances of batting, bowling, innings, and wicket-taking but failed miserably. She did laugh when he described the different fielding positions, such as silly mid-on, gully, long leg, square leg, and long off.

'You English are crazy,' she said.

'We prefer to think of ourselves as mildly eccentric.'

'That proves my point,' she said.

As they finished dessert, Irina looked around and said, 'It looks like we are the last ones again.'

'Just like Moscow,' he said smiling, 'Can you come back to the flat?'

'I want to, but I can't. Remember, sex is merely a tool that I use only when necessary.'

'It feels very necessary to me,' he said glumly.

Outside the restaurant, he flagged down a cab for her. They kissed, and she said, 'Show C the order of battle. We need to wake the Americans up. Don't forget what I said about the assassination,' she said as the cab pulled away.

50

24th February 1965

Nic walked into Seb's office and said, 'I have the evidence to show C.'

'Tell me more,' Seb said. Nic handed him the piece of paper Irina had given him. Seb slipped on his reading glasses. After reading the document, he said, 'Bloody hell. This should do the trick.'

Ten minutes later, they were in C's office. As he read, the colour drained from his face, 'If this is genuine, we have a big problem.'

'Sashkaya says that this is just the next phase of an operation that has been going on for four years,' Nic added.

C stared intently at Nic, 'Do you believe her? It could be an elaborate hoax designed to provoke us.'

'We will probably know very soon, Sir. She also told me that Kosygin has approved a mission to assassinate an American civil rights leader.'

'Recent reconnaissance reports show Soviet troops amassing near the Finnish and Iranian borders,' added Seb. 'The Soviets say they are conducting training exercises, but that could be a lie. I don't think we can ignore it; we must alert the Americans.'

C leaned back in his chair, 'You must admire their audacity. If this is genuine, they have completely fooled us. I agree; it is time to brief the Americans. I will talk to Admiral Raborn, the new head of the CIA. He has only been on the job for a month, so this will be an unpleasant welcome for him.'

'Sir, we were also thinking that Slater could talk to their MI6 liaison officer here in London,' Seb suggested.

'Yes, yes. Good idea, but only tell him about the assassination. I will handle the rest.'

Once he was back in his office, Nic picked up the phone and spoke to the switchboard. 'Get me Moses Ranger at the American Embassy, please?'

'Yes, Mr Slater, I will connect you.'

He heard a series of clicks as the number was dialled. After three rings, a high-pitched sing-song voice answered and said, 'This is the Embassy of the United States of America. How may I assist you this fine day?'

'I have Nic Slater from the UK Foreign Office for Mr Moses Ranger.'

'Let me see if Mr Ranger is available.'

The line went silent for a few seconds before a distinctive baritone bellowed, 'Slater, how the hell are you?'

Nic heard two clicks as the switchboard operators disconnected and the tape started recording.

'Not bad, how are you?'

'Just peachy, my friend. Are you in London?'

'You know I am.'

'You would not be calling about an unprovoked attack on one of my men yesterday by chance?'

'It certainly wasn't unprovoked. Your two clowns nearly destroyed a year's worth of work,'

'If you had briefed us properly, it would not have happened.'

'BS, as you Americans say, your guys screwed up.'

There was a loud sigh, 'Yeah, they screwed up. I have just ripped them a new one.'

'What was their story?' Nic asked.

'They lost contact. As they tried to re-establish contact, one of them ran smack into her as he turned a corner. He says she got the jump on him.'

'Sounds like he got what he deserved. Can you have your guys back off? I am close to getting to her to share some dynamite intelligence.'

'Like what?'

'Let's just say it will make Washington rethink its whole strategy towards the Soviet Union.'

'Are you serious?'

'Deadly,' Nic replied.

'Okay. But you must keep me in the loop if I am going to keep Langley off your back.'

'Deal! Fancy a pint tonight?'

'Roger that, when and where?' Ranger responded.

'There is a nice little boozer, just south of Tower Bridge, called the Anchor Tap. Walk over the bridge, turn left onto Shad Thames and then immediately right onto Horselydown Lane. Does seven thirty work for you?'

'Sure does, buddy.'

Ranger put down the receiver and smiled. He had hoped the surveillance on Sashkaya would trigger a response. Moscow station had tracked Slater's movements. At first, it seemed he may have formed a connection with a Brazilian SNI agent. However, more recent reports described a series of meetings with a known KGB agent. His sudden move back to London, almost immediately followed by that agent, confirmed a connection. But who had recruited who?

Ranger liked Slater; they had bonded over beer and burgers in Langley. Nic was intelligent and curious and exhibited the creativity essential for an effective field agent. Ranger didn't think he had been turned but was not completely discounting it.

Langley was frustrated that London had not shared any details of the operation. Ranger had been ordered to find out what was happening, hence the surveillance that Sashkaya had blown up.

He spent the afternoon reviewing Slater's CIA file. He was relatively inexperienced but had performed well in Moscow. MI6 Moscow Station chief, Sir Roderick Barker, had told his CIA opposite number that Slater showed great promise. Ranger knew much less about Sashkaya, though last night's debacle showed she was no amateur.

Darkness was falling as Ranger walked across Tower Bridge. The rush hour crowds had abated, and lights from barges navigating along the river illuminated the inky black water.

As he reached the south bank, Ranger felt like he was travelling back to the time of Charles Dickens. Wharves and warehouses lined the riverbank. The streets were narrow, cobbled and dimly lit.

Bermondsey was one of the poorest areas of London, an odd juxtaposition of commerce and community. The gulf in affluence between the City, the financial hub of the empire and the docks was stark despite only being separated by the river.

He took the steps down from the bridge onto Shad Thames. Warehouses lined both sides of the street with wrought iron bridges connecting them. Most had been abandoned in recent years as London's docks had moved steadily east to accommodate larger container ships.

The Anchor Tap stood a few yards down Horselydown Lane. Ranger had to duck as he entered. Most of London had been designed for people no taller than 5'10". The head of every patron turned; not many 6' 4", 250-pound black men were seen in Bermondsey.

The clientele reflected the local economy. Dockworkers with arms like Popeye mingled with City office boys who made the short journey across the river to toil in the offices of the banks, insurance companies, and stockbrokers in the City of London.

Ranger saw Nic sitting in one of the small side rooms off the main bar with two pints in front of him. Ducking again, he joined Nic at his table.

'Good to see you, bro,' he said.

Nic nodded, 'Sorry I didn't contact you sooner.'

'No, you're not,' Ranger said, smiling. 'Why is this place called the Anchor Tap?'

'It serves as the taproom for the brewery next door. You can sample their wares fresh from the barrel.'

'Well, we better get started,' he said, downing most of his pint in one gulp. 'Your food may be crap, but your ale is pretty darn good.'

Nic smirked, 'No one in England has said "ale" since Robin Hood was a lad!'

Ranger pulled a packet of Marlboros out of his pocket and lit up. After taking a deep drag, he downed the rest of his pint and said, 'Are you going to tell me what the hell is going on?'

'Can't two friends get together for a drink?' Nic teased.

'Cut the crap, Slater.'

'Your boys got a little too close for comfort. They have spooked her.'

'I know, but did she really have to beat one of them up?'

'He was stupid,' Nic responded. 'He got too close.'

Ranger nodded. In her position, he would have done the same. He slid another Marlboro from the packet and lit it.

'Looks like you need a refill,' Nic said, nodding at Ranger's empty glass.

He returned with two fresh pints and two bags of crisps. 'I have been working for almost a year to recruit Sashkaya,' he explained.

'Why is she willing to work for you?'

'She is disillusioned with the failure of the Soviet system to benefit anyone but the political elites. Far from creating a worker-led nation, she thinks the Soviet Union is rapidly becoming a failed totalitarian state.'

'Tell me something I don't know,' Ranger said sarcastically.

'I will,' Nic said. 'The economy may be a mess, but we are seriously underestimating their military capabilities.'

'Are you sure? Every report says their military is poorly trained and stuck with World War II era equipment. As for their nuclear arsenal, it is no match for ours.'

'According to Sashkaya, that's not true. They have been investing heavily in both their conventional and nuclear forces. At the same time, they have been conducting a series of clandestine operations aimed at undermining NATO.'

'Do you believe her? I think you are being played, my friend. It's classic disinformation.'

'Don't you think I haven't considered that?'

Ranger sighed, 'Nic, you are a smart guy, but you don't have much experience. What evidence do you have?'

C had insisted he not share the Kosygin memo yet. That only left him with the information about the assassination attempt, which Irina had told him not to share. He wished she had never told him. She must have known it would put him in a difficult position. Maybe KGB agents had no moral compass?

After much soul-searching, he decided to ignore her advice. There was little chance the Soviets would ever find out he had warned the Americans.

'The Soviets are going to try and assassinate a prominent civil rights leader sometime in the next two weeks,' he said to Ranger.

'Shit. Who, when, and where?

'I don't know.'

'Not exactly actionable intel, is it? We pick up threats against civil rights leaders all the time. It is usually some drunken redneck. Why is this any more credible?'

'It has been sanctioned by Kosygin.'

Ranger cursed; Nic could tell he was disturbed by the news. It must be a sensitive topic for a black American working for the FBI.

'King is the obvious target. He just won the Nobel Peace Prize and is by far the most visible civil rights leader.'

'I don't know much about the civil rights movement. Wasn't a law passed last year banning discrimination?' Nic asked.

Ranger laughed, 'It will take more than one law to erase generations of racial prejudice. Don't get me wrong, it is a positive step, but there is a long way to go. I passionately want to see an end to racial prejudice. My Pops served in the Navy during World War II. He experienced the full effect of racial segregation growing up in Alabama but was still a fierce American patriot. In the Navy, he faced some hostility from white seamen, but he earned their respect over time. He believes change is possible through integration rather than violence and passed those beliefs on to me.'

'He sounds like a good man.'

'The best,' Ranger replied, 'Now tell me about your mole in the KGB. What is she like?

'Intelligent, driven, passionate, and very beautiful.'

Ranger smirked, 'Lucky you!'

'She is highly thought of within the KGB. We believe she has the ear of the Politburo Secretary, Constantin Chernenko.'

Ranger whistled, 'Quite the package then!'

'Yes. But you need to get your guys to back off. I cannot tell you everything yet, but she could be our most important source since the war. The assassination attempt is only a minor part of the Soviet plan. The last thing we need is for her to get spooked and return to Moscow.'

'You are worrying me. What are you implying?'

'Just the biggest intelligence failure since the Trojans allowed the Greeks to roll a horse into Troy. You need to be patient and trust me. I have no intention of cutting you out, but we cannot scare her off.'

Ranger knew Nic was not telling him everything, but the CIA had no equivalent source. 'We don't have much choice, do we? Want another pint?'

'Of course,' Nic replied, finally relaxing a little.

When Ranger returned with two fresh pints, their conversation moved onto other topics. It was almost closing time when they got up to leave. Once outside, Ranger scanned the street for a taxi.

'You won't find a cab here at this time of night,' Nic said. 'I will walk you to London Bridge; you will find one there.'

They turned onto Tooley Street, passing St. Olave's Grammar School. The warehouses along the Thames cast eerie shadows across the street.

'Have you boned her yet?' Ranger asked.

'If I have, it was purely in Her Majesty's service.'

'Bullshit!' Ranger said, laughing.

Before Nic could reply, a cab turned onto the street. Ranger stepped into the road and tried to flag it down. Nic was not sure the driver was going to stop, so he raised his own arm. The taxi pulled to a stop, and Nic opened the door.

'Thanks, buddy,' said Ranger. 'It is the same the world over. Maybe one-day people will look at a black man and not be intimidated.'

51

Nic woke drenched in sweat. Every muscle was tense, and he had tears in his eyes. A hand was resting on his shoulder. He relaxed a little, turned and saw Irina lying next to him.

'Are you alright?' she whispered.

'Sorry, just a bad dream.'

'Tell me about it.'

He laid his head in her lap and said, 'I have been having the same dream a lot since my encounter with Philby. I am in a concrete-walled, windowless room lit by a single, bare lightbulb. I am naked. My arms and legs are bound, and every muscle in my body aches. A small, balding man is standing before me; he has pure hatred in his eyes. His shirt is soaked with sweat and spattered with my blood. I am crying as I tell him that you are a traitor. He laughs, telling me I am pathetic and weak. Then he delights in describing what his colleagues are doing to you in the room next door. I can hear your cries— that's when I wake up.'

Irina stroked his head, 'It is just a dream. Our job is to make sure it does not become a reality. We know the risks, but we are doing the right thing.'

Nic nodded, 'Will it ever be normal?'

'What do you mean?'

'This? Us?

Irina shook her head, 'Of course not. This is our life. We must make the best of it.'

She wrapped her arms and legs around him and hugged him tight. He marvelled at her inner strength and surrendered to the security her presence offered.

When he woke, Irina had gone. He lay on the bed staring at the spider's web slowly creeping across the ceiling. His fear had subsided, sharing with Irina had been cathartic.

An hour later, he knocked on Seb's office door. A raspy voice bellowed, 'Come.'

Seb lay on his office sofa, looking the worse for wear. His jacket lay draped over one of the chairs, his bow tie was askew, and his wispy hair pointed in multiple directions.

'Did you sleep here last night?'

Seb nodded.

'Looks like Mr Jameson kept you company,' Nic said, nodding towards the empty bottle on the coffee table.

'Yes. He is a wonderful night-time companion, but he is not so bright in the morning,' Seb said ruefully. 'Take a seat, dear boy and tell me what you need from Uncle Seb.'

Nic waved a piece of paper he had just ripped from the teleprinter. 'Irina was right,' he exclaimed.

'What do you mean?'

'Malcolm X was assassinated yesterday in New York.'

'Who is Malcolm X?'

'A civil rights activist. Until about a year ago, he was one of the leaders of a group called the Nation of Islam, a black nationalist organisation. However, he fell out of favour and has been in open conflict with them ever since. The FBI thinks they may have killed him. But we know better, don't we?'

Seb groaned, 'You know what this means?'

'I do. Suppose Irina was telling the truth about the assassination. In that case, there is a good chance she is telling the truth about the invasions.'

'Yes, we could be days away from World War III. I need to make a few calls. Let's catch up later.'

Nic returned to his office. He felt guilty. He had betrayed Irina's trust, but it had been for nought; he had not saved a life. He may even have put her life in danger.

His phone rang, lifting the receiver, he said, 'Slater here,'

'Damn,' said a subdued-sounding Ranger.

'I'm sorry,' Nic replied.

'Yeah, I need something sweet to take away the sour taste.'

Ranger suggested they meet him at the back entrance to Fortnum & Mason's in one hour.

'Okay,' Nic said, putting down the phone.

He walked over Waterloo Bridge, through Parliament Square and St. James Park, towards Piccadilly. Ranger was standing by the rear entrance of Fortnum's, smoking a Marlboro. When he spotted Nic, he dropped the half-smoked cigarette, grinding it into the pavement with the leather sole of his brightly polished black Oxfords. He looked angry.

They walked in silence along the south side of Jermyn Street. Ranger spoke first, 'Shame your commie bitch could not be more precise with her information.'

Nic was startled, 'Hey, that is a bit unfair. If it wasn't for Irina, you would never have known anything,' he retorted.

Ranger grunted, and they walked on. When he spoke again, he was calmer: 'You are right. I am just angry we could not prevent it from happening. We made the wrong bet, assuming King was the target.'

'What happened?' Nic asked.

'Malcolm X was about to give a speech in New York when a man with a sawn-off shotgun walked up and shot him. Two other assassins with semi-automatic pistols then opened fire. He was shot twenty-one times. The FBI thinks they were members of the Nation of Islam. There are no signs of any direct Soviet connection yet, though we know Moscow was channelling funds to the group.'

Nic nodded, 'Do you believe she is genuine now?

'It looks that way.

'She says there are more operations in the works.'

'I need to meet her,' Ranger said, 'everyone at the agency is going crazy, and the FBI is giving us hell for not having better intelligence. We need her help.'

'I will see what I can do. Irina would be taking a big risk meeting with both of us.'

'She is already taking a big risk!'

Without waiting for Nic to reply, Ranger flagged down a cab and was gone.

For the next month, nothing much happened. Irina and Nic met several times, but she had no new information to share on Vanquish. The world's focus was on escalating tensions in Vietnam, the American military occupation of the Dominican Republic, and Soviet claims of having discovered an extra-terrestrial civilisation based upon radio signals emanating from a distant quasar.

52

Irina knew how to make an entrance. She walked into the pub, and every man turned to look. She had been shopping again. She wore a tight white sweater, a red miniskirt, and a pair of black high-heeled boots. It was an eye-catching ensemble. She strode confidently across the room with a look that said, 'Look all you like boys, but don't mess with me.'

Nic felt an irrational surge of pride. She was here to meet him. As she sat down, her skirt almost disappeared. He was left gazing at her thighs, sheathed in black tights.

'Eyes up!' she commanded, 'I clearly don't need to ask if you like my new outfit.'

'You look stunning, though it's not exactly a discreet look. Everyone in the pub will remember you.'

'Didn't they teach you at spy school that the best disguise is to hide in plain sight?'

'I don't think you are hiding!'

She smiled and kissed him on the cheek. 'Cheer up. Every man in this pub is jealous of you right now.'

'Modest, aren't we.'

'Lucky, aren't you!'

He admitted defeat.

'You were right about the assassination.'

'Didn't you believe me?'

'It doesn't matter what I thought, I believe you now. Have you seen the news from Alabama? The police attacked a civil rights march in Selma. It was all captured by the television cameras. Was that your lot as well?'

'I'm not sure, but it is consistent with fomenting racial unrest. The Kremlin analysts believe America is on the road to a race war. Combined with their growing involvement in Vietnam, it further reduces their focus on Europe. The hardliners are pushing to launch the invasions as soon as possible.'

'Why bother with Finland and Iran? Why not just roll through West Germany?'

'The Kremlin thinks that an invasion of West Germany is the one thing that will get America's attention. The US invested billions in rebuilding Germany through the Marshall Plan, saved West Berlin with the airlift in 1948, and led the move to create the Federal Republic by merging the American, British, and French sectors. They won't stand by and let all that effort go to waste. Finland and Iran are seen as soft targets and are not NATO members. The Kremlin is betting NATO will not go to war. If that calculation proves correct, the next moves will be against Greece and Turkey before tackling West Germany.'

Nic nodded, 'I see the logic. When will the attacks be launched?'

'Planning is complete. All that's needed now is for Kosygin to give the green light. The Red Army has over forty divisions along our western and southern borders. They don't expect to meet much resistance.'

It sounded a lot like Hitler's strategy in the late 1930s. Then, it was Austria, Czechoslovakia, and Poland. When the Allies failed to respond with anything more than words of appeasement to the invasion of Czechoslovakia, Hitler felt emboldened to go after Poland. That turned out to be one step too far. Would history repeat itself?

'The target date is the sixth of June.'

'No symbolism there! That is the twenty-first anniversary of D-Day.'

'I know,' she replied.

'I must leave and talk to Seb.'

'Go ahead, I'm sure one of these handsome young men will keep me company.'

Nic frowned.

'Don't you trust me?' she said, smiling.

'Not dressed like that.'

An hour later, Nic was sitting with Ranger in Seb's office. He shared what Irina had told him. Ranger was incredulous, 'They seriously think we will let them roll into Finland and Iran?'

'Can you stop them?' Nic asked.

Before Ranger could reply, Seb said, 'It's doubtful. NATO forces are only at about sixty per cent of the target. Over 200,000 American troops have been withdrawn in the last two years. The Russians know that NATO without the Americans is nothing.'

Ranger sighed, 'You may be right. Johnson seems intent on fighting both the Soviets and Chinese in Vietnam. We need that meeting with Sashkaya as soon as possible. I need something pretty convincing to get Washington to pay attention.'

'I will set it up when I meet her tomorrow,' Nic said.

53

13th April 1965

Parks and pubs—did spies ever meet anywhere else? Nic sat on a bench by the entrance to Brompton Park, waiting for Irina. He wasn't sure how she would react when asked to meet with Ranger. He was right; she was already in danger, but if anyone found out she had met with a CIA agent, it would be disastrous.

He saw Irina walking towards him. Despite the coolness of the day, she was wearing the same outfit that had made such an impact in the pub. He stood, and they kissed.

'How did Seb react?' she asked.

'Initially, shock. Ranger was there as well; he was angry. The CIA had no idea. If it ever became public, it would be politically devastating. He wants to meet you as soon as possible. He is in "trust but verify" mode. He doesn't want to set Washington ablaze unless he is certain.'

'It better happen soon.'

'How about this weekend?' Nic asked.

'Okay. Where?'

'Let's talk about it in the pub,' Nic said.

'You just want to show me off again, right?'

'Who wouldn't?'

They walked through the park to the Harewood Arms, another of Fulham's traditional pubs. Irina's entrance elicited the same reaction as before. Every man stared while every wife, girlfriend, or mistress frowned. Nic went to the bar while Irina found a table.

As he ordered their drinks, a man wearing a tight-fitting grey suit, pink shirt, and orange tie made a beeline for Irina. Nic watched, intrigued to see what happened. The man leaned forward and whispered something in Irina's ear. She smiled and whispered something back. A look of shocked surprise appeared on the man's face, and he quickly turned around and walked away, blushing.

The barmen placed Nic's pint and Irina's double Stoli on the bar, 'Quite the bird you've got there, mate,' he said admiringly.

'Tell me about it,' Nic replied, handing over a few shillings. He walked over to the table and set the glasses on beer mats adorned with the Guinness toucan.

'What did Casanova have to say?'

'He said I was wasting my time with a nonce like you. Apparently, he has a lot more to offer.'

'What did you say to scare him off so quickly?'

'I told him that under my skirt was a huge cock and balls, and he seemed to lose interest.'

'I am not sure they would fit under that skirt!'

She laughed, 'Tell me about this meeting.'

'Seb suggests we meet at his country estate. It is in the middle of nowhere, so we should be able to avoid detection. We can stay at the pub in the village nearby.'

'Would this be what you English call a dirty weekend?' she said mischievously.

'I hope so,' he replied. 'I suggest we leave London separately. I will borrow my sister's car; you can take the train. I will pick you up at a station out in the country near Seb's estate. On Saturday morning, we will give the impression we are going for a day's walk in the countryside. A footpath from the village follows the perimeter of the estate. It will be quiet this time of year, so any tail will be easy to spot. Seb will meet us at an agreed-upon spot and take us to the house.'

Irina looked thoughtful, 'That should work. I will tell the Embassy we are going away for the weekend—after all, I am supposed to seduce you as part of the job.'

'Good. Pack your pyjamas,' Nic said, finishing his pint.

'Will I need them?' she said with a wink.

'How about we get some practice in back at my flat?' he said hopefully.

'I like that idea,' she said, standing up to leave. As she crossed the room, the throng of drinkers around the bar parted like the Red Sea. Nic followed in her wake. As he edged through the crowd, he heard a whispered, 'Nice one, son,' and, 'Give her one for me.'

They walked arm in arm towards Fulham Broadway. Nic worried she might cause an accident as distracted drivers whistled and blew their horns as they drove past. She pretended to be oblivious to the attention she was attracting. They walked in silence, enjoying a rare moment of calm in each other's company.

It was just past closing time when they walked past Stamford Bridge, the home of Chelsea Football Club. A group of drunken men rolled out of a nearby pub, almost knocking Irina over.

'Hey darling, give us a kiss,' one of them said in a slurred voice.

'I can give you more than a kiss,' said another. 'Come home with me and find out what a real man can do for you.'

Nic bristled, but Irina said, 'Leave this to me.'

She turned and stepped towards one of the men. Before he knew what had happened, she had raised her right knee and slammed it into his groin. He doubled over in pain. One of his mates shouted, 'Hey, bitch, you can't...'

He never finished the sentence. Irina wheeled around and struck him in the throat with her outstretched fingers. He staggered backwards, gasping for breath. Shock registered on the faces of the others. They backed away, leaving their stricken friends howling in pain.

Irina looked down at her victims, 'If I ever see you again, I will rip your balls off.'

She grabbed Nic's hand and calmly said, 'Come on. I'm ready for bed now.'

Nic was exhausted. Irina looked at him, 'Are you shocked?'

'A bit, but I am not complaining. Where did that come from?'

She smiled ruefully, 'It is always there under the surface. Our training teaches us to suppress anger, but sometimes, you must let it go, or you will explode. My trigger is men who demean women. First, it was the man in the pub, then those drunks. They think they can abuse women without consequences. Usually, they are right. I was fourteen when one of my teachers started defiling me. The instructors at the KGB training school were worse; abusing the female students was seen as a perk of the job. I vowed I would learn to stand up for myself. Now, I fight back whenever possible, although it's not advisable to knee a member of the Politburo in the groin!'

Nic was impressed and a little intimidated. He subconsciously understood that women were subject to unequal treatment. Even at home, when his father returned from work, he would sit in his armchair being waited on by his mother.

Slippers, an ashtray, and a glass of beer would be laid out ready. She would cook and serve dinner, wash the dishes, and iron while he read the paper and watched television.

Mags had shared stories of the casual sexism she experienced at university and in chambers. Senior partners considered young women to be fair game for innuendo, groping and more. Never mind that she was paid considerably less than her male colleagues. He had accepted it as usual—but maybe not for much longer if his sister and Irina had anything to do with it.

She lay back down and stared at the ceiling, 'Are you ever going to get rid of those cobwebs?'

They slept late, and after showering together, she returned to her apartment. Nic watched from his bedroom window as she descended the steps to the pavement in her heels. When she stuck out her arm to hail a cab, two converged from opposite directions, eager to secure the fare. She looked up as she opened the cab door; that smile was there.

54

Plans were finalised for the weekend. Nic made a reservation at the pub for Friday and Saturday nights and called Mags to arrange to borrow her car for the weekend. She had finally replaced the ageing Sadie with a brand-new Mini Cooper S, which she named Pet, after her favourite singer, Petula Clark.

Seb marked up an Ordnance Survey map of the area for Nic, highlighting the pub, footpath, and the spot where he would meet them. Despite having been to the estate before, Nic had little appreciation for its size. The main house was a good four inches on the map from the meeting point, four miles in the real world.

'Is all that land yours?'

'Of course, dear chap. We even own the village.'

'You must be worth millions,' Nic said.

'Not really. The estate costs a bloody fortune to maintain and is not exactly a liquid asset. You could say we are asset-rich and cash-poor. Daddy had to sell a couple of Gainsborough paintings last year to pay for a new roof. Half the rooms are mothballed to cut down on heating costs, and the staff have been reduced from twelve when I was a nipper to just a cook, butler, and gardener today.'

'My heart bleeds for you,' Nic replied. 'I will have a whip round for you in the working men's club next time I go home.'

Seb smiled, 'I know it is wrong to plead poverty, but I will probably have to sell the estate when I inherit to pay death duties. It is happening all over the country.'

Nic nodded but was unable to summon up much sympathy. The house in Eaton Square, the fishing lodge in Scotland, and the villa in Capri would ensure Seb was not homeless.

'Will your family be home?' Nic asked.

'No, the 'rents and my two sisters are in Capri until the end of the month. We will have the place to ourselves.'

'Except for the cook, gardener, and butler, of course,' Nic said, smirking.

55

23rd April 1965 – Oxfordshire

Nic took the train from Waterloo to Esher on Thursday afternoon to pick up Pet. Mags and family were out, but she left the keys on top of the rear tyre. Nic was excited to try out her new car; the Mini Cooper had just won the Monte Carlo Rally.

On the drive back into London, he tried to re-familiarise himself with the art of driving. It took a few attempts to master the clutch; he stalled twice and crunched a few gear changes. By the time he reached the Hammersmith Roundabout, he felt more confident. Hopefully, he would not embarrass himself too much when Irina was in the car. Fortunately, he found a parking space on a side street just off Edith Grove.

Friday morning was spent at Century House reading the latest intelligence briefings on Soviet military activity. There were further signs of troop build-up north of St. Petersburg and in Azerbaijan. Time was running short if NATO was going to mount any meaningful response.

Before leaving, he ate a sandwich at his desk. He then took a convoluted route back to Pet, using the tube, bus, and taxi; no one appeared to be following him.

The evening rush began to build as he zigzagged his way north to the A40. He did not expect to pick up a tail but wanted to be clean as he headed out of London to Oxford. Irina was taking a train from Marylebone to Princes Risborough, a small town about twenty miles from Oxford, where he would pick her up.

The traffic lightened considerably as he cleared the outskirts of London, heading towards High Wycombe. He decided to see how fast Pet could go before the new 70mph speed limit went into effect. The small but mighty 1275cc engine smoothly accelerated to 110mph. It felt exhilarating until one of the front wheels hit a pothole, and the car slewed left. Nic managed to keep the car on the road but decided 60mph was fast enough.

Irina was pleased to find no Chuck following her as she left the Soviet Embassy for Marylebone. She reclaimed the suitcase she had deposited at the left luggage office the night before and bought a return ticket to Oxford. She was only going as far as Princes Risborough, but it always made sense to lay a false trail if possible. She boarded the six-coach train just before it departed.

The train was packed with workers heading home to start the weekend early. What had Nic told her? Friday was POETS Day (Push Off Early Tomorrow's Saturday). The English had such quaint expressions.

For the first part of the journey, the railway ran parallel to the Underground. Irina could see the faces of the passengers squeezed onto a Central Line train as they passed Ruislip—all except those in the smoking carriages, who were shrouded by a dense smog.

As the suburbs gave way to gently rolling countryside, she sat back and thought about the weekend ahead. She could be walking into a trap. She trusted Nic, but would he know if Seb or Ranger were using him as bait?

Despite her doubts, she was excited about spending two nights with Nic, meeting the infamous Viscount Weston, and having her first encounter with the CIA.

Nic shaded his eyes from the setting sun as he drove west. Just past High Wycombe, he spotted a signpost for Princes Risborough and turned onto the A4010. Twenty minutes later, he pulled up outside the station.

A train had just arrived. Commuters poured out of the station. All the men wore dark suits, white shirts, and ties topped by a trilby or Homburg. Bankers or lawyers, Nic thought, heading home to dutiful wives ready to meet their every need after a tiring week at the office. The few women amongst the throng were younger, perhaps the unmarried daughters of the bankers and lawyers, returning from their jobs as shop assistants or secretaries in the big city.

Ten minutes later, the next train pulled into the station. Nic got out of the car and walked towards the ticket barrier. He looked up and down the platform, confident Irina would stand out from the crowd. Then he saw her. For once, she was dressed conservatively in a dark green sweater, tweed skirt, sensible shoes, and understated make-up.

Seeing Nic's expression, she said, 'I have done my research. The country set do not wear miniskirts!'

Twenty minutes later, they pulled up outside The Leathern Bottle, a 300-year-old pub in the village of Lewknor, not far from Sangster Hall. Irina still drew admiring looks from the ruddy-faced farmers standing at the bar despite her subdued dress. Their bedroom was tucked under the eaves at the back of the pub. The furnishings would not have looked out of place in the 16th century.

They enjoyed a hearty steak and kidney pudding, which was washed down with a couple of pints for dinner and retired early.

However, any energetic activity was curtailed by the creaky bed, floors, and walls.

56

24ᵗʰ April 1965

Nic woke with a start; another dream interrupted. He tried to get his eyes to focus. Irina was sitting at the dressing table applying her make-up. She turned and said, 'Good morning, sleepy head. About time you moved yourself. It's past eight.'

Nic rolled over, swung his legs over the side of the bed and stood up, not altogether steadily.

'What a fine sight first thing in the morning,' she said, staring at his naked body. Nic stumbled into the bathroom.

When he reappeared, Irina stood up and twirled, saying, 'Will this do for Viscount Weston?'

She had been shopping again and looked like an advertisement from Country Life. A high-necked brown wool sweater was paired with a mid-length green checked skirt, which gave way to a pair of knee-high, low-heeled brown leather boots with shiny brass buckles. A brand-new Barbour jacket hung on the back of the door. Nic thought that KGB agents must have very generous expense budgets.

'You look like the Queen ready for a hike around Sandringham. The only thing missing is the corgis.'

'Hurry up and get dressed,' she ordered, 'I need breakfast.'

Nic donned the outfit he had purchased at an astronomical cost for a shooting weekend at Seb's estate the previous year. At least today's wearing would halve his average cost per use.

Irina wolfed down her first full English breakfast, although she did baulk at eating the black pudding. It was just after 09:00 when they set off. Nic consulted the map; the trail started just across the road from the pub. The previous day's sunshine had been replaced by more typical English weather. Heavy, grey clouds hung low in the sky, and a fine drizzle soon coated them both in a sheen of moisture. Irina had complemented her ensemble with a floppy, green waterproof hat. Nic wore one of his father's flat caps.

The trail was wet underfoot, and their boots soon squelched through the mud. High hedgerows lined both sides of the path, obscuring any view of the surrounding countryside. Prickly hawthorn twigs occasionally snagged their sleeves.

'What is the point of walking on a path where you cannot see anything?' Irina asked.

'Hedgerows are a defining feature of the English countryside,' Nic said indignantly.

'In Russia, we find fences work just as well,' Irina said, smiling. 'They have the added benefit that you can see through them!'

'Yet another triumph of the Soviet collective,' Nic replied sarcastically. They walked on in companionable silence. Periodically, Nic consulted the map. After an hour, he said, 'We should be approaching the meeting point.'

'Good, because I am cold and wet,' Irina declared.

'Welcome to England!'

Just then, the peace of the countryside was shattered by the deep roar of an engine in a nearby field. Nic peered over a farm gate set into the hedge. A battered old, mud-splattered Land Rover was bouncing towards them across a muddy field. A single windscreen wiper valiantly battled the drizzle. Just short of the gate, the vehicle skidded to a stop. Nic and Irina jumped backwards to avoid a wave of flying mud.

The driver's door flew open, and Seb lumbered out, followed by two exuberant golden retrievers. Seb looked the epitome of a country squire. Green wellies, brown corduroy trousers worn to a shine at the knees, and an ancient shooting jacket topped by a deerstalker. Irina stifled a laugh as he plodded through the mud towards the gate.

'Settle down, boys,' he said to the dogs as they tried to climb the gate. 'Don't worry about Disraeli and Gladstone; they are harmless.'

He opened the gate and enveloped Nic in a bear hug before stepping back and looking at Irina, 'You must be the notorious femme-fatale, Irina Sashkaya.'

'And you must be the entitled and patrician Viscount Weston,' she retorted.

'Touché,' he replied. Irina offered her hand, but Seb also grabbed her in a bear hug. Nic froze, fully aware of what Irina could do in such a situation. Thankfully, Seb was able to step back unmolested.

'What a fine-looking filly,' he bellowed to Nic.

Nic flinched again but saw Irina was smiling. 'Nic has told me a lot about you,' she said, 'and if first impressions are anything to go by, it is all true.'

'I like her,' Seb said to Nic. They walked over to the Land Rover, and the two dogs leapt into the back seat. Seb opened the passenger door for Irina. 'Slater, you are in the back with the dogs.'

Seb gunned the engine, and they set off across the field. A wet dog smell filled the air. The ride was unnecessarily bumpy as Seb insisted on driving as fast as possible.

Irina wiped the condensation off the windows and peered out. She let out an involuntary gasp, 'Is that your house?'

'Not yet, but it will be one day,' replied Seb.

'It looks like a palace,' Irina exclaimed.

'Not quite, although George V did stay for one night in 1913.'

'It's huge,' she said.

'Not really, we only have forty-seven rooms. The Marlborough's have one hundred and eighty-seven at Blenheim.'

'How old is it?'

'The oldest part is 15th century. My lot has been here since the early 1700s. One of my ancestors was a close aide to John Churchill, the 1st Duke of Marlborough, during the War of the Spanish Succession. He got the estate and a baronetcy for services rendered.'

'Sounds very Tsarist,' Irina commented.

Seb drove through the arch to the side of the main house and brought the Land Rover to a halt in the courtyard Nic had parked in on his previous visit. There were a couple of battered old cars next to Seb's Bentley in the barn, and a horse had its head out of one of the stable doors, no doubt wondering what all the commotion was about.

As Nic opened the rear door, he was trampled as the dogs leapt over him. Seb opened the door for Irina, who stepped out and walked over to pat the horse's muzzle.

'Do you ride?' Seb asked.

'Only English spies,' she replied. Seb roared with laughter. 'Feisty, isn't she?'

'You don't know the half of it,' said Nic

A large wooden door set into the side of the main house was opened and Hayes appeared.

'Slater, you remember Hayes, don't you?'

'Welcome back, Sir,' Hayes said.

'Thank you,' said Nic before remembering Hayes' admonishment not to keep saying thank you on his previous visit

Turning to Irina, Hayes said, 'Madam, would you follow me.?'

'This is the servants' entrance,' Seb explained. 'Father insists everyone use it. He reckons it costs half a crown in lost heat every time the front door is opened.'

As they walked down the corridor, Hayes said, 'I have set up morning tea in the library, Milord.'

'Good,' replied Seb, 'it is the warmest room in the house, so you can thaw out in front of the fire.'

'When will Ranger get here?' Nic asked.

'In about half an hour. That is if he remembers which side of the road to drive on.'

The library was much cosier than the drawing room where Nic had met the family on his previous visit. A set of French doors opened onto the garden. Arrayed before the roaring fire were two leather armchairs, a three-seat sofa, and two damp golden retrievers.

'What a gorgeous room,' Irina exclaimed.

'Aren't you supposed to say it is decadent and was built on the sacrifices of the proletariat?' Seb said.

'All true, but it is still impressive.'

Irina sat down on the sofa. One of the dogs lazily raised himself up to sniff her fingers. He was rewarded with tickles under the chin, which prompted his companion to walk over in search of his fair share of attention.

'Ignore them,' Seb said, 'they are fat, lazy, and spoiled.'

'A bit like their owner,' Nic whispered. Irina giggled.

'I heard that, Slater,' he said as he walked over to the sideboard. Ignoring the tea and coffee, he poured three large whiskies. He handed the drinks around and tossed a couple of logs onto the fire. Sparks shot up the chimney and onto the rug as the dry wood crackled.

Settling into one of the armchairs, Seb started to quiz Irina. He tried to probe into her background, mission, motives for working with Nic, and even her mother's supposed relationship with Chernenko. She deftly deflected every question, limiting her responses to the spy equivalent of name, rank, and serial number. Nic could see Seb was frustrated. He was not used to being so effectively stonewalled. Finally, he gave up and poured himself another whisky. Nic saw a hint of that smile on Irina's face.

There was a knock at the door, and Hayes said, 'Milord, may I present Mr. Moses Ranger.'

Ranger walked through the door with a broad smile. 'I could get used to this,' he said, nodding at Hayes.

'Welcome to my humble abode,' Seb bellowed.

'Some place you got here, Viscount Weston,' Ranger said. 'Nic, good to see you, and you must be Comrade Sashkaya, a pleasure to meet you,' he said, offering his hand.

She shook it firmly and said, 'A pleasure to meet you too, Colonel Ranger.'

'Just call me Ranger,' he replied.

'Help yourself to drink,' Seb said, gesturing to an array of bottles on the sideboard,

'Got any bourbon?' Ranger asked.

Seb chuckled, 'No, we only have proper drinks here.'

Ranger shook his head and poured himself a whisky. Once seated, Seb said, 'We all know why we are here. Based on information from Agent Sashkaya, it appears that the Soviet Union is about to launch two major military operations in Finland and Iran.'

Irina and Ranger both made to speak at the same time.

'You first,' said Irina.

'No, you first, ma'am,' said Ranger.

Irina shook her head in irritation, 'Let me make two things clear,' she said before switching to a near-perfect New York accent, 'I want none of your bullshit American courtesy, and if you ever call me ma'am again, I will kick your ass.'

Nic looked at Ranger to gauge his reaction. He was staring at Irina, who was smiling back at him. Ranger turned to Nic and said, 'That is some broad you have got there.' The ice had been broken.

After a few minutes of small talk, Ranger said, 'Let's get down to business. Irina, what are your motives for betraying your country?'

Irina smiled, 'How very American, straight to the point. It is a fair question. If I were in your shoes, my first thought would be that I am a plant sent to pass on misinformation. I assure you my motives are genuine. The Soviet Union has strayed far from its Marxist-Leninist roots. Our leaders have abandoned the working class, the economy is failing, and we are falling further behind the West technologically. The government's response is to increase spending on the military and engage in a pointless space race to distract people from the reality that they live in a failing state. The sad thing is that it is working. If the invasions succeed, they will be hailed as proof the Soviet Union is the dominant superpower and embolden our leaders to take even more aggressive action.'

'That is delusional,' Ranger said.

'Let her finish, and you may change your view,' Nic cautioned.

For the next hour, Irina described Vanquish. Khrushchev's use of his "peaceful coexistence" doctrine as cover for a series of successful missions shocked Ranger. Still, all he said was, 'Damnit.'

Irina saved the best for last: 'There is one other Vanquish mission I must tell you about. But before I do, you need to promise it stays inside this room.'

'Are you sure you want to go there?' Nic asked.

Irina nodded, 'To trust each other, we must be completely honest. Do I have your word?'

Both Seb and Ranger looked puzzled. Seb responded, 'Yes, if that is what it takes.'

She looked at Ranger. 'You are making me nervous,' he said, 'but yes, I agree.

'What was your government's conclusion about the assassination of President Kennedy in Dallas?'

Ranger looked perturbed, 'What do you mean?'

'Exactly what I said.'

'The official inquiry concluded that Lee Harvey Oswald acted alone.'

'Do you believe that?'

'Based upon the evidence, it was the logical conclusion. There have been numerous conspiracy theories but nothing definitive.'

'Were you aware of Oswald's Soviet connections?'

'I remember reading something, but the inquiry discounted Soviet involvement.'

'They were wrong,' Irina stated.

'Are you serious?' Ranger exclaimed.

'Yes. Lee Harvey Oswald defected to the Soviet Union in 1959. He was recruited by the KGB while living in Minsk in 1960 and married a Russian, Marina Nikolayevna, in 1961. Marina was a trainee KGB agent; her father was a Ministry of Internal Affairs colonel. Oswald, his wife and their first child moved back to the US in June 1962 as part of a wave of so-called ghost spies. These Soviet agents would live normal American lives until activated by Moscow for a specific mission. Oswald's was to assassinate Kennedy.'

Ranger was speechless.

'After shooting Kennedy, Oswald botched his escape, killing a police officer. He was arrested and charged with Kennedy's murder. The KGB panicked. They were convinced Oswald would talk, so they ordered the Mafia to arrange a hit. Jack Ruby, who ran a Dallas nightclub for the Mafia, was ordered to kill Oswald, which he did two days later.'

Ranger said nothing. Seb said, 'It sounds plausible.'

Irina looked at Ranger, 'You understand why I asked that this stay between the four of us?'

He nodded but said, 'You have put me in an impossible position. This is explosive; if I do not report it, I am breaking my oath to serve.'

'That makes us all equal then,' she replied.

Ranger looked up and said, 'I suppose you are right.'

They took a short break during which Hayes served a ploughman's lunch of freshly baked bread, cheese and pickles, accompanied by two bottles of chilled Chablis. Seb polished off one of the bottles all by himself.

As they ate, Irina tried to draw Ranger back into the conversation. She knew she had tricked him. He was now burdened with knowledge so explosive that it could trigger calls for a revenge attack on the Soviet Union.

'What is it like being a black man in America? Moscow thinks an all-out race war is imminent?'

'I hope they are wrong. There is a lot of anger in the black community. Prejudice is ingrained in America; it will take years for attitudes to change. However, with the passage of the Civil Rights Act, there is now a mechanism to address discrimination. The problem is a lack of trust in government, which sometimes manifests itself in violence.'

Irina nodded thoughtfully, 'Being black in America sounds a lot like being a woman in the Soviet Union.'

After lunch, Ranger seemed to come to terms with the new knowledge he had gleaned from Irina. He probed Irina for more details about the attacks on Finland and Iran. He acknowledged that America was becoming distracted by events in Southeast Asia but was sceptical that the Russians had the capability to pursue two invasions simultaneously.

'The Kremlin is counting on the element of surprise. They think NATO will struggle to decide how to respond given that neither country is a NATO member.'

'We need to convince the Kremlin they are wrong, then maybe they will reconsider,' said Nic.

Irina nodded, 'The problem is we have to move quickly. The invasions are currently scheduled for early June.'

Ranger frowned, 'I am not sure it is doable. We must convince the Pentagon that every assessment they have made about Soviet strategy, military capability, and operational intent for the last decade has been wrong.'

'Do we, though?' Irina questioned.

All three looked at her.

'What are you suggesting?' Seb asked. He had moved from wine to brandy, cradling a large snifter in his hands while puffing on a cigar of Churchillian proportions. Despite consuming a vast amount of alcohol, he showed no visible signs of impairment.

Irina stood up, walked over to the French windows, and looked across the gardens. She turned back and said, 'Isn't it enough to convince the Kremlin that NATO knows about the planned attacks and will respond?'

'You mean without any real action to back it up?' Ranger asked.

Irina nodded. Seb looked thoughtful, 'You mean call their bluff?'

'Precisely. It worked for JFK over Cuba,' she said. 'Three things need to happen. Moscow must know that NATO is aware of the planned attacks. They must believe the Americans will not abandon Europe and that any invasion will be met with a proportionate military response.'

'It might just work,' said Ranger.

They spent another hour trying to hash out the details. Irina committed to alerting the group if there was any change in the planned invasion date and serving as the conduit for feeding details of the bluff back to Moscow. Ranger would report to Langley and try to wake the Pentagon up to the imminent threat. Seb would lead the planning of what they christened Operation Artifice, or as Nic called it, a cunning plan.

Dusk was falling as they wrapped up the discussion. While saying their goodbyes in the stable yard, Irina said to Ranger, 'I am sorry I had to compromise you like that.'

'Don't be; I would have done the same in your position.'

They watched as Ranger climbed into the Triumph Spitfire he had borrowed from a colleague at the Embassy. After turning the ignition on, he gunned the engine, engaged first gear, and shot down the driveway, sending up a shower of gravel.

Seb looked at Irina and said, 'You were very impressive today. I hope to God you are telling the truth.'

Irina smiled, 'You will find out soon enough.'

Seb instructed Hayes to drive Nic and Irina back to the pub. Nic hoped for a ride in the Bentley, but Hayes reversed what appeared to be a battered old Rover P3 out of the barn. It had probably been green once but was now a muddy rust colour.

Once they were back at the pub. Irina sat on the edge of the bed, levering her boots off. Dried mud flaked onto the floor. Nic lay beside her, his wellies discarded by the door. 'How do you think it went?' he asked.

She thought for a moment, 'Probably as well as we could expect. I was worried about how Ranger would react when I told him about Kennedy. He seemed more upset than angry.'

'I agree. He will struggle with the moral dilemma, but he is smart enough to see the big picture.'

'I hope so,' she said.

'What did you make of Seb?'

'He was exactly as I expected. A classic upper-class twit, as you English would call him. Except he is no twit. It is all an act to disarm people who then underestimate him. Did you notice how his behaviour changed as the day went on? The false front dissolved, and an intelligent, analytical brain was revealed. Although if he keeps drinking like that, it won't last for long.'

Nic was impressed. It had taken him much longer to get the measure of Viscount Weston.

'Aren't you going to ask me about Ranger?'

'Why should I?'

'Yes, because he is gorgeous! I bet he has muscles on his muscles. I think I will make him my next mission,' she said.

Nic sighed. He was pretty sure she was teasing him, but he still felt a pang of jealousy.

'Stop sulking.' she said as she unzipped her skirt, removed her top, and lay beside him. 'You have work to do, Agent Slater.'

57

25ᵗʰ April 1965

They barely made it down to breakfast before service ended. Nic picked up a copy of The Sunday Times and pointed to the front-page headline: 'Russian Walks in Space.'

Irina smiled, 'Another triumph for Mother Russia—the first man in space, the first woman in space, and now the first spacewalk. The Americans have a lot of catching up to do.'

After breakfast, they went for a walk around the village. The church bells rang, and the locals, dressed in their Sunday best, headed to church. Nic and Irina walked arm in arm-around the village green.

The pealing of bells was shattered by the sound of a car horn. A dark green Bentley sped around the corner and stopped in front of the church. The door swung open, and Seb stepped out. He doffed his hat to an old lady about to remonstrate with him. 'Sorry, Mrs Meade, one cannot be late for the Lord,' he said, hurrying up the path to the church door.

Irina and Nic walked back to the pub and retrieved their bags. Nic stowed them on the back seat of the Mini, and they set off for London. They took their time, avoiding the main roads and stopping for a Sunday roast at the Angel pub in Henley-on-Thames. Irina was pleasantly surprised by the Yorkshire pudding, even though Nic insisted it was not a patch on his mother's.

The added pounds from lunch caused Pet to struggle a little on the climb up Remenham Hill out of Henley. But once they reached the A4, she ate up the miles towards London. Nic dropped Irina off at Osterley tube station before turning south through Richmond and Kingston to Mags' house in Esher.

He pulled into the driveway and parked Pet in front of the garage doors. Before he got out, the front door flew open, and his six-year-old niece, Helen, ran out shouting, 'Uncle Nic's here.' Close behind was her four-year-old brother, Hugo. Nic adored his niece and nephew. He often wondered if the day would come when he would be a father. Given his career choice, he thought it unlikely.

Mags appeared in the doorway, 'Is my Pet still in one piece?'

'Just about,' Nic replied, 'although she could do with a wash.'

'Typical,' said Mags. 'Come in, Norman's golfing as usual.'

He climbed the front steps somewhat awkwardly, Helen and Hugo entwined around his legs. He gave his sister a peck on the cheek and disentangled himself from the children.

Once seated with cups of tea in the living room, Mags said, 'Tell me all about your weekend. Did you take a girl with you?' For years, she had been trying to pair Nic off with every single woman she knew.

'I went alone,' Nic replied. He did not like lying to her but could hardly reveal that he had spent the weekend with a KGB spy. 'Seb invited me to his country estate near Oxford. We mostly talked about work while taking long walks in the countryside. I stayed over last night as I drank a little too much.'

Mags tutted, 'Little brother. What have I told you about getting drunk?'

'What does drunk mean?' Helen asked from the doorway.

'It means Uncle Nic was a naughty boy,' Mags said.

'Will he be sent to his room?' Hugo asked.

Nic and Mags both laughed. 'Run along, you two. Let me

talk to Uncle Nic for a few minutes.'

Reluctantly, the two children disappeared upstairs. Their conversation followed the usual pattern. An update on the children's progress at school, further enquiries about Nic's love life, and a discussion about their parents. Mags never asked about his work, though he was certain she knew what he did. She had once hinted that MI6 was a client of her chambers.

It was not long before the children reappeared. Hugo insisted on showing off his latest Dinky car, a 1964 Rolls-Royce Silver Cloud, while Helen sashayed across the kitchen wearing her new frock. Before Nic left, the children insisted he come for Sunday lunch sometime soon. He agreed, said his goodbyes, and walked to the station.

Back at his flat, he felt tired but elated. The weekend had gone better than expected. Irina had established her credibility with Seb and Ranger; there had been no hint either suspected what he and Irina were really doing, and the sex had been great.

58

It had been over a month since the weekend in the country. There was no new news about the planned invasions. Seb, Nic and Ranger discussed every possible permutation—full invasion or minor incursion, conventional or nuclear, land or air. Irina warned them they would be lucky to receive more than 72 hours' notice of an imminent attack. Any response could only be limited in scope.

Nic decided to walk to the office. There was something about walking through London he found calming. You could avoid the crowded tube trains or busses, take a different route every day, and there would always be something new to see. He headed down Edith Grove to Cheyne Walk. As he walked past Town Records on the Kings Road, a large crowd of young people had gathered, waiting for the shop to open. A poster in the window indicated that The Beatles' new album was being released that day. Nic noted the odd title, 'Sgt. Pepper's Lonely Hearts Club Band.' Nic doubted it could be as good as their previous album, Revolver, which contained his two favourite Beatles songs, the hauntingly sad, Eleanor Rigby and the Indian-sounding Tomorrow Never Knows. A second poster announced the release of another album called David Bowie. Nic had never heard of him.

Nic was surprised to see a reflection in the shop window indicating that he had picked up a tail. It looked like a Boris. Was this Irina's doing, or were the KGB independently checking up on him? As he was only going to the office, there was no need to try to lose him; however, he ensured that his tail knew he knew he was being followed.

He crossed the river at Battersea Bridge and turned into Battersea Park. He was surprised to see Boris pull a two-way radio out of his coat and start talking into it. Surely the KGB were not planning to abduct him in broad daylight? It would be difficult to pull off as there was no vehicular access, and the park was full of early-morning dog walkers. He stopped by the Old English Garden and checked behind him. There was no sign of his tail. What was going on?

He turned to continue walking and saw Irina walking towards him. It made sense now; the tail was communicating his position to her. Something serious must have happened for her to intercept him like this. He knew better than to acknowledge her presence, so he kept walking.

When she was within a few feet of him, she stumbled, dropping her bag and newspaper on the ground. Nic did the gentlemanly thing, bending down to help pick up her things and ask if she was alright. She assured him she was and thanked him for his help. To anyone looking, it was just a random meeting between two strangers. They parted ways, with Irina's newspaper now safely in Nic's hand.

As soon as he exited the park, he flagged down a cab. Once back in the office, he spread the newspaper on his desk and turned to the crossword on the inside back page. It was partially completed, but none of the answers were correct. This was a code he and Irina had developed that needed no code word or code book. The first letter of each answer was the key. He took a piece of paper and wrote down the first letter of each answer. Whenever the last letter of an answer was an X, it signified the beginning of a new part of the message. When he had finished, he had a three-part message: 'VGO ITOM HPNOON.'

He looked at the sequence, trying to decipher the meaning, HPNOON was easy. Irina wanted to meet in Hyde Park at NOON, one of their predefined meeting locations. VGO must mean Vanquish was a GO. The invasions would begin on the 6th of June as planned, only five days from now. He was left with ITOM. I must be Irina, so TOM must be TO Moscow.

They did not have much time. He hurried upstairs to Seb's office, and remarkably, given the early hour, Seb was at his desk.

'Vanguard is a go. We have five days.'

'Bugger,' Seb exclaimed.

The rest of the day passed in a whirl. Coded messages pinged around the globe. Prime Minister Harold Wilson, President Lyndon Johnson, NATO General Secretary Manilo Brosio, the Shah of Iran, and the Finnish Prime Minister were all alerted. C met with the CIA London Station chief and briefed the Foreign Secretary.

Nic called Ranger and simply said, 'Elvis has left the building,' the code they had agreed to signal that Vanquish was a go. Just before noon, Nic slipped out to meet Irina in the park. The sun had finally returned, and all of London seemed to be picnicking, playing football, or canoodling in the park. Irina was waiting for him by the Rangers Lodge just north of the Serpentine.

'I leave for Moscow tomorrow, and then I am going to Azerbaijan,' she said. Gromyko has ordered me to serve as the KGB liaison for the attack on Iran.'

'Why you?' Nic said, worry written across his face.

'It makes sense. Yuri and I are the only KGB agents who have been involved in the planning of the operations. He will be doing the same thing as me in Finland.'

'How will you warn the Kremlin that we know what's afoot?

'I have already messaged Chernenko. He will get me in to see Gromyko when I stop in Moscow.'

'What do you think he will do?'

'He will have to tell Kosygin, then one of three things will happen. They choose to go ahead regardless. Given the success of previous Vanguard operations, that is a real possibility. They may delay or modify the plan or cancel it altogether.'

'Have you contacted Yuri?'

'Yes. He is already on his way to Helsinki. He will deliver a similar warning through Semichastny. Hopefully, with two independent sources, they will reconsider.'

'Are you scared?' Nic asked.

Irina turned to face him, 'Of course.'

He pulled her towards him, hugging her tightly. She responded in kind. For the first time, her affection felt spontaneous. His thoughts were interrupted by a loud sigh of disgust. 'Disgusting behaviour, and in a public place with children present!'

They broke their embrace. A matronly-looking woman with tightly permed grey hair the texture of steel wool stood scowling at them. Nic saw that Irina was blushing; he had never seen that before. He looked at the woman and said, 'You are just jealous, aren't you?'

The woman frowned and stomped off down the path while Irina laughed. The incident released the tension they both felt.

'I am going to cook dinner for you tonight,' Nic said, 'who knows when we will see each other again.'

'I like the sound of that. Can you cook anything other than burnt toast?'

'Cheeky. Be at my flat at seven.'

'Yes, sir,' she said, mockingly saluting him.

When he returned to the office, Seb told him President Johnson had sent an urgent coded message to all NATO leaders. 'He is on the phone with Wilson right now,' he said.

'What do you think will happen?' Nic asked.

Before Seb could answer, his phone rang. He picked it up and listened without saying a word.

'Ranger is on his way over. Johnson's talking about using nukes!'

'What?' exclaimed Nic.

'He is saying it is the only option, as NATO cannot stop an invasion with conventional forces alone.'

'We cannot let that happen,' Nic stated. Seb nodded in agreement

When Ranger arrived, Seb asked, 'What is this nonsense about using nukes?'

'Not using them, just threatening to use them,' Ranger replied.

'One often leads to the other,' Nic said.

'Johnson hopes not, but he is fuming. He thinks the Soviets have been negotiating in bad faith and wants to teach them a lesson. He has ordered the joint chiefs to develop a plan to use limited tactical nuclear weapons against the invading forces. He has already spoken to the Finnish President and the Shah and got their agreement. Wilson is resistant, but he will cave in the end.'

'When will he warn the Soviets?' Nic asked.

'He plans to wait until they cross the border. He wants the world to know who started it.'

'We need to talk to C,' said Seb. 'Ranger, you come with me. Nic, can you warn Irina?'

'Yes, I am meeting her tonight. Are you suggesting we go behind Johnson's back?'

'We have to prepare for anything.'

'Agreed,' said Ranger.

Seb and Ranger went off to see C. Nic felt slightly left out. Everyone else was rushing about, and there he was, the source of the information, sitting and twiddling his thumbs. He headed downstairs to the research library for want of anything better to do. He walked into the middle of a shouting match between Simon and Charlotte.

Charlotte stood with her hands on her hips, glaring at Simon, 'How dare you undermine my authority!'

Simon rolled his eyes, 'I do not work for you; I work with you.'

'Bollocks,' Charlotte shouted.

'Look, I have said I am sorry,' Simon said.

Charlotte's expression softened a little. She turned to Nic, 'Why are all men pricks?'

Nic assumed the question was rhetorical.

'Can I interrupt this little domestic?' he inquired.

'What do you think?' Charlotte said, looking at Simon.

'Anything to avoid your wrath,' he replied.

'Don't be such a baby. I will make it up to you later,' she said while winking at Nic. 'What can we do for you, Mr Slater?'

'Tell me everything you know about Russia, Finland, and Iran.'

Three hours later, he was mentally exhausted. Simon and Charlotte were a formidable double act; when one stopped talking, the other took over. They were like a talking encyclopaedia.

By the time he left, he knew that Finland had been part of both Sweden and Russia at various times. During World War II, the Finns fought the Red Army to a standstill. After the war, Finland remained neutral in the Cold War but remained wary of the bear next door.

Iran, formerly Persia, had connections with Russia dating back to the 16th century. Between 1651 and 1828, the two countries fought five wars. After the Russian Revolution, thousands of Russians fled to northern Iran, but since an American-sponsored coup in 1953, Iran had been under Anglo-American influence, much to the annoyance of the Soviets. Charlotte asserted that the Soviet Union believed it had historical claims over both countries.

Nic could not find Seb or Ranger, so he left to prepare dinner for Irina. An hour later, he had finished setting the table. The wine was open, and candles lit. He hoped the food would match the atmosphere. He served smoked salmon with a lemon garnish and crusty brown bread for the appetiser. The main course was Coq au Vin with steamed vegetables and au gratin potatoes. He was using a recipe from the chef at Chez Solange, a small French restaurant Seb had introduced him to near Leicester

Square. He had made his mother's apple crumble for dessert, which he would serve with fresh cream. He had decided not to spoil the evening by sharing what Ranger had said.

As he made the final preparations, he sipped a relatively strong gin and tonic, his second. He was folding the napkins when the doorbell rang. He whipped off his apron, downed the last of the G&T, and checked his look in the mirror. Not bad, although the gin was making his cheeks a little rosier than usual.

He hurried downstairs and opened the door to find Irina leaning on the door frame with a broad smile on her face. She held a bottle of champagne in one hand, although Nic barely noticed it. Like the model Jean Shrimpton, her long dark hair fell in waves over her shoulders. Her lips were coated in bright red lipstick, and a chunky necklace hung around her neck. The tight black top served to frame her breasts. A white, patent leather belt with a giant gold buckle hung loosely around her waist. A miniskirt was peeking out below. It was even shorter than the one she had worn to the pub. Her legs were bare, and she wore white, patent high-heeled shoes.

'Put your eyes back in, lover boy,' she whispered in her huskiest voice while running her hand over his chest. 'I'm hungry!'

She could not keep the act up and burst out laughing.

'You had better come in before you get arrested,' Nic said.

'Are you complaining?'

'Not at all,' he said, taking the champagne and giving her a kiss on the lips. Even her lipstick tasted good. He thought about abandoning dinner altogether.

'Something smells good, and it is not you,' she said as they climbed the stairs.

'Champers first, I think,' he suggested.

'Good idea.'

By the time the champagne was finished, they were feeling very relaxed. Dinner was a success, exceeding Nic's low expectations of himself. Between courses, assorted items of clothing were discarded as they energetically cleansed their palates. The crumble never made it into the oven as they retired to bed.

Sometime later, as they lay entwined in bed, Irina looked at Nic and said, 'What are you not telling me?'

'Is it that obvious?'

'Yes, but it didn't spoil the evening, did it?' she said.

When Nic finished telling everything, she sighed and said, 'I am not surprised. We have to make sure our plan works.' They talked for a few more minutes before falling asleep in each other's arms.

Nic's arm flailed around as he tried to silence the alarm. Irina lay next to him, curled up in the sheets; she had that smile on her face even as she slept. If it had been their last night together, it had been worthy of the occasion. He tiptoed out of the bedroom and made two large mugs of strong tea. When he returned, Irina was sitting up, a sheet pulled across her chest. She smiled and said, 'I could get used to this if the world doesn't end.'

'So could I,' he replied. 'Who knows when we will get to do it again.'

'Don't spoil it,' she said. The sheet dropped from her chest. The tea went cold.

59

2nd June 1965

Nic knocked on the door of the Foreign Office conference room. A voice bellowed, 'Come in.'

There were five people seated around a large mahogany table. At the head of the table was Michael Stewart, the new Foreign Secretary, who had replaced Gordon-Walker when the latter failed to win re-election to parliament. To his left sat Dick White, and to his right was a blond-haired man Nic did not recognise. Ranger sat next to White, and Seb sat opposite Ranger.

'Slater, please take a seat,' C directed.

Nic sat down and poured himself a glass of water from the jug on the table. His throat had gone dry. The Foreign Secretary gestured to the man on his right, saying, 'This is Matti Astana, the Finnish ambassador,'

'Pleasure to meet you, Mr Slater,' the man said in unaccented English.

'Likewise, Sir,' Nic replied.

'I will hand the meeting over to C,' said the Foreign Secretary.

'Thank you, Sir. Thanks to Slater, we have confirmation that the Soviets plan to attack Finland and Iran on Saturday.'

'Maybe they think we don't work weekends,' interjected the Foreign Secretary. No one laughed.

C recapped everything they knew about the planned attacks. Then, the Foreign Secretary provided an update on the discussion between the Prime Minister, President Johnson, and the other NATO leaders. As Ranger had suspected, Wilson had caved into Johnson's demand to threaten a nuclear response. Stewart said, 'We must tread very carefully to avoid this escalating. Success hinges on the Soviets backing down when they learn how NATO will respond. No one wants a nuclear war.'

'The President thinks the Russians are bluffing,' said Ranger. Nic hoped he was right.

'We have already put our plan into motion,' C said, looking at Nic.

Nic nodded, 'Our source is en route to Moscow as we speak. They will communicate that we know about the planned attacks and will be ready to deliver an appropriate response. There will be no mention of anything nuclear at this stage.'

C took over, 'We have agreed on a small retaliatory action if the Soviets go ahead with some form of attack. The hope is that it will discourage them from triggering the nuclear option. With the consent of the Finns,' C said, looking over at Astana, who nodded, 'A small SAS force is en route to the Finnish border to disrupt any Soviet activity that does take place. As for Iran, there are no ground troops available. However, the US Air Force has some local assets that will be mobilised.'

'We have two squadrons of aircraft and helos based in Iran. Their primary mission is conducting joint surveillance missions with the Iranians; however, if Soviet ground forces cross the Iranian border, they will launch an airborne attack,' said Ranger.

C turned to Nic, 'Slater, you will leave for Helsinki this evening. Ambassador Astana has consulted with his government, and they will provide whatever support they can. However, everything must be done covertly. Finland is bound by a 1948 Mutual Assistance pact with the Soviet Union.

Moscow must violate the agreement first. We understand that a Soviet contact of yours, Yuri Kovlev, is in Helsinki. We can only surmise that he is there in relation to Vanquish. You will contact him and tell him that recent A12 reconnaissance flights have detected the build-up of Soviet forces near the Finnish and Iranian borders. Warn him NATO has assured the governments of both Finland and Iran it will protect the sovereignty of both nations if asked. You should also hint that the Americans are considering a nuclear response.'

'We expect Kovlev to report back to Moscow. He will corroborate everything your source has told them but also raise the spectre of nuclear action.'

Nic was impressed; it might just work. The Foreign Secretary wrapped up the meeting with a few platitudes about how Nic was the best man for the job and doing his country a great service. As they headed for the door, Ranger pulled Nic aside and said, 'Walk with me.'

After leaving the Foreign Office, they walked down Whitehall. The usual crowd of tourists was gathered in front of 10 Downing Street. Another group was taking pictures of the mounted Lifeguards at the entrance to Horse Guards Parade. Everyone looked happy. Nic wondered how they would feel if they knew the world was edging ever closer to nuclear war.

As if sensing Nic's thoughts, Ranger placed a hand on his shoulder and said, 'Hey buddy, this is what you have been trained to do.'

'I know,' Nic said. 'So far, it has felt like I have been playing a game, but now it has become very real.'

'Not just for you, but also for Irina,' Ranger replied. 'That is what's bugging you, isn't it? You have broken the first rule of this job; you have become emotionally involved.'

Nic nodded.

'Listen,' Ranger said, 'you have done an outstanding job so far, do not screw it up now.'

Nic nodded. They reviewed the final aspects of the plan. It helped. He started focusing on the job at hand.

60

3rd June 1965 – Helsinki

Nic boarded the evening flight to Helsinki, while Irina would already be en route to Moscow. He fell asleep soon after takeoff, only opening his eyes as the plane started its descent for Vantaa Airport. After deplaning, he walked through the customs area and saw a uniformed driver holding a sign saying, "Mr. Nicholas Slater." They had it wrong again. Everyone assumed his first name was Nicholas, not Dominic.

'Welcome to Helsinki, Mr Slater. My name is Seppo, I will take you to your hotel.'

'Thank you,' Nic replied, handing him his bag.

Despite the late hour, it was still daylight. The sun barely set at this latitude at this time of year. Seppo opened the rear door of a dark blue Volvo, and Nic settled into the back seat.

After checking in, Nic took a shower but was too tense to sleep. He ran through his script for meeting with Yuri multiple times. The objective was to corroborate what Irina would be telling Gromyko while also hinting that the Americans were considering the use of tactical nuclear weapons against any aggressive Soviet action. The message was that NATO would not tolerate any expansion of Soviet influence regardless of whether the target countries were NATO members.

He woke to find the sun shining through the thin curtains even though it was only 03:45. He gave up on sleep, got dressed, and went for a walk. Helsinki is a city made up of almost 300 islands. Founded in the 16th century by the Swedish King Gustav I, it had been part of Russia for over a century before gaining independence after World War I. To Nic, the city looked quite Soviet with its functional, minimalist architecture. He had heard somewhere that film directors often used the city as a "double" for Moscow.

London had confirmed that Yuri was staying at the Hotel Tomi, so Nic decided to put his plan in motion. The hotel was easy to find, being the tallest building in the city. Nic entered the lobby and walked over to the deserted reception desk. He rang the bell, and a hunched old man appeared from the back office. He looked slightly irritated at being disturbed. Nic asked, in Russian, for a pen and paper and wrote a note for Yuri.

"Yuri,

What a coincidence! We are both in Helsinki. We should meet at the café in Kaivopuisto Park at 14:00.

Nic"

He slipped the note into an envelope and wrote Yuri's name. He handed it to the old man and asked for it to be delivered promptly. He received a grudging nod in reply.

He had no doubt Yuri would come to the meeting. With the invasion about to begin, Yuri would know that Nic being in Helsinki was not a coincidence.

As he returned to his hotel, the city was slowly waking up. Trams trundled down the streets, the smell of fresh-baked bread wafted through the air, and the first commuters emerged from the railway station. Nic managed to get a few more hours of sleep before leaving for the meeting. He was pleased to see that a two-man team was tailing him—Yuri had got the message.

He strolled through the city centre, past the docks, towards the park. He wondered if Irina had met with Gromyko yet and, if so, what his reaction had been.

Kaivopuisto Park bordered the Gulf of Finland, the easternmost part of the Baltic, stretching from Finland to Estonia and the Soviet Union. Nic bought a drink at the café and sat at a table in the warm sunshine. He watched the shipping traffic moving through the gulf. The steam pouring out of the funnels created the only clouds in the sky.

Bang on time, he felt a slap on his back, and a voice said in Russian, 'Slater, what are you doing here? Working on your tan?'

Nic stood up, 'Good to see you, Yuri. I could ask you the same question.'

Yuri smiled wryly. Nic liked Yuri and could imagine that, under different circumstances, they could be good friends.

'How is Irina?' Yuri asked.

'She is a very capable cultural attaché,' Nic replied.

Yuri laughed and sat down next to Nic. After a few minutes of small talk, Yuri's expression turned serious, 'So why are you in Finland?'

'I think you know why,' he said, studying Yuri's face for any reaction. There was none.

'I am here to warn you. The Americans know what is about to happen. They showed me some interesting images from recent reconnaissance flights over the Finnish and Iranian border regions.'

Yuri's brow furrowed. Nic continued, 'I have been instructed to warn you that NATO will not tolerate any incursion into the sovereign territory of either country.'

'Your intelligence is, as usual, flawed,' Yuri responded in a cold, dispassionate voice. All sense of friendly bonhomie had disappeared. 'Our northern and southern commands are conducting defensive military exercises. There is no intention to take any action beyond our borders.'

'Good,' Nic replied, 'because the Americans are considering using tactical nuclear weapons in the event of any incursion into Finnish or Iranian territory.'

That got a reaction; Yuri's face went ashen. He quickly recovered his poise and said, 'You are bluffing! They would not resort to nuclear weapons in defence of non-NATO members.'

'Can you afford to take the risk?' Nic asked. 'You should know two things. First, the governments of both Finland and Iran have requested NATO support in case of any breach of their borders. Second, the CIA is beginning to connect the dots about Vanquish. They don't know the whole story, but Johnson has been briefed that the Soviet Union may have been conducting missions inside the United States while trying to negotiate arms reduction treaties. As my American friends say, he is mad as hell.'

Yuri frowned before saying, 'This is just another idle threat, my friend. You are being duped by your supposed allies.'

'If you say so, but I strongly suggest you pass this information on to Moscow.'

Nic got up and started to walk away. He had gone no more than ten yards when Yuri shouted, 'Wait.'

What he said next surprised him. 'Thank you, my friend. Our leaders seem hellbent on leading us into the abyss. Hopefully, this will make them stop and think about the consequences of their actions.'

Irina had been telling the truth, and Yuri was on the same side. Yuri offered his hand, and Nic shook it. 'I hope we get to meet again. Maybe next time we can have a drink or two.'

'I will look forward to it,' Nic replied.

Yuri turned and walked down the path to join his two colleagues.

Nic watched them go. In the gulf beyond, he could see two young boys paddling a canoe in the wake of a large cargo ship. Nic thought the waters he was navigating had just become considerably choppier.

61

3ʳᵈ June 1965 – Moscow

Irina was surprised to see a ZIL 111 waiting for her on the tarmac at Sheremetyevo airport. Commonly used exclusively by the Politburo, it was a sign of her temporarily elevated importance. The driver explained he would take her to her apartment and pick her up again in the morning for her meeting with Gromyko at 10:00.

Despite her luxurious ride, Moscow looked drab in comparison to London. It was early evening; London would be just coming to life as people headed out for a night on the town whereas Moscow was shutting down for the day.

Would she ever see London again? The bright lights, upbeat music, vibrant nightlife, and risqué fashions were exciting compared to Moscow's austere dullness.

Arriving back at her apartment building, little seemed to have changed in the six months since she had left. The crack in the glass by the front door had not been repaired, the entry lights were not working, and the lift was still out of order. She checked her mailbox; there was a little post, a letter from her aunt and a couple of notices from the apartment management company.

Climbing the stairs to the second floor, she heard a piano playing in the apartment below hers. It would be Mr Bellus. He was a Polish Jew who had escaped to Moscow ahead of the German advance in 1941. His wife and two children had not been so lucky. They had the misfortune to be on a train heading east that was stopped and searched by the Gestapo. All the Jews on board had been sent to Auschwitz; none had survived. Bellus rarely ventured out; there were still a lot of anti-Semitic feelings in Russia. He had been kind to Irina when she had first moved in, treating her like the daughter he had lost. She cursed herself for not getting him a present. She usually brought him a bottle of Polish vodka, which he insisted was superior to any produced in Russia. She made a mental note to visit him when or was it if she returned from Azerbaijan.

She opened the door to her apartment and heard the phone ringing. She picked up the receiver and heard a female voice, 'Comrade Sashkaya?'

'Yes,' she answered. The driver would have reported dropping her off.

'Your meeting with Comrade Gromyko has been rescheduled for eleven o'clock tomorrow morning.' She was relieved; at least it had not been cancelled.

She decided to go for a walk to clear her head after the flight. She was not surprised to immediately pick up a tail; the security services would be checking up on her. It felt good to stretch her legs. She wondered if Nic had connected with Yuri yet. Their plan was shaky at best. Was it realistic to think that the Politburo would change their minds based upon largely unverified information?

After wandering aimlessly for a time, she stopped at one of the ubiquitous street corner kiosks and bought a bottle of cheap vodka—perhaps not the smartest thing to do, but she needed some sleep.

It did not work. Three hours later, she woke with a headache, spending the rest of the night alternating between cups of tea and cigarettes. Finally, it was time to get ready to leave for her meeting with Gromyko. It felt strange to put on a skirt that fell below the knee, apply 1950s-style make-up, and wear sensible low-heeled shoes.

The Zil arrived promptly at 10:30. She asked the driver to drop her by St. Basil's so she could walk the final part. He was reluctant, insisting he had been ordered to take her directly into the Kremlin. A smile and a promise to tell no one secured his agreement.

Out of habit, she walked past the lamppost. Was it only forty-eight hours ago that she had been curled up in bed with Nic in London?

Crossing Red Square, she walked past the Lenin Mausoleum to the Nikolskaya Tower entrance to the Kremlin. She introduced herself to the guard, who made a quick phone call. Shortly thereafter, a young KGB officer appeared. 'I will escort you to Comrade Gromyko's office,' he said.

He looked very young, probably a trainee at the academy. His sharp facial features and dark hair marked him out as a Tatar of Crimean descent. Tatars were still an unusual sight in Moscow. Stalin had forcibly resettled more than 200,000 to Uzbekistan and Kazakhstan after the war, accusing them of collaborating with the Nazis. Only now were some beginning to find opportunities in government service.

Irina said, 'Thank you, what is your name?'

'Emir Abdul,' he replied, 'but I go by Eric Andreev in Moscow.'

Irina understood. Despite official pronouncements that the USSR was an egalitarian society, there was still significant prejudice against ethnic minorities.

She followed Eric through the maze of Kremlin buildings. Upon reaching Gromyko's office, a secretary showed Irina into a large but soulless office. Seated behind a utilitarian metal desk was Andrei Gromyko, the Soviet Foreign Secretary. He stood up as Irina entered and said in English, 'Irina, it is lovely to see you again. Have you been enjoying your time in London?'

'Very much, Comrade Secretary.'

'Good, good. Do you mind if we speak English? I like to practice when I get the chance.'

'Not at all, comrade.'

Gromyko continued, 'I hear London has become quite exciting in a depraved sort of way. Everything was very drab when I was there in the early fifties, though I enjoyed the pubs. Have you been to the Goat near the Embassy?'

'Many times,' Irina replied, smiling.

'I spent many a happy evening there,' Gromyko replied, 'I developed quite a taste for Fuller's Bitter.' He motioned for her to take a seat.

'Wasn't that around the time of the acid bath murders?' Irina asked.

Gromyko nodded, 'Just after. John Haigh met his first victim there. Apparently, after having dinner together, he enticed him to a nearby building, killed him and dumped the body in a tub of sulphuric acid. He went on to do the same to the man's parents.'

Irina shivered, 'Pretty gruesome.'

'Ironically, it was good publicity for the pub; it was always packed when I went there. Anyway, enough of my reminiscing. I understand you have information relevant to Operation Vanquish?'

'Yes, comrade,' Irina replied. 'My MI6 contact has informed me that NATO knows about our plan to attack Finland and Iran.

American spy planes have detected our troop movements, and NATO listening stations have intercepted radio traffic that suggests we are not conducting routine military exercises.'

Gromyko sat back in his chair frowning, 'Did your contact indicate how NATO will respond?'

'Not explicitly, but I think it will be more Poland than Czechoslovakia.'

Gromyko nodded. He knew she was referring to the Allied response to Hitler's actions in the 1930s. The Allies allowed Hitler to annex Czechoslovakia but drew the line at Poland and declared war.

Gromyko frowned, 'I suspect you may be right, but with the Americans moving troops to Indochina, NATO forces are inferior to ours.'

'In terms of conventional forces, yes.' Gromyko frowned; Irina's implication was clear.

The phone on Gromyko's desk rang. He picked up, listened for a few seconds, and put the receiver down without saying a word.

Turning back to Irina, he said, 'What do you recommend?'

She needed to be careful what she said. Soviet leaders were notorious for asking such questions. If you give the wrong answer, your career, if not your life, could come to a sudden end. Many of Stalin's most senior confidants had perished for failing to read their leader's mind accurately.

She needed to balance her personal agenda with what was realistic. Plans were too far advanced for the Politburo to abandon the attacks. She said, 'The success of Vanquish to date has relied heavily on the element of surprise. If we have lost that advantage, we must ask whether we are prepared to engage with an enemy expecting an attack and likely to respond. Launching a preliminary action to test NATO's resolve might be a viable middle ground. We could use the false flag attacks to justify a proportionate response before embarking upon a full invasion of each country.'

Gromyko looked thoughtful, 'Interesting. That is a clever stratagem, comrade. I must consult with Comrades Kosygin and Brezhnev immediately.'

There was a knock at the door. 'Enter,' Gromyko said, switching to Russian. Semichastny walked in. He was breathing hard, with beads of sweat on his forehead. He looked surprised to see Irina. She got up and made to leave, but Gromyko motioned for her to stay.

Semichastny frowned slightly before turning to Gromyko and saying, 'Comrade, we have just received an urgent message from Yuri Kovlev, one of our agents in Finland.

'Go on,' said Gromyko.

'Kovlev was contacted by Slater, our source inside MI6.'

Gromyko glanced at Irina and said, 'Comrade Sashkaya just told me he warned her that NATO suspects we are about to attack Finland and Iran.'

Semichastny frowned again. He did not like being upstaged. 'Yes, comrade,' he said irritably.

'Kovlev says Slater met him face-to-face in Helsinki. He warned him that the Americans are considering using tactical nuclear weapons in the event the invasions go ahead.'

'Is it a bluff?' Gromyko asked.

'We don't know,' said Semichastny. Irina hoped Gromyko did not feel the confluence of events was contrived. She and Nic had talked about it but hoped the urgent need to make a decision would overcome any doubts.

'Come with me,' Gromyko ordered, 'Irina, please wait here.'

Gromyko did not return for an hour. He looked agitated. 'You must leave for Baku immediately, he said. 'A military jet is waiting for you at Kubinka airbase. Kosygin thinks the Americans are bluffing but has accepted your suggestion. He has decided to scale back the attacks. We will make limited advances in both countries in response to the false flag attacks. We will hold our position for forty-eight hours to gauge NATO's likely response.

You will meet with General Ivanov in Baku and develop a modified attack plan. Kovlev will do the same for the Finnish assault.

Irina kept a straight face. It was not the ideal outcome, but it bought time. 'Good work, comrade Sashkaya. You have done an outstanding job. Vanquish is a long-term strategy; we can adjust tactics as events dictate. This is one of those times. Now off you go to Baku.'

'Yes, Comrade Secretary,' Irina replied as she stood and headed to the door. As she left, Gromyko said in English, 'Good luck and be careful.'

62

4ᵗʰ June 1965 – Helsinki

Nic was sitting outside a café on the Helsinki waterfront when a messenger from the British Embassy arrived and handed him a note. It read:

Kovlev to Leningrad

Nic smiled. Yuri's hasty departure would be a direct result of their conversation. Hopefully, he had already conveyed Nic's warning to Moscow, which would corroborate what Irina had told Gromyko. How would the Soviets respond? Nic suspected he would find out soon.

As he stood to leave, the radio inside the café started playing a song he had never heard before. It was not a typical pop song. The lyrics were dark, and the singer's voice was very gravelly. The lyrics were haunting and perhaps prophetic—a battle was raging, windows were shaking, and the times were changing. He listened to the end. The artist was an American, Bob Dylan. Nic had never heard of him.

He returned to the British Embassy and sent coded messages updating Seb and Ranger on events. His orders were to remain in Helsinki and await further instructions.

Ranger replied immediately. Irina had been seen entering the Kremlin early yesterday morning; she left three hours later. Ranger said Soviet troops were still massed on the two borders, and there had been no change in the tone of the radio traffic. Nic's mood darkened. Had they failed?

It was another hour before he received a reply from Seb containing new orders from C. Nic was to leave immediately and rendezvous with the British Special Air Service (SAS) team on the Finnish-Soviet border. Everything must be done covertly. Only the Finnish prime minister and Astana, the ambassador in London, knew British troops were in Finland. If discovered, it would cause a major international incident and provide further ammunition to the Soviets.

Nic felt his adrenaline levels spiking. He was excited to be doing something. Before returning to his hotel, he went to the Embassy library. There, he got the latest maps of the area where he was to rendezvous with the SAS team.

As he left the Embassy, he was not surprised to see Yuri's henchmen following him. The Soviets would try to find out what he was up to and where he was going. Losing them would be time-consuming but not difficult.

He took three buses and a taxi and walked through a crowded indoor market, confident he had thrown them off. They would assume he would return to his hotel and wait for him there. Sure enough, one was standing across the street from the hotel entrance; his colleague was probably sitting in the lobby.

He ducked down a side street, circled to the back of the hotel, entered through the staff entrance, and took the service elevator to the floor above his room. As he exited, he nearly knocked over a chambermaid. He apologised and explained in Russian that he was meeting his mistress and could not be seen entering the hotel as her husband was very suspicious. She giggled and put her fingers to her lips. He waited for her to enter one of the rooms and took the stairs down to his floor. He wanted to ensure one of Yuri's men was not waiting outside his room.

Peering round the stairwell door, he saw the coast was clear and quickly walked to his room. Once inside, he changed into army fatigues and stowed his torch, water bottle, rain cape, dry socks, MRE (Meal, Ready to Eat) meals, and his Colt M1911 pistol in a backpack. As the name implied, the gun dated from 1911 but still widely used by the US military. It was a semi-automatic, .45 calibre. Nic had first handled one while training with the CIA. He had liked the weight and balance so much that he had asked the MI6 armourer if he could be issued with one. Two bottles of Glenfiddich had done the trick.

Before leaving his room, he made sure the coast was clear, walked down the corridor and entered one of the communal bathrooms shared by guests on each floor. Looking in the mirror, he saw bags forming under his eyes due to lack of sleep. He slipped a pill box out of his pocket, took out a round white tablet and washed it down with water cupped in his hands. The tablet contained Benzedrine, an amphetamine used by soldiers in World War II to stay awake. It was standard issue for agents in the field.

Rechecking the corridor, he returned to the stairwell and took the stairs to the basement. Thankfully, he did not see the chambermaid again. It would have looked like an embarrassingly short liaison if he had.

In the basement, he found the entrance to the tunnel referenced in his instructions. It connected the hotel to the department store's basement on the opposite side of the street. He switched on his torch as he entered the tunnel; wartime posters were still affixed to the walls.

The door at the far end of the tunnel was stiff from lack of use but succumbed to a hefty shove. He took the stairs, which opened out onto a deserted corridor at the back of the store, which should lead to the loading dock.

A dark grey Volvo Duett was parked in the service road behind the store. A few minutes earlier, an embassy staffer had left it there. Nic retrieved the keys from the exhaust pipe, opened the driver's door, and dumped his backpack on the passenger seat.

Soon, he was driving at a sedate 40kph through the Helsinki suburbs. His orders were to rendezvous with the SAS team near Joukio—320 kilometres northeast of Helsinki. Reconnaissance photographs showed a heavy concentration of Soviet forces in the area. The drive should take about four hours.

Once clear of the city, the traffic volume diminished, and Nic increased his speed to 100kph, which felt close to the Volvo's limit. It was still daylight even though it was approaching 22:00.

He could feel his heart beating faster, probably from the combined effects of the Benzedrine and natural adrenaline. The scenery was an endless sequence of lakes and woods. The car's low-powered headlights started to pick out dark shadows amongst the trees as the sun finally set around midnight. Two hours into the journey, he pulled to the side of the road, relieved himself and ate one of the ready-to-eat meals. The packet said it was pork and rice, but he could not detect any trace of either.

63

A Tupolev TU-28 sat on the tarmac, waiting for Irina. It was a long-range fighter fitted with reserve fuel tanks that enabled it to fly to Baku nonstop. The pilot helped Irina into the rear seat and ensured her seatbelt was correctly fastened. Her bag was stowed behind her seat.

After the excitement of the take-off, the plane quickly reached its cruising altitude of 50,000 feet at twice the speed of sound. Irina felt no sensation of speed or altitude and fell asleep.

She woke up when her ears popped as the plane started to descend. It was a bumpy approach. Baku is Asia's Chicago, a city known for its winds. Under the circumstances, the pilot executed an exceptionally smooth landing and taxied to a halt by a Soviet Air Force hanger.

A member of the ground crew placed chocks under the wheels; another jumped onto the wing and helped Irina out of the cockpit. She thanked the pilot and jumped down to the ground.

The heat was oppressive; it must have been over 100F/38C. Beads of sweat formed on her neck. Even at ground level, there was a strong wind. Irina was thankful she had changed into her army fatigues before boarding the plane. A skirt would have proved troublesome.

Two plain-clothed agents stood beside a black Moskovitch. One of them opened the rear door for her before getting into the seat next to her. His colleague climbed into the passenger seat and told the driver to head to the local army headquarters.

'How long is the ride?' she asked.

'About an hour. The roads are shit,' one of them replied.

The agent beside her tried to engage her in conversation, but she was in no mood for small talk, much to his frustration.

While he continued trying to chat her up, she composed in her head the message she wanted to send to Nic. They had set up a communication protocol before she left London. She would send a telex to Seb, care of the landlord of The Jackalope pub, which was just around the corner from Seb's mews house and was another of Baron Ebdale's wartime acquisitions. The landlord was the son of Hayes, the butler at Sangster Hall.

They had agreed on a simple substitution cypher using Ian Fleming's Moonraker, the third James Bond novel. Each letter of the plain text message would be substituted by the number of the first word starting with that letter in the book. For example, if the message began with the word 'PLAN', the letter P would become the number 88 as Pointed was the first word in the book to start with the letter P. L became 69, A, 21 and N, 286. So, PLAN became 85 69 21 286.

By the time they arrived at the army headquarters, Irina had composed the message in her head; she just needed time to code and send it. As the car pulled to a stop, the agent next to her made one last futile attempt, 'Why don't you join us for a drink at the hotel later?'

'Why would I want to do that?' Irina retorted.

The agent in the front muttered, 'Bitch.'

Irina got out of the car, turned around and said, 'Make sure my bag gets to my hotel room. You are dismissed.' As she walked away, she heard them both mutter obscenities.

A junior army officer approached, 'Comrade Major, welcome to Baku Station. I am Lieutenant Spassky, General Ivanov's aide. Please let me escort you to the General's office.'

She nodded, and he led the way up the steps, holding the door open for her. The building was standard issue post-war Soviet design. Dull grey concrete stained with rust from the action of water on the iron used in the construction. The windows were covered with a thick layer of sand.

Spassky led Irina upstairs to a room at the front of the building. He knocked on the door, and a gruff voice granted admittance. A large bear of a man sat behind a metal desk with a cigarette firmly clasped between his lips. The overflowing ashtray showed it was not his first of the day. A slow-turning fan failed to dissipate the smoke or cool the room; sweat stains were visible under the General's armpits.

Ivanov had a formidable reputation. He was a veteran of Stalingrad and the battle for Berlin. At Stalingrad, he had been instrumental in defending a tank factory on the banks of the Don River during the battle that turned the war against the Nazis. After earning several promotions as the Soviets moved west, he was among the first soldiers to enter Berlin. He took part in the storming of the Reichstag.

After the war, he continued to rise the ranks under Stalin but, like so many others, fell out of favour with the notoriously volatile leader. He had been lucky to escape death and now was in command of a division in Azerbaijan. He had the red nose of a serious drinker, and his uniform strained to contain his girth. It was hard to discern the vital, energetic soldier of his youth.

He looked at Irina with disdain. Like most of his contemporaries, he did not approve of women being anywhere except in the kitchen or bedroom. Easing himself out of his chair, he moved slowly around the desk, which was covered with maps. The top one showed the Azerbaijan-Iran border region.

'I hear our plans have changed,' Ivanov said as he offered her a sweaty hand.

'Yes, Comrade General,' Irina replied. 'Moscow has decided to delay the full invasion. We will only pursue limited objectives in the first phase. The false flag attack will go ahead as planned. Then, a small force will advance as far as Bileh Savar. We will hold that position for forty-eight hours to see how the enemy responds. A decision will then be made as to whether to push on.'

The General shook his head in disgust and said, 'What is the point of such a minor effort? If we stop, we will be sitting ducks.'

'I am afraid that is classified,' Irina replied.

The General grimaced. He did not appreciate a woman, especially one more than twenty years his junior, telling him he was not privy to certain information.

He studied the maps for a few minutes, barking orders at Spassky, who had remained in the room. He then dismissed them both. Spassky showed Irina back downstairs, where a car awaited to take her to the hotel. Thankfully, the two agents were nowhere to be seen.

Once in her hotel room, she saw that her bag had arrived safely. A cursory check confirmed that the contents had been searched. She thought at least one pair of knickers was missing.

She sat at the desk and took a piece of notepaper from the desk drawer. She wrote out the message to Nic and used her copy of Moonraker to encode it. She addressed it to James Merriweather, two of Seb's many Christian names, care of the Jackalope pub in London.

She went down to the lobby and asked the receptionist to telex the message immediately. Upon looking at the sequence of numbers, the receptionist looked puzzled but said nothing. Irina was not worried about raising any suspicions by communicating with London. Moscow knew she was running a double agent, so using a coded message to contact him would not seem unusual.

She waited until the receptionist returned and gave her the receipt for the transmission. Rather than return to her room, she decided she had earned a drink.

The bar was just across the lobby, and judging by the hubbub emanating from within, it was busy. She walked over, entering through the open double doors. The light from the once elegant chandeliers cut through the cloud of smoke that hung over the room like the early morning sun through the mist. She almost turned and left when she saw the two agents who had met her at the airport sitting at the bar. One of them smiled and signalled for her to join them, obviously thinking she had changed her mind. She ignored him and took an empty seat at the bar.

She ordered a Kvasya, a popular Russian cocktail that combines kvass and vodka and is flavoured with cinnamon syrup. The bartender went light on the kvass and heavy on the vodka, which Irina appreciated.

She reflected on her day. While the attacks had not been cancelled, they had been scaled back. The prospect of all-out war had at least been delayed. However, she worried the Americans would overreact and use nuclear weapons anyway.

She wondered if anyone else in the bar knew how crucial the next forty-eight hours could be for humanity.

The first two cocktails slipped down very easily. She had better stop; tomorrow promised to be another busy day. Before retiring, she needed to get some fresh air after spending so much time on planes and in smoky rooms. The crowd in the bar had thinned, but the two agents were still knocking back the vodka. She signed her check, leaving a generous tip for the barman—the Kvasyas had been perfectly mixed.

Slipping from the barstool, she walked across the lobby and down the steps at the front of the hotel. Turning left, she started walking through the streets of Baku Old Town. Much of the city had been built in the twelfth century. The streets were narrow and cobbled, with three—to four-story stone buildings lining both sides.

It was still warm, but the constant wind provided some relief. She took long strides, trying to shake the stiffness out of her legs. Few civilians were about. Armed soldiers stood on the street corners, but they did no more than stare as she walked past.

Turning into an alleyway, she climbed a set of steps that led up to the Maiden Tower, a 12th-century monument overlooking the city. As she neared the top, she heard footsteps behind her. She did not turn to look but quickened her pace a little, and the sound faded away. Relaxing, she stopped and looked out over the city before making another left turn to complete a loop back to the hotel. She had walked no more than twenty metres before an arm reached out from a doorway and grabbed her around the waist while a hand clamped across her mouth. She tried to kick backwards at her assailant's leg, but he was well-trained. An alcohol-soaked voice slurred, 'Time to teach you a lesson, bitch. Whores like you have no place in the KGB.'

The two agents must have circled around in the opposite direction to intercept her on the way back to the hotel. She felt one of the men force his leg between her knees and try to rip her skirt off while the other grabbed her hair, pulling her head down. She heard a zip being undone.

As her training had taught her, she did not resist. The key was to use the attacker's leverage against them. Hopefully, their inebriated state would have dulled their reflexes. As she hoped, the first man's grip loosened ever so slightly. This was her chance. She let him continue pushing her head down, allowing her to bend at the waist and raise her right leg. She kicked backwards, knowing she had hit the target when she heard a loud cry, and the grip on her hair was released. One of the assailants crumpled to the ground.

At the sound of his accomplice's pain, the other attacker tried to tighten his grip around her waist, but it was too late. Irina turned her body through ninety degrees, breaking his hold, before launching a vicious uppercut with her right hand into his chin. He staggered backwards, giving her just enough room to launch a roundhouse kick to the chest. He twisted away and put his hands out to break his fall.

Irina turned to where the first man was trying to get up. She grabbed one of his outstretched hands and bent the fingers back using his own momentum. The sound of bones cracking elicited another pained scream. She unleashed a jab with straight fingers to the throat as she had done to the drunk in London, only this time it was with her full force. The man staggered back and collapsed, gasping for breath as his windpipe compressed. She finished off the second man with a swift kick to the head, knocking him unconscious.

Straightening up, she smoothed out what was left of her skirt. Looking down at the one still conscious attacker, she said calmly, 'I think your next assignment will be on the Mongolian border.'

The man scowled, so Irina decided to stamp on his groin, heel first, as a parting gift.

When she entered the hotel lobby, the night porter, seeing her dishevelled state, brought her a blanket. He asked if she needed anything else. She asked for a bottle of chilled vodka to be brought up to her room.

In addition to the vodka, the porter brought a large bucket of ice and some towels. Irina thanked him and plunged her swollen hand into the ice. In addition to taking a large slug of the vodka, she used it to clean her wounds. Now, her emotions kicked in, and she started sobbing. Violence always affected her the same way. She would maintain her composure, sometimes for hours, while in the heat of battle, but as soon as she was alone, she would break down and cry, not for her victims, but as a release from the tension that had built up.

After gathering herself, she took a long hot shower to soothe her aching body. Somewhat refreshed, she sat in bed sipping another tumbler of ice-cold vodka, surveying the darkening bruises on her body. Her cheek was red from a glancing blow during the struggle. She had two cuts on her arms and a large purple bruise across her ribcage. Other than that, she was in decent shape. Certainly better off than her assailants. She would be sore in the morning.

64

4ᵗʰ June 1965 – London

Seb and Ranger sat waiting for some news. They had heard nothing since Nic's message from Helsinki. There was a knock on Seb's office door.

'Sorry to interrupt,' said Seb's secretary, 'a Stephen Hayes from the Jackalope pub, just left this message at the front desk for James Merriweather. I assume that is you?'

'Quite correct,' said Seb, taking the note.

Once she had left the room, he said to Ranger, 'It's from Irina.' He moved to his desk and took his copy of Moonraker out of his desk drawer.

'Good choice for a code book,' Ranger said, laughing.

Seb turned to the first page and began decoding the message. When finished, he handed it to Ranger, who read it aloud:

"Plans changed. Limited force advances 20 clicks. Hold forty-eight hours. Test response. Then attack or retreat."

'It worked,' Ranger said.

Seb's phone rang, and he picked up the receiver and listened. 'C wants us upstairs, now,' he said to Ranger.

'Sit down,' C said as Seb and Ranger entered his office, 'We have just received intelligence that some of the Soviet forces are pulling back from the border.'

'Yes, Sir,' said Seb. 'Sashkaya has managed to send us a message.'

Ranger handed over the decoded message. After reading it, C said, 'Good. This corroborates what the latest reconnaissance photographs show. President Johnson has spoken with all

NATO members. All agreed on the plan of action to disrupt any Soviet advance across either border. I want you in the operations room to keep track of both fronts. Keep me and the CIA fully apprised.'

'Yes, Sir,' they said in unison.

C dismissed them with a wave as he answered his phone.

65

5th June 1965 – Eastern Finland

The Benzedrine was working. Despite being awake for almost forty-eight hours, Nic felt alert and energised. It was 02:00 as he approached Joukio. The eastern sky was already brightening even though the sun would not rise for another two hours.

A heavy mist draped the landscape, casting eerie shadows in the car's headlights. Nic reduced his speed; he did not want to miss the turn to the farm track near the bridge over Lake Joukionsalmi, where he was to rendezvous with the SAS team.

The headlights picked out a piece of white material tied to a tree ahead on the left. The SAS had thoughtfully left him a sign. He turned onto the track and switched off the car's lights. He was not far from the border and did not want to alert any Soviet patrols.

The Volvo bounced down the rutted track. He pulled to a stop where the car would be hidden from the road. He got out of the car and took his backpack from the passenger seat. It was eerily silent. His instructions were to walk down the trail and wait to be contacted by the SAS team.

He had gone no more than ten metres when two pairs of hands emerged from the gloom. One pair clamped around his mouth, and the other grabbed both his arms, immobilising him. He had heard nothing.

A voice whispered in his ear, 'Hamilton.'

He responded with, 'Academicals.'

Both pairs of hands simultaneously released their grip.

'Welcome to World War III,' said a voice with a strong Geordie accent. 'I am Sergeant Carr. These two turkeys are

Corporal Martin and Private Evans,' he said, gesturing to his companions.'

'I am glad you are on my side,' Nic responded, 'I never saw or heard you.'

'That is the general idea,' Carr replied.

Carr ordered Evans to move the car; it would be needed later. Turning to Nic, he said, 'Follow me, Sir. Captain Rodway and the rest of the team are stationed in the woods near the Soviet border.'

An SAS troop consisted of sixteen men split into four four-man squads. Carr led the way through the trees to a small clearing. Four soldiers had formed a perimeter to guard against any curious visitors. Carr introduced Nic to Captain Rodway. 'Welcome, always good to have a spook along,' Rodway said. Nic was not sure if he was joking or not.

'We have completed a recce across the border. The Soviets are about one click away—four tanks and plenty of infantry.'

'Doesn't sound like an invasion force,' commented Nic.

As Rodway was about to continue, the troop's radio operator emerged through the trees. 'I have a message for Agent Slater.'

Rodway nodded, and the man handed Nic a piece of paper. Irina had confirmed that the Soviets had postponed the full invasion. However, they still planned to use the false flag attacks as justification for making incursions across the Finnish and Iranian borders to test NATO resolve. Nic handed the note to Rodway.

'Well, that explains the group of soldiers we saw dressed in Finnish Army uniforms. They must be the team that will carry out the false flag attack. The main invasion force must be to the rear.'

'How does it change your plan?' Nic asked.

'It makes our life a lot easier. I was not thrilled at having to take on a whole Soviet division,' Rodway replied, smiling. 'Now, we can really give them something to think about. Our orders are not to engage until they cross the border; when they do, we will stop them by disabling the lead tank. The woods on either side of the trail are so dense they cannot manoeuvre to get around the disabled tank. In the confusion that follows, one of our squads will grab their most senior officer, who we expect to ride in the second tank. The rest of the team will keep the infantry occupied. We will use their confusion to make good our retreat. A plane will be waiting at a disused airfield about ten clicks west of here, and before you know it, we will be back in Helsinki.'

Nic was impressed, not just by the plan but by Rodway's supreme confidence in his team. After the briefing, three squads moved off to their observation posts. Nic stayed with Rodway and the fourth squad. One of the men brought him a mug of hot tea and a bacon sandwich, which he gratefully accepted. The MRE was not sitting well in his stomach.

The next few hours passed slowly. Rodway issued updated orders to Carr, who trotted off to deliver them to each squad. Nic needed rest; the effects of the Benzedrine had worn off, and he did not want to take a second tablet. Rodway showed him to a small bivouac the SAS team had set up. He lay down and immediately fell asleep.

When he woke, it was dark. He looked at his watch— midnight. He had been asleep for eleven hours. Stumbling out of the tent, he found Rodway sitting on a log.

'Well, if isn't sleeping beauty,' Rodway teased.

They sat and talked quietly until the sky started to brighten again. An early morning mist hung like cotton wool above the ground before slowly dissipating as the air warmed up. Rodway ordered each of the squads to undertake a final recce. Nic joined Carr's squad. They worked their way through the woods, tracing a wide arc from the trail to the lakeshore, taking care to avoid making any unnecessary noise. At one point, Carr whispered to Nic that they had crossed the border into the Soviet Union.

A few metres further on, the soldier on point dropped to the ground and held a clenched fist in the air—the signal to stop. Nic could hear voices up ahead and to the right. It was a Soviet patrol. The squad lay still until the patrol moved off. They made their way a little further along the lakeshore before stopping again. Carr signalled for Nic to follow him. They crawled up to the edge of the tree line. Ahead, in a large clearing, Nic saw the four Soviet tanks. Soldiers were sitting around smoking and drinking tea. Nic took out his binoculars and scanned the scene. A mess tent had been constructed under a large fly sheet. He was astonished to see Yuri sitting at one of the tables dressed in a Red Army uniform. He was no more than fifty metres away. He wondered if Irina was as close to the front line in Azerbaijan. He hoped not.

Carr tapped him on the shoulder, signalling that they should leave; twenty minutes later, they were back at camp.

66

5th June 1965 – Baku, Azerbaijan

Spassky was waiting for Irina in the lobby. The porter who had helped her the night before was still on duty. She walked over and thanked him again, pressing a ten-rouble note into his hand. He smiled broadly. It was probably the biggest tip he had ever received, almost a week's wages.

Spassky said, 'The car will be here shortly.'

While waiting, she studied the ornate but faded hotel lobby decoration. Like every other pre-revolution building in the Soviet Union, it suffered from a lack of maintenance. The ceiling had probably not seen a paintbrush in half a century.

The car pulled up in front of the hotel, and Spassky motioned for her to follow him. It was still searingly hot and very windy, whipping up eddies of sand. They arrived at the military headquarters a little after 06:00.

Ivanov was already in the operations room. If anything, his cheeks were even redder than the day before; no doubt there would be an empty bottle lying somewhere nearby. He turned and glared at her. She suspected she knew why.

'Two KGB agents were attacked in the Old Town last night,' he barked, 'do you know anything about that?'

Irina was confident neither of the agents would ever tell the truth about what happened. To admit they had been beaten up by a woman would be too humiliating. She put on her best-shocked expression and said, 'No. What happened?'

'They say they were attacked by a gang of young Muslim men near your hotel.'

His tone showed he was sceptical of the explanation. If only he knew the truth, Irina thought.

'How terrible. Are they alright?'

'They will live. One of them will be in the hospital for a few days with severe damage in the groin area.'

Irina tried not to smile.

'Did you see either of them last night?' Ivanov asked.

'Only briefly. I went down to the front desk to send a telex, and they were sitting in the lobby bar.'

The General nodded as if not surprised, 'What time was that?'

'About quarter past ten.'

'That was the last time you saw them?'

'Yes, Comrade,' Irina replied.

The General stared at her but moved on, 'Spassky has arranged transport for you to join up with our attack force. You should leave immediately. Good luck,' he said begrudgingly.

'Thank you, comrade General.'

The journey to the border would take about five hours, given the sorry state of the roads. As far as Ivanov was concerned, Irina's role was to gather intelligence in preparation for the full-scale invasion. He did not know that Gromyko had instructed her to report back on the performance of the military. Moscow was concerned that Soviet military readiness had dipped in the twenty years since the end of the war. Vanquish envisioned military action in both Western Europe and Indochina. If the Soviet Union was to establish itself as the preeminent superpower, it needed a first-class military.

Spassky showed Irina to an army jeep waiting outside. Thankfully, it had a roof, offering some protection from the wind, sand, and sun; however, the suspension was suspect, and every jolt sent a shock wave of pain through her bruised ribs. By the time she reached Bilasuvar, she felt like she had been attacked all over again.

Tanks and troop carriers lined both sides of the road as they approached the border. When they reached the front of the convoy, the driver pulled up outside the command tent. He jumped out and opened the door for her. She stepped out, trying not to show that she was in pain.

A soldier escorted her inside the command tent. Captain Karpov, the company commander tasked with the first incursion into Iran, rose and saluted as she entered. Irina, as a Major, outranked him. The wind was still blowing hard, causing the guy ropes securing the tent to vibrate wildly. The sound reminded Irina of a boat's rigging rattling against the mast or boom in a windy harbour.

Karpov was younger than most army officers Irina encountered. He was too young to have served in the Great Patriotic War. Tall and handsome in an angular way, his Stalin-style moustache did him no favours. Unlike many of his older peers, he had an easy manner and seemed to have no problem dealing with a woman.

He explained that the initial invasion force comprised four tanks, six self-propelled guns, and a company of 120 infantry. The tanks would lead the assault, followed by the infantry. No resistance was expected, as there was only a token force of Iranian soldiers at the border post, and no further units were reported in the area. The attack would commence at 08:00 local time to coincide with the Finnish mission. Azerbaijan and Iran were two hours ahead of Finland.

Karpov suggested Irina travel with one of his infantry commanders behind the tanks.

'I will ride with you,' Irina said. It was not a request; Karpov simply nodded.

An aide brought some tea, and they sat and talked about their lives. He explained that his father and elder brother were in the KGB. His father had helped set up and train the East German Stasi after the war, and his brother was a KGB colonel based in eastern Russia. This was his first major operational command, and Irina could tell he was anxious for it to go well.

'Why did you join the army?' she asked.

'Apparently, I showed an aptitude for leadership while at Pioneer Camp. The army recruited me when I was sixteen.'

'Do you have a family?'

His face lit up. 'Yes. My wife is called Kateryna. We have two sons, Oleg and Piotr. They are back home in western Ukraine. I miss them terribly.'

Two hours before the assault was due to begin, Karpov suggested she get some rest. She was not tired but accepted the offer to lie down on a camp bed set up behind a curtain at the rear of the tent. She wondered if her message had made it through to Seb. If so, how would NATO respond?

67

The final patrols went smoothly. Rodway received another message from London. The Soviets were expected to try to destroy the bridge over Lake Joukionsalmi, effectively cutting off access to a large part of northeast Finland. This would prevent Finnish forces from moving to blunt a subsequent Soviet invasion further to the north. The latest reconnaissance reports showed the main Soviet force forty kilometres behind the border and moving north.

Nic was confident the SAS troop could blunt the initial assault. Rodway explained that the Soviet force was commanded by General Vito Vykonen. He had been born in Finland, but his parents, both of whom were avowed communists, had moved the family to Leningrad when Vykonen was ten. He spoke fluent Finnish and Russian and knew the terrain, making him an ideal choice to command the mission.

He had a reputation as a fearless leader who liked to ride up front with his troops, in the mould of George Patton. A fact that underpinned Rodway's plan. One squad would set up observation points along the trail inside Soviet territory. Their job was to keep eyes on the General as the Russians advanced. They would radio confirmation of Vykonen's position to the rest of the troop. Two squads plus Nic, nine men in total, would be stationed by the side of the trail. It was the only accessible route from the border to the main road and, therefore, the obvious route for the Soviets to take to reach the bridge. Charges had been laid to disable the lead tank, which would block the trail. One squad would cover fire while another grabbed the General.

The remaining squad would organise transport to the airfield to complete the extraction. Only Nic, Rodway, and the captured General would board the plane. Sergeant Carr and the others would use the truck they had arrived in to drive to a military airport outside Helsinki, where an RAF plane would take them back to the UK.

As Rodway reviewed the plan one final time, his men showed no fear or doubt about their ability to pull off the mission. Nic could tell Rodway was a strong leader highly respected by his men.

At 05:00, the squads moved to their assigned positions. Rodway, Nic and the rest of the abduction team stationed themselves by a rickety, wooden gate crossing the trail. Explosives had been placed along the bottom of the gate and on each gatepost. The lead tank would probably try to barrel straight through the gate. A Soviet patrol had been seen examining it the previous day.

Vykonen was expected to be in the second tank. Two SAS team members equipped with anti-tank weapons would disable its tracks. The abduction squad would toss smoke grenades behind the tank to obscure the infantry's vision. Covering fire, fragmentation grenades, and a few mines they had planted earlier would give the Russians the impression they were being attacked by a sizable force.

Once the second tank had been disabled, the team would take the General prisoner and subdue any remaining members of his tank crew. The element of surprise should create sufficient confusion to allow the team to make good their escape before the Soviets knew what had hit him.

03.30 GMT: Bilasuvar, Iran-Azerbaijan border

'Comrade Major, we move out in thirty minutes,' said a voice from outside the tent. Irina woke with a start; she had fallen asleep after all.

'Thank you, comrade,' she replied, shaking herself awake. It was still dark outside, the only light provided by a crescent moon.

Irina walked over to the jeep at the head of the column. Karpov was already sitting in the passenger seat. When he saw her approaching, he jumped out to let her climb in the back.

'Ready?' he said.

'Ready,' she replied.

The driver handed her a scarf and made a motion indicating she should wrap it around her mouth and nose. The wind was still whipping across the desert landscape, and the sand was sure to blow.

At a signal from Karpov, the company moved off, with the tanks rolling along behind Karpov's jeep. Clouds of dust whirled in the air as the tanks' tracks carved ruts in the sand-covered landscape. The border was about twenty kilometres away. Irina wondered how Nic was faring in Finland.

As the attack force rolled along, Irina thought she saw the dark silhouettes of two aircraft streaking like comets across the sky. Dawn was breaking, making it difficult to be certain. Ivanov had said that no Soviet aircraft would be used in the operation due to the lack of expected resistance. She tapped Karpov on the shoulder, 'Did you see that?'

He nodded; his expression sombre. 'Probably American,' he shouted over the noise of the convoy.

As they approached the border, Irina saw the minarets atop a mosque on the Iranian side of the border. Karpov signalled for the jeep to stop. He climbed out and gestured to one of the troop carriers. About twenty soldiers got out, all dressed in Iranian Army uniforms. Karpov walked over to the group and started issuing orders. Irina was too far away to hear. When he finished speaking, the soldiers returned to the unmarked truck, which split off from the main force and headed north. A jeep followed. Irina saw a film crew sitting in the back. She almost laughed at how stage-managed the whole affair was. No doubt, newsreels across the Soviet Union and abroad would soon be showing films of unprovoked Iranian attacks on the Soviet Union.

For the next hour, they sat and waited until a green flare soared into the sky to the north. The false flag attack had been successfully completed. Karpov signalled for the column to advance.

About 100 metres short of the border, the jeep stopped again, and Karpov, together with two soldiers, walked towards the border post, which consisted of a wooden pole across the road and a dilapidated hut next to it. Three soldiers in scruffy Iranian army uniforms appeared from the hut.

One of the Soviet soldiers stepped forward and spoke to the soldiers in Farsi. When he had finished, the Iranian soldiers looked at each other before walking over to a battered US Army jeep parked next to the hut. Seconds later, they drove off at high speed toward Bileh Savar, leaving a cloud of dust in their wake.

They had been given one hour to warn the town of the impending attack.

Karpov returned to the jeep. One of the soldiers lifted the barrier, and the convoy rumbled across the border. Irina looked up and thought she saw two more black dots on the horizon.

As the minutes ticked by, the tanks and remote-propelled guns moved into position. Their orders were to attack and then occupy the town. Irina looked at her watch. She was angry; innocent people were about to die for no good reason.

The first salvo created a deafening roar as the tanks and artillery pieces simultaneously launched their high-explosive shells into the sky. Multiple gun recoils shook the ground. Seconds later, she saw the first explosions.

The bombardment only lasted ten minutes, but the effects were devastating. As the smoke cleared, Irina could see that one of the two minarets at the mosque had disappeared; smoke and flames rose into the sky. Irina could see people running out of the town into the nearby fields.

Two tanks, followed by infantry, moved slowly into the town. The rest of the division took up positions along the road parallel to the nearby Aras River.

Irina stepped down from the jeep and walked with Karpov towards the town. 'There does not appear to be any resistance,' he said.

'I am not surprised,' Irina said. 'Did you see those aircraft again?'

Karpov nodded, looking grim, but said nothing. 'Do you think everyone was able to evacuate?' Irina asked.

'Unlikely,' Karpov replied. 'We did not give them enough time to get the elderly and sick to safety.' There was genuine remorse in his tone.

They walked down the main road through the town. It looked as though it was carpeted with diamonds as the rising sun reflected off shards of broken glass. A couple of bodies lay in the road; Karpov signalled for a medic to check them.

Just ahead, in the shop doorway, Irina saw a young woman cradling an infant. She bent down to look. The mother was dead, a large piece of shrapnel lodged in the side of her head, but the baby was crying. Irina eased the baby out of the mother's grasp. As she did so, the baby stopped crying, opened its eyes and smiled. Irina struggled to control her emotions.

'I am going to find a medic,' she said, gently holding the baby in her arms. She walked back towards the convoy, shouting for help. A medic appeared and took the baby from her. 'Make sure this child is looked after,' she ordered. The medic nodded. Karpov was at her shoulder. He sighed and said, 'Why must we do this to innocent people?'

'We don't,' Irina snapped.

A look of surprise flashed across Karpov's face, then he nodded. There was a human being somewhere in there, she thought.

03:45 GMT, Eastern Finland

'The Soviets are preparing to move out,' Rodway said. 'We have confirmation the General is in the second tank.'

Nic nodded. It was 05:45 local time. They would not have to wait long. Rodway handed Nic a Heckler and Koch MP-5 machine pistol. 'This will serve you better than that peashooter,' he said, nodding at Nic's Colt.

The abduction team took up a position on the south side of the trail to take advantage of the shadows cast by the sun as it rose above the trees. At 06:00, Rodway's radio crackled and emitted two beeps, the signal that the Soviet column was moving. There was a one-click response from each squad confirming they were in position. Nic's throat was dry. This was his first experience of combat. Nothing in his training had prepared him for the excitement and fear he now felt. He heard the rumble of diesel engines in the distance. Rodway signalled to his team and got a thumbs-up in reply.

Turning to Nic, he said, 'Don't shoot unless you have to, but if you do, shoot to kill.' Nic nodded. The radio clicked again. The lead tank was fifty metres from the gate. The roar of the engines was deafening. Nic could see the head of the tank commander sticking out of the hatch. He was wearing a headset but no helmet.

As the first tank hit the gate, the explosives detonated. Flame and smoke followed by a deafening roar, and Nic was rocked backwards. The tank seemed to levitate in slow motion before crashing back to earth. The turret was a mangled mess of bent metal; there was no sign of the tank commander. Rodway raised his arm and signalled for his men to move forward. They tossed smoke grenades to obscure the enemy's view.

As he ran past the disabled tank, Nic saw the second tank trying to pass its stricken mate. He saw a helmeted figure poking out of the turret, gesticulating wildly. Then, from his right, the two M72-LAW anti-tank rocket launchers fired. The tracks on the second tank appeared to vaporise.

Rodway was already climbing up onto the tank. He pointed his machine pistol at the stunned General. Nic climbed up beside him and shouted in Russian for the General to get out of the tank. He did not appear to have heard, so Nic leaned forward and repeated his command. This time, the General reacted, slowly raising his hands to show he was not holding a weapon. Rodway helped him out of the turret. He started complaining loudly that he was still in Russian territory. Nic moved to the General's side and shouted, 'Shut up. You are on Finnish sovereign territory. We are taking you prisoner.'

The General glared at Nic. He knew that if he ever made it back to the USSR, his career and maybe his life would be over. The Soviet ethos had little tolerance for failure.

Rodway pushed the General in the back, encouraging him to climb off the tank. The other squad members provided covering fire as they shepherded him along the trail. The sound of scattered gunfire rattled through the trees.

Nic saw his Volvo reversing down the trail towards them at great speed before stopping. Vykonen resisted Rodway's attempt to push him into the car. A swipe across the head with the butt of the machine pistol persuaded him to cooperate. Nic sat beside the General, and Rodway got into the passenger seat. The driver gunned the engine, and the Volvo set off down the trail. The Volvo bounced down the trail and made a sharp right turn onto the highway. Nic looked at his watch. The whole operation had taken less than three minutes.

Rodway looked at Nic and said, 'Nice work.'

'Thanks. How long until we reach the airfield?'

The driver shouted, 'Five minutes.'

Vykonen was cursing loudly despite Nic telling him to shut up. Rodway looked at Nic and said, 'Turn your head.'

The next thing Nic heard was the sound of a gunshot and the shattering of glass. He turned and saw the now silent General's stunned look. Rodway had fired a single shot, barely missing the General's left ear, before it smashed through the rear window.

We are here,' said the driver as he swung the wheel of the Volvo and slid the car sideways through an opening in the trees. A wide expanse of open land sat before them. A small plane with its propellers slowly turning sat out in the open. The car skidded to a halt, and Nic pushed the General out of the door. Once on board, the plane bounced down the grass airstrip before lifting off and barely clearing the tree line.

'We should be in Helsinki in thirty minutes,' Rodway said.

'You guys are something else,' Nic said.

'Just doing our job,' Rodway replied with a smirk.

04:00 GMT, Bileh Savar, Iran

An hour had passed since the attack had been launched. The medics were tending to the civilian wounded. An initial count estimated that twenty-three civilians had been killed, with many more injured. Irina checked on the baby she had rescued. Remarkably, he was uninjured. His mother's final act had been to save his life.

Irina found Karpov beside his jeep. He offered her a cigarette, and an orderly brought them mugs of hot, sweet tea. All they could do was wait, either for orders from Moscow or for signs of a counterattack.

Irina wandered over and sat down on a rock by the riverbank. Karpov stayed talking to his unit commanders. As she sipped her tea, she saw what looked like a swarm of insects approaching from the south. As they got closer, she could tell they were not insects but helicopters. The distinctive thwap of the rotor blades increased in volume.

She shouted to Karpov, 'We have company.'

He turned and looked at the approaching aircraft and immediately started issuing orders. Soldiers rushed to man their guns. Turning to Irina, he pointed to his left and shouted, 'Take cover behind those rocks.'

She threw away the tea mug and jumped over the rocks bordering the river. Once she was lying down, she peered through a gap and saw small plumes of smoke billowing out from the side of the helicopters as they fired their missiles. There was only sporadic return fire. Seconds later, one of the tanks exploded, then another and another. She tried to see Karpov, but smoke obscured her view.

There was an almighty explosion on the other side of the rock she was sheltering behind. The next thing she knew, she was lying flat on her back, half submerged in the river. She pulled herself up the riverbank. The rock had disappeared. As the smoke cleared, she saw the hulking wreck of a tank. Overhead, the helicopters were wheeling away and turning back to the south. It looked like they would not be making another run. Despite being in shock, she identified them as Bell H-1 Iroquois or Huey's, as they were more commonly known. The missiles were most likely French SS-11s, which the Americans had recently started using in Vietnam.

She gingerly rose to her feet and looked along the line of the convoy. The commanders of the remaining tanks were loading up and trying to get moving. The ground was littered with the bodies of dead or wounded soldiers.

She felt dizzy and had a pounding headache but otherwise seemed unscathed. She walked slowly towards Karpov's jeep, which appeared to be undamaged. However, she saw Karpov lying on the ground. He was bleeding heavily from a shrapnel wound to the upper thigh. She knelt by his side. His eyes were moving, and a faint smile appeared on his face. Irina took the scarf from around her neck and wrapped it around the wound to try and staunch the bleeding. She feared the shrapnel had ruptured the femoral artery.

Karpov tried to speak. She leaned closer. In a whisper, he said, 'Tell my wife and children I love them.'

She held his hand tightly and smiled while saying, 'Don't worry; you will be able to do that yourself.'

His smile widened but then froze. She felt tears welling up in her eyes. They were tears of anger at the unnecessary death of a good man. He was a dedicated soldier who did his duty despite questioning the moral justification for his actions. She closed his eyelids and said a silent prayer.

Nearby, another soldier lay on the ground; he was crying out for his mother. Irina moved to his side. His face was still pitted with the remnants of teenage acne. He could not be much more than nineteen years old. He had a head wound, and there was a piece of shrapnel lodged in his arm. Irina ripped a piece off her shirt to make a tourniquet.

She shouted for a medic, but her cry was lost amidst the cries of the wounded. She bent down and shouted into the young soldier's ear, 'This will hurt, but I need to move you.'

The boy nodded. Irina slipped her arms under his armpits and gently levered him up against the side of the jeep. He screamed in pain.

'I need to get you in the jeep. Can you help?'

Nodding, he put his uninjured leg on the running board and hooked one arm over the side of the jeep. While he held on, she managed to roll him into the seat.

She jumped in the driver's seat, pushed the starter button, and eased the jeep forward. She had seen a medical truck and tent set up near the border post about two kilometres away. She was unsure how long the boy had got, so she put her foot down, accelerating through the gears. Despite weaving to try and avoid the debris and the potholes, each bump elicited a cry of pain from her passenger.

A medic ran out to meet her as she approached the aid station. She slammed on the brakes and brought the jeep to a sliding stop. The medic helped her carry the soldier into the tent.

The scene was chaotic; injured men were all over the place. Outside, a row of dead bodies already lay covered by blankets. A doctor and nurse went to work on the boy. The nurse attached a drip, removed Irina's makeshift bandage, and cleaned the wound. The doctor used a pair of forceps to remove the shrapnel. They dressed both wounds, and the doctor gave the boy an injection of morphine. As he did so, he turned to Irina and said, 'That was one of the bravest things I have ever seen. You almost certainly saved his life. If those fragments had stayed there for a minute longer, they would have killed him.'

Irina was too tired to respond; she slumped onto a nearby chair, exhausted and angry.

07:45 GMT, Helsinki

The plane touched down at an airfield outside Helsinki. Vykonen was now handcuffed. He had gone very quiet after initially insisting that his kidnapping was a war crime.

Two Finnish soldiers escorted him into a single-story building that normally served as the airport's waiting room. Posters for flying schools dotted the walls, and a noticeboard displayed adverts for everything from second-hand aircraft to slightly used parachutes.

Five men were seated at a table in the middle of the room. Nic saw Ranger standing in the corner, trying to keep a smile off his face.

Rodway motioned for Vykonen to sit down; Nic moved to stand beside Ranger, who leaned over and whispered, 'Nice work, buddy. We have caught the bastards red-handed.'

'Any news from Iran?' Nic asked.

'Our helos made a bit of a mess of the Soviet force.'

'Any word about Irina?'

Ranger shook his head. Nic silently prayed she was safe.

A bald man with glasses, sitting at the head of the table, called the room to order and started speaking, 'General Vykonen, I am Urho Kekkonen, the President of Finland. I am joined by the British, American, and Soviet Ambassadors and a representative from the United Nations.'

He made no mention of Ranger.

'General, you have been captured on Finnish soil in charge of a hostile military force, a clear breach of the 1955 Agreement of Friendship, Cooperation, and Mutual Assistance between our two nations. We would be within our rights to hold you in custody until a trial can be arranged. However, we know that you were simply obeying orders.'

The glum-looking Soviet ambassador tried to interrupt but was ignored. 'A message has been sent to Prime Minister Kosygin demanding an explanation. We will await his response.'

07:45 GMT, The Kremlin

Alexei Kosygin sat in a large Kremlin conference room. His mood was bleak. Brezhnev and Gromyko stood to either side of him. The rest of the Politburo and a small cadre of military chiefs were arguing amongst themselves. News of the debacle in Iran had just filtered through.

The aggressive American response had shocked everyone in the room. As usual, everyone was trying to shift the blame onto someone else. First, reports from Baku indicated that at least thirty-eight men had been killed, with many more injured. They had badly miscalculated NATO's resolve. Brezhnev was furious. He accused Kosygin of humiliating the Soviet Union with his determination to overpower the West.

Gromyko thought back to his conversation with Irina. She had been right. He took some satisfaction from having been the only person to question the wisdom of the attacks. At the time, he had been accused of defeatism, but now he was the only person in the room who could say, 'I told you so.' That would be useful one day.

There was a loud knock at the door. An army signals officer entered. He handed a piece of paper to an aide, who walked over and gave it to Kosygin. As he read the message, his face flushed with anger. After a few seconds, he said to no one in particular. 'The Finns have taken General Vykonen prisoner, and our force has been routed. The Finnish President is demanding an immediate explanation of our actions.'

A collective gasp echoed around the room. Gromyko leaned forward and whispered in Kosygin's ear, 'You must speak to the Finnish President immediately.'

Brezhnev nodded his agreement. Kosygin's face flashed anger, 'Get me the Finnish President,' he barked.

A phone was placed on the table, and Gromyko ordered everyone except himself, Brezhnev, and Kosygin out of the room. They hurriedly discussed what Kosygin should say. After a short delay, the phone rang, and Kosygin snatched up the receiver.

08:00 GMT, Helsinki

Back in Helsinki, Kekkonen answered the call. He did not wait for Kosygin to speak before launching into an angry denunciation of the Soviet Union. Vykonen and the Soviet ambassador looked glum.

When he had finished, he demanded an explanation. He listened to Kosygin's initial response and handed the receiver to Vykonen. Kosygin asked him to confirm his identity and verify that everything Kekkonen had said was true.

When Vykonen did so, Kosygin swore and slammed the phone down. Vykonen stared at the receiver before handing it back to the Kekkonen.

'Now, we wait,' Kekkonen said in English, 'Your superiors have one hour to meet our demands. If they do not, you will shortly appear on Finnish television, and your face will be on the front page of every newspaper in the world by tomorrow morning.

Kosygin turned to Brezhnev and Gromyko and said, 'The Finnish President is demanding the immediate withdrawal of our forces. If we refuse, General Vykonen will appear on Finnish state television to admit his role in an attempted invasion of Finland, and a news release announcing his capture will be sent to all United Nations members and international news agencies. We have one hour to respond.'

08:00 GMT, Moscow

Gromyko said nothing. He was subordinate to the other two, and this was not his problem. Kosygin knew his standing would be irreparably damaged by his approval of the attacks. Brezhnev would seek to capitalise on his failure, but that was a topic for another day. Kosygin said, 'Comrades, we have no option but to withdraw from Iran and Finland. It is our only hope of avoiding global humiliation.'

'I agree,' said Brezhnev.

'We should be thankful Agent Sashkaya's warning saved us from an even bigger defeat,' said Gromyko.

Brezhnev nodded. Kosygin looked like he was about to explode.

After leaving the aid tent, Irina tracked down Karpov's second-in-command, Lieutenant Fischer. He was awaiting orders from Moscow.

'We don't have time to wait,' Irina insisted. 'We must withdraw back across the border immediately. They could launch another attack at any time.'

While reluctant to act without orders, Fischer knew they were sitting ducks. After giving it some thought, he said, 'You are right. I will give the order to withdraw. Hopefully, Moscow will agree with my decision.'

As the remnants of the company prepared to depart, Irina went to check on the baby and soldier she had rescued. Both would survive, though the soldier would probably lose a leg, and the baby would grow up an orphan.

She commandeered Karpov's jeep and started driving back to Baku alone. She had mixed emotions. She was pleased the attack had been thwarted but angry at the senseless loss of life. The Kremlin had badly miscalculated.

She just hoped Nic was safe.

09:00 GMT, Helsinki

Rodway's radio buzzed, breaking the silence in the room. 'Excuse me,' he said as he stood up and stepped out of the room. Less than a minute later, he returned, 'The Soviets are pulling back across the border.'

Everyone except the Soviet ambassador and Vykonen clapped. The celebration was interrupted by the phone ringing. Kekkonen answered it and sat listening for some time before replacing the receiver. 'Moscow has agreed to all our demands,' he announced triumphantly. 'They have also requested immediate talks with our government to reset relations. Their only condition is to keep news of today's events secret.'

He turned to the Soviet ambassador and said, 'We will hold General Vykonen until a suitable prisoner swap can be negotiated.'

Nic was only half listening. He was worried about Irina. When Kekkonen finished speaking, he said, 'Sir, is there any news from Iran?'

The US ambassador spoke, 'The Soviet force was attacked by our fighters, sustaining significant losses. The last I heard, the Soviets were retreating back across the border into Azerbaijan.'

68

13th June 1985 – London

A week had passed since the attacks on Finland and Iran. The news blackout had worked; there had been no leaks to the press. All Soviet forces had returned to base. General Vykonen was still being interrogated by NATO. It would be some time before he returned to Russia.

The smoking ruins of Soviet tanks on the Iranian border showed up clearly on the latest reconnaissance photographs, and the two tanks immobilised by the SAS were still in the woods outside Joukio.

NATO estimated at least fifty Soviet soldiers had been killed during the two actions. The only incident on the NATO side was a member of the SAS team who sustained a minor injury when a Soviet bullet grazed his arm.

Upon his return to London, Nic was greeted as a hero. He could not have cared less. All he wanted to know was whether Irina was safe. However, there was a communication blackout regarding the operation. C refused Nic's request to have the Embassy in Moscow check on her. He had big plans for Irina and did not want to risk Moscow becoming suspicious of her.

Nic was angry. Without Irina, MI6 would never have known about the attacks. She had proven herself the most effective double agent MI6 was running. He tried complaining to Seb, who sympathised but reminded Nic that MI6 could do nothing that might expose her. He knew Seb was right, but it did nothing to ease his concerns.

Feeling sorry for himself, he went out for a few lunchtime pints at his new local, The Hollywood Arms, just round the corner from his flat. About halfway through his third pint, he had an idea. He drained his glass, found the pay phone in the corridor by the toilets, and looked up the number for the Brazilian Embassy. He called the switchboard and asked for the telex number for the Moscow Embassy. Five minutes later, he walked into the Post Office on Fulham Broadway and wrote a message to Rosa Klein.

69

14th June 1965 – Moscow

Irina found herself sitting outside a Kremlin conference room once again. After ensuring that the baby and soldier were adequately cared for, she drove Karpov's jeep back to Baku, where she intended to debrief General Ivanov. However, she found him so drunk that she headed straight to the airport and hitched a ride on a military transport bound for Moscow. Back to her apartment, she called the Lubyanka to inform them she was taking a few days leave. Semichastny demanded she appear for a debrief; she refused, knowing he would not dare force the issue. Despite having thwarted the invasions, she was livid. Soviet leaders had once again shown their arrogance and disregard for life. The blood of the young Iranian mother, Karpov and the others could now be added to that of the tens of millions of Russians who had perished because of flawed leadership. She was also worried about Nic but dared not try to find out if he was safe until it was clear that they were not under suspicion.

Aside from visiting her mother, she did not talk to another human being for a week. Then, she received a phone call from Chernenko. He listened patiently while she vented. He acknowledged the operations had failed but reminded her that her actions had saved many lives. He also reminded her how successful earlier Vanquish operations had undermined the West and encouraged her to return to work.

'You are a hero,' he said. 'Brezhnev has personally acknowledged your contributions. You must take advantage of your new status.'

Irina knew he was right. There was a narrow window of opportunity for her to increase her influence. Instead of sulking, she needed to focus on the next stage of her and Nic's plan. She wondered how Chernenko would react if he knew how she would wield her newfound power.

The next morning, a limousine arrived at her apartment. The driver informed her that he was to take her to the Kremlin for an important meeting. As the car pulled away from the kerb, two motorcycle outriders appeared in front and proceeded to clear their path. Red lights meant nothing as they raced towards the Kremlin. This was special treatment indeed, but was it good news or bad?

The car dropped her off at the entrance to the Palace of Congresses, where she was met by an army officer who escorted her to a reception area near the Politburo conference. The door to the conference room opened, and a secretary beckoned for Irina to enter. Three men sat at a table: Kosygin, Brezhnev, and Gromyko, the three most powerful men in the USSR.

'Thank you for coming, Comrade Sashkaya,' said Brezhnev, motioning for Irina to sit. Like I had a choice, Irina thought.

Brezhnev smiled at her, which was a little disconcerting. Politburo members were not known for displaying any emotion other than anger.

'First of all,' he said, 'I must thank you on behalf of the peoples of the Soviet Union for your service,' Brezhnev said. Irina relaxed a little; however, this could still be the preamble to a punishment. She wondered if the fact that Brezhnev, not Kosygin, was speaking indicated a subtle shift in the balance of power.

Brezhnev continued, 'The Soviet Union has suffered two

significant reverses in our patriotic struggle, but it would have been much worse were it not for your patriotic actions. The intelligence you provided saved many of our fellow comrades' lives.'

Irina noted he made no mention of the lives that had been lost. Still, this was as close to an admission of culpability as Irina had ever heard from a Soviet leader.

Gromyko said, 'Your service developing a new source inside MI6 over the last year has been outstanding. He is proving to be a source of valuable high-grade intelligence. He must remain in our service. You will return to London immediately and continue serving as his handler.

Irina's heart leapt. Did this mean Nic was safe and back in London? She dared not ask. Gromyko continued, 'Before we let you go, we have something else for you. In addition to your exemplary work with Slater, we have learned of your heroic actions in Iran. You single-handedly saved a comrade's life while under intense enemy fire.' Irina noted there was no mention of the baby.

'Please stand,' Gromyko said.

They all stood up. Gromyko continued, 'By order of the Presidium of the Supreme Soviet, you are being made a Hero of the Soviet Union and the Order of Lenin. Congratulations, Comrade Major.'

Irina was flabbergasted. She had walked into the room half expecting to be shipped off to Siberia, yet here she was, receiving the Soviet Union's highest honour for bravery.

Kosygin said, 'This is a great honour. You are only the 87th woman to be honoured out of over ten thousand recipients.'

Brezhnev picked up a box off the table, opened it and took

out the medal, a gold star with a red ribbon. He stepped round the table to pin it onto Irina's blouse.

'Congratulations, Comrade,' he said.

Irina bowed slightly and said, 'I am honoured and will continue to serve the people to the best of my abilities.'

She saluted, turned, and walked out of the conference room, still shaking.

A secretary was waiting for her outside. 'Chairman Semichastny wants to see you immediately. Please follow me.'

They walked down a long corridor. The secretary motioned for Irina to knock on one of the doors. A deep voice said, 'Enter.'

She turned the handle and entered. Semichastny looked up and said, 'Congratulations, comrade. You have performed great services for Mother Russia. Let us hope that continues.'

Irina detected a slight edge to his voice. He must find it galling to praise a female agent.

He motioned her to sit. 'Before you return to London, you must be fully debriefed.'

Irina knew what that meant: hours of being asked the same questions in multiple ways to find inconsistencies in her story. She would get little sleep and not much food. Despite being a hero of the Soviet Union, she would be guilty until proven innocent. There was no point in complaining; it would only delay her return to London.

As Semichastny explained the process, Irina saw the hint of a smile on his face. The bastard was enjoying himself.

The debriefing was three days of near torture. The lights in her room were left on twenty-four hours a day, loud music played constantly, and she was given the bare minimum of food and water. None of the treatment was a surprise, she had often been on the other side of the process. It seemed a strange way to treat your own people, but the level of paranoia in the Soviet Union knew no bounds.

When she finally returned to her apartment, she took a long shower and lay on her bed with a chilled bottle of vodka. Unusually for her, the bottle lay unopened, and she immediately fell asleep. She did not wake for fifteen hours. Sunlight seeped through the flimsy curtains. Slowly, her body and brain began to function. She reflected on the absurdity of the last few weeks.

She and Nic had betrayed their respective countries, potentially prevented the outbreak of World War III, and been instrumental in causing the Soviet Union's most embarrassing post-war debacle. Then, she was honoured by the very people she had betrayed.

Rolling out of bed, she began to feel sick, probably caused by the release of tension. She went to the bathroom and threw up. She had just finished getting dressed when her doorbell rang. That was unusual; no one had ever called on her. She pressed the buzzer to unlock the front door and waited.

There was a sharp rap on the door. Irina peered through the spyhole. An attractive, blonde-haired woman stood outside; she looked vaguely familiar.

Irina opened the door. The woman smiled and said, 'Hello, Irina. I am Rosa Klein. We met briefly a few months ago. You were having dinner with Nic Slater.'

Irina nodded. She remembered. Nic had made too much fuss trying to reassure her that Rosa was just a friend. She had teased him about it.

'Nic asked me to check on you,' she said.

'You better come in,' Irina said, standing to one side.

Once inside, Rosa said, 'I am not sure what the two of you have been up to, but he is worried about you.'

Irina felt dizzy and started to cry. Rosa stepped forward, hugged her, and said, 'Sit down. I will make some tea.'

Irina was not sure what had come over her. When Rosa returned with the tea, she apologised, 'I am sorry. I don't know why I am feeling so emotional.'

They talked for hours. Rosa could sense Irina's feelings for Nic were not just professional. After Rosa left, she got the vodka out of the freezer and poured out a good measure but then decided she did not feel like drinking.

70

22ⁿᵈ June 1965 – London

Nic arrived early for his meeting with Ranger and Seb, so he stopped by his office. There was a massive stack of paperwork in his inbox. He marvelled at the government's ability to generate masses of meaningless paper. He filed it all in the wastepaper basket. If any of it was important, a bureaucrat somewhere would be sure to chase him down.

There was one envelope sitting in the middle of his desk. His name was written on the front, but there was no address indicating it had been hand-delivered. He sat down and opened it. Inside was a short telex printout. It read,

"Our mutual friend is back from her holidays. She had a great time and will see you soon. Rosa"

Nic yelled, 'Yes!' so loudly that one of the secretaries put her head round the door and asked if everything was all right.

'Never better,' he said.

He rushed up the stairs to Seb's office; Ranger was already there. 'Irina's safe,' he exclaimed, 'and she's returning to London.'

'Hell, yes,' said Ranger.

'Splendid news,' said Seb. 'This calls for a little celebration.'

The next few hours were a blur to Nic. They started at the White Hart and visited several other drinking establishments before ending up at a pub in Mayfair as last orders were called. They had been drinking for six hours. Nic had no idea how much or what he had consumed. Seb tried to cajole him to go to Ronnie Scott's, a jazz club in Soho. Nic slurred his excuses, and, for once, Seb did not insist.

Ranger and Seb guided him out of the pub. The combination of fresh air and an empty stomach set the world in motion, and he threw up in the gutter. He could hear Seb and Ranger laughing. They flagged down a taxi, poured him inside, and instructed the driver to take him to Edith Grove.

Nic slumped onto the back seat. The driver looked in his mirror and said, 'Sir, let me know if you plan on throwing up.'

Nic tried to nod an acknowledgement. The next thing he knew, the driver was helping him out of the cab. Nic handed over a pound note and told him to keep the change.

He felt a little better but took his time climbing the steps. He took immense pleasure in successfully inserting his key into the lock on the first attempt. He made it up the stairs without mishap and was about to unlock the front door to his flat when he saw a shaft of light under the door. He suddenly felt a lot more sober. He was certain he had not left a light on.

Bending down, he removed his shoes and inserted his key in the lock, turning it slowly. In the quiet of the hallway, the click as the lock opened sounded very loud. He slipped his gun out of the shoulder holster, eased the door open and saw light escaping from under his bedroom door. Was someone in there?

He slid his feet over the polished, wooden floor to minimise any sound. Stopping outside the bedroom door, he listened for any sound from within. He could not hear anything but was not going to take any chances. He crouched low and gently eased the handle down. When the catch disengaged, he flung the door open, rolled inside, and rose to a crouch. He scanned the room while holding the gun somewhat shakily with both hands. He heard a slow clapping sound coming from the bed. Lowering his weapon, he stood up and saw a naked Irina sitting up in the bed laughing.

'Nice entrance,' she said, 'you can put your gun down now.'

Nic did as instructed before tumbling forward onto the bed.

He woke up with a throbbing headache and tried to recall the events of the previous evening. Had it all been a dream? He turned on his side, but no one else was in the bed. He slumped back onto the pillow just as the bedroom door opened, and Irina walked in. She was naked and carrying two mugs of tea. She handed one to him, 'I think you will need a few of these this morning.'

She slid back under the covers and gave him a kiss on the lips. 'That was quite a performance last night. You burst through the door like a drunken acrobat waving your gun around. Then you start talking incoherently about how you are a real-life James Bond before falling onto the bed and passing out.'

He smiled sheepishly. After a second mug of tea, they managed a leisurely reunion, although Nic was a rather passive participant. They lay in bed and shared everything that had happened in the last few weeks. Nic laughed at the fate of the two agents who had attacked her. When she described saving the baby and the young soldier, he felt both sad and proud.

He was sobering up nicely, and they made love again. Afterwards, as they lay in each other's arms, she said, 'There is one other thing I must tell you.'

Nic gazed at her, thinking how beautiful she looked in the early morning light.

'What?' he asked.

'I'm pregnant.'

The Behind the Curtain Series

False Flag is the first book in the Behind the Curtain series of Cold War novels.

Book two, Berlin Bitte, continues the story of Nic and Irina. Nic is based in Berlin and regularly crosses the Berlin Wall to stir up trouble between Moscow and its satellite states. Irina has been banished to the basement of the Lubyanka. When an opportunity to rehabilitate her career presents itself, she risks everything. They reunite as the seeds of revolt grow across the Warsaw Pact and find themselves caught up in events leading to the Prague Spring. At significant personal risk, they undertake a humane mission that again threatens to expose their traitorous pact.

Book three, Detente Dawn, finds Nic and Irina struggling to adapt to a changing world where superpower tensions are replaced by moves towards détente. The threat of nuclear war has diminished and is being replaced by random acts of terror conducted by extremist groups. The world of espionage is being redefined. Can Nic and Irina adapt? Can their relationship survive new tensions as the world is redefined during the 1970s?

The Behind the Curtain books are works of fiction set during the Cold War (1947-1991), when the defining geo-political construct was an ideological battle between capitalism and communism in the aftermath of World War II.

While fictional, many real places, events, and people appear throughout the narrative. As far as the author is aware, JFK's assassination, the Cuban missile crisis, the Profumo affair, and Malcolm X's assassination were not part of a coordinated Soviet plot. The events did take place contemporaneously with the book's fictional action. I have tried to be as accurate as possible in describing events and locations.

Khrushchev, Semichastny, Kosygin, Brezhnev, Chernenko, and Gromyko held the positions described. Dick White was head of MI6, Harold Wilson was Prime Minister, and Patrick Gordon-Walker and Michael Stewart both served as Foreign Secretary. Nic, Irina, SirRod, Seb, Yuri, and Ranger are (mostly) fictional creations.

Any errors are the author's own. Thanks to my wife, Donna, for reviewing multiple drafts, my editor, Kieran Devaney, for his insightful guidance, and Nick Castle for the cool covers.

Find out more at www.davidaxson.com

www.ingramcontent.com/pod-product-compliance
Lightning Source LLC
Chambersburg PA
CBHW020525110726
47899CB00004B/1245